Parrot and Olivier in America

Peter Carey received the Booker Prize for *Oscar and Lucinda* and again for *True History of the Kelly Gang*. His other honours include the Commonwealth Prize and the Miles Franklin Award. Born in Australia, he has lived in New York City for twenty years.

PETER CAREY

PARROT

and

OLIVIER

in America

faber and faber

First published in 2010
by Faber and Faber Limited
Bloomsbury House
74–77 Great Russell Street
London WC1B 3DA
This export paperback first published in 2010

First published in Australia by Penguin in 2009
First published in the United States by Alfred A. Knopf,
a division of Random House Inc. in 2010

Printed in the UK by CPI Mackays, Chatham

The right of Peter Carey to be identified as author of this work
has been asserted in accordance with Section 77 of the
Copyright, Designs and Patents Act 1988

Design by John Canty © Penguin Group (Australia)

Illustrations copyright: p. 2: *célérifierè*, Mary Evans Picture Library;
p. 226: *Liberty Leading the People* by Eugène Delacroix, Imagno/Getty
Images; p. 260: T. J. Maslen's map reproduced courtesy of Mitchell
Library, State Library of NSW.

A CIP record for this book
is available from the British Library

ISBN 978–0–571–25330–2

2 4 6 8 10 9 7 5 3 1

FOR FRANCES COADY

'Can it be believed that the democracy which has overthrown the feudal system and vanquished kings will retreat before tradesmen and capitalists?'

❧

'It is not good to announce every truth.'

❧

ALEXIS DE TOCQUEVILLE

OLIVIER

I

I had no doubt that something cruel and catastrophic had happened before I was even born, yet the comte and comtesse, my parents, would not tell me what it was. As a result my organ of curiosity was made irritable and I grew into the most restless and unhealthy creature imaginable – slight, pale, always climbing, prying into every drain and attic of the château de Barfleur.

But consider this: Given the ferocity of my investigations, is it not half queer I did not come across my uncle's *célérifère*?

Perhaps the *célérifère* was common knowledge in your own family. In mine it was, like everything, a mystery. This clumsy wooden bicycle, constructed by my uncle Astolphe de Barfleur, was only brought to light when a pair of itinerant slaters glimpsed it *strapped* to the rafters. Why it should be strapped, I do not know, nor can I imagine why my uncle – for I assume it was he – had used two leather dog collars to do the job. It is my nature to imagine a tragedy – that loyal pets have died for instance – but perhaps the dog collars were simply what my uncle had at hand. In any case, it was typical of the riddles trapped inside the château de Barfleur. At least it was not me who found it and it makes my pulse race, even now, to imagine how my mother might have reacted if I had. Her upsets were never predictable. As for her maternal passions, these were not conventionally expressed, although I relished those occasions, by no means infrequent, when she feared that I would die. It is recorded that, in the year of 1809, she called the doctor on fifty-three occasions. Twenty years later she would still be taking the most outlandish steps to save my life.

My childhood was neither blessed nor tainted by the *célérifère*, and I would not have mentioned it at all, except – here it is before us now.

Typically, the Austrian draftsman fails to suggest the three dimensions.

However:

Could there be a vehicle more appropriate for the task I have so recklessly set myself, one that you, by the bye, have supported by taking this volume in your hands? That is, you have agreed to be transported to my childhood where it will be proven, or if not proven then strongly suggested, that the very shape of my head, my particular phrenology, the volume of my lungs, was determined by unknown pressures brought to bear in the years before my birth.

So let us *believe* that a grotesque and antique bicycle has been made available to us, its wooden frame in the form of a horse, and of course if we are to approach my home this way, we must be prepared to push my uncle's hobby across fallen branches through the spinneys. It is almost useless in the rough ground of the woods, where I and the abbé de La Londe, my beloved Bébé, shot so many hundreds of larks and sparrows that I bruised my little shoulder blue.

'Careful Olivier dear, do be careful.'

We can ignore nose-bleeding for the time being, although to be *realistic* the blood can be anticipated soon enough – spectacular spurts, splendid gushes – my body being always too thin-walled a container for the passions coursing through its veins, but as we are making up our adventure let us *assume* there is no blood, no compresses, no leeches, no wild gallops to drag the doctor from his breakfast.

And so we readers can leave the silky treacherous Seine and cross the rough woodlands and enter the path between the linden trees, and I, Olivier-Jean-Baptiste de Clarel de Barfleur de Garmont, a noble of Myopia, am free to speed like Mercury while pointing out the blurry vegetable garden on the left, the smudgy watercolour of orchard on the right. Here is the ordure of the village road across which I can go sailing, skidding, blind as a bat, through the open gates of the château de Barfleur.

Hello Jacques, hello Gustave, Odile. I am home.

On the right, just inside, is Papa's courthouse where he conducts the marriages of young peasants, thus saving them military service and early death in Napoleon's army. It does not need to be said that we are not for Bonaparte, and my papa leaves the intrigues for others. We live *a quiet life* – he says. *In Normandy, in exile*, he also says. My mother says the same thing, but more bitterly. Only in our architecture might you glimpse signs of the powerful familial trauma. We live a quiet life, but our courtyard resembles a battlefield, its ancient austerity insulted by a sea of trenches, fortifications, red mud, white sand, grey flagstones and fifty-four forsythias with their roots bound up in balls of hessian. In order that the courtyard should reach its proper glory, the Austrian architect has been installed in the Blue Room with his drawing boards and pencils. You may glimpse this *uppity* creature as we pass.

I have omitted mention of the most serious defect of my uncle's vehicle – the lack of steering. There are more faults besides, but who could really care? The two-wheeled *célérifère* was one of those dazzling machines that are initially mocked for their impracticality until, all in a great rush, like an Italian footman falling down a staircase, they arrive in front of us, unavoidably real and extraordinarily useful.

The years before 1805, when I was first delivered to my mother's breast, constituted an age of inventions of great beauty and great terror – and I was very soon aware of all of this without knowing exactly what the beauty or the terror were. What I understood was drawn solely from what we call the *symbolic aggregate*: that is, the confluence of the secrets, the disturbing flavour of my mother's milk, my own breathing, the truly horrible and unrelenting lowing of the condemned cattle which, particularly on winter afternoons, at that hour when the servants have once more failed to light the lanterns, distressed me beyond belief.

But hundreds of words have been spent and it is surely time to enter that château, rolling quietly on our two wheels between two tall blue doors where, having turned sharply right, we shall be *catapulted* along the entire length of the long high gallery, travelling so fast that we will be *shrieking* and will have just sufficient time to notice, on the left, the conceited architect and his slender fair-haired assistant. On the right – look quickly – are six high windows, each presenting the unsettling turmoil of the courtyard, and the gates, outside which the peasants and their beasts are constantly dropping straw and faecal matter.

You might also observe, between each window, a portrait of a Garmont or a Barfleur or a Clarel, a line which stretches so far back in time that should my father, in the darkest days of the revolution, have attempted to burn all the letters and documents that would have linked him irrevocably to these noble privileges and perils, he would have seen his papers rise from the courtyard bonfire still alive, four hundred years of history become like burning crows, lifted by wings of flame, a plague of them, rising into a cold turquoise sky I was not born to see.

But today is bright and sunny. The long gallery is a racetrack, paved with marble, and we swish toward that low dark door, the little oratory where Maman often spends her mornings praying.

But my mother is not praying, so we must carry our machine to visit her. That anyone would choose oak for such a device beggars belief, but my uncle was clearly an artist *of a type*. Now on these endless stairs I feel the slow drag of my breath like a rat-tail file inside my throat. This is no fun, sir, but do not be alarmed. I might be a slight boy with sloping shoulders and fine arms, but my blood is cold and strong, and I will swim a river and shoot a bird and carry the *célérifère* to the second floor where I will present to you the cloaked blindfolded figure on the chaise, my mother, the comtesse de Garmont.

Poor Maman. See how she suffers, her face gaunt, glowing in the gloom. In her youth she was never ill. In Paris she was a beauty, but Paris has been taken from her. She has her own grand house on the rue Saint-Dominique, but my father is a cautious man and we are in exile in the country. My mother is in mourning for Paris, although sometimes you might imagine her a penitent. Has she sinned? Who would tell me if she had? Her clothes are both sombre and loose-fitting as is appropriate for a religious woman. Her life is a kind of holy suffering existing on a plane above her disappointing child.

I also am sick, but it is in no sense the same. I am, as I often declare myself, a *wretched beast*.

Behold, the dreadful little creature – his head under a towel, engulfed in steam, and the good Bébé, who was as often my nurse as my tutor and confessor, sitting patiently at my side, his big hand on my narrow back while I gasped for life so long and hard that I would – still in the throes of *crisis* – fall asleep and wake with my nose scalded in the basin, my lungs like fish in a pail, grasping what they could.

After how many choking nights was I still awake to witness the pale light of dawn lifting the dew-wet poplar leaves from the inky waters of the night, to hear the cawing of the crows, the antic gargoyle torments of country life?

I knew I would be cured in Paris. In Paris I would be happy.

It was the abbé de La Londe's contrary opinion that Paris was a pit of vile miasmas and that the country air was good for me. He should have had me at my Catullus and my Cicero but instead he would drag me, muskets at the ready, into what we called the *Bottom Hundred* where we would occupy ourselves shooting doves and thrush, and Bébé would play beater and groundsman and priest. 'You're a splendid little marksman,' Bébé would say, jogging to collect our plunder. '*Quam sagaciter puer telum conicit!*' I translated. He never learned I was shortsighted. I so wished to please him I shot things I could not see.

My mother would wish me to address him as *vous* and *L'Abbé*, but such was his character that he would be *Bébé* until the day he died.

I was a strange small creature for him to love. He was a strong and handsome man, with snow-white hair and shrewd eyes easily moved to sympathy. He had raised my father and now I trusted myself entire to him, his big liver-spotted hands, his patient manner, the smell of Virginian tobacco which stained the shoulder of his cassock, and filled me with the atoms of America twenty years before I breathed its air. 'Come young man,' he would say. 'Come, it's a beautiful day – *Decorus est dies*.' And the hail would be likely flailing your back raw and he would marvel, not at the cruel pummelling, but at the miracle of ice. Or if not the ice, then the wind – blowing so violently it seemed the North Sea itself was pushing up the Seine and would wash away the wall that separated the river from the *bain*.

The meek would not swim, but Bébé made sure I was not meek. He would be splashing in the deep end of the *bain*, naked as a broken statue – 'Come on Great Olivier.'

If I became – against all that God intended for me – a powerful swimmer, it was not because of the damaging teachings of Jean-Jacques Rousseau, but because of this good priest and my desire to please him. I would do anything for him, even drown myself. It was because of him that I was continually drawn away from the awful *atmosphere* of my childhood home, and if I spent too many nights in the company of doctors and leeches, I knew, in spite of myself, the sensual pleasures of the seasons, the good red dirt drying out my tender hands.

And of course I exaggerate. I lived at the château de Barfleur for sixteen years and my mother was not always to be found lying in her pigeonhole with the wet sheet across her eyes. There was, above my father's locked desk, a large and lovely pencil portrait of my maman, as light as the dream of a child that was never to be born. Her nose here was perhaps a little too narrow, a trifle severe, but there was such true vitality in the likeness. She showed a clear forehead, a frank expression, inquiring eyes that directly engaged the viewer, and not only here, but elsewhere – for there would be many nights in my childhood when she would rise up from her bed, dress herself in all her loveliness, and welcome our old friends, not those so recently and swiftly elevated, but nobles of the robe and sword. To stand in the courtyard on these evenings with all the grand coaches out of sight behind the stables, to see the fuzzy moon and the watery clouds scudding above Normandy, was to find oneself transported back to a vanished time, and one would approach one's grand front door, not speeding on a bicycle, but with a steady slippered tread and, on entering, smell, not dirt or cobwebs, but the fine powder on the men's wigs, the lovely perfumes on the ladies' breasts, the extraordinary palette of the *ancien régime*, such pinks and greens, gorgeous silks and satins whose colours rose and fell among the folds and melted into the candled night, and on these occasions my mother was the most luminous among the beautiful. Yet her true beauty – evanescent, fluttering, deeper and more grained than in the pencil portrait – did not reveal itself until the audience of liveried servants had been sent away. Then the curtains were drawn and my father made the coffee himself and served his peers carefully, one by one, and my mother, whose voice in her sickbed was thin as paper, began to sing:

> *A troubadour of Béarn,*
> *His eyes filled with tears . . .*

At this moment she was not less formal in her manner. Her slender hands lay simply on her lap, and it was to God Himself she chose to reveal her strong contralto voice. I have often enough, indiscreetly it seems now, publicly recalled my mother's singing of *'Troubadour Béarnais'*, and as a result that story has gained a dull protective varnish like a ceramic captive in a museum which has been inquired of too often by the overly familiar. So it is that any tutoy-ering bourgeois and his wife can know the comtesse de Garmont sang about the dead king and cried, but nothing would ever reveal to them Olivier de Garmont's fearful astonishment at his mother's emotions, and – God forgive me – I was jealous of the passion she so *wantonly* displayed, this vault of historic feeling she had hidden from me. Now, when I must remain politely at attention beside my father's chair, I had to conceal my emotion while she gave away a pleasure that was rightly mine. Our guests cried and I experienced a violent repugnance at this private act carried out in public view.

His eyes filled with tears,
Sang to his mountain people
This alarming refrain:
Louis, son of Henri,
Is captive in Paris.

When she had finished, when our friends remained solemnly still, I walked across the wide rug to stand beside her chair and very quietly, like a scorpion, I pinched her arm.

Of course she was astonished, but what I remember most particularly is my wild and wicked pleasure of transgression. She widened her eyes, but did not cry out. Instead she tossed her head and gave me, below those welling eyes, a contemptuous smile.

I then walked, very coolly, to my bed. I had expected I would weep when I shut my door behind me. Indeed, I tried to, but it did not come out right. These were strange overexcited feelings but they were not, it seemed, of the sort that would produce tears. These were of a different order, completely new, perhaps more like those one would expect in an older boy in whose half-ignorant being the sap of life is rising. They seemed like they might be emotions ignited by sinful thoughts, but they were not. What I had smelled in that song, in that room full of nobles, was the distilled essence of the château de Barfleur which was no less than the obscenity and horror of the French Revolution as it was visited on my family. Of this monstrous truth no honest word had ever been spoken in my hearing.

My mother would now punish me for pinching her. She would be cold, so much the better. Now I would discover what had made this smell. I would go through her bureau drawers when she was praying. I would take the key to the library. I examined the papers in my father's desk drawers. I climbed on chairs. I sought out the dark, the forbidden, the corners of the château where the *atmosphere* was somehow most dangerous and soiled, well beyond the proprieties of the library, beyond the dry safe wine cellar, through a dark low square portal, into that low limitless dirty dark space where the spiderwebs caught fire in the candlelight. I found nothing – or nothing but dread which mixed with the dust on my hands and made me feel quite ill.

However, there is no doubt that *Silices si levas scorpiones tandem invenies –* if you lift enough rocks, you will finally discover a nest of scorpions, or some pale translucent thing that has been bred to live in a cesspit or the fires of a forge. And I do not mean the letters a certain Monsieur had written to my mother which I wish I had never seen. It was, rather, beside the forge that I discovered the truth in some hum-drum little parcels. They had waited for me in the smoky gloom and I could have opened them any day I wished. Even four-year-old Olivier might have reached them – the shelf was so low that our blacksmith used it to lean his tools against. One naturally assumed these parcels to be the legacy of a long-dead gardener – dried seeds, say, or sage or thyme carefully wrapped for a season some Jacques or Claude had never lived to see. By the time I pushed my snotty nose against them, which was a very long time after the night I pinched my mother, they still exuded a distinct but confusing smell. Was it a good smell? Was it a bad smell? Clearly I did not know. Not even Montaigne, being mostly concerned with the smell of women and food, is prepared to touch on this. He ignores the lower orders of mould and fungus, death and blood, all of which might have served him better than his ridiculous assertion that the sweat of great men – he mentions Alexander the Great – exhaled a sweet odour.

The old blacksmith had died the previous winter. Gustave was the new blacksmith, and Jacques his apprentice. They had recently restored our damaged gates with fierce spikes along their top and were presently rehanging them. While Gustave barked at Jacques, I quietly laid the first of these musky parcels outside on the flagstones. They certainly did not look like death or horror. The yellow wrap of newspaper, being very old, broke apart like the galettes we ate at Epiphany although in this case, they contained not the delicious almond cream called frangipane but – what was I looking at? – no more than the desiccated body of a bird, a pigeon from whose dried remains there issued a line of small black ants, and it was the ants who caused me such upset. That is, they swarmed along my arms and down my neck, and bit me. I was soon running up and down the courtyard crying and it was not until Gustave removed my tunic that I was saved.

So loud were my screams that my father rushed from the court in his judicial gown and wig. A robust bride and big-nosed groom came after him and peered at what I'd found. Gustave and Jacques now produced dozens of these parcels and laid them, according to my father's instructions, in a neat line along the side of the building. When they were all formed up, my father gave orders that they should be destroyed, which I naturally assumed was because they were filled with horrid ants.

Odile, drawn by my screams, came out to see. So did Bébé. This was a considerable crowd to be in such a place. But then my mother drove through the open gates in The Tormentor – which is what we called her swaying carriage – and in a moment she had descended and was in the thick of it, against my father's wishes.

'No, Henriette-Lucie, you must not.' Those were his words, exactly.

My mother snatched the crumbling paper from my father's hand. 'My pigeons!' she cried.

I did not understand, not for a second, but I had found the very explanation of my life.

My mother held her handkerchief across her mouth. It seemed she might be vomiting. She was blind to me, half dead with noble shame. She would not be attended to by servants, only by the aristocratic Bébé who now escorted her to the château. No one noticed me, and I remained behind while my father ordered his bride and groom back into the court. I stayed to watch the cremation of the pigeons, but even so I did not understand that each parcel contained a victim of the revolution.

Inhabiting the wainscoting, as it were, I easily rescued a single fragile sheet of paper and, careful of it as if it were a lovely moth, carried it away into the woods to read.

II

The horrible Austrian stared at me as I fled toward the oratory whose door I hammered at until the latch jumped free. I threw myself before the altar, blood pouring from my nose. Would God not protect me from that hideous thing I carried crushed inside my hand?

Then my Bébé kneeled beside me. He took my hand as if to comfort me, then forced it open. Firmly he held my wrist, gently he brushed the fragments from my palm.

'What is this my child?'

It was a drawing from the old newspaper that had wrapped a pigeon.

It showed a machine, an awful blade, a set of tracks, a rope, a human head severed from its body. It was the king's head; I knew his noble face. A hand held the head separate from the butchered neck whence the blood did spurt and flow. An ornate typography declared: *Que le roi soit damné.*

Bébé offered his rumpled handkerchief. It was not the *complete and total inadequacy* of this that frightened me but that he, my own Bébé, should look at his Olivier with eyes so dull and tired.

'This *happened*?' I demanded.

He held out his big hands in resignation. This was terrifying but worse than that, far worse – he *shrugged*.

'It is horrid.' I cried as bats cry, flying through the dreadful dark.

Below me was a great abyss, no floors, no walls, and my mind was awash with the monstrous terrors of decapitation. The king's head was a perfect living head that might smile and speak, and its eyes were perfect eyes, and the hair was dressed as a king's hair should be dressed, and everything about him was so fine and good except for this vile machine, these flying drops of blood, this filthy squirt and gush.

'Is this why my mother cries? Does she know this?' I meant was this what she saw when she lay with the damp sheet across her eyes?

'Yes, my darling, alas.'

'Then who made this dreadful thing, Bébé? Who would *imagine* such a horrid sight?'

'It is thought to be kinder,' said Bébé.

'It was Napoleon who did this? This is why we hate him?'

'No, this is the father of Napoleon.'

I did not understand what he could mean – a *father*.

'Bébé, who killed so many pigeons?'

'The peasants put the birds on trial for stealing seeds. They found them guilty and then they wrung their necks.'

'But we don't have pigeons, Bébé. The loft is empty. We have never had pigeons.'

'Your grandfather kept pigeons. The peasants felt oppressed by them it seems, to have them eat the planted seeds.'

Can you imagine such a flood of horror washing over so young a child? But so it was, at six years of age, I had my first lesson in the Terror which had been the flavour of my mother's milk. My parents had been thrown into Porte Libre prison where every day one of their fellow nobles was called 'to the office' and was never seen again. In these months my father's hair turned white, my beautiful mother was broken in that year of 1793, when the *sansculottes* came up the road from Paris.

My family had been at table, Bébé told me, as he 'got the boy outside', out past the forge, beneath the linden trees. They had been at dinner, my mother and father and grandfather, when the gardener had come hurrying inside and stood before them with a pair of secateurs in his gloved hands.

'Citizen Barfleur,' he said to my mother's father, 'outside are some citizens from Paris asking for you.' Even allowing for the fact that it would have been against the revolutionary law for him to use the respectful form of *you*, it was a very unusual way for my grandfather to be addressed by a servant.

'Did no one strike them for their impudence?' I asked.

As we walked in the fields beside the river, the air was sweet with new-mown hay. There was a stench of drunken peaches in the orchards – why not? – each fallen fruit attended by its circus troupe of bees and gnats and wasps climbing and falling from the pulp. In the midst of this bright maggoty celebration I had now found the secret, as old and musty as a walnut locked inside a woody shell.

'Why did my father not strike them?'

My grandfather had been Armand-Jean-Louis de Clarel Barfleur. His name was the name of his town, his river, his long noble line unbroken to the Normans and, beyond that to Clovis, and beyond Clovis to Childeric, king of the Salian Franks, massing with his warriors in the forests of Toxandria, and who was he to let his life be taken by some drunken sansculottes?

'It is difficult to explain,' my Bébé said.

Indeed. It was beyond belief. There were only two men from Paris, as far as I could gather. My family had been as timid as the pigeons, I thought. They had let their necks be wrung.

'Was it to this that they took my grandpapa?' I asked.

'Where, my child?'

'This *thing*.'

'Yes, that thing.'

As we walked down through the *Bottom Hundred* the secret quail rose from the grass. I was outraged by my family, and very fierce in my judgement of my father particularly, that he had not drawn a sword and slaughtered his tormentors.

My lungs were clogged, my heart was disturbed, but my Latin declensions must still be learned. As the day ended, Bébé and I *hic-haec-hoc*'d our way through the strange pale grass, up to the old mill on whose steps we rested to eat an apple. It was not yet dark, but I could see, through the heavy branches, the golden lights of our home. I understood it then, as for the first time, not as a castle of pride and strength, but as a weak place, a soft thing in the coming night. I saw my grandfather and my father sitting unprotesting in their chairs. I imagined the murderers with their bare bottoms and huge moustaches coming through the gloom along the road from the village, the air dark with stolen wine, the sky alight with burning faggots, oily black smoke curling into the opal sky so that the wispy threads of smoke drew lines on an ancient mirror which should have reflected back heroic scenes – my papa with his sword drawn putting the enemy to flight.

'I would have smote them, Bébé. I would not have been a coward.'

The dear old abbé remained silent while we crossed the village road, while the porter unlocked the heavy gate. Then he waited and watched while the servant retreated to his lodge.

'Bébé, are you angry?'

I was frightened to feel so alone, to see that he who only ever loved me had ceased to do so. It was time for my bath, but I could feel myself transfixed by his dark eyes while moths brushed against my hair and settled on my shirt.

When he spoke he did not even say my name. As the colour

left the sky and the porter closed his door and the light from the gallery windows lay down upon the earth, he lectured me. The infinite universe soon showed itself above us, and my child's opinion was nothing but spilled salt.

My breathing coarsened but he showed no mercy. My arms itched and my legs ached, but I was too afraid to complain while Bébé told me about the man who had sat at the table on that dreadful morning. This was my mother's father, the great Barfleur, who was no more to me than a name. Barfleur had so loved the king, it seemed, that he hectored him and chastised him when his advisers were leading him to ruin. It was Barfleur who dared instruct the king to tax the nobility, make the Jews citizens, let the Protestants worship legally in peace.

'This is courage,' said Bébé. 'It was the comte de Barfleur who told the king to cut the extravagances in court. He told him to remember the history of Charles I in England. Do you remember what that was?'

'I forget the year, Bébé. I'm sorry.'

'The year does not matter. He told our king, "You hold your crown, sire, from God alone; but you are not going to deny yourself the satisfaction of believing that you also hold your power due to the voluntary submission of your subjects."'

'The king,' said the abbé de La Londe, whose voice was echoing around the courtyard so clearly that I was afraid, imagining the blacksmith, the porter, the gardener listening from the shadows of the doors. My dear wise Bébé suddenly seemed the most reckless of men.

'The king was not a bad man,' he told me, 'but he was surrounded by vain and selfish men and women.'

Now my breath turned very rough, most likely because my mother, whose windows were wide open to the summer air, would not hear a word against the king.

'It was Versailles,' Bébé said, 'that brought down the monarchy, and the Court's blindness and foolishness that led us, not only to the guillotine, but to this thief Bonaparte who has made France no better than a pickpocket and a burglar.'

'Bébé, should we not go inside?'

'No,' said Bébé, 'for you have been raised in a most peculiar way, poor child. And now I see you have no idea who you are or who your father is. Did he ever tell you he saved my life?'

'No Bébé.'

'Your father is a brave man. To do battle with the citizens from Paris would have been as foolish as fighting against a swarm of wasps. Did your father run around shrieking at his pain?'

'No Bébé, I suppose not.' In my mind I saw my father standing in a field, a cloud of wasps around him.

'That is courage,' said Bébé, 'that is character. You do not blame the poor ignorant people, my darling. Do you understand me? The court of Versailles brought this down upon us all.'

Even then I knew he did not mean the people were wasps but that is how I pictured it and in my imagination I was no longer the noble with his sword, slaying those who hurt my kind, but a frightened boy, screeching, running through the darkened fields, stung, hurt, throwing himself from the bank and drowning in the Seine.

That night my breathing was so bad neither garlic nor brandy could cure me, but it was not till dawn that they fetched the doctor from his bed.

III

The guillotine now cast its diamond light on scenes which had hitherto existed in the domestic shadows.

That is not to say my life was ruined. I swam and hunted and feasted on green plums until my belly ached. I made a friend, Thomas de Blacqueville, who once stayed with us for sixteen days. On my seventh birthday I travelled to Paris and ate mille-feuilles at the house of Mme de Chateaubriand. I am said to have made the company laugh but no one can recall my witticism. I was precocious. I was a genius for the piano. I had a high opinion of myself. By 1812, the year I turned seven, I was accomplished in Latin and Greek.

It was during this very particular summer that the Hero of the Vendée arrived at the château de Barfleur. It was my father's birthday but the visitor brought no gift – or left arm either, the latter presumably sliced away by some horrid machine. His empty white-silk sleeve was like a ghost, but what I noticed most of all was my mother.

She had, until the moment of the young visitor's arrival, occupied a *chaise* in the Gold Room, blinds drawn against the shrill heat, a damp cloth across her face in such a manner that a stranger to the house might assume her dead.

The footman approached my mother. He bent stiffly and spoke in that ridiculous whispering way they learn in Italy but to see how my mother responded, you would think he had shouted in her ear.

She fairly *sprang*.

If the footman fell over she did not notice for she was – as the servant scurried blushing from the room – *bowing* to a visitor. That is, my mother, she whose status required her to give no more than a polite curtsy to anyone, bowed deeply to a man whose arm had been chopped off. Later I thought that bowing was surely some private *reference*, a play, a quote, a joke: Molière?

The visitor was Marie-Jean de Villiers, *écuyer*, marquis de Tilbot, sometimes known as the Hero of the Vendée, although I seldom heard him called anything but Monsieur. Whether this was the fruit of modesty or pride I do not know. He was big and ruddy as a side of beef, a noble warrior who had led the peasants of Calvados and Orne against the revolution. If only, my mother later said, there had been one hundred Monsieurs.

In the Gold Room, Tilbot spoke very quietly to my mother. He had brought a 'little something', a folio of engravings of exotic species, such as were popular in the lost libraries of the *ancien régime*. I suppose he planned to sell it to her, but I did not know that then. They both examined the item, sheet by sheet, exclaiming with delight at the bizarre botany of Australia. As to what they said to each other, I heard nothing, but I felt the air shiver and knew this horrid one-armed soldier was about to steal my father's birthday from us.

That dinner was to be a grand affair of fricasseed chickens, and minced partridges, and ember-cooked pies and chickens with truffles, and so it was, but the feast was now laid waste, not by the awful thunderstorm, but by the visitor who talked too much in a way quite clearly intended to hide the truth from a child. When the songs had been sung, Bébé excused himself and I understood he was angry. My father? He became exceedingly formal and his skin took on a shining waxy sheen as if he were a clever copy of himself. My mother twice remarked on the amounts of paperwork awaiting him and complained, as if in sympathy, that no one in Paris thought sufficiently to honour him with a copyist or secretary. Nothing was said of the engravings.

I was an excitable child, now in a distressed condition. When my father spoke, as he was often wont to do, of the young peasants he was marrying off to save their lives, Monsieur smiled directly at my mother. What this meant I did not know, but if I had been my father I would have taken the visitor's empty sleeve and slapped his face with it. I wished it so violently that my lungs rebelled against me and I was taken off to receive my final gift – not the crystallised fruit, but Odile and her leeches, and sheet lightning all that August night.

The next incident I recall was on a morning some months after the departure of M. de Tilbot. I had discovered my mother in her quarters.

'Where is Céleste?' I named her maid.

My mother did not answer. She was filling a travelling trunk with white cockades. She set her head to one side, smiling, just so. I thought, Good grief, what is the matter? Is she happy?

'Maman, what has happened?'

I sat quietly, prickling inside my scarf which I wore to hide the leech marks. My mother, I saw, was playing the part of servant. Finally she locked her trunk and the real servants were called to take it down.

In later years she would always insist that she could not tell me the truth because I was too *frail*, but when she locked herself in her boudoir with Céleste she only brought me to a higher pitch.

By the time she emerged I had scratched my arms until they bled, but all this discomfort was forgotten when I saw – she had got herself up in costume, like a pretentious bourgeois in a play.

She dragged me into her apartments where she squeezed me into what was called a skeleton suit, short red jacket and tight trousers. I wondered why it would have such an awful name.

There then followed a completely unexpected audience with my father. This took place out of doors in the midst of all the confusion caused by my mother's imminent departure. He was dressed as a Garmont in the Titian portrait, as a noble of the robe, his gorgeous ancient sword hung at his side occasionally making that small sound like gold coins in a purse. He smelled of talcum powder and raven oil and I apprehended him with a feeling very close to awe. Thus, very formally – Olivier in his skeleton suit, the M'sieu l'comte in all the glory of his rank – we faced each other. It was exceptionally hot and bright although the sky was completely grey.

'Your mother has explained to you?'

'No, Papa.'

'King Louis is returning,' my father said, clearly in a state of high emotion. 'The comtesse will be a dame du Palais to the queen. I will sit in the Chamber of Peers. You will one day be the comte de Garmont. I am going to Paris to greet His Majesty,' he said, his eyes glistening. 'Your mother refuses to remain at home. She will go in her carriage.'

How could I continue breathing? I thought, I will not be left behind.

As always when observed by servants, my tender father embraced me stiffly.

'Good man,' said he, and swung himself upon his stallion to whose proud body he had restored scabbards, halyards, saddle-cloths, all the signs of ancient rank. He galloped away with no more reliable news than that which is always blown along the Paris road, no more educated than the opinions of men with burning faggots in the night. I thought, They will guillotine my papa and then I will kill them in their swarms, God forgive me. Yet I was also very proud to see him leave with no other company to protect him. He set off to Paris where, as everybody now knows, the Russian prisoners and wounded Frenchmen were carried through the gates in carts. Some, half dead, fell beneath the wheels which they stained with blood. Conscripts, called up from the interior, crossed the capital in long files to join the army. In Paris all was still turmoil. That very night, my father would hear artillery trains passing along the outer boulevards. No one could know if the explosions meant victory or defeat.

'From the towers of Notre-Dame you could see the heads of the Russian columns appearing, like the first undulations of a tidal wave on the beach.' So wrote Chateaubriand and it is likely true, or most of it.

Paris was in the process of being invaded or liberated, and the cannons split the trees in the Bois.

At the château de Barfleur my mother was brave and fright-ened, calculating and careless. She had dressed as a bourgeois, as I said before, but then she called for the coach which declared her an aristocrat without apology. She embraced me and whispered I must stay safe with Bébé, but then she was in the kitchen person-ally packing a hamper, ignoring the cook and maids, whose sulky offers of cold meats and fruit she firmly refused. And this was how I knew I would go to Paris: I saw her choose a series of small and sweet surprises for her only son – crystallised fruits, rose-scented Turkish delight, *caprices de noix*, those Périgord walnuts, glazed in sugar and coated with bitter cocoa.

I rushed to Bébé and demanded that he come to Paris. I thought, I will be the comte de Garmont now. I thought, Why will he not obey me?

I ran and clambered into my mother's great Tormentor, leaving Odile and the other servants to follow, crammed like pickled turnips in the coach behind. It was an ordinary day, grey and overcast, very quiet as we escaped our exile. I thought, We are like the cicadas who live so many years entombed beneath the earth.

Then the coach wheels rolled across the courtyard stones and my mother rose up singing and I with her, leaving behind our yellowed skins, our sad bedclothes for the laundry maids.

IV

My mother's carriage was like its patron – heroically resistant to change. That is, no modern suspension could fit it.

I would, on any other occasion, have begged to travel with Odile in the second coach.

'*Vive le roi*,' my mother whispered when we were finally alone, without our audience of spies.

I kissed her wet cheeks.

'*Vive le roi, Maman*,' I cried, trembling at what might lie ahead.

She held me to her little bosom. Her brooch pressed against my cheek and hurt me, but everything the breathless bleeding sleepless Olivier had wished for seemed as if it might now really come to pass. The days of glory were returned. Everything smelled of jasmine and leather, but I did not forget the horrid cartoon of Louis XVI's spurting head, nor was I blind to my mother's disguise. Whether we were returning to our friends or enemies, I was not sure, nor would I ask the question in any forthright way. These unspoken anxieties may very well have contaminated our return but such was my mother's experience of life that she knew the value of distraction – had not the aristocrats in the prison of Porte Libre staged Racine and played whist? Neither of these activities being suitable for this occasion, she had placed a hamper between us in the coach.

The peasants were ploughing their fields and the air was rich with dung and dirt. My mother's memory of the weather was completely different, but I distinctly remember that the first hawthorns were in bloom, while inside The Tormentor's ancient painted carapace we supped on sugar flowers, so delicate and lovely, each one wrapped in pale blue paper, as grand and gorgeous as a noble of the robe.

'All gone,' she would cry.

But then my newly playful mother would produce one more pretty blue skirt, and untwist it to reveal a white rosebud which would dissolve like nectar on my tongue.

'Will I see the king, Maman?'

'But of course.'

'What will I say to him, Maman?'

'Olivier. Look. What can this be?'

And what she had produced, now from her basket, was a familiar object from my father's desk, where it had long stood in company with sundry botanical and sentimental curios. Here, on what I could confidently announce was the most exciting day of my life, this pink glass flask with its tear-shaped bottom and its bound cork stopper, might have been a magic balm for one of Cervantes' wounded knights, and if Maman had told me it was filled with frankincense or myrrh I would have had no reason to doubt her, except for the embossed letters MADE IN NEW YORK.

It was, as my mother told me later, on a calmer, less ecstatic day, a gift to my father from the American who claimed to have invented electricity. It was *soda water*.

My mother gave not a fig for the American who had not even known to wear a wig to the château de Barfleur, and yet she unwound the copper wire from around the cork with a certain reverence and when she placed it in my hand I understood I was to keep it as a relic. I folded the wire and tucked it into the pocket of my skeleton suit. My mother then removed the cork. The *soda water* produced none of the percussive force of champagne, but its own distinctive effect, something rounder and softer, rather like, if I may say so without disrespecting his beloved memory, dear Bébé farting in his sleep.

We were *rocketed* toward Paris, lifted upward, shaken sideways by the beastly Polignac springs, but in the midst of this turmoil my mother carefully filled one goblet and I witnessed my first soda bubbles, never guessing the gas had been gathered from the top of dirty brewery yeast, seeing only an ascension of my own spirit, fragile orbs of crystal rising in the golden light.

My mother and I drank and laughed and shrieked. Bubbles burst inside my nose, behind my eyes. We were, I swear it, drunk.

And then we were very sober, and I have a clear dark recollection of our arrival at the banks of the Oise where we found my father waiting for us, I suppose by prearrangement, although I had not been told of it. There were battles still being fought, apparently, and this is why we approached Paris by this route. I was not in the least surprised to see my papa looking so handsome and noble on his horse, his sword at his side and the great plumes of black smoke rising from the street behind him. As we approached him, my mother hurried the empty bottle back inside her hamper but my father barely had time to speak before he wheeled his horse around, shouted to our driver, and so escorted us toward our house on the rue Saint-Dominique.

Above our heads sat the coachman and our blacksmith, the latter with a musket across his lap and the former with his whip cracking the road lest anyone approach. The sun set along golden boulevards as we veered away from the Cossacks, whom we feared, and cantered beside the Austrians, whom we trusted, although both, together with the Prussians, were our saviours come to destroy the tyrant the revolution had brought forth.

As we crossed the Seine the sun was at the horizon and the ancient river flowed beneath our path like mercury, carrying the bodies of our own French sons and fathers like so many sawn-up logs. You would think the enormity of this sight, all this blood paid to remove Napoleon, would disgust me, squash my child's happiness like a stinking rose petal in the street, but you see, my noble father was ahead, the blacksmith above, and as we arrived on the Left Bank I was in fact a thoughtless disgusting little thing, a general returning in glory from the wars.

Vive le roi, I thought. *Vive la France*. I kissed my mother's cheek and squeezed her little hand. The house of Garmont was restored.

V

Abandoning the blackened silver of the Seine, emerging from behind the solemn sooty shadow of the ministries, we found the rue Saint-Dominique. Broken bricks and cobbles were everywhere beneath our wheels. The air, previously sulphurous, was here foul and fetid. Gustave the blacksmith dismounted and, having fired his musket at the sky, shouted instructions so the coachman might ease the carriage around a bloated horse whose shiny green bowels rose like an awful luminous bubble from the chiaroscuro night. There were very few lamps burning in the great houses and this, the absence of our kind, was not comforting. I had only visited the rue Saint-Dominique twice in all my life, but it loomed massively in my imagination – Blacqueville's family lived here too, so we would both be neighbours of King Louis XVIII.

'No, no,' my mother cried when the light of Gustave's lantern revealed a high thin townhouse with its eyes gone blind. My mother had been born in this street. She knew each house by family name. 'There, Blacksmith, there,' she cried. 'Onwards.'

At that moment there appeared, on the penumbra of the wavering light, some towering phantom, as tall as a house, pressing down toward the carriage, bleeding black against the charcoal sky.

'Maman,' I shrieked.

'What is it?' she demanded, her voice rising to a pitch quite equal to my own.

I was literally dumb with terror, all the hairs on my neck and head bristling. I could do no more than point.

'Oh.' She saw, then *slapped* my leg. 'It is the Blacquevilles' wisteria.'

If it was the Blacquevilles' wisteria it was also a living thing, abused, attacked, wounded, hacked, pulled away from the house so it teetered in a mass above our heads. This was the house of my friend Thomas. I felt sick to see how it had been punished, as the pigeons had been punished, as it was said the printers of rue Saint-Séverin had held a trial and hanged their masters' cats.

'Maman, where is Thomas?'

But she shrugged off my hand.

Our iron picket gates were now opened to us by our blacksmith, who, it seemed, could think of nothing but the gold fleur-de-lys which had been melted down for bullets. I heard the grind of steel on steel, the heavy hinges swinging, and my heart was beating like the devil, my blood sluicing through my arteries and veins. Then – *another fright* – the high front door opened and I beheld a pair of deep dark staring eyes. Standing hard against my mother I slowly understood that the eyes belonged to one of ours and she – that is the chatelaine – was refusing to admit her mistress.

'Don't fret,' my mother reprimanded me, but she was the one who was fretting. I could feel the heat of her body. In a moment she would enter the grand dining room, where she planned to welcome the king himself amid a sea of lilies.

Imagine my confusion when I discovered, by the light of twenty candles in that same room, a large black gelding, eighteen hands high, shitting on the parquet floor.

Among the manure and straw, I beheld a broken vase and silverware, damask curtains in a pile – small damage if you consider what was happening across the Seine, but horrid violence just the same. A shudder passed through my bowels.

Behind the horse, the servants were still assembling with their candles and my mother was on show once again and I, her son who had imbibed her terrors in the womb, knew she could not possibly endure this public trial. For instance, what would she call them? I made a horrid smell. The comtesse de Garmont squeezed my hand once, briefly, and then she laughed, not desperately at all, rather girlishly in fact, as if the awful sight was a very droll amusement.

'Come,' my mother said, but I dared not move. My mother touched me lightly on the head and then, having addressed her servants from the chilly distance of her majesty, gracefully ascended the curling marble stairs. Thus was I abandoned to the violence of the room.

I thanked the chatelaine for greeting us. She answered me appropriately. She explained that the horse was there because the stables had been burned down and that Hobbes thought him certain to be stolen by the Cossacks. She made me understand my nose was bleeding.

Six strange servants escorted me to bed.

Then Odile arrived carrying a large rose-tinted Ch'ien-lung goldfish bowl. This contained my leeches. She set it on an English giltwood stand and removed the muslin cloth from around its neck. These *vieilles amies* had always been in her charge and she was constantly ready, at whatever hour her bell rang, to scoop out the starving parasites with an instrument I have seen nowhere since – an English tea strainer strapped with leather shoelaces to a wooden spoon. Odile was slow and heavy-limbed but extraordinarily dexterous and, when required, she would select a single creature and hold it between thumb and forefinger and then, when the doctor had departed, she would – without fail – fix one to her nose and through the kindness of her heart, to lessen my distress, roll her eyes at me as it wagged its vile body in the air.

Thus for our first two days in Paris I was declared an invalid, and although I complained bitterly it was not so bad. The Blacquevilles had not returned from Normandy. I watched for them from my window and saw, if not my tall young Thomas, then many other visitors arriving by coach and foot, carrying their baskets or parcels or portmanteaus or simply holding the trains of their dresses high. I could also see my mother's coach, in no way hidden but standing on call, with its team in harness all day long. People of the most surprising type stood in the street to stare at this, and when one urchin rushed through the gate it was not to slash the horse's tendons but to tenderly place a white daisy in the harness before the poler's ear. So did my blood spill over, my lungs rip and roar, the louder for witnessing the guildsmen and market women arrive at our gates with gifts of furniture and mirrors and other items 'taken into safekeeping' during the revolution.

As my father had refused to join the nobles' flight into exile, the house, no matter what spiteful damage it had suffered, had always remained his property, and the items now returned had been, even by the laws of the Directory and Empire, quite frankly stolen.

I lay in bed and Odile brought me chamomile relentlessly. If this calmed me I do not know. My mother visited me often but was always in a rush to see a returning friend, sometimes carrying a broth, sometimes no more than her glad and nervous heart. I had never seen her eyes so bright, and these visits, ever so brief, filled me with happiness, and gave birth to a very clear expectation of what my life might now become.

And I was not disappointed. For when I rose from my sickbed she brought me a new sailor suit. As for her own dress, she had moved from black to white, from age to youth. She had raised her hair. She descended those wide marble stairs dressed in white lawn from head to toe, pleated beyond perfection, her long floating sleeves held with flocks of white silk ribbons. She was an angel, a noble princess, with a long and lovely neck, her artful curls twisting down each cheek, her white bonnet decked with live bouquets, which may have had the rather prosaic purpose of disguising the odours of the street.

The servants, crowded like geese inside the entrance, applauded.

This shocked the comtesse clearly. She stopped on the third-to-last step and her entire forehead erupted in a frown of disapproval while her dark eyes shone in undiluted triumph. In this style she ran the gauntlet of her audience and I behind her, still clutching my letter to the abbé de La Londe. Through the gates I beheld a crowd of men of all sorts wearing white cockades, and women too, some very rough. My mother, not knowing whether to acknowledge them or no, wrapped her shoulders with a shawl of fleur-de-lys, and this simple action raised another cry.

'*Vive le roi*,' they cried.

'In, in,' my mother hissed.

I jumped into the dreaded Polignac monster and she followed

quickly after me. '*Vive le roi*,' she whispered in my ear, brushing my cheek with the fresh blooms in her hat. '*Vive le roi*, my treasure.' And so we rolled along the rue Saint-Dominique to the rue de Rivoli where we called on Mme de Chateaubriand. M. de Chateaubriand was not at home but many other aristocrats were gathered around the dining table which was stacked high with papers bound with bright green printer's cord. Even as we entered these cords were cut and the pamphlets divided between la marquise de La Tour du Pin and Mme de Duras and Mme Dulauloy and many others whose names I did not know, although I do believe Mme de Staël was of the party, but in any case we all rushed out onto the rue de Rivoli, not to our many waiting carriages but down along the street so the coachmen followed us, at what you might have called a funereal pace, and we, in shining white, spread like a flock of splendid birds, rare flamingos perhaps, out across the boulevards and squares down from the faubourg Saint-Germain into the faubourg Saint-Antoine, giving away M. de Chateaubriand's pamphlet which, at the time, I assumed to be some sort of announcement of the king's return. In fact it was a pamphlet written by M. de Chateaubriand, and it had a very great impact on the population as it legitimised the restoration.

Louis XVIII later said that 'Of Bonaparte and the Bourbons' was worth a whole regiment to him. It never did occur to Chateaubriand that he had been mercilessly flattered, but in that he is no worse than every other writer ever born.

Dear Little Bébé,

I wish you a good day. I am going to tell you something. I am to have a new suit for His Majesty's visit. The statue on the place Vendôme has just been knocked down and they have put in its place a white flag with fleur-de-lys on it. Goodbye, little Bébé, I kiss you with all my heart. My friend Thomas is now here with all his sisters. He asks after you and demands you come to join us very soon.

Olivier

VI

The gates were repaired and painted. There were new curtains, cream and silver, luminous by candlelight, which had been sewn and hung in just two days, one of them a Sunday. Our horses were lodged with the young nephew of the duc de Berry, who was a neighbour, and the entire rue Saint-Dominique echoed with hammer blows as our stables were rebuilt by a group of Marseillais who ate so gluttonously that a cook was engaged to deal with their unreasonable demands. Every day the king was expected in Paris. Every day he was delayed until, finally, my sleep was quite destroyed by nervous expectation.

'Why does the king not come to Paris?' I asked.

'He is not only king of Paris, Master de Garmont. He is king of all the French.'

'Then he is the king of murderers!' I cried, and was dispatched to my room where Odile was ordered to prevent me writing letters to Thomas. I doubtless made an appalling noise. Who knows, I might have gone on all day had I not been witness, in seeking a sight of Thomas, to a conversation in the garden beneath my window. That is, I heard, very clearly, the duc de Blacqueville tell my father that the *préfet* had left for Boulogne to greet His Majesty.

'Then tomorrow?' my father asked.

'Or the next,' said M. de Blacqueville.

Vive le roi, I thought, with great relief. He will be here soon.

The Blacqueville wisteria was reattached to its ancient stone and we were permitted to play in the Luxembourg Gardens. A new wave of visitors arrived with articles that could be used to make our house to *fit a king*, among them a splendid Sèvres service with views of Paris sent by the wife of a newly appointed Gentleman of the Chamber. This meant my father would soon be made a peer, Odile said.

Vive le roi, thought Olivier, and if his lungs hung like rags on the bony rack of his little chest, he remained a strong and wilful boy. *Vive, vive, vive*, I thought, inflating myself with the intoxicating smell of lemons that had been used to clean the brass. I was a lunatic child staring wide-eyed, unprotected, at the moon which – at that very moment – must be shining on the waving plumes of the shakos, the splendid black royal carriage splattered with hard hot sprays of mud. In my imagination, I urged on the sweating horses through the night, past the flares and faggots of the king's *good honest* people. I prayed for him. Oh do not fear, my king.

I was still engaged in this journey, driving away his enemies, twisting in my sheets, when Odile returned from her evening off. My pulse was racing, and I myself was very hot, but not so hot as Odile, and I will tell you how I knew: When she leaned to kiss my forehead I could feel her blushing down her chest.

'What has happened Odile?'

'The king has been detained again.'

'No, do not tease me.'

'This time it is the flour dealers of Amiens.'

'But *flour dealers*, Odile? Do not the flour dealers want his head?'

'No, no, my small master.' She placed her hot hands on my cheek. 'It is the millers' ancient privilege.'

Millers, I thought. How *preposterous*.

Good Odile stroked my forehead until I slept and when I woke she had gone, although I soon understood that she was sobbing in her room. The daughter of a peasant, I thought, but she is no different from Blacqueville or myself. Neither of us can bear to wait another day.

At breakfast she did not wish to be bothered with me, so I pulled at her broad fingertips until she slapped my leg.

I said I would tell my mother.

'Tell who you like,' she said. 'It can't be worse than this.' She said she was to be sent back to the château de Barfleur that very day.

'Oh poor Odile,' I cried, 'you will never see His Majesty.'

Odile's small round nose was red with her own misery, and yet she smiled and shook her head. I thought, It is not so bad for her as it would be for me.

'Little Olivier,' she said, 'your silly Odile has fallen in love.'

I thought, It is the king, of course.

'Who will look after me, Odile?'

'Oh,' she cried, 'you poor little creature.'

I was briefly puzzled to hear her speak this way. Yet it was not uncommon that her generous affections would lead her to forgot her place.

Shortly before lunch I observed, with some alarm, a swarm of the strange Paris servants piling various items of my clothing, willy-nilly, upon the billiard table. Having at first taken exception to their appalling method, it took me a moment to see, among the tangle, the Ch'ien-lung bowl. Then I finally understood why she, a servant, had called me a *pauvre petite créature*. I was to be sent away with her.

When my mother confirmed these fears, I threw up on my shoes and declared myself too sick to travel. In any case, why must I be banished because a *servant* had misbehaved?

'You must study your Latin,' my mother said formally, and again many hours later, by which time I lay exhausted on my bed. It had been a horrid, horrid day. The leeches had finally fallen off and been cast into the flames. 'Bébé is waiting for you at home, my darling.'

'Maman, you know I cannot possibly leave before the king arrives. Bébé must come here.'

'Olivier, the abbé de La Londe will not come to Paris.'

'I cannot travel, Maman. I simply can't. I will study my Latin with Blacqueville. He will teach me Greek as well.'

'Young man, you are a Garmont not a sparrow. You cannot sing the same song all day.'

'It will be much better for everyone if I remain.'

And so on.

The very next morning, having been permitted a tearful farewell with Thomas, I was carried to my tumbrel, a quilt wrapped around my *poor thin legs*. How dare they, I thought. How dare my own parents treat me so stupidly.

I was of noble blood. It was my right to stay but instead I was sent into exile, the horses plodding through mud and drenching rain, *through melancholy, to melancholy*, as the poet has said.

The servant steadied the Ch'ien-lung bowl on the seat between us and it was then that she confessed – we were being sent away to *safety* because she had fallen for a splendid Austrian guard and my mother would not have it.

I thought, What has this to do with me?

'You will have the abbé anyway,' she said, lighting her little clay pipe and filling the carriage with her dusty smoke.

It is not Odile who is to blame, I thought. It is Bébé.

'Bébé is afraid,' I said. 'He is afraid Bonaparte will put him to the sword.' I had never said such a vile thing in all my life and I waited to be shamed for it, but Odile shifted the Ch'ien-lung onto her lap and clutched it to her stomach as if it were her child.

'Everyone should be afraid,' she said. 'They are not afraid enough poor creatures.'

'You are a poor creature, too, Odile.'

And at that she began to laugh. 'Aye,' she said. 'Look at us.'

We entered the gates of the château de Barfleur at that time of day when – so dreary, so predictable – no lights were lit and the dark beached mass of château bled into the gloom. How I dreaded it, the very air of my home, the dusty smell like that of a reliquary built to house the thigh bone of a tortured saint. I would be the only person of my age.

In the great courtyard we were greeted by Gustave the blacksmith, whom I had imagined to be in Paris, and by Bébé who, to my private shame, was so kind and affectionate toward me. He announced that we were, immediately, to make a *bivouac* in the unwalled pavilion my father had built beside the pond. We would sleep there and study there. We would botanise.

So Odile was left to take her leeches and grief into the château which, with so many of the servants in Paris, must have been a very lonely place indeed. Although, I thought, perhaps they like it, perhaps they have secret balls and grand dinners where they wear my parents' clothes and drink the best of our cellar and perform plays and juggling tricks when Bébé has gone to bed.

Let them dance, I thought, poor creatures.

But of course there were no dancing parties in the château. Or they were not visible. From the pavilion we could see only a single lighted candle in a window below the eaves, a very lonely flame compared to the rushing sparks from Bébé's splendid fire. The rain soon stopped. The sky cleared. We ate grilled rabbit below the great eternal wonder of the stars.

If you had observed Olivier's greasy face in starlight, you might have supposed he had been cured of his bleeding, vomiting, gasping upset. Yet this was a very wilful constant child and he did not, not for a moment, forget his king. So while you see young Olivier admire the reflection of the moon in the pond, you must not doubt that he was, even as he turned to smile at the abbé de La Londe, picturing the royal coach, the spinning wheel hubs decorated with painted suns, the spokes like shining rays ending in the firmament portrayed by the signs of the stars. He was a good boy. He said his prayers. He lay down beneath his uncle de Barfleur's bearskin. He closed his eyes and pictured the great ship of state ploughing through the night.

VII

The rudimentary comforts of our first night suggested only a brief diversion. Who would have expected we would live there all that summer and that our bivouac, of necessity, would assume an established character, with Turkey rugs and armchairs and my grandfather's campaign bed, an antique brass construction held together with verdigrised butterfly nuts and wire cross-bracing.

A refectory table was discovered in the old pigeon loft, and when this was scrubbed and waxed it was where we spent our mornings, classifying the previous day's botanising according to Linnaeus.

We had a wide low roof over our heads and if, from time to time, the rain blew in from the river, the summer was warm and our rugs were easily resuscitated in that gorgeous dry air, ripe with the perfumes of hawthorn blossom and grass and manure and fresh rich hay. Black honeybees and bumblebees danced around me as I studied. More than once we had speckled wood butterflies basking on our table, and once the sexton's cow awoke me with a dreadful bellow in my ear.

M. Blacksmith constructed an Indian's fireplace, that is, a *babracot,* and the servants split firewood and the English cook finally consented to grill the game as Bébé ordered.

My mother wrote a letter every day. I looked forward to her pale-blue *tutoiements* with a simple joy one would never feel in approaching her quite formal person. One broke the sealing wax with a dreamy sort of pleasure such as an eagle might feel lazily gliding on a warm delicious current. It was as if the windows had opened in my mother's life and the air was filled with cyan dragon-flies. Today it is my sweetest memory of Henriette-Lucie, the jasmine escaping from its paper shell.

These love letters were delivered by means of the postal system my father had designed as an improvement on that arrangement the emperor so famously devised. In our corner of Normandy there was no household, be it as low as a charcoal burner's, where a letter would not arrive as quickly as it did at the château. It was as a result of my father's particular system that we were blessed to have Marie-Claude, the sexton, deliver our mail directly to the pavilion. He had no horse, nor did he require one, for we were less than a kilometre from the village and every morning – provided there had been no death in the night – he would amble, long-armed and poke-necked, as if demanding that the peculiar world explain itself. He would stumble through the dew-wet pasture to that place where he would be pleased to withhold my mail while he inspected the botanical samples spread across our table.

I was infuriated by the sexton but also nourished in all my dreams and expectations by what he brought me, that is, my mother, in all her blindness and bubbling intoxication.

From inside the sexton's pocket, she sang to me like a captive bird: *Lovely boy*, she called me, and *brave boy* and *good boy* too: the king had not yet dined at the rue Saint-Dominique but she and my father had been to the Tuileries. This visit, she wrote, meant that the king had not forgotten the service given by her family nor by the valiant Barfleur who had died for Louis XVI, and she was confident that, for this reason alone, my father might reasonably expect to be made a *pair de France* and sit in the Chamber of Peers.

My father wrote less often and, far from calling me a boy, seemed to have forgotten I was not a man. His tone was both sophisticated and familiar – wry, ironic, fed by a disenchantment that I could not have named. The taste of his letters stayed with me, producing in me a profound unease. For instance:

'I shall never forget the impression Louis XVIII made when he came out to receive us; we saw an enormous mass emerge from the king's study, shuffling and waddling; this mass was topped by a fine and noble head but the expression of the features was entirely theatrical; the king came forward with his hand over his heart, his eyes raised to heaven. He said a few perfectly well-judged words to us, delivered in the most sentimental manner. It was clear from this that he had rehearsed his performance. We retired from his presence with gratitude for the special kindness that he showed us, and with the conviction that as a king he would make a most excellent actor.'

This less-than-respectful tone makes no sense until you know what was omitted from my parents' loving letters. My father did not say that he found himself severely disadvantaged for not having fled the revolution. He did not point out that the émigrés were also now returned. The king, of course, was of their party. I did not understand that my father's loyalty was neither celebrated nor valued, and he had been finally granted what the English call the leftovers – not a seat in the Chamber of Peers but the prefecture of the département of Maine-et-Loire. This was an insult, but he was a Garmont and so he set out for his new residence.

My mother would have none of it. She remained in Paris.

Autumn came and the servants packed away my campaign bed, the specimen table, the Turkey rugs, all the contents of the pavilion except my bear rug which I would not relinquish. Bébé and I withdrew to the château, where we were appalled to find that the preposterous architect and his assistant had expanded their territories. The Blue Room had proven insufficient for their needs and now they occupied the library where they had taken up the incense habit. Bébé and I retreated to the second floor and here we also took our meals and I developed what was thought to be a sleeping sickness.

Bébé wished to *get the boy outside* but all those useful extending legs and springing arms, those Olivier-in-the-box explosions, saved me. It was not until the ice had melted on the *bain* that I ventured out, my bear rug still wrapped around my shoulders.

And it was on a late March morning in 1815 that my parents returned from Paris and I came rushing to them, dripping wet with the waters of the *bain*, me and Bébé, wet and dry, bear and man, hand in hand, in such a hurry that we were both almost crushed beneath a screeching gun carriage drawn by a company of soldiers up the Paris road.

My mother burst out from her box.

'Hoorah,' I cried. She did not hear me. She shook her feathers, and rushed toward the château leaving the servants to unload the coaches. The servants, like their feverish mistress, carelessly abandoned precious items where they fell. For instance, here – a grand ball gown lying on the architect's spilled earth like pink hydrangea blooms.

I saw my mother fly past the gallery windows, unwinding like a muslin curtain, a white train floating above the stairs, spiralling around the former pigeon loft. Soon I saw her draw her apartment blinds, although not her window sash. Everyone in the courtyard could hear their mistress weeping. I was ashamed for her. Bébé took my hand to calm me but I tugged free and rushed inside, more like my mother than I knew, wet and white and naked, my childish sex exposed, the bearskin trailing behind me and dragging fallen hats and ribbons in its train. I tripped on the stairs and hurt my leg running toward this dreadful howl of wind bursting from the same dear pipes that had sung 'A Troubadour of Béarn'. I entered the blood-rich cavity of sound, and discovered my maman on her *chaise*, her face all raw and wet as if flayed by grief.

'Bonaparte is back,' she said. 'It's over.'

'Over?' I was terrified. 'Over!' I yanked the bearskin once again, brought down something with a crash. I heard the rattle of the deadly blade in its grooved oaken track. I fled out down the stairs, sprinted naked along the gallery to my father's office, where I found him behind the great leather-topped desk which was piled high with papers accumulated in his absence.

'Ah, Master de Garmont,' he said, as if we had been separated for only a few minutes. 'There you are.' He said nothing of my undress or bloody leg. He laid his hand on my head and looked at me but I knew he was blind, that he could know nothing but my mother's shocking distress which was carried to us even here, so many stairs and walls away.

He had in his hand the soda-water flask my mother and I had drunk from now so long ago and he was turning this object over and over and peering into it. He was a great man but he could no longer help us.

Only Odile knew what to do. She rushed on her big flat feet to my mother's rooms, carrying her Ch'ien-Lung bowl before her. I followed close behind, a lace cloth to hide my naked skin. In my mother's apartments, Odile lit the candles, thumping from place to place making a deep soothing noise of a type one might imagine would persuade a cow into her bails. She arranged my mother on the *chaise* and, having wet the noble lady's brow and wiped away her rouge and powder, turned her attention to the bowl.

Squatting beside her, shivering, girlish in my lace, I saw the great oily stillness of our neglected leeches in their prison, unneeded and forgotten, starved to scum, their sucking stilled, all my glory dreams turned broth and black corruption.

PARROT

You might think, who is this, and I might say, this is God and what are you to do? Or I might say, a bird! Or I could tell you, madame, monsieur, sir, madam, how this name was given to me – I was christened Parrot because my hair was coloured carrot, because my skin was burned to feathers, and when I tumbled down into the whaler, the coxswain yelled, Here's a parrot, captain. So it seems you have your answer, but you don't.

I had been named Parrot as a child, when my skin was still pale and tender as a maiden's breast, and I was still Parrot in 1793, when Olivier de Bah-bah Garmont was not even a twinkle in his father's eye.

To belabour the point, sir, I was and am distinctly senior to that unborn child.

In 1793 the French were chopping off each other's heads and I was already twelve years of age and my *endodermis naturalus* had become scrubbed and hardened by the wind and mists of Dartmoor, from whose vastness my da and I never strayed too far. I had tramped behind my darling da down muddy lanes and I was still called Parrot when he, Jack Larrit, carried me on his shoulder through Northgate at Totnes. My daddy loved his Parrot. He would sit me on the bar of the Kingsbridge Inn, to let the punters hear what wonders came from my amazing mouth: *Man is born free and is everywhere in chains.*

If that ain't worth sixpence what is?

My daddy was a journeyman printer, a lanky man with big knees and knubbly knuckled hands with which he would ruff up his red hair when looking for *First Principles*. Inside this bird's nest it was a surprise to find his small white noggin, the precious engine of his bright grey eyes.

'Children remain tied to their father by nature only so long as they need him for their preservation. As soon as this ends,' so wrote the great Rousseau, 'the natural bond is dissolved. Once the children are freed from the obedience they owe their father and the father is freed from their responsibilities towards them, both parties equally regain their independence. If they continue to remain united, it is no longer nature but their own choice which unites them; and the family as such is kept together only by agreement.'

More or less that's it.

My daddy and I were two peas in a pod. The acquisition of knowledge was our occupation, but of my ma I knew nothing but that she had a tiny waist which would fit inside her husband's hands. I missed her all my life.

I knew Adam Smith before I reached fractions. Then I was put to Latin which my father liked no more than I did, and this caused us considerable upset, both with ourselves and with each other. It was due to Latin that my father got in a state and clipped my lughole and I grabbed a half-burned bit of kindling and set to drawing on the floor. I had never seen a drawing in my life, and when I saw what I was doing, dear God, I thought I had invented it. And what rage, what fury, what a delicious humming wickedness I felt. All over the floor and who will clean it? I had seen my daddy's hand reach for his belt buckle and I was, *ipso facto*, ready for the slap. Yet at this moment I entered a foreign jungle of the soul. I drew a man with a dirty long nose. A leaping trout. A donkey falling upside down.

But my daddy's belt stayed in his trousers.

He stared at me. His hair stood up like taffy. He cocked his head. I permitted him to take my charcoal stick and kiss me on the head. Not a cross word, or a kind one. He led the Parrot downstairs where he ordered the landlord pour me a ginger beer. Then he sat and watched me drink, and what was he pondering, do you reckon?

Why, the benefits of having an engraver in the family.

Thereafter I was a mighty protégé and we forgot about our upsets and our Latin and our fractions, and even though my drawings were not always wanted where I placed them, he encouraged me at every turn, always on the lookout for a quiet church porch on account of the quality of its slate. As to subjects, he was not fussy, although once he gave me a pound note to see what I could make of it.

On another occasion he was compelled to scrub clean the Dartmouth footpath on which I had drawn the great bloody head of Louis XVI. My father said he didn't mind the scrubbing, it being a pleasure to make any tyrant vanish from the earth. It was suggested we might leave the town. There was no work in Dartmouth anyway. But up in Dittisham – Dit'sum as they called it – we found a strangely isolated printery, situated just at the place where the estuary became the River Dart, and there we found members of that better educated class – I mean printers. There is nothing like them. Having spent all their day with words and proofs, they are monstrously well read and disputatious beasts, always – while setting up the type, tapping in the furniture, rolling out the ink – arguing. If it was not that they spoke varying types of English, you might think yourself in France. It was the drunken height of revolution and all was Girondins or Cordeliers, Hume or Paine.

The printers at Dit'sum were family-genus-species *Textus miraculus*. They would shut up only at the long deal table which they shared with their master, Mr Piggott, and his wife, them both being Catholics of a put-upon variety and very sarcastic about Tom Paine in particular. Mrs Piggott was a young Frenchwoman easily made tearful by events in her country, which left the men with nothing they could safely say at table – but I am ahead of myself. I did not say our single aim was to find shelter and a decent meal.

We arrived from Dartmouth at dinnertime. My father knocked and hallooed, until we discovered seven full-grown humans, all supping at a table, quiet as Lent.

We finally sat down the end with big bowls of stew and lumps of rough bread and a cup of rainwater and about twenty cats mewling about our legs. No sooner did my daddy have a mouthful than the master wished to know who he was. He replied he was a press or case man, whatever was needed worst. In fact Piggott required a case man – that is, a compositor – who would lift types for sixpence a thousand, but at first he said nothing of it, for he was staring hard at me. No matter how girlish his wife, Mr Piggott himself was all of sixty. He was almost bald, with a little lump of a nose.

'The devil, are you?' he demanded.

'Me, sir?'

'You, lad.'

He had a very short neck and colossal shoulders that seemed as wide as the table and when he stood to see me better he began to butt his big head against the ceiling, like a goat.

I would have run but my father clamped my thigh.

I said that I was ten years old and, being too young to be apprenticed, I was accustomed to taking the job of devil.

My father was occupied cleaning the tines of his fork with his shirt tail.

Many is the dirty job I did, I told old Piggott. I would rather work than play. I could clean the proofing press, I said. I was a dab hand at dissing which is what they call putting the type back in its right case.

'See him draw a racehorse,' said my father.

This comment caused some puzzlement but finally I was given pencil and paper. The result was then passed around the table. No one made a comment but when the horse arrived in front of Mrs Piggott, she rose up from her chair.

The mistress could not yet have been twenty, but I saw a small old person, camouflaged like a lizard, and she came around the table at me flicking out a measuring tape like some enormous tongue.

My face and neck burned bright red while I stood in front of all these men and Mrs Piggott, with no word of explanation, having completely ignored my racehorse, measured me, not only my height but around my chest, from armpit to extremity.

'Ah, ain't that lovely?' said my da who would say anything to get a nice hot feed. 'See that Parrot – you are to be measured. What a treat,' he said to Mr Piggott.

Mrs Piggott slipped her tape measure into the pocket of her pinny. Mr Piggott thumped his fist twice against the ceiling, which was even more alarming than the butting. At this signal each printer bowed his atheistic head.

'*Benedictus benedicat per Jesum Christum dominum nostrum.*' Then, moving from Latin to English without a cough, Mr Piggott formally employed my father, passing down to him, from hand to hand, a copy of Miss Parsons's *The Castle of Wolfenbach* which, just published in London for ten shillings, he would soon have on the roads at six shillings and sixpence.

My father said, 'Good-oh,' and did not seem to worry about

what might happen to me on account of the measuring. My racehorse was left with all the breadcrumbs. I never had so little praise before.

Even when we went out after dinner my dad said not a word about what had happened. Instead he lit his pipe and told me this was certainly the River Dart. It was a place where cattle crossed, so the bank was bad-smelling from their droppings mixed with earth. 'Lovely night,' my father said, turning with one arm behind his back to survey the printery which occupied what might have once been a grand house but had long been encroached upon by woods, tangled in wild creeper, guarded by thistles on the riverbank, surrounded by carts and wheels in such a style you would think it the graveyard for old carriages.

Piggott's was what was called a *black house*, not because of the grimy slate tiles that wrapped themselves around the soft contours of the roof, but on account of printing what was *on the cross*. To make this cheap edition of *The Castle of Wolfenbach* was an offence against the Crown.

Soon Mrs Piggott gave us each a bundle of bed linen and when my father paid her a florin, she silently showed him to a bed by the dormitory door. Me she led to the far end and left in what was once a kind of scullery. My da said it was a fine accommodation but this was like him, to become most enthusiastic when most oppressed by life. He showed me how I could lie in bed and watch the cattle go home for milking. His bright eyes were a fright to see.

On this first night, I was sitting on my bed, wondering if I dare walk outside to do my business, when something attacked my shoulder, I thought a bird or bat but discovered a pile of quarto proofs wrapped in string.

My da was always at me with a book and I was not displeased. When I had unwrapped the bundle I was excited to find engravings for a picture book. Alas, these were depictions of human congress too disturbing for a child. I could chop the head off a king, but I was not strong enough for this.

I never told my father what I had seen, or why I abandoned my own place and walked the length of the dormitory in my nightshirt and squeezed into his narrow crib.

'Oh, this is a grand place,' he said, and I agreed it was and got ready to protect myself from his nightmares and his bruising knees.

II

That first morning our bathing in the river provided amusement for the printers whose yawning faces appeared in a line of windows like noggins at a fair. One of them asked us were we mermaids – it was not what he said, but he was a Londoner with all his lovely London sounds, and I did adore the voices of mankind.

'Meer-mayds,' said the Parrot to his da.

My dad tried to wad the washcloth in my mouth. If I was a good boy I should have let him, but I squirmed away as wicked as a slippery eel.

'Meer-mayd,' I called.

'Shush,' he said. And ran away, my da, sausage bouncing, splashing nudey through the water, lurching toward the riverbank with the idea, I suppose, that I would have no one left to talk to if he was not there.

'Oh, lor!' I shouted from the middle of the stream. 'Blow me down. It must be a meer-mayd.'

Came my father's voice, faintly, from the shore: 'Shush.'

'Meer-mayds!' I cried, making a funnel with my hands. 'Meer-mayds!' I had the lovely vowels, I was a Pearly King.

My daddy dressed and walked back to the printery, head down, combing at his wet hair in such a way I knew he was trying to hide his grin. He had a soft sweet heart, it was a burden to him. 'How *do* you do that?' he would often say. He could not whistle either although he often tried.

When breaking fast the cockney fellow winked at me and I knew I had made a friend not the enemy my father must have feared.

After breakfast we were taken to the printery. The cockney announced he was known as Gunner and proceeded to show my da his frame. Piggott watched suspiciously, it seemed to me, as my dad set up the implements of his trade and mounted a pair of cases full of shining type in readiness for *The Castle of Wolfenbach*. Then I was set to clean the proofing press.

It was not only Gunner who had a nickname. There was also Weasel, Bunter, Chooka, Chanker, to name a few. Gunner was a pressman who operated his machine with the darting little Weasel. Bunter was tall and gone to fat, a slovenly worker, scrambling and shovelling his types together without any regard to the exact mechanical neatness which is an instinct with the good compositor. All this I observed as I cleaned the ink slab. When that dirty task was done I was set to work humping heavy bundles of the Dit'sum newspaper from the back door to a trolley. After this, with my hands already harrowed and scarified from binding twine, I was ordered by Bunter to clean myself with spirit and printer's soap, and this hurt a great deal as it had the texture of coarse sand. Then I was ordered to drag this four-wheeled monster up a rutted road and then along a maze of lanes and footpaths which – being always unsure if I could find my way home again – I did not like at all.

Dit'sum being a decent size and the people of a secretive disposition, it took the best part of the day to get the newspapers to their subscribers. I was relieved to find my way back to the old printery, grey and lumpy, like a turtle in the mud.

After supper my father and I bathed again. He had the hands of a drowned man, my dear daddy, blanched to death by endless washing. When we were dry and decent we found the men gathered by the broad dormitory steps pursuing what was clearly an ongoing argument about the utility of kings in a republic. My father was excitable by temperament but cautious by habit, and he smoked his pipe, nodded his head but offered no opinions.

In the night he was alarmed by some bad turn his dream was taking and nearly took my eye out.

The second day involved washing in the river and then getting dirty and then delivering a job lot of docket books to the Swan. This was formally received by an older girl who looked me up and down like I was the living filth. She took me into a dark parlour where some old ladies sat wetting their hairy chins with stout. Thus it was at a table in a pub I first saw the quality of Piggott's engraving which was what you might call *cack-handed*.

She said, 'What happened to Sniffy?'

I said I did not know.

She said, 'Did Sniffy die?'

'I don't know, Miss.' I thought I could draw a swan much better. I was bursting to show her what I could have done.

The third day began just the same. I washed. I got dirty. Mr Piggott himself came to give me my instructions.

'Get the trolley, lad,' he said. 'Today it is a pickup.'

I set off at a great speed in order to get the heavy trolley up onto the road, but he snatched the machine from my care, and shoved it underneath a pussy willow. He then led me through some stinging nettles arriving hard against the backside of the house, at a place where there was a stink of moss and lichens, also a peeling grey door, which I was told to open. I found myself in an empty dark stale-smelling room which had once been a kitchen. From here I was shooed like a hen into another room which held nothing but a big fireplace of grey carved stone.

'Now,' said Piggott, 'come in the fireplace and I'll show you.'

I said I was not allowed in fireplaces.

For answer Mr Piggott threw his head back against his wide shoulders. Then he folded himself up, all shoulder, head and knees and – maintaining this strange arrangement of his limbs – edged himself inside the fireplace.

'Come here with me,' he said, taking off his spectacles and sliding them inside his apron.

'I'm going to fetch the trolley,' I said.

'Forget the blessed trolley. We need no trolley.' He came crabbing out to snatch at me, his naked eyes gone wet and fishy. He twisted up my shirtfront in his fist. I tore away and broke my buttons and rushed out into the dappled woody light of morning, bawling in fright, but I wanted a sleep and a feed and so fetched the stupid trolley from its hiding place and brought it back to the main door of the printery where I met my father rushing the other way, a stick of type grasped in his hand.

Mr Piggott rounded on us, arms swinging, head nodding.

'What's he done now?' my father said.

Mr Piggott removed the stick from my father's hand, assessed the type composed there, before laying it carefully on a windowsill. Then he led my da away from me, down toward the stream. I saw the water sparkling behind their dark figures, light shining like a halo through Mr Piggott's ring of hair. The master stroked my da on his long back, then watched as he returned to his son.

'What?' I asked.

He attempted to mimic me but he did not have the ear. He was hangdog, red neck, and could not look at me. 'Come on, my Parrot,' said he at last. 'Master needs your help.'

'No,' I said slipping from his grabby hand.

My daddy permitted himself to be led into the stinging nettles, through the empty kitchen, to the empty fireplace. I followed.

This time I noted Piggott took the trouble to explain, and when he did this his voice became both whispery and loud.

Said he, 'I have a very good pressman working in a very hard-to-get-to place.'

My father squatted and peered toward the chimney.

'That's right,' said Mr Piggott, jerking his head at my father. 'That's it, John.'

My father winked at me.

'Nothing's going to hurt the nipper,' said Mr Piggott. 'All he has to do is.'

I took a step back but my da had already locked his arm around my shoulder.

'That's it,' whispered Mr Piggott. 'All he has to do.'

He got down on his hands and knees and crawled into the fireplace. 'Come on, young 'un,' he whispered, and I smelled an airy rush of peppermint.

'See up there?' My da pointed, squeezing in. 'See that?'

I allowed myself to be pulled in beside my da and Mr Piggott, who had a tussock of white hair growing out of his wattly ear.

'See that?'

'No,' I said, but I did see: a little metal door inside the chimney.

'Yes, it looks all dark, don't it, but once inside, young 'un, why, you'll find an oil lamp burning. It's like bloody Christmas.'

'Well, so to speak,' my daddy cautioned.

'Yes, so to speak,' said Mr Piggott. 'In a way of speaking. Not Christmas, of course, but plenty of surprises. You see, young 'un,' he said, plucking at my open shirt, 'hold your lamp up high, you'll see there's a passage tailor-made for you, and even though it goes this way and that, it keeps on going just the same, and you come to a bit of a step which you climb up, and then there is another door. Doesn't look like a door at all, even when your nose is hard against it, but you give it a good hard knock. You will, I know you will. Because what's inside but a printer like your father, not so tall or so handsome. Mr Watkins is his name. And he's going to give you something.'

'What?' I asked.

'See,' said Mr Piggott. 'It's not hard.'

'What will he get given?' my father asked.

'Well, it's a funny thing when you say it, but it's as regular as your daily bread.'

'What is it?' I asked.

'It's his chamber pot I suppose,' said Mr Piggott, 'and the printer fellow would be very grateful if you could bring it back out here so we can nicely deal with it.'

I was tremendously relieved to hear all this, and I was ready to set off immediately, but my father was now edging me back out into the room and Mr Piggott had no choice but follow, although the three of us continued bunched together as if packed into a box.

'How was this job done previous?' my daddy asked.

'We had a lad, of course. It requires no training,' said Mr Piggott, who must have seen which way my father's mind was working.

'Ah, there you are,' my daddy said. 'Then he's better than an apprentice.'

'How's that?' said Piggott.

'No training. Less eaten. Less laundered. Less found,' my father said. 'And why was he measured? Well, it's obvious. It was an act of employment. Speaking legally.'

'A penny,' said Mr Piggott.

'Threepence each way,' my father said, 'and another threepence for each time he's needed.'

'I could get anyone to do this,' Piggott said. 'Threepence in and out this first time. And a penny each way thereafter.'

By now my father had his hair combed up into a big mess and he was scratching at his neck in an attempt to hide his happiness, but I had been there long enough to decide that the previous boy had been Sniffy, and although I allowed my father to lift me to the dark door, the tiny red hairs on my boy arms were standing up on end.

It was a tight fit in there but passing clean, and the so-called passage bent and twisted and arrived at a wall that I did not understand. This was what Mr Piggott had called a step.

Then I was over this and soon I came to another dead end and, just as my throat was closing up with terror I knocked. A hidden door swung open. And there it was – the printer's chamber pot, filled to overflowing, thrust right in my face.

'Take it,' the pressman said.

He was a fright, I won't pretend he wasn't. For although he was a young man and had therefore often walked the earth and seen the sun, he seemed, at that moment, like one of those transparent creatures they say live in rivers far below the earth. His hair was fine as silk, and long and white, not like the English but the Swedes. His forehead was very tall, and so white and smooth it seemed as if it must be carved from ivory. He had pale projecting eyebrows, and eyes like water.

'Now put it down,' he said.

'What?' I asked, having heard him perfectly.

'Put down the filthy pot,' he pleaded, 'on the stinking floor.'

I saw no reason to be afraid of such a nervous creature, but when I obeyed he gave me an awful cuff across the head and took me by the ear and twisted it.

'If you ever leave me waiting again,' he whispered, 'I will come out *the hard way*' – that was how he put it – 'and Piggott don't want that. Smell it,' he cried, his voice cracking. 'Smell.'

He meant his room. I looked above his shoulder and saw he was like all men who work with black ink and white paper. That is, his printed sheets were as clean as sawn timber and his narrow bed was tightly made. He shared his snug space with a guillotine and the first iron hand press I ever saw. He was all hunched over, his arms were long and thin and he held them across his chest in a way that made me think of the roots of a pot-bound tree. I could not make out how tall he was.

It would be many years, on the other side of the world, before I understood that Piggott's house had been designed by Nicholas Owen, a clever fellow who had devised the many hiding places for priests in the reign of Elizabeth I. Whether Piggott had inherited or purchased the property, I still don't know. At the time, of course, I did not care, for while it had been easy enough to crawl along the tiny passageway, it was quite another matter to return, nudging and sliding the sloshing chamber pot. Gently gently catchee monkey. This was now my job – penny both ways, a fortune – to bring Mr Algernon Watkins his sandwiches and take away his slops three times a day and if I was ever to breathe so much as a word to anyone, then I would be murdered and my body bricked up inside the house. 'That's an exaggeration,' my father said.

III

I had never set eyes on a silkworm and I dare say young Watkins was in no way like one. Yet it is a silkworm that I think of when I recall him in 1793, a poor pale secret thing at the service of a Chinese emperor, sitting on his heels before his press, playing it like a dice box, and with all the papery essentials within the reach of his long arms. It will be no surprise, I reckon, that I got to know Algernon Watkins well enough, although the path will be curly, and not as you expect.

Piggott was as sly as a fox, as clever as a poacher. So well did he cover my tracks (and his own) that not even Weasel, the Jacobin, or Chanker, the Benthamite had any idea what was taking place above their heads. As for my revolutionary father, it is a sad fact that you could kill his famous curiosity with less than threepence. So when I slipped away after tea he knew better than to ask me why.

It took a good many nasty trips to Watkins' dark door before I crossed the threshold, and only then did I really comprehend his terror of the chamber pot. As anyone who has served at His Majesty's Pleasure will tell you, the smells that make your guts first heave soon become your home sweet home. But Watkins was, put plainly, a more fastidious and secretive young fellow than all your sisters put together.

There was ventilation of a sort which we will come to, but because he must clean his press, the air always contained white spirits – which he feared would blow him to kingdom come. This sensible concern had him pulling on the ventilator pulley with one hand even while he worked the press, so he was – as he said himself – like one of the Jack Puddings you see outside the George and Dragon with twenty instruments, the left foot beating drums, the right one cracking walnuts, this not being a bad picture of Watkins for he also – apart from being both pressman and ventilator – kept vials of aromatics – oil of cloves, sweet geranium – in a row before his knees and was constantly dabbing these onto the silk scarf he wore across his nose and mouth.

But it was not only the straight thin nose he covered. He had white cloth draped everywhere, across the chamber pot, the press, the guillotine, his paper stock, brush box blocks, and the burins which were to play so painful a part in my life I have sometimes wished to God I never saw them.

You do not know what a burin is, and nor did I, mistaking it for a shiv, a murdering steel shaft with a hemispherical handle.

It was very tight inside Watkins' *shop*, as he called it, but he offered a place for Parrot to sit, jammed in a corner just inside the door. His place was also just inside the door, but on the other side, and there he remained, with his pot-bound arms around his knees and his high head bowed beneath the ceiling so we were like a pair of ill-matched firedogs.

Although he could have been no more than twenty, he had clearly forgotten what it was like to be a boy. He conversed by means of questions, answers, commentary, as if I was there to learn my catechism.

He would ask me what I had seen that day. This was mostly birds and animals, and his commentaries, particularly about the birds, were very queer and very personal and often of surprising length.

When my da was in his cups, we had some strange conversations, but none like this. For Watkins' memories could turn him so suddenly and wildly happy, and he would make a picture of stomping on the moor and all the colours of the birds and gorse he could count off on his fingers. You would think he was a saint with the light of heaven on him. In this condition he could make you share his wonder at plain old tomtit, for instance, and it was by catching this intoxication that I drew a fieldmouse for him, showing off, right on his floor.

I had done this trick so often, I knew I was a prodigal. So when Watkins peered at my mouse and twisted himself around and I saw his hand burrowing under a cotton cover, then why, I thought it was my just reward. I was in no way surprised to see a big square of chocolate.

I put it in my mouth and saw him laugh at me. It was hard and brown, would break your teeth.

'What is it?' I asked. I was used to beer for my daddy or taffy for myself. Not this, this cold hard thing inside my palm.

'You are not an artist's bootlace,' said he.

'What is it?'

'It is a brush box,' said he, 'and if you are an artist it is butter beneath your knife.'

I asked him was he an artist.

For answer he would only smile and I thought how large his eyes were when they hid behind his purplish lids. He retrieved the square of steel-hard wood like a cardsharp on the Strand, not letting me touch it but allowing me to glimpse the very artful drawing of a quail he had made upon one side. I hated it and was angry that he would not praise me. At the same time he was a mystery like none I ever knew. He was uncanny, pot-bound, excitable. He was watchful and ugly but graceful too. He was close as a tomb but on that same day I drew the mouse he revealed to me, a boy, his great ambition and the reason why he had sold his services to Piggott. He planned to amass sufficient *Geld* to produce and print the best book of birds the world had ever seen.

Saying this, his watery eyes were very bright and everything in that dreadful little tomb seemed illuminated by his joy.

'What are you smiling at?'

I said I was thinking how nice it would be to see a book like that.

'You can't imagine, boy.'

I supposed I couldn't.

'You don't know what I am,' he said.

'I am just a boy.'

He looked at me very close as if sizing up my utility and, without shifting his gaze, reached out for the shiv, that lethal-looking object we have been waiting for. I bolted for the door but he stuck his leg out so it would not open and then, picking up the brush box, he began to work. I understood he would not murder me, but he did not look up at me or speak to me for a very long time, and even then he had not finished his work but I saw how he wielded that burin.

When he had done all he planned to do he let me touch it very briefly. I was not his bootlace. He sent me out so he could do his business in the pot.

IV

A fortnight previous the precocious Parrot had been Leonardo, Cicero and the perfect future of the workingman. Now he was plucked and naked, a printer's devil, the silkworm's fag. There were more suitable skills to be acquired – for instance – holding the piss pot off the floor with my elbows and pushing through the darkness on my knees, a painful business.

The first pot I dispatched into the hydrangeas, and for this I got my ears boxed and would have got my bum whacked except Jack be nimble Jack be quick. It was a case of dig hole, bury shit, return empty pot. No time for drawing on the Church of England's slate. Collect empty water pail. Fill pail in stream. Other matters besides – ink – trolley – don't get lost. At the end of each long day I received from Watkins some ten parcels the size of four house bricks, sealed with red wax and wrapped tight with brown paper. These I pushed along the burrow one at a time, as instructed by Piggott, leaving them hidden inside the trapdoor to be taken in the night.

What happened to these parcels was a mystery I would not solve for many years. They disappeared, leaving no clue but a mess of broken sealing wax like the remains of something eaten by a dog. The wax was hard as broken glass and I was mostly concerned about the pain it caused my skin. But whether I was torturing my knees or strapped in the harness of the dog cart, I thought about not much else except how to make Mr Watkins teach me to engrave. The deep green oaks arched above my head but I was blind to all their splendour. I imagined the burin in my hand, carving with a flick and a push, feeling the steel moving through the hard wood like a knife through butter. I arrived in Mr Watkins' presence like a beggar on my knees.

I could hardly look at him, nor did he deign to glance at me.

If I had asked him to teach me he would have been haughty as a goose. So I sat in my place beside the door. On sufferance, I observed his long fair hair falling like a curtain across the mystery of his hands. I dared not ask to touch that unforgiving steel. I saw how his four long fingers were drawn back and curved and how he pressed the tool against the ball of the thumb. It looked so easy, but on the fetid night when at last – without warning – he pressed the tool into my warty hands, I found it completely resistant to my passion.

'You see,' he said to me, 'it is a gift.'

And took his burin back.

I was not worthy, but I would not go away and something in my wilfulness must have stirred him for he finally allowed me to ruin one of his brushwood blocks. How many nights was this for? Three? I sat cross-legged in the stinky hole, trying to engrave – not the rural scenes I had imagined, but ten straight lines close together. That was all he would let me do.

I was tired. I was very angry. I would not quit.

'You'll never be an engraver's bootlace,' he said. I will not say this did not hurt my feelings.

'Yes sir, I know.'

'Then go.'

With his long spidery arms he opened the door for me and was nice enough, on this occasion, to personally hand out the wrapped parcels of his day's production. Then the door closed as usual, and I was outside in the blackness. No skerrick of light snuck around his door and I knew he had put out his lamps and set to clean his equipment in the dark, his long hands fluttering across blade and type bed like a blind watchmaker. When his labour was done, he had earlier informed me, he would lie in bed pulling the rope of his ventilator, removing the flammable white spirit in time for work. Lighting the first lantern each morning, he feared he would be blown to bits.

One overcast dawn I arrived inside the fireplace to find an entire red wax seal broken as a biscuit. Then, deep in the dark of the crawling space, I came upon an item that must have spilled from the parcel – a sample of Mr Watkins' labour, a job so fine, I decided when

I brought it into the light, that he would have found employment anywhere on earth. The strange pale silk spinner was an artist, and although I already knew this from watching him work the burin, this single *assignat* confirmed him as the highest of the high.

Of course you, monsieur, know that an assignat was, at that time, the paper currency of the revolutionary government of France. Although the Parrot was only an ignorant printer's devil who had no clue about the assignat, the hair on my neck prickled. I recognised the power and danger of this ornate and clever forgery. I had only seen one British banknote in my life, the one my father had me draw, and that had been as pale and ordinary as a cabbage moth, requiring the endorsement of Lord Hob-Knob or I knew not who. The assignat was a power unto itself, a goldish colour, one part butter yellow, the remainder mustard, printed on pearly linen paper – *DOMAINES NATIONAUX*. Although I was no lawyer I believed that a man could be hanged for printing what was in my inky hands. A wise boy would have destroyed it, but was a wise boy ever born? I could not kill such a lovely thing. Nor could I bury it, for it was too beautiful. So I folded it until it would fold no more and then I thrust it in my britches and kept it like you keep a treasure you can worship under the bedclothes in the early light of morning.

I was always tired, always busy, falling asleep when my head hit the bed, being awoken by my father to get myself washed. The printers had long given up finding our *public ablutions*, as they called them, amusing. So we were left alone to clean ourselves and, on Sunday mornings, to wash our clothes as well.

The Sunday I will now recall was hot and overcast, and we found ourselves in company, not only with a hatch of mayflies, but a gentleman I had observed the night before at dinner, a tall Frenchman with a broad chest and a rich man's manner who was noteworthy on account of the glint in his small grey eyes and the mass of curling red hair around his big head – this latter making him look like a Scots laird – but all of these distinctions were trumped by his left arm which was *completely missing*.

At dinner he had mostly engaged with Mrs Piggott who I saw was tremendously excited, and although she was a little bantam with fretful eyes, she now began to bat them like a girl. She was suddenly so talkative she hardly touched her food. Back and forward they went – *parlez-vous* and so on.

We were told to call our visitor Monsieur but he did not seem so ordinary to me, and all the while he talked with Mrs Piggott, sugaring her with *d'accord*s and *madame*s, he had his eyes on the men around the table, engaging each of them, even me, letting us know he was very fine and fancy and that we would be unwise to cross him or betray him or even dream of such a thing.

We were at war with France yet we were in Devon very near the coast, and at Piggott's it was always ask no questions and you'll be told no lies. We never knew where the fruits of our labours would come to rest, in Louvres or Auxerre or Oxford Street. The Piggotts were always feeding up their customers, plying them with brandy and Madeira, and after they had slept off their dinner they were on their way.

I expected the Frenchman to be gone by morning. But there he was, nudey in midstream, and all I could see was the shocking violet skin shining in the place where his arm had been, and nothing left of it but a kind of flap, or turtle fin. Elsewhere his body had been pierced more times than Saint Sebastian, and each site of injury was like a patch of angry silk.

My father was a terrible talker who wanted to know everything at once, but here he had a powerful wish to know not a bloody thing.

'Bonjour,' the Frenchman called to us.

My father's eyes went dead and milky.

'Bonjour,' he called again, but my father was taken by the sights downstream.

It was I who called back, not from wickedness but because I could. Perhaps I might never draw a proper mouse, but I was a perfect mimic. That was a talent. Vowel for vowel, a parrot on the wing.

Says I: *'Bonjour.'*

Says he: *'Parles-tu français, monsieur?'*

Says I: *'Parles-tu français, monsieur?'*

He had a face like stone. I squeezed a grin out of it. *'Vous,'* said he. 'Ah, *vous?*' said I.

I wish you could hear me now because you would understand the unholy jumble – that rough little English boy falling over his *vous* and *tu*s in the perfect accent of the faubourg Saint-Germain. I dived into the stream in triumph, scraping my bare boy chest along a gravel bed as lightly as an old brown trout. Surfacing, I saw my father had retreated from me, scrambling to the bank to fetch our laundry.

'Où habites-tu?' the Frenchman asked me. You could hear the money in his voice.

*'Où habites-*tu?' I replied.

The Frenchman was not sure what was being done to him, whether he should be offended or amused.

My father came splashing toward me, the clothes clutched to his chest. It was rocky and difficult but he never once looked down.

'Wash-oh,' he cried to me. 'Wash-oh!'

Monsieur was a great wide bear, the hair on his chest pale and tight and curly. He sent a splash to me, a kind of kiss. I splashed him back, like a mad creature, in a frenzy of happiness.

Then I joined my daddy in the middle of the stream where, in the midst of a shallow run, he was already beating my britches against the river rocks. He turned the left pocket out and left it hanging empty as a spaniel's ears. I arrived at his side as he turned his attention to the other where I had hidden the assignat.

I dared not say a word but set to rubbing at my collar while my father, not inches from me, coughed and passed his hand across his mouth. All the while he scrubbed my britches I knew he had the forgery inside his mouth.

At last the Frenchman left the river and, once on the cattle path, shook himself like a great wild dog. My father watched him as he returned to that grey lumpy printery with its dragon's-back roof giving up its dew, mist rising, bleeding into the grey sky, and all its windows dark and secret, declaring its business was not for you to know.

When the Frenchman went inside my father finally spoke. 'That's the job then.'

He stared at me, pointing with his big burned nose like some fierce ostrich.

'What job?'

'Shut your mouth,' he said.

My father was a plucky man. But now I knew him seriously afraid, and his fear made him hard and unkind toward me.

'Tell no one,' he said. 'Here,' he said, throwing my britches at me like they were the skin of a dead beast. 'Here.' He handed me a bar of soap. And so we occupied ourselves as usual for a Sunday but I had never, on any day, in all my life, felt my heart so heavy or seen my father's eyes so dull and far away.

At last, we brought our clothes ashore and spread them on the gorse, hoping some breeze would come before the thunderstorm, to put it mildly.

V

It was a Sunday, and the revolutionary factions of English printers dispersed themselves around the woods and riverbank in endless arguments about the rights of man. There, amid Piggott's graveyard of wheels and broken axles, my father and the Weasel conferred together. I fancy I can make an honest sketch of this: the single iron ring springing free of a rotting wheel, the humpbacked printery, the elder bushes, the oaks and poplars, the fuzz of hatch above the shallow stream, the Piggotts' cat rubbing around the Weasel's bandy legs, my lanky daddy with his hands pushing violently into his pants, and there, in Jack Larrit's white scrubbed hand, an assignat, all golden in the sun.

I had no idea that thousands of these assignats were forged in France and Britain and the Netherlands. Their purpose was to devalue the currency and thereby, by dint of ink and paper, destroy the beloved revolution. All I knew was that forgery was a capital offence. Witnessing the two printers examine Mr Watkins' work I understood I had betrayed the poor queer creature, trapped inside his cage.

Of course I should have confessed to Mr Watkins, but I wished him to like me and I was so ashamed that, on that Sunday night, I would not take my burin lessons. I said I was needed by my father.

'Indeed,' he said. His eyes were as frail as plover eggs, the prey of raging boys.

VI

Next morning the Weasel slung his misbegotten bedroll across his narrow shoulders and headed off into the woods without, it seemed, a word to anyone. Concerning this departure the printers – arguers and complainers to a man – made not a boo, although the absence of our best pressman would make more work for everyone.

So it was that my father, a compositor of the first water, was removed from his tray of type and ordered to take Weasel's place at the press. Da would now work with Chooka, five foot tall, a proud pernickety pressman with chin and nose like Punch. My da's poor work would have Chooka in a rage, I knew it. But it was worse than that, for Piggott had contracted to produce a fancy chapbook on expensive linen paper, and the pressmen would be fined for spoilage.

Yet after the third sheet was thrown away, I witnessed little Chooka, who had a famous temper, reach up and pat my father's back while he, my da, grinned and shrugged in shame.

And still no one blamed the Weasel. Which meant – there was a Higher Cause. And although I was only a printer's devil, I understood that every one of these men was sworn to this cause in secret. They were comrades, solid as a wall.

Piggott ordered me to perform a hundred dirty chores, including a message to the Dit'sum Swan which meant running across the stubbled fields with the beery harvesters calling me to them *cootchum cootchum coo*. I returned alive, with a fierce stitch in my side. I was late for Mr Watkins who was so kind to me I almost cried. I mean, he offered me the burin, but how could I touch it after my betrayal?

'Sorry Mr Watkins.'

'You won't sit, boy?'

'No time sir,' I said. I was certain the Weasel had gone to report Watkins to what you might call *the authorities*. I thought, This fellow will never make his book of birds.

'What is it, boy? What happened?'

I thought, I have destroyed you. 'Nothing sir,' I said.

He brushed his fine white hair back from his high forehead and considered me directly, long and slow until I felt my ears burn red.

'Sorry sir,' I said, and carefully manoeuvred his doings through the doorway.

'No time for Mr Watkins, boy?' he called.

I snaked away from him, holding his piss pot high, pulling myself forward on my elbows.

That afternoon, when the men took their tea-oh on the steps, I drew my da away among the rotting wheels.

'Where did Mr Stokes go?' I asked, for I was not permitted to call him Weasel.

My father looked directly at my face which I imagine thus – dry
lips parted, brow furrowed, heat showing on the cheeks and mottling
down the smudgy neck. He reached a hand toward me and I went
to hold it tight, but he ducked inside my cover and got his fingers in
my ribs and when he had me wailing and shrieking without breath
he grabbed me by my ankles and held me upside down so that my
penny and two favourite stones fell to the ground.

I was upside down, blood filling my head like a bucket, crying
loud – 'Where is he?'

'Good old Weasel is a journeyman,' my father said, setting
me back the right way and helping me pick up my treasure. 'He's
journeying. It's his nature,' he said, and gave me back my penny
and another one besides, but even this did not persuade me. If
the Weasel had been a French printer, that would be his nature
sure enough – always on the road, travelling to jobs as far away as
Switzerland. The French printers got paid for the time they were
on the road, but the English printers had no such excitements and
don't argue if you please, for this is true.

I knew my father was lying to me about the Weasel's nature, but
if I was worried about the assignat and worried about Mr Watkins,
I was worried about my daddy even more. If you were ever a boy
you will remember the worries of a boy and how they swarm around
you, and if I have had no reason to name mine for you until now, it
does not mean they were not my constant companions. A boy's life,
like a bird's life, is not what is generally assumed. For bird examples,
watch the whitethroats gorging in the bramble patches, the warblers
gluttoning among the blackberries, the blackcaps swinging off the
rosehips, all in a panic to get fat before the summer ends. I, for my
part, was forever in a fret lest my daddy die like my mother and
leave me with no one to care for me, no one to save me from my
cheeky nature, my mimicking, my fear of strangers on the road or
in the woods at night, tramps, scamps, hermits, men who put paper

noses on their face to frighten boys.

He was a dear tender man, and if he lied to me it was only because he loved me, and his eyes were moist when he gave me the penny and I put my hand inside his and walked back to the printery and worked very conscientious until tea.

Only two days later I was on the lanes with my cart of newspapers, and all around me bindweed, bluebell, chamomile and coltsfoot, ferns uncurling like a thought, white butterflies around my shoulders. All these things I could name and draw, although not so well as I imagined, but they were my deep familiars and they must have given me that comfort a boy does not know he has until it is lost to him and he finds himself robbed of names by providence. There was heather, wild primrose, and around the corner of the rutted lane there came a man walking, duck-footed and bandy-legged, a new white straw hat upon his head.

It was the Weasel and I saw him lift his staff and was afraid.

But of course – you guessed already – he greeted me with a punch to the arm and a sticky dust-covered humbug from his pocket. I sucked on my lolly and he picked a paper from my cart and read through Bunter's setting, finding fifteen faults in as many column inches. 'Home sweet home,' said he.

And after that everything was calm, and I was able to visit Mr Watkins and take up his burin once again. It was still summer. My da and I saw glow-worms in the night. Then it was almost autumn. I found hazelnuts, hawthorn berries, and sycamore seeds among the leaves. The harvest was ending and as I cut across the paths to Dit'sum I would see the drunken workers at their games, throwing their reap hooks at a sheaf. Now I had worn the sharp edges off my guilty conscience Mr Watkins became cooler to me once again. Just the same, he instructed me in what is called the crosshatch. After that I was finally permitted to attempt a creature. I chose a butterfly and he was very fierce about it but I knew I did it well enough because he recognised it as a silver-washed fritillary and taught me how to spell its name.

Then I was sent to deliver a box of wedding invitations to the next village after Dit'sum, I forget its name, and I cut across the commons toward its spire only to find myself set upon by a mob of harvesters who came rushing out of the deep shade of an oak and chased me across a ridge and down toward a sluggish stream, and by the time I emerged onto a road through a hedgerow I was cut and bleeding and had lost my invitations and my courage. I set off crying, having no idea of where I was.

I passed a group of men with scythes who did not speak to me, although I suspected them of being the ones who chased me so I would not ask them the way. The hedgerows were high and it was impossible to get any bearing and when a carriage came along I had to press myself back into the buckthorn. It was a very large and black affair, doubtless with some fancy name I did not know, and I can remember no more than the single line of gold along its trim. When its gleaming back wheel was almost past me it stopped, leaving me imprisoned, so to speak, behind its bars. I would have ducked beneath the axle, but feared being squashed and so I remained, black-faced, slashed with red, pinned like a butterfly. I was thus easily identified by the gentleman inside the coach, who poked his smooth-shaven face out the window to consider me.

'Printer's devil,' called he. His voice was very Windsor arsehole and he had a hat like an admiral's.

I pulled my forelock although my father would have wished I did not. 'Yes sir.'

'And where is your printery, devil?'

'Near Dit'sum, sir.'

'Is it old Piggott who is your master? You know a chap named Weasel?'

'Yes sir.'

'Isn't it a little late in the year for bird-nesting?'

'I was on a message sir. I was chased sir.'

'By whom were you chased?'

'Farmers sir.'

He lowered his spectacles on his nose. It was a good-sized nose at that, not fat, but long and bossy. I could smell the wheat-starch powder of his wig.

'Well, Piggott's boy,' he said at last, 'let me give you a ride home.'

'I'm lost sir. I don't know where to go.'

'Then you're an exceptionally fortunate devil,' said the gentleman who was – as he told me when I was sitting in his coach together with two gents who I took to be his gamekeepers or something of that nature – Lord Devon himself. His men were Mr Benjamin and Mr Poole and they also told me I was a lucky little devil and please not to put my filthy hands on his lordship's seats. I had never travelled in such style before and I sat up very straight with my bleeding legs held away from where they might touch anything and, with my hands clasped in my lap, I was left alone to enjoy the privilege of being able to see, above the hedgerows, a peregrine falcon sailing high up in the pale sky.

'That's a hawk, that is,' Mr Poole said. So he was not a game-keeper, even if he did have leather patches on his jacket elbows. I looked to his lordship to see what he would say it was.

'What do you say, devil?' he asked me, smiling so his beaky face became suddenly very kind. 'Is it a hawk?'

'It's a peregrine falcon, sir.'

'And what does a peregrine falcon eat, devil?'

'Birds, sir. Although I heard it will eat a fish,' I said. 'My father saw one take an asp.'

'In fact,' Mr Benjamin said, 'almost everything.'

'Including printers,' said Mr Poole.

His lordship said nothing to that but took an urgent and violent interest in what was outside his window – a great flock of birds, as it happened, about fifty of them, attacking some mystery inside the hedge. This seemed to engage his attention for a very long time.

'You are an enormous fool, Poole,' he said at last.

Waxwings, I thought, but did not say.

VII

Mrs Piggott held her locks back from her appley face.

Then Lord Devon clamped my upper arm, and together we marched to her doorway. She must have been astonished to see the Parrot in the company of a lord.

'*Madame?*' Devon asked. *Je suppose que votre nom est Marie Piggott?*'

Mrs Piggott curtsied as if very pleased. '*Mais oui, monsieur,*' she said. 'That's me.'

'Did you know, madame – and here he used his cane to flick a dead oil beetle from her steps – 'did you know, Mrs Marie Piggott, that the Alien Act of 1793 requires all foreigners to register with customs officials of the police office?'

'What?' she said.

But his lordship was not waiting for an answer or an invitation, and he charged on up the steps with the Parrot still attached.

A small girlish cry from Mrs Piggott. A fast retreat.

Benjamin and Poole were hard behind us. Their hats were small black dinghies beached upon their wigless heads. All four of us pursued the fleeing mistress through the hall and into the dining room where she awaited us, standing alongside Mr Piggott, the pair of them in check against the panelled wall.

For a moment both residents and intruders paused to consider their positions. Then Piggott thrust himself one square forward, all eighteen stone, rubbing his hands together. What larks, he seemed to say.

'Bert Piggott at your service, sir.' He would not tug his forelock. He gave his head a little bob instead.

His lordship did not so much as lift an eyebrow. He removed his topcoat, revealing himself in his waistcoat like some dangerous red-chested bird with gold embroidery around its buttonholes and pockets. An older boy would know to be afraid of all this Tory needlework, but I was thrilled to see Piggott in a state of terror.

His lordship threw his coat across a chair. So peaceful did he seem that it was a wonder he did not call to have his slippers fetched.

'Have you registered your wife, sir?'

Piggott lifted up his thirty-pound bucket of head and thrust out his chin. 'As you say, sir, she is my wife.'

'Then you understand your legal position, Mr Piggott. You must take her to Exeter tomorrow. You will register her, do you understand?'

'She is as good as English, sir, please.'

His lordship must have been a funny fellow when with his mates, for he bugged his eyes up very big. 'She is *what* exactly?'

'In a manner of speaking, sir.'

Devon turned to Poole and Benjamin. 'Mr Poole,' he said, 'you are the wicket-keeper. Mr Benjamin – you are silly mid-on.'

They are playing cricket now, I thought. His lordship retrieved his coat, a silky thing as light as butterfly wings, and tossed it to Poole. 'Bees sting,' he said. 'Ants bite. Do keep an eye out.'

This was not cricket or any other game I ever heard of and the hidden language was very frightening. I knew it time to see my father. However, his lordship, as if reading my mind, lifted a finger and raised his eyebrows and I understood I was under his orders.

'So I shall take her to Exeter,' said Mr Piggott, shoving his hands into his apron pockets. 'I do business in Exeter, so it is quite convenient.'

'So, this is your property, Piggott. *En avez-vous hérité? Vous avez cambriolé une banque?*'

'I'm afraid I don't parlez the lingo, sir.'

'Your house. A lovely old place,' said his lordship, running his hand admiringly over the tight curling grain of the panels. 'Nicholas Owen,' he said.

'Sir?'

'Are you a Catholic yourself, perhaps?'

'I am sir, yes.'

'Poor old Owen was a Jesuit, I think. They were bad times for Catholics, when he designed this place.'

'Could I fetch you some refreshment, sir? A brandy?'

'Brandy?' Devon raised his cane and smashed it down upon the panelling. Mrs Piggott was not the only one to flinch. 'No one told you your house was famous?' he asked, not looking at Piggott but tapping on the wall with his knuckles.

'Famous, sir? Ha-ha.'

'Famous, sir,' said Lord Devon, who was now caressing the house as if it were a horse, casting an extraordinary smile across his shoulder at the Piggotts. You would think he loved them half to death.

There was a sharp clear click.

'There you are, madame,' he said, sliding a small panel sideways. 'Here's a nice place for your prayer book.'

'Monsieur?'

'*Un endroit parfait pour cacher un livre de prières* if you were here two hundred years ago.'

'Good Lord,' cried Piggott, stepping forward urgently. 'Good heavens sir. Who would credit it?' He was so set on inspecting the secret cubby-hole that he would have jammed his big booby head inside, but his majesty detained him. 'Ha-ha, sir. Nice place to hide a bottle, your lordship.' He wiped himself with a rag, leaving printer's ink upon his neck.

His lordship smiled so sweet, he might have been the printer's mother. 'Oh there is much much more than this, Piggott,' he cried. 'All manner of holes and chapels contrived with no less skill and industry. They've hidden traitors in this house, Mr Piggott. Can you imagine?'

'Good grief.'

'Oh yes, Mr Piggott, in chimneys.'

'Chimneys sir?' said Piggott. 'I have a lovely brandy. Let me fetch it now.'

The fireplace was set and ready as it always was, and it was certainly the talk of chimneys that drew Lord Devon to inspect it. Piggott hovered at his back, a fat white presence which his lordship seemed at first put out by, but then –

'Ah yes, sir.' He beamed. 'A brandy would do the trick.'

Piggott bobbed his head and winked his eye and tapped his nose and soon I heard him on the stairway, an unexpected direction for the brandy bottle.

His lordship nodded amiably at Mrs Piggott. She tucked her curls inside her hat as if she might, in doing this, make herself more English.

'Printer's devil', he said to me. 'Fetch back your master. Have him bring the brandy now.'

I used the door through which Piggott had departed and immediately found him on the staircase which now revealed itself to be a clever hiding place. The first three steps were steps indeed, but Piggott had now lifted them like a hatch and inside was revealed the one-armed Frenchman who had reappeared last night at dinner.

Said I, to no one, 'He wants his brandy, sir.'

The man with one arm pushed Piggott violently. And as the stair returned to its rightful place, Piggott took me by my neck and turned me back the other way and forced me through a door and down the stone steps into the cellar. Finding what he came for, he pushed me very cruelly up the stairs and I barked my shins and cut my hands upon the stone.

On my return I found Lord Devon kneeling before the fireplace. Behind him, Mrs Piggott wrung her hands and silently beseeched her husband please to save her, from what I did not know.

'Do you mind?' his lordship asked politely, encouraging the little flame he had begun with his flint and tinder.

'Oh no sir, please sir,' cried Piggott in alarm.

'No sir?' queried his lordship who now, as his flame took hold, seemed in a very jolly frame of mind. 'Please sir, no sir, is it?'

'It's a summer's day sir.'

'Oh I do like getting warm,' Lord Devon said, as the kindling – which had lived a lifetime in the house – fairly leaped to its own destruction.

His lordship stood, brushing down his stockinged knees.

'Now,' he said. 'That drink you promised.'

Piggott, you will remember, was a big man with a big head and he was, even when malicious, slow as a cow in his manners. By now, however, both Piggotts were in a state they no longer could disguise. Mrs Piggott left for the scullery; Mr Piggott ran after her. They returned by different doors, each holding a different-shaped glass.

'Here's a riddle,' said Lord Devon, considering the choice. 'Bless me if I won't have them both.' He clasped his hands behind his back where the fire was crackling fiercely, exploding in the way of dry pine logs, showering tiny grenades into the room.

Piggott filled the glasses with clearly trembling hands.

'Thirsty weather,' said his lordship, raising both in a toast. He sipped. He giggled. Then, in sheer delight at his own wickedness, he threw the brandy on the fire which now leaped at him, licking with its yellow tongue, leaving a glowing bite upon his wig which Piggott, in his panic, attempted to pat out.

For this he was poked right in the belly.

Lord Devon removed his burning wig, astonishing me with the hard bony brightness he revealed. He patted out the damage, keeping his eye on me as if I had some news to give. But it was only the genius forger Watkins I was thinking of, and I would not betray him now.

It was hot inside the dining room and no one would move away from the fire. To admit the heat, I saw, would be to confess to something worse. Lord Devon rested his gloved hand on my shoulder and carelessly jabbed his stick into the fire. The stick was handsome black oak with a silver top to it, but he used it like a common poker, jabbing it and banging it, until it was charred and glowing on the tip which he showed to the Piggotts with no nice meaning I was sure.

'Your stick is burning.'

'So is your hearth, sir.' And with this he gave a good hard jab into the heart of the fire and Piggott watched dumbly as the burning logs were knocked onto his dining-room floor and the charred walking stick was stabbed again and again into the hearth as if it were a spear to kill a dragon.

'You see, Piggott,' his lordship said. He was having a great old time, careless of the choking smoke, the soot on both his face and hands. As for his silver stick, he now reversed it so he could use it like a navvy's crowbar.

'You see,' he said, and – completely indifferent to the heat and burning wood, thrust in his hand like a farmer at a calving and drew into the light a fistful of smouldering currency – not assignats.

The dreadful Lord Devon, who was later paid a bung by Mr Pitt for services to king and country, held up his treasure – pale white notes carrying the promise of the Stockton and Cleveland Bank to hand over five pounds of gold for each and every one.

Behind my back I heard a noise, and turned to see both

Piggotts on the floor, poor devils, him kneeling, her curled up in a ball, her stockings showing.

VIII

As a lizard drops its tail to save its life, so must the Parrot sacrifice his sleeve to escape Lord Devon's grip. Out the door I fled into the inky evening, not a living soul in sight except the house martins scything across the sky. I stumbled coughing, spitting, down the dark side of the mansion, flushing a quail from beneath the pussy willow. The bird was much more wily than the boy, for while I was heading straight for Watkins' secret hole, she pretended a broken wing and hobbled and fluttered toward the river, intending to lead me away from her nest.

I had reached the stinging nettles, just before the door, when the designated wicket-keeper caught me.

Mr Benjamin dropped on me like a spider, wrapping his huge hands around my chest, binding me to him, so close I could smell the inside of his nose.

'Got you,' he cried.

The Parrot slid right through his nasty knot, surrendering the remainder of his shirt. I feinted toward the house, cut back toward the river, crashed through the pussy willow where Mr Poole was waiting for me.

'Got you.'

He had fair hair and blue eyes and a red blush to his cheeks like a toy soldier. He was slight but as hard and stitched together as the leather casing of a ball, and though I kicked and spat and scratched at him, there was no escape from the bony shackle around my wrist.

'I'll break your frigging arm,' he said.

'Where is he?' That was Lord Devon, hollering from the steps.

'Here sir,' called Poole, dragging me brutally, skidding me on my knees, a half-skinned hare.

'Not him, you fool!' Lord Devon had a captive of his own – Mrs Piggott – tripping and stumbling after him. 'Not him, not him!'

'Who sir?'

'Try to remember,' cried Lord Devon. 'Lord Jesus save me, whom did we come to get?'

'Piggott sir? Where is he?'

'I do not *know*,' his lordship cried, advancing with his still-burning stick. Poole jerked me backward and away. The red-waistcoated dervish continued closing and was only halted by an awful bang. *Deus ex machina*, as they say. And what a *machina* – a hot wash of light bathed his lordship's upturned face and there, for all to see, his cold gleaming rage was caught and held by a writhing rope of fire running along the ridge line of the house.

'Shit,' cried the member of the House of Lords, and I had time to be astonished he would speak like that.

The printers came running down their stairs, tumbling into the evening, walking backward, faces illuminated, necks craned, their gazes on the smoking humpback ridge. The first line of flame had died, but what was left behind were three conflagrations, flames bursting from three beds of tiles.

Mr Benjamin clipped me across the ears. The show contin-ued – exploding squibs now bloomed like wildflowers in the gloom. These also whacked my eardrum, five times, as hard as anvils. Then came bursts of fire, broken tiles erupting from hips and valleys and places not in my view.

The sky was now a cloudless shade of green, and as Benjamin dragged me from the hail of heavy tiles, I feared for Mr Watkins' life. Poor Watkins – he had dreaded fire above all things, and now there were at least eight separate fires all erupting from his roof. Then – from where I do not know – a great flock of bats burst forth, and in among the bats, at first almost indistinguishable from them, a thousand sheets of paper tipped with Pentecostal tongues. It was as if Piggott's brain had exploded through its bony casing and all its greed and argumentative confusion, its secrets and whispers and smugglers' boats, had burst in smithereens and scattered through the darkening air, landing like stinging wasps upon our arms and faces, and through all of this my captor was transfixed, as if he had seen the assumption of the Virgin Mary in the Devon sky.

All nature was disturbed. The nightjars, who would have normally stayed quiet till dark, came diving and flapping around their territories, swooping down above Lord Devon's smoking wig. In flight they made a soft *coohwick* and a dreadful hand-clapping with their panicked wings. The printers were equally disturbed, shouting, running to the stream with buckets.

I politely asked to be let go.

Poole knew not what to do. He watched Lord Devon who, like someone drunk or dreaming, stared at the men carrying water into the house.

Then came a great soft thump like a chaff bag thrown out of a loft.

'Good God,' cried Poole.

On the ground beside the steps I saw the broken body of a man. It was Piggott. When Benjamin dragged me to his side I saw the printer's big white carcass twisted like a doll, his eyes wide open, the most horrific look of triumph on his face. This expression was not diminished one iota by the wailing of his wife to whom he spoke impatiently. *'Marie, il n'y a plus aucune preuve ici. Tout est brûlé.'*

Lord Devon quickly decided Mrs Piggott was worth not a damn to him. He set her free to moan.

'Fool,' he cried to Piggott, as burning five-pound notes fell to the dark ground like cherry blossom. 'Fool, it is *raining* evidence.' Then: 'Let the house burn,' he ordered the printers, but they were Jacobins and they hated him and all his kind.

Understanding his position, Devon rushed to his carriage, from which he produced a heavy tangle of chain and threw it hard against the ground.

'That's one lesson for you,' he shouted at the men.

He disappeared for a moment and emerged waving two pistols. 'And here's another.' One of these pistols was quickly taken by Benjamin while Devon confronted the bucket brigade with the other.

'What's that you say?' he cried. 'What's that?'

He struck Bunter on the shoulder and, by dint of a great deal of barrel-poking, 'persuaded' the bucket brigade to stand in line while he walked up and down, reviewing them like Grenadiers.

Not once taking his eyes off his captives, he ordered Benjamin to pass Poole his pistol so the latter's hands were free to fetter these good men's ankles with the chain.

While Devon snatched evidence from the sky, my flame-licked father smiled at me. He shrugged, dear man, dear father.

'Come,' called Devon to Poole. 'You can help as well. You're not a bloody nursemaid.'

'But I have the boy,' said Poole.

'Yes, yes, yes,' cried Devon.

My daddy was tossing his head at me, as if he had a flea in his ear. 'I have the boy, sir,' said Poole.

'Devil,' Lord Devon said, 'I will blow your brains out if you move.'

'Yes sir,' I said.

Chooka tossed his head. He meant that I should flee.

'Run,' my father cried.

Devon swung around. But now Poole shrieked. He pointed, and who – even Lord Devon – could not follow his gaze? A fiery angel had appeared upon the roof, its hair ablaze and streaming upward, fire right down its spine. It ran along the ridge and *flew* into the air, smashing into an old oak through whose ancient branches it crashed nosily before passing out of sight. Three others followed, forgers rising like hatchlings in the night, their cries beyond the edge of nightmare.

'Run,' my father cried. 'Parrot, run.'

I heard the shot go past my ear and Devon screaming. I ran like a rabbit, through the smoke and haze, through the gloom, through the field of broken wheels. The men were cheering me, a pistol roared. I ran, shirtless, into the open woods, through the broken bracken, into dark, so many years ago.

OLIVIER

I

'It's over,' cried my mother, rushing along the hallways of the château de Barfleur in 1814. 'It is finished. It is done.'

And yet, madam, monsieur, it was *not* over, not in the least. Or, if it was over, it was only for as long as it took Napoleon to be defeated at Waterloo. One hundred days later he was finished, packed off to exile, and Louis XVIII returned as planned. My mother could dash off to Paris any day she wished.

Vive la roi, you might suppose. How happy we Garmonts must be.

To which I answer, not at all. First, my father was treated unfairly. Once the monarchy was restored he should have been a power in the land, but he had failed to flee from the revolution so he was not of the party of émigrés who returned beside the king.

Who loses, and who wins; who's in, who's out;

My father was made a prefect of a department in the provinces. He accepted this insult with good grace, although his own wife would not leave Paris to share his bed.

You might reckon my mother in heaven to live so near the king, but no – she now judged him too weak and modern. In the house where she had once planned to receive His Majesty she now formed a salon for ultra-royalist priests who feared democracy would be the death of religion.

My father did not argue against her, except to mention to me, *en passant*, that His Majesty felt the merest wisps of democracy as a physical assault on his royal person.

As for my own beliefs, they were changing. Thomas and I decided we had finished with the Holy Catholic Church. We became deists. If my mother had prayed a little less she may have noticed. Instead she observed that Thomas and I were 'good scholars with our books'. Indeed we were – a sixteen-year-old boy could see that France was a house of cards. The king died. Another king was crowned. You would think these changes calamitous, but it seemed to us that all the kings had a natural inclination to wish things to be as they had been before the revolution. Louis XVIII was more placatory. Charles X was most pigheaded. He did not understand that if he removed more rights from the people the edifice would collapse.

Blacqueville and I grew up aboard this teetering structure built between the old and new. Years and years went by in this same unstable state. By the time I arrived at the law courts in Versailles I was ten centimetres taller, but the monarch and his ministers were still intent on turning back the clock.

I was now twenty-six years old, a salaried lawyer. I had imagined I would be fairly good at my new profession, but I had deceived myself. Public speaking was a horror to me. I groped for words and cut my arguments too short. Beside me were men who reasoned ill and spoke well. The exception my constant friend Thomas with whom I shared a small grey house on the rue d'Anjou.

In Normandy, Thomas had taught me the art of racquets, rescued me from the chestnut tree in which I had wedged myself, and introduced me to his extraordinary cousin, Louise. Now, all these years later in Versailles he was again my tutor, and I do not mean he coached me in matters of oratory, or English wives or the d'Aumont sisters but, rather, set the example of a noble who every day refused to be trapped inside his history. Thus it was history itself that became our subject, our enemy, our ambition. Together we *hammered* at its pages, windows, doors. And why? Because Blacqueville's family was as ancient as mine. Because, in our home districts we were surrounded by men whose names appear in the roll of Norman conquerors. Because it was impossible that we become nonentities.

Yet the curtain had fallen on gore and glory, and we found ourselves in a theatre where we were revealed as poor pale creatures, blinking in the artless light. Monstrosities and giants no longer walked the bloody streets. Malesherbes, Diderot, Rousseau. The great men were dead. Danton even, Robespierre. Do not take my word. Look at the works of our painters – the people were dwarfed by nature. As for the novels, the characters were blown like fallen leaves, without volition, not worth reading. Worse, we were overshadowed by our own family trees. I was a Garmont, but a lowly judge advocate. My colleagues saw that I was slight and myopic. They could not imagine the secret life of my body or my mind. I was thought reticent, even cold, but I was ablaze with violent contradiction.

Blacqueville and I were stallions bred for racing, now condemned to pull a cart of night soil.

But what would we do in this present age? What sort of nobles might society still permit? Would we stamp on wasps' nests? Would we drown swimming against the tide of history? Would we break open the door we could not yet locate, and enter the salons of a glorious time as yet unborn? Or would we spend our lives between the thighs of actresses?

Dear Blacqueville was the more handsome but at heart we were no different. I said we read like schoolboys? We read like warriors. We attacked all ten volumes of Adolphe Thiers' *Histoire de la Révolution française*. We deemed ourselves liberal modern men but we were nobles still. So we felt a violent hatred of the author who blamed the aristocrats for the sins of the revolution.

That was our paradox, our impossible position.

For while the king's advisers tried to push back against the revolution and the bourgeoisie tried to push forward, we occupied a category of our own, trusted neither by our own side nor the other, living in a constant state of contradiction and confusion, unable to imagine what our futures held.

It was in this thirst and fury that we were drawn to the lectures of a certain Protestant from Nîmes named Guizot. It was this severe man, with a black stock around his neck like a clergyman, who forced us to understand that democracy could not be turned back.

Thus Blacqueville and I attended a great many of these lectures, side by side with citizens of all descriptions, very few of them with friends at court. We were diligent and earnest. We made notes. We had no idea of the dangerous nature of the game that we were playing.

II

A dreary Monday in Versailles. Our servant having been dismissed on an embarrassing matter, and Blacqueville having taken the coach to Paris, I returned to an empty house where I immediately began to change my clothes so that I might go into society. And then, when I was in my shirtsleeves – what was the point of this? – I crawled into my bed.

It was in this depressed condition I was awakened by a footman bearing an invitation from the marquis de Tilbot. The reader will recall Monsieur for no other reason than that he had his arm hacked off. My own recollection was pretty much the same, except I had not liked him as a child when he was first my mother's friend. This evening, it seemed, Monsieur was visiting Versailles and in urgent need of company.

Monsieur was, as they say, *eccentric*. In England, where the aristocrats lounge in the House of Lords like farmers exhausted by the hunt, he may not have appeared so alarming, but in my France, his France, we insist on the uniform, and he could not be bothered to accommodate us. As if to underscore the point, he now provoked me with a timeworn servant of an unsettling democratic *grammar*, a liveliness in the eyes, a broadness of speech, an open curiosity which would certainly have excluded him from my mother's household. Monsieur had spent many nights sleeping next to peasants in the hedgerows of the Vendée, so perhaps this fellow amused him.

When I accepted the invitation – my own handwriting was appalling, no match for the calligraphy of the invitation – I expected the evening would conclude with Tilbot trying to sell me a folio of etchings or some Sèvres supposedly rescued from the ashes of the revolution.

Clearly it was boredom that got me from my bed, but the invitation was also a welcome escape from the company of bourgeois lawyers. I will be disliked or even killed for saying this, but it is only with nobles, those of my own blood, that I have ever felt completely at home, even an extreme conservative like Tilbot.

It was early summer, the most asthmatic time of the year. I strolled toward the hôtel Juste through the Saint-Louis quarter. Closed mansions. Neglected gardens. No matter the seasons, Versailles was, generally speaking, stone dead. Of the two hundred hotels that had thrived before the revolution, there were perhaps fifty doing any sort of trade at all. If Monsieur had expected the Hôtel Juste to be as it had been in the years of Louis XVI, he would be correct only to the extent that it had no water closet. Certainly he would no longer find a *mixed crowd*, comtes side by side with opera singers, or eager dancers who had just performed a gala for the king. All dead. All gone. At the Juste I came upon an attendant who, like a common actor cast to play a duke, gave no more service than waving a gloved hand toward the staircase. Such was the state of servants since the revolution. They consented to serve but were ashamed to obey. They had begun to treat their masters as the unjust usurpers of their rights.

I set off up the staircase whose walls revealed the flaking common paint which had once affected to be marble. How sad to live in the shadows of the dead.

I knocked and discovered, to my pleasant surprise, apartments very like the *Autumn Room* of the château de Barfleur.

Monsieur welcomed me from a strange position, his single arm resting along the mantel which, being Carrara marble, was a monument to the taste and glory of Louis XVI.

'Complete?' he asked, not me, another. For me, his visitor, the great man betrayed no speck of interest.

'Don't move,' this other said.

And there I beheld the awful footman or factotum. *Reclining* on a canopied *chaise*.

Dear God, I thought, now here's a comic turn, for he was affecting to make a charcoal portrait of his posing master, who would *not* turn his head toward me. If dogs stood up and walked I could not have been more discombobulated.

'Perroquet,' I heard Monsieur call him.

So he keeps company with a parrot. Of course.

The creature, who had previously spoken in the most *higgledy-piggledy* patois, now answered in tones identical to his master. 'Just one moment,' said he. I thought, Dare he mock him thus? Does his master tolerate it? But what were these eccentricities to me?

Monsieur posed with his body arranged so that his amputation was cleverly denied. The glowing fire reflected in the fluted columns, and danced like wraiths across brocade and upholstery – laurel leaves, bellflowers, shepherds and shepherdesses. The scene had the warmth and glory of that earlier time – four arched openings separated by carved pilasters, walls covered with tapestry and brocade – and yet there, on the periphery of the canvas, was this fraudulent parrot. Velázquez, I thought, with no one to share my wit. Monkey, dwarf, parrot.

I snuffed my candle and set it on the mantel.

'I had imagined you would be taller,' my host said at last.

I had imagined he would have more teeth. He had grown older, balder, with his mouth set in a peculiar sarcastic mould.

'You have the Barfleur family markings,' he continued, alluding to the tiny wounds where leeches had bitten me so recently. The familiarity this sentence presumed might have been offensive and yet it was offered with a strange and unexpected tenderness. What to make of this ruined warrior.

The missing arm indicated his misfortune, but his eyes showed you he was, even at the age of seventy, a man still dedicated to excitements and danger. When his royalist war against the revolution failed he had become like a stream that enters an underworld of lakes and tunnels, from which secret life it will emerge where no geographer could predict. Where this stream had travelled during the reign of Napoleon, I did not know, although the peculiar relationship with this servant suggested something very subterranean indeed.

'Ah,' said Monsieur, 'you've already met M. Perroquet.'

Monsieur, seeing with what hesitation I took the servant's proffered hand, made a comic face. I wondered was he drunk.

He joined me on the settee and although I was supported with all the strength and grace of the royal workshops, my host occupied his territory less neatly. He was broad of shoulder and chest. Like an American, he wore no wig and this, paradoxically, served to magnify his leathery head – twenty-five centimetres from ear to ear, at least, a fringe of curly red-brown hair around his pate. He smiled at me. Those teeth were awful.

'Mr Parrot,' Monsieur said, nodding to the creature who had once more set to sketching, 'is a man of many parts, not one of which will you find in Linnaeus. A gentleman who travels cannot be at the mercy of servants.'

I thought, What is this leathery creature?

I was angry. Yet now – as I saw the dishes begin their majestic procession through the doors – I understood he wished to do me a signal honour. We were to start with the melon and follow with the eels and carp, and the larded rabbit on the spit. To this end we sat at table.

'So,' said Monsieur, 'you've been at Guizot's lectures.'

I thought, The servant must be told to leave the room.

'Six times you attended,' said Monsieur. 'Blacqueville, ten times.'

The Parrot caught my eye a moment but returned to drawing.

'It is not the Parrot you should worry about,' Monsieur observed. 'He is the only one you should trust.'

'And you, sir?' I asked with all the distance our language so thoughtfully makes possible. 'In what way should I trust you?'

For answer he produced a small chapbook from beneath his napkin. I thought, He wants to sell me something. Then I understood it was only a cloth-bound order book. From this he now read the following, pausing for effect, raising his eyes like an actor at the Comédie-Française.

'"The Middle Ages,"' he began, '"were the heroic age of France, the age of poetry and romance, the true realm of fancy, when fancy was stronger than we may think possible in the lives of men."'

It was Guizot. That is, he was quoting *evidence*. The hair on my arms rose inside my shirt.

'"On the other hand, gentlemen, the hatred that the Middle Ages have aroused is even easier to explain."'

Three weeks before, I had transcribed these very lines at a lecture. It was now clear to me, and to my bowels, that someone had observed the very movement of my pencil.

'"The common people were so unhappy during that period of their existence, they emerged so damaged and with so much effort from the condition into which it plunged them, that a deep instinct makes its memory agonising . . . The French Revolution, gentlemen, is no more than a defining explosion of hatred against the ideas, the manners, and the laws which were bequeathed to us by the Middle Ages."'

In the time of Bonaparte the secret service had bred like peasants, and there were many who detested the regime but took the pay. Might M. de Tilbot, I wondered, have become one of that sorry caste? He had lost his lands in the revolution. What income might he have? Was he spying for the Court?

'You imagine I agree?' I demanded.

Monsieur lifted his wine the better to examine it against the candlelight. 'You, Olivier de Garmont, are in a very bad position.'

'You will tell my mother, that is what you mean?'

'Your mother is a more supple and subtle creature than you could ever imagine.'

'I am sure you know her well, sir.'

He stared hard, and then his features softened. 'You are a Garmont,' he said quietly. 'The liberals see you and have no doubt you are a spy. The monarchists see you and know you for a traitor. You are in danger.'

'I will be out of favour?'

'For God's sake' – he pushed away his Pauillac lamb – 'your mother knows what danger is. If she wishes to save you it is because she has lost so many.'

I thought, Do not dare to tell me who my mother is, she has saved my life so often I have almost died of it.

'How did Chateaubriand save himself in the middle of the Terror?'

'You wish me to flee to America like Chateaubriand?' I said while thinking, She is calling the doctor for me once again.

'My dear Olivier, he did not flee. He went to write a book!'

Indeed, I thought. What vulgar hysterical sentences, what overblown chrysanthemums he put in the nation's vase. I could smell them now like the wreaths left too long inside a church.

Monsieur took my wine and poured half into his own glass, and there I saw, in my untidy passion, the great dark wave of it, the bloody grapey drunken *demos* which would wash us all away, and I took my own crystal goblet and downed the portion he had left me, imbibing in one long surging undulating swallow that brought my host to his feet, the bottle in his hand. It was because he was smiling that I downed this second glass.

'There,' cried the impossible creature, my mother's noble friend. 'We understand each other now.'

III

When Blacqueville walked into a room, eyes followed, not only the eyes of the men who doubtless envied him, but of the women with so many of whom he had been intimate. To see him pass between the tables of Les Lilas on the rue du Temple was to witness a minor wonder, this modest man emanating a golden light, although the light, of course, came from those delicate lamps, each one in the shape of a tulip, each whispering the secrets of the burning gas.

There was no question of being incognito when one was Blacqueville, not at Les Lilas or at the Sorbonne. So although

I had not planned to attend Guizot's next lecture, I set off to Paris to prevent my friend attracting the notice of spies. It was ridiculous that I should leave so early on the morrow, but no surprise to anyone who knew my character.

By the middle of the morning I found myself striding through the streets of the Latin Quarter, still in a state of considerable confusion, with nothing to occupy me until the night.

Inevitably I visited the rue Saint-Dominique where I was astonished to find my father at breakfast with my mother, a rare event, and all around them on the long bright table, a number of books which they, although aware of my arrival, seemed loath to tear themselves away from.

It was not extraordinary that my father would read a book in this intense manner, with quill and paper at his side, but that my mother should be so occupied was suspicious. The comtesse's mind was normally much occupied with theology so the laws she contemplated were those of God, and those she judged to be better studied upon her knees. So when I apprehended that they were now united in this charade and that this must be somehow related to their parental affections toward me, I was moved exceedingly. Of course I expected, soon enough, to be warned off Guizot and his democratic lectures, but I embraced my parents passionately, knowing myself to be their love and treasure.

I asked them what they were so fascinated with. My mother replied she had discovered that the Americans had invented prisons which would reform the people they contained.

So, I thought: *America*. I did not laugh, although this enthusiasm for prison reform was in violent – even comic – opposition to the views of her ultra-royalist friends who understood prison as a place to keep felons until they should be punished, whether by execution or hard labour. Yet I was very touched to hear my noble mother exclaim at the ingenuity of the Americans, who had, she declared – in one of those strokes of genius which mark *their extraordinary charac-ter* – turned the matter upside down.

'Someone should do this,' she said. 'This is an *extraordinary* idea. Montalivet should set up a commission,' she told my father. 'He won't deny you.'

'Certainly someone must go there,' my father said, looking thoughtfully at me.

His poor dear face showed all his love for me. I turned to my mother and saw from the crêpe skin on her cheek that she was already hearing the thundering clocks of history which she knew were about to strike their awful bells.

On the pretext of finding me some spending money for the day, my father soon led me into his office and shut the door.

I expected he would be explicit about his plan to get me to America, and I dreaded the exchange for I would not be a coward no matter how much I wished to please him. But now he had me alone he began to whisper, briefing me hurriedly on the dire situation of the government which had pressed so hard upon the king that he was prepared to sign the ordinances now laid before him. That is, His Majesty was about to dissolve the Chamber of Deputies and reduce the already tiny electorate to almost nothing. In other words, he would kill what small democracy he had not already sliced away. This would cause a public uprising, and in the ensuing chaos every Garmont and Barfleur would be at risk.

I immediately declared that I would stay with my parents at the rue Saint-Dominique and thereby protect them both, but my father passionately begged that I take no public position, that I act with extreme caution and present myself at Versailles and wait for word from him. I listened quietly, thinking only that I must speak with Blacqueville.

My father was of no importance to this government, but his absence from the palace would be a political act, and so he soon departed and I joined my mother who spoke, bravely and brightly, about the curious sect of Quakers in America. I watched her silently, thinking only how the revolution had drowned her beauty in a lake of fear.

In the early evening I bathed and was preparing to leave the house when my eye fell upon some dreary botanical engravings – or so I had always thought them – that had previously adorned the hallways at the château de Barfleur. In the past I knew only that they were a gift from Monsieur and that they meant one thing to my mother and something quite different to my father. One can imagine why a child might develop the habit of avoiding them. But now my eyes had chanced to alight, not on the leaves of *Eucalyptus globulus*, as it is still called, but on the neat label that proclaimed it so. This was the very same hand which had composed the invitation to the Hôtel Juste, not that of Monsieur but of his awful Parrot. If it had been a different day, perhaps this would have burned into my brain forever. But when you see what follows you will forgive me for forgetting it.

It was late. I was now rushed to the Sorbonne in my mother's coach whose unsuitable royalist decorations ensured that my arrival was well noted by the crowd outside. There I waited, feeling myself reviled, until I saw Blacqueville strolling toward me with that very careless elegance which marked his character. As we kissed I whispered to him that he should not attend the lecture.

'Ah,' he cried out loud, 'very nice to have met you again.'

And he set off back the way he had come. A few minutes later we were reunited at Les Lilas. Here we were shown to a banquette that was, as they say in this sort of place, 'the bower', which the owner reserved for Blacqueville and his friends and which I would never think to occupy without him. Here I related what I had heard from my father, that the extreme conservatives had pushed the king to sign the ordinances and that we were being spied on, that our situation was, as they say in London, very tight.

You might think there was a great deal to discuss, but we quickly agreed we were honour-bound to defend the king however wrongheaded we thought his actions. What an awful day. We wished it had not come. We therefore amused ourselves as the circumstances demanded: that is, we drank champagne. The bower was shortly full, and Blacqueville was occupied with a very pretty young Bourbon princess whom I will not name but who was soon the occasion of my friend bidding me goodnight. We agreed we would both present ourselves at the Versailles law courts on the morrow.

It was then, as my eyes followed the graceful couple's passage through the golden light, that I saw Monsieur's servant sitting not two tables away. So it is: we have never seen a person in our life and then they are everywhere we go. Although, let me confess, it was his companion who first took my eye, an actress with a glory of black hair, creamy white skin, and a generous bosom. I heard her laugh, a kind of throaty call, and I was doing my damnedest to catch her eye when the identity of her companion forced itself upon me. M. Perroquet was changed, not physically, but by his situation; and his green eyes were bold and alight and his nose now seemed hawkish, wild, exhibiting a dreadful kind of confidence, attractive yet repellent at the same time.

Was he the spy who had observed me in Guizot's earlier lectures? How could he be? Did he steal his master's silk waistcoat? No, no. He would have swum in it. He whispered in the actress's tiny perfect ear. She bowed her neck to let him kiss her. I had a fresh champagne, perhaps two; in any case I had not finished when my lovers stood to leave. I found myself on my feet, quite steady. I did not think to bid my friends goodnight. I am not sure that I even meant to leave. I made no definite decision, merely put one foot in front of the other, and by this innocent procedure, following them down whatever lane they turned in to, soon enough found myself

in a disgusting part of Paris. There was no lamp boy, only darkness. A flint was struck but nothing followed it. I heard the actress
laugh once, then a silence, as long as that which follows the last
notes of Mozart's *Requiem*.

'Monsieur Perroquet?' I called.

I was a noble, alone in darkness, held in my place by ten
centimetres of stinking mud, and having paid little attention to the
details of my chase, I had only the most approximate notion of how
to reach the rue Saint-Dominique.

What streets I walked along I cannot say, except I breathed
the miasma of the cesspools, the copperas of the factories, the air
the revolution had left for those it claimed to love. The dark was
horrid, suffocating, cloacal, dead, but when I finally emerged on a
long well-lit boulevard I had reason to wish I had kept myself well
hidden. For soon I was at the place de Grève, and all around me,
hollow-eyed emaciated children who seemed to hold my embroidered coat responsible for their present condition.

I threw what few coins I still possessed and walked southward,
swinging my stick, walking boldly right across the open ground
where the guillotine had once stood, and I thought, even in the
middle of my fear, Is this why you murdered my grandparents
and cousins, so you could have this, so you could gather in your
beastly warrens and prisons and spread your vile calumnies and
wish me dead while all these years no one has done a damn thing
for you, and if you wish to see what has been done, why then, do
not shout at me, a Garmont, sworn to protect and care for you
with his last breath, but look instead at the new bourgeois houses
along the avenue de Neuilly. For this you spilled your blood and
our blood – the bourgeois who turns his back upon the street, who
eats your bread and drinks your blood while his fat arse blocks
your way.

Oh monumental figures of the revolution, great figures of

our past. Oh mammoth fools, mighty sansculottes, elephantine dupes.

That night I dreamed of M. Perroquet, an annunciating angel fluttering around me like a moth. 'Hail full of grace,' he said, ascending. I woke in sudden darkness, disgusted by the blasphemy.

PARROT

I

It was bad enough being a servant to the dreadful Tilbot, paid to blow his nose and pour his wine. But I must then become a spy, required to write up every word of certain conversations which were later delivered to the comtesse de Garmont, by which I mean Lord Migraine's mummy, who would not rely on Monsieur's recollection of conversations with her son. She told him frankly that his cranium lacked the second bump and he therefore had no interest in her child.

Monsieur then reminded her that his mind had been created by God and all this phrenology was anathema.

'Never mind that Marie-Jean,' she said. 'I must know what Olivier says.'

I know this because I was in the room. I watched Monsieur's brows descend. For a soldier he had a very touchy equilibrium. On the right tray of his scales you had his infatuation with the comtesse de Garmont. On the left, there was his mad impatience. I have seen him break a man's neck, in an instant, and now would you like a cup of tea, Monsieur? But with Lord Migraine's maman he was like a boy in love, not that he threw pebbles at her window or climbed a ladder like the Sorel fellow, only that he was a fool before her translucent skin, her long swan's neck, the ancient fire still glowing beneath the quartz. I never saw the like before or since, the way they blushed and whispered, travelling in closed coaches, and me up on the box seat in the dark with nothing but a whip to save me from the pistol men in the Bois.

Monsieur told Lord Migraine, 'A gentleman who travels cannot be at the mercy of servants.'

And me, Parrot, pretending to draw a portrait, wrote this down, thinking all the time – but what compositor would ever set such language?

Monsieur had held me in this trap so many years I had come to accept it as my rightful place. I had food and shelter of a type my da could never have imagined. I handled prints and folios the most cultivated men in Europe wished to own, and there were not a few occasions when I gazed at myself in admiration. A fly on the wall, I thought, might mistake me for Monsieur's junior officer, or his disinherited brother, or his bastard son sired when he was twenty, but then hey-ho, enough of that my lad, and off along the frigging Paris road in the wind and rain, and *Chevalier* – it amused him to call me Chevalier – *Chevalier, do take us to the bishop*. Then hell's gate for the bishop. I hope he dies.

Where was I?

In July 1830 the Frogs had once again become maddened by their king and went around the capital smashing anything that reminded them of their own stupidity. As far as I could see, this so-called July Revolution was not my business. I ignored it in favour of visiting some English printer mates at their rooming house on the rue Saint-Honoré. I was expecting some ale and beef, but my old friends had come out for the revolution. They were set upon assembling a body of our countrymen whom they reckoned might *signalise themselves*, as they put it, *in the cause of freedom*. So there they were – pressmen, compositors, tramping up and down the stairs in such excitement that one of them was bitten by the dog. This was sufficient warning. Saying I would signalise myself immediately, I left them to their madness.

Soon I was obstructed by a fat old bourgeois with a rifle. He advised me to make my route in another direction – *une barricade* was forming, so he said. That was the first time I ever heard of *une barricade*. On reaching the Pont Neuf I had some difficulty. There was a fracas with the populace at the Tuileries – soldiers advancing slowly with level bayonets turned the mob away.

During all of this it was still my job to be the secret nurse of the son of the comtesse de Garmont. He would not have been the only aristocrat to join the mob so I kept my eyes out for him everywhere I went, and I say this only to illustrate my own ignorance of the ways of the noble class. Olivier de Garmont was unhappy with the king, but what I did not understand was that he was, so to speak, *on the same team*. So no matter what a nutter the king was, Olivier de Garmont was a noble, duty-bound to protect him from the mob

So on the following dawn, while my English printers were storming toward the palace with pikes and tricolour, his mother's own Olivier, without my knowledge, got together with his mate, young Blacqueville, and lined up some national guards before the palace gates.

As it turned out, the mob was not the problem. Instead the two nobles and their men found themselves the object of a violent action from the *rear*. That is, the fellow they had come to protect came charging at them incognito, a common burglar with all the silver he could carry in his bags. The king's carriages galloped by and Olivier de Garmont wept to see the last of the Bourbons departing, mud smeared like so much shameful shit across the royal escutcheons.

That all this spying should become my business was in no way to my liking. Yet it was more agreeable than smuggling folios and ivory carvings past the customs posts. In the second week my responsibilities were broadened so it was my job to observe the poor pale creature swear a loyalty oath to another king. I knew it was not his wish. He neighed and snorted, but on orders from his parents he complied. I transcribed the oath myself and when it was stamped and sealed by the marquis I was the one who delivered it to the *parquet*, that is, the law court at Versailles.

For making this oath his own team, the Bourbons, declared he was a rat to swear loyalty to the House of Orléans. As for the new team, they did not like him either. He was from the Bourbon side no matter what he signed and swore. He was therefore called back before the court and told he would have to swear a second time, just to make sure they heard him right.

Watching this, I considered it advisable for him to do a bunk. I could have smuggled him to London immediately. I made the offer, but this was much too straightforward for the family of Garmont. So I was sent not to Calais but to the *booksellers* to buy more important volumes concerning *prisons*, for goodness' sake.

Thus Olivier de Garmont was being helped to develop an interest in *penal servitude*. Let me see if I can put it plain – if he was prepared to write a report *On the Penitentiary System in the United States and Its Application in France*, it was his patriotic duty to go abroad and do so.

Then it was communicated that the new government would not spend a sou on a Garmont, but if he wished to pay for himself – well, they were happy to have him find out how felons should be best tortured in the world to come.

During this great fuss I was busy with another matter entirely. I mean, Mathilde Christian. It was she who came into my bed, she with the fragrant oil paint still beneath her nails, my gorgeous creamy-skinned, raven-haired, plump-armed, nestling, rutting, smiling creature who spent her days painting in the canvases her master sketched, and her evenings with her pencil and her pen.

Mathilde.

II

Elisabeth Vigée-Lebrun once complained about the fate of female painters – Women used to reign, she said, until the revolution dethroned them. The revolution dethroned Elisabeth Vigée-Lebrun of course, but by the time of this second revolution, my Mathilde was hard at work in the salon of comtesse X and marquise Y. Indeed, she had once been called to paint the comtesse de Polignac, a portrait that turned out so well her master was pleased to sign it himself. This was the turbulent and shining soul who was my lover and my teacher, and when I woke by her side I knew myself, most mornings, a lucky man.

We might sleep in Monsieur's *petite maison*, which he had built in the garden of a relative in the faubourg Saint-Germain, or we might choose Mathilde's studio in the faubourg Saint-Antoine, it mattered not to me. In the middle of the night I would turn and see her wide dark lips in the blue moonlight and think how many hard roads she had travelled, how many rivers I had swum, sailed, canvas slapping and thwacking in the dark, to arrive at this moment. She had that rare combination of strength and femininity, not like Rosa Bonheur, who had to be issued a certificate to dress in men's clothes, but like herself.

Was it because I had no mother that I so passionately sought her breast or fell asleep with my face nestled between her legs, or was it only that I who had no home was at home with her? In any case we both sat with brush and pen before the so-called quality, and it was her lot to grant the grand ladies the luxury of forgetting their lack of chest or wealth of chin.

For all that, we somehow tricked ourselves into believing we were not their servants, and at night in her studio, while her mother soaked her weary feet, she worked by lamplight on *Un tableau de deux figures en pied représentant une femme peignant et un ange déchu.*

It was partly a self-portrait – herself in her studio – but there was the shocking secret in the shadows, the fallen angel – her bare-legged Parrot sleeping in the morning light. This was later judged blasphemous and destroyed but the real outrage was that she had ravished me and that I, and every male who looked upon it, was thereby unmanned. This was contradicted by that truest judge of these situations, my manly instrument itself.

Yet the truth about the painting was much more ordinary, for when we were together in her studio – which we frequently were – we also had her aged mother to care for, and only when the old lady from Marseille, her spine twisted sideways, her veins blue and aching, set off down the stairs for Les Halles did we enjoy the golden pleasures the painting suggested.

All around us the world rose and fell, people went hungry, the days were hard, kings fled, nobles fretted, but we had, until now, occupied a tea-sweet backwater. Mathilde, whose master was a noble of a sort, had arranged that her mother should have a grace-and-favour apartment in the Louvre, no small thing, but once the old woman attempted entrance this grace was denied. So old Mme Christian was our burden, although a burden I was pleased to accept and it was no terrible duty to rub her ugly old feet and knead her little knotted shoulders. She was not quite there but not quite gone, and although she had a tendency to talk to herself, and therefore to reveal her gums, she set off each day to market and returned with the best and cheapest and freshest of everything, laying out her findings on the windowsill where we must inspect each item and then hear the full adventure of its purchase. There was also a flagon of good wine from a merchant with his own vineyard in the Loire which we all, madame most of all perhaps, enjoyed too much.

Thus, by our own lights, we were doing very well.

Very soon after the fall of Charles X, the last Bourbon, and the coronation of the fellow from the House of Orléans, I was ordered to present myself urgently at the *petite maison* where Monsieur received me, not in the anteroom but in the salon.

Of course I knew this room, right up to its domed ceiling whose amorous scenes had been painted by Mathilde's master. Mathilde herself had lain up on the scaffolding and, although Monsieur did not know this, and I was forbidden to tell, the most personal aspects of the cherubs had been made by her.

The salon, at once so beautiful and commonplace to me, was a most particular paradise. The candles were alight, all thirty of them, held by a chandelier and girandoles of Sèvres porcelain arranged in brackets of gilded bronze. These thirty candles were reflected in beautifully crafted mirrors set in lilac-coloured panels. With the room arranged as for a scene in a play, I entered.

There were a pair of gilded chairs placed in comfortable relation to a low table, its surface painted by none other than Proudhon.

'Sit,' Monsieur said, tapping his table with the stem of his pipe.

Then I was afraid.

'I want you,' he said, 'to take young Garmont to America.'

I imagined Mathilde, her mother shelling peas, her portrait of her studio, her portrait of the comtesse de Polignac. I am not leaving my place for anyone, I thought. I have walked down too many roads, slept under too many hedges, lost too many homes. I am almost fifty years of age and if my body is still strong it is also scarred like an old cat.

My refusal came out so fast and rough it startled me.

Monsieur studied me. Then his lips twisted and his eyes opened wide.

'Your floozy,' he cried.

I could have killed him.

'Oh, Chevalier.' He laughed. 'Please.'

Please nothing, I thought. I am a free man. I have pleased enough.

'You know, Chevalier,' he said, 'her master has been working the Bourbon side exclusively. The tide will be against him now. The portrait of the comtesse de Polignac will do her no good now,' he said. And when he said this he looked so happy that I was even more afraid.

'If so,' I said, 'she will need me even more.'

He considered me as if appalled. 'She is pretty enough,' he admitted.

This from him, always in a lather about the scrawny comtesse de Garmont.

'You are English,' he said at last. 'You can't hear how she speaks.'

'And how might that be, sir?'

'Like a fishwife, Monsieur le Chevalier. Like a fishwife from Marseille.'

I took it.

Monsieur smiled agreeably. He was one of the few men alive who knew my history. He had known me first at twelve years of age and in certain respects he was my intimate, in other ways a stranger. He was a man of amazing strength and extraordinary limitations. As he had spent many years selling off his father's library, he had a considerable reputation as a connoisseur but in truth he had no eye – I could show him the engravings I had done for Jean-Baptiste Staley's *Lettres* and all he could see was that the ducks were not French ducks.

At this point he rose and I heard him rustling in the bedroom, and when he emerged he had some engravings which he flung across to me.

'Here is what I'll do for you,' he said.

I imagined he was making me a gift of these landscapes, both of which showed small neat cottages on a high hill above a broad river. I guessed this was America.

'What do you think, Chevalier?'

'Very pretty.'

'Which would you like?'

Both works were very poor, but the smaller one had some dexterous crosshatching.

'This one.'

'No, no, no,' he cried, snatching it back from me, laying it on the table, holding it flat with his big blunt hand. 'Which one?' And he jabbed his thumb at the bigger of the houses which had two storeys and perhaps ten windows. Only then did I understand he was up to his old tricks – he was offering me a house.

'It is never cold,' he said. 'It is like summer continually.'

'It is America?'

'The Hudson River.'

I was thinking of the other house he had tricked me into leaving. Even now, years later, he would not admit his fault or the hurt he had caused those I'd left behind. Enough. There is no cause to talk about that business.

'Why would I need a house in America?'

'In New York, houses are cheap.'

'Which one is cheap?'

'All of them. They are the same price as a cow.'

I knew this could not be true. He knew I knew it and was already moving rapidly along. 'You could speak English there,' he said.

'I can speak French here.'

At which, of course, he pursed his ugly lips and rolled his eyes.

'Sit,' he ordered, although I was already sitting and he meant, Please stand. 'Have a drink with me. You must.'

At the cabinet I found Scotch whisky.

'No, the Armagnac. Bring the bottle.'

I obeyed him like the lackey I had let myself become and was not even rewarded with a drink. Instead he used the Armagnac bottle, together with its cork, his pipe and his glass, to explain his plan – I would be a spy and protector of Lord Migraine and his friend. As both young men were presently reluctant to commit to the plan for their own rescue, it was I who must make the preparation for their journey. I would buy their clothes, pack their trunks, and arrange whatever financial instruments they would require. In packing my own trunk I would, on no account, omit the clever invention he would shortly show me.

Among my many duties, I would serve as a *secrétaire* much as I did for the marquis. This would include making fair copies of correspondence and taking dictation for the report his lordship would later submit to the government.

'I will demonstrate,' Monsieur said. 'Do not roll your eyes you scoundrel. There is much you do not know.'

Then, bustling back and forward, for he only had one hand to carry things, he assembled before me the instruments required for dictation – quill, ink pot, a secretary's notebook.

'Write this down,' he ordered. 'Dear Perroquet,' he cried.

'You wish me to write to myself?'

'Write this – Dear Perroquet, the great land of America calls you across the waves, ha-ha. There, that will do.' And he snatched the notebook back and in the process sent a great splash of ink across the Proudhon.

'No, no, don't worry about that. It is nothing in comparison.'

He held the book in his teeth and removed a piece of very thin black paper he had secreted within the pages.

'Look,' he cried, the notebook still clenched between his teeth. I watched his hand turn black before my eyes. I removed the notebook from his mouth, rather as one takes a ball from a Saint Bernard, and here was revealed to me a second secret page which contained an extraordinary duplication. This was the first time I saw carbon paper. It was this spanking new invention which would allow me to make copies for Garmont's mad mother who was almost as anxious for his safety in his place of refuge as in his homeland.

'Take your floozy to America,' Monsieur said, holding out his blackened hand as if the cherubs would descend to bathe him. 'She can paint in America. All that space, and never cold.'

'She has no patrons in America.'

'Pish. There are no end of patrons. Chevalier, you know these new countries.'

'I do?' I said, for I knew very well what other new country he referred to and I wished, with the fierceness of my eye, for him to admit my loss.

'You do indeed,' he said, avoiding my gaze. 'No end of patrons, no end of walls. It is *culture* that they lack. In America they will think she is a genius. You too, if you like. In America there is no one who can paint a horse.'

'You know this, sir?'

'I have been there, Parrot. I have been there. It is a country for an artist and all you need to do is write down what his lordship says.'

'She has a mother, sir.'

'We all have mothers.'

'I hope we do, sir.'

'She can take the mother. Why not? It is a large country. Your *petite amie* can paint. You can be his lordship's *secrétaire*. It will be amusing. You can go around the prisons with him. Why, citizen, I'll lay you a gold louis you'll meet men you already know.'

He was not drunk, but he was entering into the kind of mood which I would almost call a fit and I chose that moment – the Hero of the Vendée drinking Armagnac with his single black hand – to leave him alone with his invention.

III

Mathilde and her mother lived up six flights in the faubourg Saint-Antoine. The landlord was a carpenter who ran two floors of workshops, employed a dozen journeymen, and owned four other houses in Paris, one of them in the rue Saint-Honoré. Yet he would not repair his own crumbling premises.

I could be sentimental about the smell of sawdust, even glue, but my stomach frequently rebelled against the stinking damp which rose up from the marshy foundations and seeped down from the roof, creating a confluence between the fourth and the third floors, a glistening sour-smelling sheet of scum.

Yet two floors above was heaven, glass panes in the ceiling and a small stove with a fearful zigzag flue which ran like Zeus's lightning bolt from the corner near the door to the uppermost sections of the roof.

Of course it was cold in winter, but now it was warm, and I returned from the *petite maison* to find the windows thrown wide open and the air perfumed by woodsmoke from the yard below.

In one corner, serving as a screen to hide the old lady's cot, stood a single painting as tall as a man – or woman – for it was Mathilde's self-portrait – the painter in her studio with her fallen angel's marble legs protruding from a silken sheet. Around the walls were models in plaster, a head of Niobe hanging from a nail, a Venus, a hand, other things all being the property of the woman portrayed in that shocking painting, no less a beauty in the living light than on the canvas. The confrontation in the painted eyes was gone that evening, and in its place such a warm and lovely glow.

Her Parrot entered. She rose, wineglass in hand, barefooted, her arms open, and all the velvet shadows of the room held inside her gorgeous clavicle. She smelled of wine and onions, and when she kissed me on the mouth I breathed her deep and pulled her hard against me. She pushed back and looked into my eyes so frankly, and I could already smell that musty rutty salty perfume our parts made in the night. Six years we had been like this, and never a day was less passionate between us. I kissed the old lady too, on her crown, and she lifted her lined face to kiss me on the lips and poured me *un verre* – *un* cup in fact – and began to recite the story of the beef *daube*. Did I think it was too early in the year? Had I felt the change of season? And so on. They were, both together, so dear, so familial, so fond of me and I of them, and if they had been at the wine an hour or two before I got there, that was how we lived. I liked it, our sour red mouths. Soon I would have to give the news of Monsieur's offer, but for now Maman sang to me, the Lord knows what it was, Provençal perhaps, quavering, Moorish. I did not doubt it was her love song to me, but who she really was or what she meant I could not say. I rubbed her swollen knuckles.

She was an extraordinary old thing, and if her spine was as twisted as the stairs, her eyes were like bright stones in water.

I sat at the yellow card table and they waited on me. The *daube* was rich and perfect and the wine flowed, and I asked my darling how would she like to come to live with me in America, and she laughed, and drank, and left gravy on her glass.

'And I will build you an enormous studio,' I said, thinking of the house on the Hudson and wondering which way it faced.

'Oh Parrot, you lovely man.'

'And we will look at the river, and have a yacht. And sail.'

'Sweetheart.' She leaned forward and kissed me, all that smeary wine and meat and fat glistening on her lips and her mother stood and took her plate to the scullery and when she had washed her plate she announced she would sit in the yard and watch the children.

'And we will have a garden, and geese.'

'Do you hear him, Maman?'

The old lady made an agreeable sighing sound and then she

was gone and we could hear her making her cautious way down the stairs.

'He is mad,' Mathilde said, and her face was now close to me, kissing, nuzzling.

'There are many walls in America,' I said, 'and very few artists.'

She cocked her head, a way of looking. She had heard another voice in mine.

'What are you up to?' she said, and she had changed, still smiling but questioning. I felt her gaze and knew I could not hide from her.

'I am asking, Do you like America?'

It was my face she was now reading, certainly not my words.

'You are running away?' she asked, as if amused by me.

'How could I?'

She pushed her chair back. 'You are running away!'

'My darling.'

'You *know* I cannot go to America. Why are you saying this? It is that dirty old marquis.'

'It is you, my love.' But she was on her feet – clatter and scraping in the scullery.

'No, it is you. *You* are running away.'

'You are mad,' I cried, not believing what I said.

In the scullery – by which I mean a wooden plank, a pail, a bowl – I found her face awash with tears.

Gently, I touched her salty cheek.

Violently she slammed my breastbone and beat me as if I were a prison door. 'Liar,' she cried, casting aside her pinny and falling backwards upon our bed, her face a seeping rock, offered to the sky.

Kneeling, bundling, I told her I loved her, would never leave her, would never go to America in all my life, and in little cautious stages, with a kiss finally permitted, persuaded my little wild creature into my open shirt, and there, in the familiar dark, she lost her armour, sloughed it off so it joined the jumble of fabrics, castings, pictures, frames without paintings, and paintings without frames, the graveyard beside our bed.

By the time Maman returned we were at peace and then the three of us did homage to the flagon and retired, the old lady to her iron cot behind the portrait, and we to our corner which resembled, more than anything, a pile of costumes for an opera or dance. When the last lantern was snuffed, the colours of the cast-offs glowed all around us, blood and anthracite in the velvet night.

We went to sleep at peace, in each other's arms, and there you would think the matter over with, all the sweet familiarity of each other's skins sucked into our pink receptive lungs. Yet to see ourselves this way it is necessary to forget – that although my strange beloved slept, she never did stop living, or arguing, or fighting, or fleeing, and there was always a drama of life and death that occupied her dreams and was no less real than anything that occurred before her open eyes.

Thus she moved from peace to war through that particular night and even though I was asleep, flat on my back, snoring a storm to shake the vineyards of the Loire, I felt her move, as if tugged from me on the tides of sleep, out of my arms, onto her side, her back toward me, and when we woke with the clatter of the streets outside, a hard cold stretch of bed separated us, and she rose without even looking at me and I listened to her heavy footfall shake the boards and, like a traveller who has been hit from behind, robbed and kicked in darkness, I felt not so much the pain or indignity but the injustice of it all. I pulled on my shirt. She was already at her canvas, painting without coffee or bread.

I glimpsed the old lady curled beneath her quilt, hands over her head, fingers in her ears. I should have paid attention, for Maman knew her daughter from the womb and what a holy hell she must have made.

I touched Mathilde's bare shoulder, and gently drew back her hair.

'Go,' she cried. 'Just go.'

'I'm not going anywhere.'

She did not look at me but went to our bed, picked up my trousers, and threw them down into the street.

'What have I done?'

She was my treasure, my ball of pain and beauty – her luminous eyes, her little curved belly, her perfect thigh. Who she was fighting I did not know, but I was old enough, had scars on my ankles and my arms, a piece missing from my ear, and saw how the moment had come, like an unexpected death, like God striking, the lightning hitting, and I was a man tipped from his bunk on the ship to find not floor but death water, bubbles, the fierce cold fingers of the salty night. There, die. Rise no more.

There was no point in asking is it fair that I should lose everything I love again. I took my duffel and threw in my tools, my better clothes, a book, and with no word to Maman I made off down the giddy seasick stairs, emerging half naked into the courtyard where the children were already playing with the trousers, from whose pockets all coin, even my good-luck acorn, was gone. It had only taken ten minutes to have my body flayed, my bones stripped clean, my squiddy soul out in the sun to dry.

I headed for my English printers, for where else could I go? The day was sunny and cruelly pleasant. Along the way I spied, in every café, the sweet familiarity of couples who had spent the night happily in each other's arms and I, who had been for six years one of them, was cast beyond the pale, a poor lonely foreign wretch. I found my friends all gone to work, and the landlady, who had always been so pleasant to me, said her house was full. Reluctantly she brought me some bottled ale and wrote the tab on my friend's account.

Then I removed to a hotel on the rue Richelieu, where on the strength of Monsieur's famous name and my good clothes – which

I was forced to lay out on the bed – I was given, for twelve francs every month, a 'parlour next to the sky'.

It sickens me to tell the rest, my many trips back to the faubourg Saint-Antoine where Mathilde finally softened enough to loan me a hundred sous. There is little that is not pathetic but in the end, no matter what injustice he suffers, a man is still a man and cannot be a snivelling wretch forever, and I set out, at an age when one expects this shit to be well past, to present myself at the *petite maison*, declaring myself ready to travel to America or hell, whatever would remove me from my present state.

IV

The trouble with the general class of Garmonts is that they cannot imagine the life of anyone outside the circle of their arse. They will hand out the Maundy money, thank you sir, but for the rest of the time you must abandon your story for their own, and you are nothing better than an ink-dipped ant who must scurry around the page at their command.

So wait a minute. Sit down, find a chair and pour yourself a tot of rum and think what I am telling you before they call me to serve their noble needs.

I was in Devon, years and years before, in 1793. My daddy had been arrested and the flames of the printery were in the night, the fir tree igniting. You have forgotten? For Christ's sake – the secret forgers were all bursting from the roof, up through the tiles, alive and dying all at once, such screams. The Parrot Larrit was a frightened boy, running, encouraged by his da and the other printers chained together. Up the hill I went, a musket ball whizzing past me like a hornet on the chase, and into the very patch of woods that had been spared the barley axe, jumping across the smoking body of a man who I, in my terror, decided was asleep. I tore through brambles, ripping skin, not daring to stop, unable to breathe, up the hill, from where I could see the fire, then down to the bank of the River Dart and along the soft path, heading always against the current, unable to think of anything but Dartmoor at the end. That I should make so wise a choice was no thanks to myself, a shitting shivering boy, but to my da who had taught me the utility of Dartmoor and the sense in keeping it nearby, for Dartmoor is a land of solitude and silence – or *almost silence* for you may hear the murmur of a torrent far below or the drowsy hum of an insect, but there will be no human voice unless it is your own.

Another boy may have run home to his mother, but the moor, in all its weathers, was my mother and I ran toward its arms. It was not until the stitch in my side brought me to a stop that I tried to understand if I was followed, but there was no sound to be heard above the River Dart, which was none other than the total of the scores of rivulets and brooks of Dartmoor, each one of which carried that haunted weirdness in their note which my daddy called the *whisht* and which here, in the dark just out of Dittisham, produced a vast melancholic wash, a dark sac of grief inside which I cried my heart out, throwing myself down on dirt and thistles, weeping until at last the moon rose on the water and I – having nothing else in life to look forward to – set off along the path which I knew would lead me, sooner or later, to Totnes, Buckfast, East Dart, and West Dart at Dartmeet on the moor.

'*Bonjour, monsieur.*'

If the language had been my own I might have fled, leaping like a goat, a moorland sheep, bleating in terror as I plunged into the dark, but it was as you have already guessed – the one-armed man. I stayed, quivering while he, in all his huge dark foreign bulk laid his single hand very gently on my shoulder, and although I could not make out the meaning of a word he said, I knew he meant to make me tame.

In all my snivelling confusion I did not know which way to turn and it was not until he pushed – or rather *encouraged* – me along the track that I understood he expected me to know a place to hide.

I walked all that night, still against the current of the river, losing paths, finding new ones, sinking up to my waist in swamps, more and more tired, walking weary and careless through Totnes, the entire town dark and not a single candle in one window, and I walked until I felt myself lifted in his mighty arm and held.

'*Fault-il suivre le fleuve?*' Something like that, for he was certainly asking should we follow the course of the river but I had as much French as I had Latin and could not answer.

I was carried by him through the night, sound asleep, somehow aware of his steady tread and then not even that.

I woke in a different season, shivering, my back pushed hard against a wall of rock. Before me a vast solitude – long ridges rising in dusky sweeps against the sky, line beyond line of them like the waves of ocean and from these waves, the rocky islands, tors, more like lions, sphinxes, and other strange monsters, and down the slope, in wild confusion, huge blocks of splintered rock. And the foreground, so achingly familiar, so forlorn without my da – brilliant green bits of bog, purple clumps of heather, red and brown rushes, and waving cotton grass in which we had once trapped rabbits and birds and eaten by the fire beneath the stars and known ourselves, a man and boy, blessed to be so free.

'*Bonjour.*'

I had already heard the crackling of his fire, but it was now a sound so sad I could not bear to turn, and would rather believe it was another man, another fire.

'*Regardez.*'

He was squatting, filthy, ash smeared across his face, his curly hair pushed sideways like his grin, and he had called me to *attention* in reference to two links of butcher's sausage which he had procured, perhaps from Mr Piggott's house or somewhere along the road at night.

His plan was not a good one, for he poked a stick into the sausage and was about to spoil our meal. I let him know I had a better idea, and so made a *Cornish pit* as my daddy had taught me, that is a little rock oven that you build the fire atop.

He let me do what I wished, although when he understood he would be waiting longer for his breakfast he puffed out his lips and rolled his eyes as I have seen him do ten thousand times since. It was then, as I dug the pit, I unwittingly entered his employ.

V

He was a great huge animal, the Frenchman, like a seal or horse, strong-smelling, with thighs as big as posts. As he had carried me and fed me I imagined him my protector, while of course he was a baby. He had a brass compass but could neither speak nor know where he was toddling, leaning forward against the wind, eyes streaming – Mama, Mama here I am – but as I had followed my father happily for so many years, I now followed him.

'O nord, O nord,' he cried. 'Monjay, monjay.' Clearly he knew nothing. The northern part of Dartmoor is a proper pig, covered by blanket bogs, peat gullies, tussocks, and hidden holes, heaven-sent for cattle thieves but no place for a bawling boy and a Frenchman without a map. Thus it was revealed that Monsieur Monjay was in no way the equal of my father, who had snared and tickled and poached and fed me, dear Daddy, with whom I had traversed the wilds near Black Tor and Yes Tor, the pair of us the only humans in the whole empty world with sheep and rabbits and grouse – the ground exploding at our feet. My da and I would talk till our throats were sore and the silence of the heather moor would be broken only by the spectral whisht and perhaps a guttural call – the grouse again – *come out, come out, come out* they cried. At those times no more was said than what you could signal by means of a loving nudge.

Monsieur tried to bring me back toward the north, striking me with his compass, straining north like a furry-footed draughthorse wanting to go home. But northward I would not go. Instead I pointed across the miles of moor, toward Princetown.

'Monjay,' said I.

I was cold and dirty, dark with grief, but I hopped like a bunny rabbit and made my hand swim like a fish. I was a scoundrel and a liar. I understood I must give him food, but by nightfall I had found nothing but a big bull oak, a single isolated tree with a hollow trunk inside which generations of cattle had sheltered. Here I made a big show of looking at the Frenchman's compass and staring in the direction of the setting sun. Showing myself by various signs to be well satisfied, I went to sleep.

We slept in our dark and dung, while outside the night sky was filled with the wild clanging of migrating birds, their hearts pumping blood I would have gladly drunk while I roasted their living flesh on a roaring fire.

In the morning we had what is called a tramp's breakfast, that is a piss and a look around, my daddy's joke.

I did not know what would be done to me if I did not find us monjay soon. Of course you are a moorsman, sir, or your uncle was before he went to Van Diemen's Land. You know there was good eating all around us at every step, the hush and the breath of food of every description – moles, pheasants, great fat pigeons – and what I needed was not a compass but a handful of corn or a little roll of wire. Certainly my da would never travel without corn to lure the pheasants to his bag. There were also, as I am well aware, very good lamb chops on Dartmoor, great bounding sheep like mountain goats. My da would lay a loop of rope along their paths and connect it to a young sapling whose top was bent down. When the silly sheep stepped on the loop it would release the sapling, and she would be wrenched upward and left hanging by her leg. In the past I hated these traps, the terror and cruelty of them, for the sheep might be there for days before we found them, raging and tearing around and scratching the skin off their legs, but now I must watch the foolish Frenchman throwing rocks, or galloping down into a bog while his prey danced easily away.

We came upon a little moorland stream. I was so cold, my skin like plucked goose, and I lay flat on my stomach looking into the water, thinking I might vomit if I had another sip, and there I saw the shadow and then the long-jawed brown trout that owned it. As I watched, the fish slid beneath the very rock on which I lay. And now I required no fowling piece or net, just gently gently catchee monkey. I held my arms as far apart as they would go and slid them into the cold water in what you might call a pincer movement. And there he was – quite peaceful – and I rubbed his underbelly with just my forefinger while I made polite inquiry which end was which and when I knew his arse from his head, I moved my hands up to the gills and, smoothly, tightened them like a vice around his head.

Right behind me I could hear Monsieur talking but I could not speak, for what I was doing was as tricky as holding wet soap in a tub. I rose on one knee and I could hear a dove nearby – *coo, coo* – and I still had my fish and he was a good one, three pounds at least, and I walked backward over the trippy rocks and gravel until I was the distance of a cricket pitch from the stream and now I saw Monsieur and I understood he was the dove, and that sweet round sound was coming from his dry expectant lips. When I had knocked the fish on his forehead and made him dead, I held him out, like the vicar I once saw with his chalice offering wine to God, and the giant marquis de Tilbot took it from me, grinning so fiercely his mouth was like a wound, slashed across his unshaved charcoal face, and he held the gleaming fish high in the air and, with his teeth shining in the yellow gloomy light, he bit a huge hunk from its back and I could hear him eating, crunching spine, and see him spitting out the grist, and I waited very patiently for my share and was too young to know the true strange nature of my life.

VI

The Frenchman had whiskers on his granitic face, scabby lichen on his chin, cracks of eyes against the wind. He was a living terror of a man. He had one broken tooth, no wonder when you saw how he made up for the missing hand, sniff this flower, bite that stone. By a broken tinner's hut his attention was taken by a dead cow, skin turned to leather, insides eaten long before. He kicked it viciously apart, dragged away its poor dead bones, smashed and bashed them with a rock.

I wished my father would come back.

'Ha-ha,' the Frenchman cried, stabbing at the mist. He had made a dagger out of bone.

My da was always very quiet and even, never any rush, just gently gently. I never had to do a thing but be with him. The Frenchman was in no way like my father. He needed every assistance and I pretended the best I could. On and on, shoes squelching, water dripping down the neck, I held out the compass like a divining rod, leading the way to nowhere. Always the queer rooty perfume of the marinated moor, bogs and boggy life: mire in the valleys, blanket bog on the higher land, marsh plume thistle, devil's bit, scabious heath, spotted orchid, saw-wort, purple moor grass, also the seething and quaking bog with a thin layer of sodden moss above black slime and water. Then finally, by chance, up from a hollow and down into a wider valley where I spied a cottage and, beyond it, tall brown reeds atop a rise. I broke into a run and I heard the great weight of the Frenchman pounding down behind me and I ran faster in my fear, and my legs were like rubber and I fell and rolled and came up running.

The Frenchman was upon me at the garden gate, taking my shoulder, turning me. I did not understand a word he said.

I pointed at tall brown reeds and said rabbit. I tried 'warrener'. No good. This was a warrener's cottage. We could eat rabbit. But then I saw something awful had happened here. The house was dead, abandoned. It was like the corpse of a beast set on by wild dogs, its inside pulled out and left scattered among the cauliflowers – bedding, tools, thatch. The only clue to the crime was the peat-digging tools which had been broken into many pieces. It was as if the bog itself had risen against its own subjection.

'Hoppity-hoppity.' I tried to be a rabbit. He did not understand but pushed past me into the cottage. The thatch was all fallen and the big roof beam had been cut in half, the cruellest act upon a house in a landscape with so little wood. What had brought this dreadful retribution on a simple warrener's head? Perhaps he had poached or smuggled. Perhaps he had been in the habit of taking peat from another fellow's *tie*, why else were the bud iron, slitting knife, and turf irons all broken? I was frightened, for the hatefulness of outlaws on Dartmoor was well known.

I took the broken turf iron and went outside to draw a rabbit in the sod. I called the Frenchman. He would not leave the cottage. I was close to tears, worried the outlaws would descend again. I came to drag him out to see my drawing but he was busy collecting peat and thatch and I saw I would have to wait until a fire was going.

He had lost all faith in me, as well he should. He made me hold a rock while he chipped at it and formed a sort of axe, then ground it. The fire was so hot it burned my legs. The sky was grey and wet above my head.

When he had his axe ready he was loudly pleased about it. I expected we would starve to death in the midst of all this food.

When at last he saw my drawing of the rabbit, he clearly did not understand. I huddled by the fire and wondered should I run away and would my daddy find his son's dead body on some lonely path, skin turned to leather, insides eaten long before. My one true comfort was the peat, which did not flame but glowed, exuding an aroma that filled my lungs with balm. I breathed it in as a richer boy might snuffle a stuffed toy, and in all my misery and intoxication, I fell asleep.

When I woke I smelled food. There was a black and battered cauldron on the fire and from it rose the most delicious smell, but Monsieur kept me at arm's length, grinning, singing to the pot, pursing his lips.

'Oppity-oppity,' said he.

I sat and watched him stir his rabbit stew. Soon I burned my mouth and filled my stomach. Then I slept, curled up like a dead caterpillar beside his smelly feet.

VII

Next morning Monsieur unearthed a warrener's net and began unpicking it, a completely useless occupation which required his long white toes and bristly mouth and single hand. He hunched over his labour like a naughty monkey, holding down a single thread with his bent toe, pulling apart a knot between tooth and pincered fingers.

By day's end I was freezing cold and near starvation. My protector had destroyed a useful snare and produced instead one hundred feet of undone netting which he wound into a ball. I removed my sodden boots and wondered at my white and wrinkly feet. I wondered where my father was. Not even sleep would save me from my misery.

It rained and rained again. There was a tall black rock upon the saddle which sometimes gave the eerie impression of a man.

I tried to catch it moving. As the night approached the Frenchman produced a second net and swept out onto the moor, the net dragging like his wedding train.

I must follow him it seemed.

In different circumstances it would have been a lovely evening on the moor, very soft and kindly, the light mellow and the gin-clear stream whispering around the edges of the bright green turf. The rabbits, having left the safety of their warren, had settled in their gentle multitudes, laying their long shadows on the sweet grasses between their front porch and the stream. How I envied them and feared their death and yearned for it.

We stretched the net taut between our growling stomachs, thus walling the rabbits' bedroom from their dinner table. Monsieur then lobbed a stone among the feeding families who lifted their heads, stood stock-still, noses twitching. One stone later they had become a stampede, a tangling jumping swarm of them, writhing in our net, and the sheer force of their collective panic near stopped my heart. We made a parcel of their writhing lives, so we thought, but in all the tangled squeaking the rabbits fell or swarmed toward a hole, and if Monsieur had not caught one by the leg we might have starved to death in spite of all our murderous intent. It was a big plump fellow, the condemned, and most unlucky to be swung through the air and have its skull slammed hard against the moor. It is a wonder he did not fly apart.

We ate the bunny, not enough, never was, that night or next. I was a scabby snotty nosey boy always tasting grass and weeds, looking out for moulds, scraps of abandoned food, and thus, next day, I discovered, high in a disused chimney, the warrener's secret hoard of pelts which he had hung like washing on a line. The skins had dried just perfectly, crinkly and crunchy on the skin side, soft and furry on the pelt.

I indicated to Monsieur that they might make a layer for our roof. In his great aristocratic ignorance he ignored me, and he was soon busy devastating them, cutting two-inch-wide spirals from one rabbit skin and then another. These ruined pelts he threw into a heap beside him.

We caught another rabbit and cooked it on the glowing peat.

I woke at dawn, shivering. I found Monsieur out on the wet grass with the strips of pelt, which he was twisting together to make a long furry tapeworm winding around his madness. He raised his eyebrows and showed his teeth as he bit a pelt. I felt my hair prickle on my neck.

Imagining all that revolting fur inside my own mouth, I ran. I did not know what I had seen or what it meant, only having some notion of a beast devouring that which should not be eaten. Our little crystal stream had turned a brooding tannic red. I leaped across it and dashed up the ridge until I lost my breath, and then I walked toward the distant tor. Then I ran once more, got a stitch, gave up, continued stooped over, my hand dug hard against the hurt. The tor remained at its great distance, but once I reached it, I expected it would be my daddy, his long loping shadow moving on the moor, the light-grey signal from his pipe.

For a long time the tor would not come close, and then – at last – I was upon it, a monolith with grey-lichened skin like cankers. I tore my knees and hands to gain its ancient back. There I squatted, bleeding and hungry, but I could see all around for many miles, right down to the smoky coast at Plymouth, but in all that huge empty space I could not see a single soul, unless a sea hawk has a soul – it rode the empty air, high and lonely and unknowable.

On this tor, a long way from any stream, I found a smooth round grey river pebble which must have been a kind of slate for I could mark it with a chip of granite. Here, with a calculation that admits no pretty explanation, I set to make a drawing of my frightening benefactor. I was not wise enough to know what I was doing, but

I was dumb with fear and cunning and I made his likeness like an emperor on a coin.

In my absence the madman had constructed a wooden frame whose corners he had bound with skin. This rack he had set up like a loom and threaded with the fur rope. He began to whistle and raise his eyebrows like a fool and I understood he had nearly finished making himself a rug. Then he pinched my cheek, and then he grasped my hand, and forced me to touch the rug and he himself brushed his big whiskery cheek against it, and kissed it as if it was his wife.

I hated him. I would not give him anything. I watched him take his bone knife and cut his blanket free and when he threw it in my direction, I took it as a taunt and I pushed it angrily away. He then took me with all his mighty one-armed force and held me while I bit and kicked and so it took an awful long time, with us both exhausted from our struggle, to understand that he had made the rug for me.

Thus in a great snotty outburst I surrendered, and he sat me on his lap and wrapped me tight and, there on the dirt floor, in the midst of all the devastation, stroked my head with his remaining hand. Then I wept, Lord God I wept for hours. I kept my stone, not knowing what the future held.

OLIVIER

Dear Little Mother – my only friend in all the world is taken from me. Blacqueville is dead and here I am, at sea, alone in my grief, in this foul bunk, dictating to this common clown whose fine calligraphy gives no inkling of his malevolence and criminality and whose only punishment for his crimes is that he must now write them down himself, and we can only trust that he is chastised in a world to come, or in America, although the former is likely to arrive before the latter.

I am informed that you know what occurred at Le Havre. Have you been told that we were visiting the château of the Countess S, as you had asked us to remember you to her? There, fleeing death as you had wished, it found us. At the countess's salon, among other persons of wit and rank, was one Monsieur d'Audloy. This gentleman, on hearing of our intention to travel to America, called me a traitor and a coward at which Blacqueville, in the full generosity of his heart, took upon himself the responsibility for both our honours and before anyone was quite aware of what had happened, seconds were appointed. Naturally I imagined the duel would take place in the early morning and was seeking counsel from the comte du Beugnot without knowing that pistols had been provided and the combatants had already presented themselves in the orchard. Learning this, I rushed to prevent the damage, but I was no farther than the terrace when I heard the single shot. Thence in the horrid grey light, in drizzling rain, I found my dear Blacqueville dead as death itself, and it may be said that my behaviour was neither dignified nor manly for all I could think was to lift him in my arms and order him to life.

Of course there was no question of my fleeing now and I determined that I would cash my ticket and return to Paris and there honour my friend in death as I had failed to do in life. I had the shipping company open their office, but when at last the manager appeared I was informed that I must now present myself to the captain on board and only then might I obtain our refund, and so, with the awful copyist at my side this is where I went.

I thought the Dutch captain exceedingly civil. He received me in his cabin with great solicitude and sympathy, and had I not accepted his brandy I doubt I would be where I am now – that is, far at sea without hope of return, surrounded by the most appalling bourgeoisie and worse, this servant you have provided, with his wretched cocky walk and his mouth always on the edge of the most horrid smirk. It would be better for me to have stayed in Paris. I would prefer being pulled to pieces by the mob. Doubtless you think me despicable, but never mind; I have clearly been dispatched, against my will, on your instructions. This is a tragedy worthy of the Greeks – that in seeking to save my life you have assured my death – for it is certain no one will survive this awful sea.

I am sure you could never imagine the conversation – if you could call it that – of the Americans. Certainly there is no talk of the tragedies, Greek or otherwise. The conversationalists include among their number a rich manufacturer of nails, a farmer turned banker, his wife, his two skinny daughters, and a Jew named Eckerd who dubs himself an impresario and is travelling with a certain Mlle Desclée, allegedly an opera singer! This Eckerd frets continually about his awful *carrier pigeons*, which poor lousy creatures he plans to release when we are off the coast of America. The birds will carry news of the opera singer's arrival to the waiting press, so all is vulgarity and ostentation, and although the banker, despite the comic name of Peek, is a good enough fellow, and I might, I suppose, benefit from his conversation, I cannot think of anything but my dear Blacqueville who died so bravely on my own behalf while I, so far from *gloire*, am sunk in ignominy on this filthy bunk with no other company but this copyist. He has no sponsor but M. de Tilbot who, if you will permit me to speak bluntly, seems capable of destroying all the good sense and religious principles which have been the guiding lights of your life.

As you can see, I have sent the servant away and am now writing with my own hand whose graceless stutterings no tutor ever could correct. More money wasted. This Master Larrit is not even who Tilbot thinks he is, I am sure. He has taken advantage of my drugged state to smuggle his paramour and her dreadful mother aboard. What with the banker and his jolly daughters, the impresario and his singer, and the servant's own menagerie *à la marseillaise*, the moral tone here is very poor, and whatever you have paid in your desire to save me from harm, your panic has once again ensured that you were robbed. I am certain you could not have imagined this confinement, or, if you did, I am sure you will beg God's forgiveness for abandoning your son to such a fate.

Goodbye.

Olivier

PARROT

This captain of the *Havre* was as hard and scrawny as a piece of rope. He had rheumy squinting eyes, a tobacco-stained moustache, a rum drinker's nose, and absolutely no arse at all. But his fingers were large and white and soft, made for the dark and secret places of a sailor's life. So when Monsieur, who had a great skill in this department, had rolled a quantity of paper currency, the captain swiftly folded himself around the bribe and found himself able to accommodate some passengers whose names had hitherto been absent from his list. That is, although he had lost one chap through tragedy, it now seemed he had gained two more, and much money needed to pass hands due to this change of plan.

How or why this situation had arisen no one bothered to inform me but it appeared that my darling Mathilde and her old maman were standing on the dock, and although my beloved would not so much as look at me, she was confidently waiting for a cabin to be free. All around her, in a great jumble of wrapped and unwrapped, was every single item from her studio. I recognised the bust of Cicero

on which the old lady sat, puffing on her pipe. I was in no state to
be a reliable witness, but you know the human mind – it will tell
you anything in order to be believed. This mind of mine informed
me that Mathilde wished to deny our private relationship at the
very moment she was publicly claiming it, but once I had her in her
cabin, she would soon have the pillow hard between her teeth. This
was very credible, and edible as well, but I also knew my tempestu-
ous darling and I did not doubt the weather would be fairer soon.

In any case, Monsieur had promised the two women passage,
and now Mathilde would oblige him to keep his word no matter
what the booking agent said.

Monsieur waited in the captain's cabin, playing solitaire. Not two
feet from his elbow lay Olivier-Jean-Baptiste de Clarel de Garmont,
drugged as death upon the captain's bunk.

I had some vague apprehension that negotiations were not
proceeding simply, but all I could think was that I would not lose
my beloved after all, and I could have wept with joy for I was really
too old to go through such grief again.

The little captain threw his sausage fingers in the air and I noticed
the marquis de Tilbot once more slip his hand into an inner pocket
in his cloak. I watched this dreamily – the silky surface of the cloak
remained as still as a mill pond but it was easy to imagine his fingers
in the dark, like the legs of some antipodean beast which makes its
living squashing bees' knees for its hungry young.

The captain now turned exceeding thoughtful. Perhaps he was
reflecting that only he and the mate, a nineteen-year-old boy from
Nantucket, were capable of performing the common but indispen-
sable business of steering, and that this was one man short, to put
it mildly. I held my breath now, waiting for Monsieur, anticipating
the single hand emerging with a golden egg within the palm.

Then, before you could say Jack Robinson, it was done. My life
was saved. Mathilde and her mother had bustled on board and,

having taken possession of a damned stateroom, had locked the door. Monsieur's carriage was soon rattling beneath the customs office arch, on its way to Paris and the rue Saint-Dominique. A pig had escaped and was swimming away from the vessel, the mate and I had carried Lord Migraine to his cabin, and I did not complain when I understood I was to share this tiny room with him. I knew not to expect justice on a ship. Mr Eckerd pleaded to have his pigeons stowed 'tween decks and he and his companion wept and remonstrated that the birds would die if left in the longboat where they had been consigned and in the midst of all this turbulence – a strong north wind was blowing with enough violence to raise a dreadful sea even in the bay – the tow-haired mate assured me that, as the sun declined it would abate, and once we had weathered Cape Barfleur we would make a free wind down channel.

'Ah,' said the Human Mind, 'let's hope this chap knows what's what.'

So I went to sit outside Mathilde's door and put my lips against the brass.

'Answer me, I'm here. I am your Parrot.'

I thought I was whispering but who can really say. I caused an awful nuisance in the gangway.

'Talk to me, please. *Sacrebleu!* Why are you angry with me?'

Some scraping.

'If you are to travel with me you must answer me. I will have you put ashore and you will have to walk.'

Silence.

'You are an irritating fool and I have no idea why you would throw away my trousers and why, if you would throw away my trousers, you would come aboard this fucking ship. To hell with you.'

Silence.

'I love you.'

Silence.

'Do you not see how much trouble you have already caused? It is not a good idea to make an enemy of Monsieur. He knows all your sitters and those not even born. M. de Garmont will want a portrait. I will talk to him.'

Silence, more silence.

'Puss?' And then it was insufferable. 'I hope you die.'

By then we were on our way to America and I was not well and I found a bench in the galley beside Mr Eckerd, who was attempting to dry his pigeons while a champagne bottle rolled to and fro across the floor and I did not trust my head to pick it up. Mr Eckerd smelled, generally, like freshly plucked poultry. A great crowd had assembled on the pier head to witness our departure, and cheered as we passed, but I could not look at them. We had set out under full sail and I waited with Mr Eckerd for the calm. Two hours went by and things got worse. Orders were given to reduce the canvas and we came back to a double-reefed mainsail, foresail, and second-sized jib. With the sail even thus diminished, the vessel, at times, almost buried herself. Mr Eckerd moaned, and then I noticed he was slipping and sliding on the deck holding a second cage of pigeons.

He had told me his plan in confidence – the birds would be released off Rhode Island and fly home to New York with news of the eminent opera singer.

My private thoughts of Mlle Desclée were interrupted by a sickening plunge, as the entire deck was buried under boiling sea which invaded the cabin and surged across my feet, then broke against the locked door behind which, even among the crashing of pigeon cages and gin bottles, I could hear enough to know my beloved was no longer well.

I cursed God, the marquis, Lord Migraine. Once that was done I vomited across my boots.

OLIVIER

My childhood friend had been done to death and in his place was nothing but a pit. I had been drugged and dragged, and left at the mercy of a vomiting copyist, and I might have expected my lungs would seize and – being denied my leeches – blood would burst right through my eyes. I had spent my whole life fearing this, or something like it, but I was a Garmont. No one would see my grief or rage.

Compared to my own cramped malodorous accommodation, the deserted main cabin was a site of healthfulness, smelling of nothing worse than salt and tar. It was here I was seated when I felt the swell preceding the first big wave, that long dreadful quiver running through the timbers of the ship, not stilled or contained by the copper sheathing of its hull but rather amplified so that a deadly vibration ran through every human bone aboard the *Havre*, and when that shiver had been doused, snuffed, drowned, and the little barque had tumbled off the edge, then I felt the first big wave break and I saw the great wash of beef and brandy erupt from the dreadful Parrot's gorge, and as the entire craft was hurled like a lobster into a kettle, I was very pleased to note that I was not afraid.

In the midst of this tempest the venal Dutch captain fled his post and stood before me, his nose and oilskins dripping, his vinous face awash, a bottle of champagne in his pale drowned hands.

'Your lordship' – he grinned – 'something for what ails you.' As the vile creature proffered his gift there was such a veritable *twist* to his body it was as if he had become a plank of his own ship, caught by opposing currents of servility and greed. I was embarrassed to look on him, so boneless and poisonous did he seem. I accepted his unwanted gift. He asked how else he could serve me.

I said that if he had an interest in my comfort he could deal with the retching varlet who had been deposited in my cabin.

'Ha-ha.' He laughed. 'Very good, sir.' His French was poor.

In English I slowly and clearly demanded that the vomiter be dispatched to the hold or the bow or whatever place such persons were normally accommodated.

He saluted me and went away.

The main cabin, I now realised, contained another traveller, a tall elegant fellow with a long nose, a shortish upper lip, and a wry smile to underline it. He exhibited such magnificent ugliness you might assume him to be French but, although we had not been introduced, I already knew him as Mr Peek, an American.

As for the introduction, it was peculiar. Mr Peek was pleased to inform me that he knew everything concerning my business, that I was in mourning for my friend, that I was a commissioner sent by my government to investigate the superior prisons of America.

While the sea entered its next stage of violence I joined him on his bench and together we gravely watched the waters overwhelm both bow and stern – great snowy rushes which were still foaming as they entered the cabin where they swept two drowned pigeons and my champagne to the aft before the shock of the next wave brought them sailing back at us. We lifted up our shoes each time the wash came our way. This, for some reason, he thought immensely funny and even I could smile.

Mr Peek reached down into the waters and retrieved the champagne bottle as it passed. Then he splashed across the ankle-deep waters and found two unbroken glasses, and a moment later I was toasting him, imbibing the tepid waters of Reims.

'Your lordship,' said Mr Peek, when the galley door had slammed, 'might I offer some advice and hope it is not ill-taken?'

I assured him of my trust in his civility, but my English was not all I had been led to believe. '*Civility*,' I said a second time.

'You see, it is the question of your servant being sent below.'

'Good,' I said, although I quickly saw his opinion would not be soothing.

'The Americans will not take it well,' he said.

I understood the word *take*, and thought *take money*.

'The expulsion of your copyist – the republicans will be against it.'

'Ah yes, but the servant is your natural enemy, an *Englishman*.'

'On the other hand you are, your lordship, an aristocrat.'

'So you seem to have been informed, sir.'

'If I had been told nothing, that much would be evident to me,' said Mr Peek. 'You possess a refinement and dignity that could have no other source. But they will not like to see you refuse to share your cabin with your man.'

'They?'

'The Americans, my lord. It will not go down well with them.'

'But do they share quarters with their servants? I am sure they do not.'

'They do not, but they believed that you did and they liked you for it. Now it would embarrass them to see the man cast out. It would strike a nerve, as we say. It would seem aristocratic to them and they would take it ill.'

'Are you sure of this, sir? It seems very strange to me.'

'We are to be two months at sea, and I can assure your lordship it is better to be all good fellows.'

He filled my glass again, and I thought, I cannot wait to tell Blacqueville this nonsense.

'Sir,' I said, 'it is my belief the scoundrel drugged me and brought me aboard.'

'Indeed,' said Mr Peck, and raised an eyebrow. 'Your lordship has suffered much.'

'Alas, Mr Peek. I lost my best friend in all the world.'

Mr Peek cocked his head at me and then, impulsively, poured the contents of his glass into mine. I dared not reject such crude kindness.

'A word of advice, your lordship, from one who admired you from the moment you spoke?'

'But yes, of course.'

'Be a good fellow sir. Play the democrat. We will have rough justice for the servant when we step ashore. I am in a position to make a promise I can keep.'

He poured back half of my remaining champagne and before we clinked our glasses in a toast, Mr Peek winked, and having finished his draught looked down his nose at me, as sly and solemn as a magistrate.

'What did we drink to, sir?' I asked.

'To deep dark prisons,' said he.

Oh, Blacqueville, you would not believe it. I raised my glass to my American and he said it was as well I had met him for he was a trustee of the board of the new House of Refuge for Delinquent Minors and could introduce me to the governors of Wethersfield and Sing Sing which latter edifice – he was the first but not the last to tell me – had been built by its own prisoners in complete silence.

Of course, I had no more interest in prisons than did my poor scarred parents who would never escape the time of Robespierre. I said I was pleased to find so intelligent a man on board.

He said he was similarly pleased – there were so many of his fellow countrymen among the passengers that it was already clear our voyage would suffer from a want of intellectual tone.

I asked him how so dire a situation had occurred in a nation so resplendent in so many ways.

'The want of intellect? Principally,' he said, 'it is the inheritance law.'

And with this he filled my glass again, this time from the bottle, and the champagne frothed excessively but was not, for that, unwelcome.

'I can still remember,' said Mr Peek, and settled himself in a manner which gave warning of a lengthy disquisition. 'I can still remember a time when my country was peopled with rich proprietors who lived on their lands like the English gentry. They cultivated the mind, and followed certain traditions of thought and manners. High morals and distinction of mind then existed among this class of the nation. But all that is gone,' he said. 'The old estates are being divided. Now a man will mostly own what he has bought himself. As for leisure, there is none.'

I thought, What am I condemned to? I asked, 'Then how do the wealthy classes take such a state of affairs?'

'What offence?'

'*Affairs*,' I said and was once again reminded that I must speak more slowly if I was to be understood. 'State of *affairs*. How do the wealthy classes regard this state of affairs?'

He grimaced so wildly that the whole of his upper lip was reduced to a single pencil line beneath his haughty nose. 'They bear it,' he said. 'For instance, the plutocrat and the lowly worker shake hands in the street. Ha-ha,' he cried. 'You like that, no? Good morning, good to meet you.'

At that moment the captain rushed in like a wet dog.

'Ah Captain,' I cried, relieved to see him. 'We have a matter to settle.'

'He looked at me bleakly.

'No, no.' My companion restrained me, allowing the captain to continue on his course. He bowed and twisted while walking backward.

'It will pass,' my new friend said, meaning what I did not know. 'Before we know it we will be in civilisation.'

I feared that most unlikely.

PARROT

One day bled into the next. I lay in my coffin, assaulted by the screams of ducks and geese being slaughtered upon the deck, the cries of passengers, the push and bustle, the plates and bottles crashing to the floor of the main cabin. So close was my pillow to the dining table that my ears were soon poured full of gravy, the voices, opinions and histories of Mr Peek and his wife and two daughters, of Mr Hill and of Mr Defenpost, and what they thought of Mr Eckerd and his actress, and all of this got mixed up with my ear wax and my nausea, so I was sick of them a week before they shook my hand. Driven from my bunk by hunger, I was in time to see my raving-mad Mathilde emerge from her cabin, frail as eggshell, in a sweeping grey skirt and a simple white blouse with a high collar *à la chinoise*. She had her hair pinned high to show the Americans her tiny ears.

When the captain finally judged it safe to set more canvas my paramour and her mother were the only ones – excepting Mr Eckerd and his pigeons – to brave the deck. I had seated myself by a doorway and Mathilde's skirt brushed my knee. I smelled her. Her jasmine. It was intolerable she would ignore me still. To be so separated from she whose thighs I had seen shining with desire, who had opened herself to me so ardently that I knew the crying tunnel of her mouth, the secret teeth, the tiny tonsil, and my own hard body shivering as she slapped the bed and cried Don't stop, to be separated by no more than the brush of a wing was an agony. My salty lover, transformed, as cold as halibut.

As for the old lady, if she knew what secret wound had opened in her daughter's heart, she dared not say. And what had I ever done but love her offspring and herself? And was I not Mathilde's model in a way that would have made another man's balls shrivel up and drop like rotten plums among the summer grass. For I loved her without limit and therefore would most happily play the vanquished male, drained lover, sucked of his juices, laid out on the sheets and dead of love and loving.

And was she not, aboard the *Havre*, still the recipient of my largesse – for what reason had Monsieur accommodated her on board at such expense? That she was mine. I loved her to death. I might have held her, screeching like a hard-eyed indignant sea bird, lifted her squirming angry body high above the rail and smashed her down into the green glass waves. There – she drowns.

She thought she knew me. My awful scars invisible. In any case, she had already found some new protectors, and before too many hours had passed I saw that the elder Miss Peek was teaching her English. This Miss Peek was a tall winsome girl with fine flaxen hair and pale, pale blue eyes, a glass of water a man might drink in a long slow draught. The two of them, dark and light, buxom and lithe, woman and girl, remained at table long after the last plate had broken and the final duck bones been removed, and then, when the lanterns were swinging back and forth, the girl helped the woman with her English lessons. In short the French beauty made herself their pet, and I could not escape her, not even with my pillow pulled across my ears.

Lord Migraine dictated a whining letter to his mother, and then, having no more need of my services, acted as if I was not born. The little bastard occupied our narrow cabin with a lack of modesty that should not have surprised me, given the gross slanders he made against me in his letter to the comtesse de Garmont. In any case, it meant nothing for him to display his member in full and proud erection every morning, its surprising size not diminishing until he had managed to pee into his pot. I never saw such bad behaviour in a boardinghouse.

Being unable to stand the sight of either Mathilde or Migraine I resorted to the poop deck, although I was obliged to move each time the captain changed his mind about his sails. When Mathilde contrived to set up with her oils and brushes by the long-boat, I retreated to the cabin. Migraine awaited me, his neat little legs folded, his pretty book in his pretty hand and his shoulders collapsed down from his neck and running to his arms like a ficus tree espaliered to catch the sun.

Back on the deck Mathilde was portraying Miss Peek in the manner of the disgusting past — that is, in the style of Elisabeth Vigée-Lebrun, who had once made Marie Antoinette look like a healthy piece of fruit. Such shameless flattery was not wasted on this new subject, or her father and the latter had soon gone mad with the lust of ownership.

I went to sleep at night hearing Mathilde tell her punters she would not sell the portrait — a comic English monologue for which she was adored.

I was at table one breakfast when she presented it as a gift to Mr Peek, and I, alone and bitter with my lumpy porridge, witnessed a new aspect of my darling. I had watched her paint and draw for hours and hours, but I had never thought of how she had managed to find her customers. This had been of as little interest to me as my work with Monsieur was to her. Now I saw how cunningly she offered a sample of her wares. It was handed from one rich American to the next.

She was warm to them, cold to me. I thought I was man enough to take her torture, but I was very wrong indeed.

The first time I found her alone, I caught her between a coil of rope and the cow cabin. It was just on dusk.

'Mathilde!'

She turned, her two balled fists pressed both against each other and her breasts.

'You left me,' she said. 'You chucked me away like an old rag.'

'Mathilde, you threw my trousers out the window.'

'Yes. Like an old rag,' she repeated, as if she had won her point.

'Then why are you here?'

'I had to leave everything,' she said. 'My studio, my patrons. Everything!'

And with that she hammered on my chest, and when she was sick of that she slapped me across the face.

'I will not be left,' she said.

As she hurried away, her skirt flying, I saw Lord Migraine and Mr Peek spying from the porthole. To hell with them, I thought. I stayed out on the deck and felt the salt wind on my injured pride and determined that, once we were landed, they could all go to damnation. With this final unwanted exile, I would have paid Monsieur back for my life.

These hard thoughts were interrupted by Lord Migraine knocking on the glass and indicating that I should come inside so that he might dictate one more letter to his mother which – it soon turned out – was not so different from the previous two, e.g. he had lost his best friend, had been prevented from attending the funeral. I – at least in the beginning – wrote exactly what he said, and therefore traced the outlines of his feelings with my hand. In spite of this, it was hard to know, as with all that class of Frenchman, what was going on. With their smooth waxy faces and their extended arms, with the careful lippy shaping of their words, these people always seemed like actors, and even Monsieur himself, a rough old man when required, would adopt this rouge-and-powder style of declamation. Maybe it was sincere enough, and when I changed a word here or there I was acting more in mischief than in malice.

Later that night I lay in my bunk and had no choice but be an audience for the conversation of Mr Peek and Lord Migraine in the main cabin, which might as well have been inside my head.

PEEK: But sir, is it the custom in your country that you would permit a servant to know your private business?

MIGRAINE: Yes, it would depend upon the servant and the business. Generally speaking, one has nothing to be ashamed of in one's conduct. What is the quality of servants in America? How would you compare them with the French?

This was me they spoke of, a thing with no volition, blown like a seed or feather from the palaces of Paris to the harsh wilds of the earth.

PEEK: Oh generally very poor I would say, but for myself I would hesitate to share my heartfelt feelings with an employee of any nation.

MIGRAINE: We would see it as no different to being dressed by one.

PEEK: Dressed, sir?

MIGRAINE: Is that not your custom?

PEEK: To stand naked? Sir I would not stand naked with my wife.

MIGRAINE: We do not call it naked with a servant.

PEEK: What do you call it?

MIGRAINE: We call it getting dressed.

There was a long pause before Lord Migraine spoke again, and then the subject had its clothes on.

MIGRAINE: Lawyers are then very common with you, I believe you said.

PEEK: Much more so, I think, than in any part of Europe.

MIGRAINE: What is their position in society and their character?

And they were off to the races, as they say, and I was so bored by them I finally dozed, not understanding that I had once again slept through history, for this is as close as damn it to the beginning of Lord Migraine's mania to interrogate Americans. On the following day – that is, about two weeks out of Le Havre – he set me to making a fair copy of his smudgy notes. It was a mistake to trust it to me, for he never had the patience for the proofs.

OLIVIER

As a child I was shortsighted but could always shoot a sparrow on the wing. I could not *see* it but still I shot it dead. On the first occasion the *Havre* was becalmed we came upon a floating barrel, and this soon became a shooting target. Of course I won. And who would know me to be a citizen of Myopia whose lands are furred like watercolour washes, whose king is as smudgy as a dancing moth. I had followed the actress from Les Lilas, but when she appeared aboard the *Havre*, why, I had never seen her in all my life.

But when she punched his chest and smacked his face I understood she must be my servant's lover and therefore, by association, that creature with a glory of black hair, creamy white skin, that generous bosom I had admired so closely, so excessively, that I had followed the pair of them into the lanes.

Like a demented man who loves again the wife he does not recognise, I was fascinated once more, not only by her extraordinary appearance but by the reckless portraits she soon produced of the other passengers – or, should I say rather, the aura she produced as she pursued this activity. What I thought was, This can save me from my awful grief. I will have her. With this, I knew, my dear Blacqueville would have heartily agreed.

Of the paintings, I was no judge. This was in no sense an obstacle. In any case, the arts that most appealed to me were those of the philosopher, the metaphysician, the economist. I could follow a rococo line of argument and find my mind led to veritable *palaces* of thought, but these likenesses she essayed seemed, quite honestly, like puddles of mud or sunshine, depending on what I did not know.

The Americans, whatever their level of connoisseurship, which I would not have expected to be elevated, had no doubt as to their ability to judge her work – it was, they declared, of the highest quality. Yet these same judges also proclaimed her attempts at English to be charming, while I, who could hear her French, knew she sounded as musical as a barrow wheel.

None of this is to suggest she was unattractive to me, for many is the country girl, around Auteuil particularly, in whose voice and smells the farmyard is everywhere apparent, and no bad thing, for my blood was never more hot than when my ennui was most deadly, when the air was rich with summer hay and the orchard fruit lay among the grass, rich rotten peaches, bees crawling the blossoms, wax melting, honey dripping from the beehive frames.

And if it be (as Plutarch reports, as Montaigne repeats) that in some part of the Indies there are men without mouths who live only by the smell of certain rich odours, then let Olivier be placed among their allies.

This woman, named Mathilde Christian, was adorable, not only in this respect but in the very particular contrast between the rough texture of her voice and the silky smoothness of her skin, and once I had seen her beat the Parrot and slap his face I saw I might further assist her with this punishment.

Next day she set to 'do' my new friend Peek, a banker who – proud and decent though he was – I would not even think to label *bour-geois*. That is, dear Peek lacked so many of the cultural pretensions with which the bourgeois, wishing to ape his betters, always cloaks himself. Of literature and philosophy he proudly declared himself a dunce. When I mentioned Proudhon, and even Elisabeth Vigée-Lebrun, he did not know who they were. And this, I supposed, was what one should expect of this new democracy which made itself without the benefit of a noble class.

To flatter her subject the she-artist invented a jacket with epaulettes – a court coat, or a misunderstanding of a court coat – a luminous pink with trim of gold, which might have you imagining the subject a noble of the sword. In a nod toward the truth, she gave to poor Peek a startled half-finished expression, as if he had just woken and was frightened to see what he had assumed. Of course one could not know what the artist had intended other than – this was blatant – to have us all believe that Peek was *what he was not*.

Was this so-called *likeness* not my nightmare of democracy – the fishwife taken to be a great lady, the banker strutting as a noble lord? Was this not the red-clawed creature I had fled? Was I now rushing to its open arms? To a place where I was instructed to share my cabin with my servant?

Standing in the main cabin, just behind the artist, where I could see the lovely loose hair that had escaped its pins and the luscious white neck and very pretty ears, I reflected that my unease with most of the arts might be not only the product of my myopia but a moral scruple, an unease in beholding *that which is not*. This painting, if one could accept the amateurish approximations, was a dangerous lie.

As a child I would get an asthma to witness my parents act on the little stage at the château de Barfleur, to see my mother be that which she was not, and on more than one occasion I wept and screeched until she removed her makeup so I should know her for who she really was.

My feelings were the same with Hugo, even Molière – this great unease with what is not. Then how should I explain my passion to be done in oils? I was hardly *persuaded* (although I pretended otherwise) by Peek who declared his mucky portrait the best *bargain* he had ever made. The ability to judge value, he told me, was really the great business of being a farmer, and this was why, he said, he had made such a success of being a banker in America. How dear Blacqueville would have laughed and marvelled and *puzzled*, not only at this notion of the bargain, but at the mercurial world of the Americans who have more stages in their lives than caterpillars.

To make my portrait it was decided that my cabin should be *dressed*. Whether this lifted my spirits or no, I cannot honestly say, but it permitted me to *act* a great excitement. My cause was taken up by all the cabin passengers and with their assistance various oriental rugs and silks were produced, and then, with a great deal of jollity, draped. To achieve this set there was no question the servant must be evicted, a course of action applauded by the *majority*. I was then persuaded to the captain's chair where I was to pose.

For the benefit of the artist I wore my court jacket, ultramarine with gold embroidery. This was not the last time I wore this jacket, but it was certainly the happiest occasion, for although it was most admired by the Americans at sea, it would prove an offence to their democratic sensibilities on land. On this highly unstable matter more anon, but for now it is enough to note that Mr Peek had a card with a crest and Latin motto which Blacqueville would have agreed was a peculiar affectation for a farmer's youngest son.

I cannot hazard whether the reader has been *done* himself but for those of you who have never *sat*, I would liken the experience to the barber's visits to the château de Barfleur where I often fell asleep while enjoying the most intimate yet innocent attentions of the comb and scissors.

Doubtless an artist of the male sex would provide a different sensation. Blacqueville told me of being painted by Proudhon and described debates so lively and engaging that the subject quite forgot the business of the day.

It was very tight inside the cabin with the artiste, the space between the narrow bunks no more than between two pews. The painter did not speak or even look at me a great deal but she was all I could think about: the rustling of her skirt, her high forehead corrugated with a frown, her breasts tightly contained in a blouse the long sleeves of which she rolled up before – suddenly – producing her palette. She was, needs be, very close to me. She made a sound not quite like humming. Her voice, when she finally spoke, occupied deeper registers, a velvety arena which doubtless vibrated in her lover's ears.

Past and future were blessedly lost to me. I inquired if everything was to her satisfaction.

Frowning, she declared herself as someone who *should*, as if by the rules of a guild, never be satisfied, and certainly not with these coarse paints. She did not know how one could paint with them. They deserved to be flung into the ocean, but still she would persist and I was reminded of those characters you see at country fairs who affect to have no interest in selling what they have.

She smelled of jasmine, very light. I told her so. She reached to touch my hair, moving the curl on my forehead a little to one side, and then, still frowning, she dipped the tip of her brush into the different pigments, not just one or another as you might expect, but moving from one to the next, light as a bee gathering pollen on its hind legs, circling rapidly. She looked as if she could not decide what colour she required but was a modern sensualist who must have a sip of every one.

I can only guess what happened – the three or four fast strokes making a glaze of blue to admit the free air to play around my hair, the hot satin sheen to my cheek, the deep shadow beneath my brimming eyes wherein she blended brown-red with burnt ochre. I swear I felt the real brush beneath my lids.

What occurred on the canvas was a thing I would not waste my time with. What occurred with my other senses made me drunk. As the hours passed deliciously, the beads of sweat gathered upon her forehead and in that place between her breasts. She worked with an unearthly glitter in her eyes, making small convulsive movements and then abating, pouring herself into long slow ululating strokes.

Out of respect for the puritan strains among my new friends I had left the cabin door ajar and now I found myself regretting my sensitivities. I felt her, as if the very brush itself were *making* Adam's sinful skin and she, although for the most part silent, and somewhat lowering in her countenance, was very charming in her concentration on my person, and I was in no sense offended to have my hair touched by her own hand, or my chin taken and lowered slightly. Why should I not enjoy the lovely small noises of approval?

Only when the sun lay low on the horizon did I realise I had not dined all day. Instead I had fed on her smell, my own desire, the brush now stroking so insistently at my stockings that my animal nature could not have been invisible to her eye. The air was suddenly drunk with turpentine, and she unfolded a cloth and laid it across the canvas. She caught my eye and held it.

I asked her price, and if that was a *double entente* it was for her alone to see.

She laughed suddenly, then held one paint-soiled hand across her mouth. And then, with what intention I did not understand, she gave a small curtsy and produced a folded piece of paper which I was disappointed to discover was an *instrument* – that is, a draft upon a bank. It was only then, as I looked up to catch the picklish twinkle in her eye, that a thought arrived in such a gust that my ardour was violently extinguished.

Lord help me, I thought, I had been a total fool. In the great haste of leaving Paris I had permitted my *parents* to arrange the financial instruments. Where were they now? What were they? I had woken on board ship without a single coin.

PARROT

Some venal clock was hidden in his lordship's vest or pants and now it struck the midnight hour. What made it chime I did not know, but I have seen English gentlemen perform the same. They are in deep mourning in their home estates, but put them below the equator and they are dancing the jig like Jews at a wedding, lifting their knees, shaking their hands, rattling bangles they do not have. So it was with Lord Migraine on the boat, shooting guns at floating barrels. The Americans did not make things any calmer. They saw what it meant for the nobleman to win, and so politely ensured him his victory. When, after an eternity, the barrel was splintered flotsam on the sea, he bought them all champagne to celebrate.

Toward me he played the icy master, perhaps not understanding that while I owed Monsieur de Tilbot my life, I had not sold myself in slavery. I was a free man, more American than any of these bankers and merchants who took their cue from Migraine and treated me like scum. The only two passengers I found humane were Mr

Eckerd and his singer. They neither spoke the other's language, so I had much to do in that department.

At first I had some idle hours to play whist with my new friends, but soon it was Jack be nimble Jack be quick. Migraine suddenly shouted he would write an *entire book* about Americans. He loudly declared them the most interesting creatures he had ever seen. It was difficult to guess what he really thought but he began to interview them one by one as if it was an agricultural occasion and he must check their weight and teeth and breeding and know who the sire and who the dame and all this he recorded in his notebook and it was my great privilege, when he was done, to transcribe his scrawl into the journal and in all cases have a carbon copy which would be sent as safety back to France. I doubt his prying mother ever found anything to make her fear for her baby's safety. Indeed, I wondered if she had the fortitude to read the tedious stuff. Was she even *curious* enough, I wonder, to endure that very long conversation – some of which later found its way into the famous book – wherein the pious manufacturer of nails asks the French commissioner to imagine France in its natural state: that is, one in which any piece of land is available to whoever is man enough to work it?

'When there is enough for all,' the nail maker said, 'there is no need for government.'

'But what of the poor?'

'No man who will work can be poor.'

The great man peed beside my ear in the middle of the night. I did not complain. He preened and postured. I played my part. But when I saw how he had his eye on Mathilde, I thought, I will sit on his chest and stuff his mouth with dirt.

She was a clever little thing, my Tildy. She painted the Peek daughter without anyone paying her very much attention. By the time she was doing Mr Peek, she had a following. Foremost among her admirers was Lord Migraine, and it was a horror for a man who loves a woman to see this flirtation acted out before his eyes. It did not matter how often I fled or how hard I pulled my pillow across my ears, they were now always in conversation, the pair of them, and when, at last, the dance was done, when he had reluctantly assented to the portrait, when they set up shop inside my own bloody cabin, I was on the rack.

I would leave them alone. I would play cards. But for Christ's sake, they would then insist I attend upon them.

'*Garçon,*' cried he.

At this command I must enter my own cabin and inhale the oil and turpentine, the perfume of our love, our nights, our days. Mathilde stood at the far end of the cabin and affected to wash her brush. I could not look at her.

Lord Migraine twisted his skinny body in his chair and asked me had I packed his bloody purse. Well frig you for a Dutchman, I thought.

'No sir,' I said, 'no purse sir.' And this was true.

'No coins, monsieur? No specie?' He was acting the cool master but he was all atwitter. I twisted the knife, asking him what arrangements he had made with the American banks.

'Arrangements?' His cheeks reddened as he held my murderous gaze. 'It was the comtesse de Garmont who made arrangements. You heard her. She insisted on it.'

'I do believe she wished to, yes. I never saw her do it.'

I held his gaze and did not tell him it was I, Monsieur's *secrétaire*, who had written the letters of introduction to the Bank of New York, and of course I knew exactly where they were.

If I were to search for some *instrument* among his trunks, I told him, the cabin must be evacuated. They must leave, the pair of them. Or not, I said. I could search another day.

'Now,' he demanded.

Mathilde was thus evicted. In being forced to pass me she gave a savage bump with her formerly familiar behind.

I removed the paints and rugs and drapery one by one. It was a pleasure, almost. I closed the door. I sat alone. I breathed the smell of her and found so little solace that I produced his bloody instruments within the hour.

I then was given the task of preparing a bank draft for twenty dollars for Mathilde Christian. When that was done he tipped me a tot and I took it to drink with the Jew and his chanteuse, dividing it, sip by sip, between the three of us. It was at this exchange that Mr Eckerd, by dint of my slow translation, finally discovered that Mlle Desclée was not a singer. He had relied on the recommendation of an associate from Nîmes, a draper it seemed, and it was only as I translated their conversation that it became clear that Mlle Desclée was a tragedienne.

'Not a singer?'

'No, monsieur,' she said gravely, and demonstrated most convincingly that this was so.

Another man might have gone stark raving mad to hear of this mistake, but Eckerd combed his strange hair and thought a moment and, before I had delivered the next three tots, he had decided on an entirely new production, a drama of the revolution which he swore the people of New York would come to like flies to honey. This story he told me – and I translated to Mlle Desclée, who listened gravely, her pale still eyes holding me with an intensity that was doubtless a benefit to her fellow actors on the boards but was completely unnerving on the deck.

I don't know what the story was exactly – you are lucky I have forgot – but it concerned, at that stage, Charlotte Corday and a certain comtesse. Mlle Desclée inquired if she might play both characters.

Eckerd announced that this was exactly what the playwright had conceived and that, although the costume changes would be a nightly terror, that was half the charm of it.

Not wishing to misrepresent the case in my translation, I asked

Eckerd was he saying the two characters were never on the stage together.

'Never,' he cried.

'Not once?'

'Not at all.'

I let Mlle Desclée know this and she bowed her head very gravely and I understood that she was formally considering the offer.

It was only to fill the silence that I asked Mr Eckerd did he have such a good memory that he carried whole plays in his head.

He looked at me with pity, smiling and supping on his rum so it made his lower lip glisten like a plum. He abandoned his glass to the deck and held up his huge rough hands. It was his brother the rabbi who was the scholar. He himself could remember nothing, he said, but he would certainly write the play to suit the situation and he would have it done in time to release his surviving pigeons with the news.

'How is that possible?'

'It is America,' he said. 'Believe me.'

I considered the grave actress, wondering if she understood exactly what would happen to her.

'It will be in French then?'

'They speak English in America,' said Eckerd whose own accent was very thick. 'She is from the opera. They do not need to understand a word in order to sing it.'

'But she is not from the opera.'

'In any case,' he said, 'I will write it. She will learn it.'

'But how can you know this?'

'For me,' he declared, 'she will learn her lines.'

'*Monsieur*' – the tragedienne spoke at last – '*je suis presque certaine d'accepter avec plaisir.*'

'She will do it,' I said, and from that hour they disappeared from public view, thus removing from me the only thing that might have distracted me from the rat inside my intestines. I drank instead – too much, of course – until I was persuaded I must rush my enemy.

I wrenched open my cabin door. The subject was absent so I did not need to hit him. I saw the court coat draped across the chair, the embroidery glittering offensively in the light of afternoon. As for the canvas, I took possession of both the portrait and its cloth. I did not touch the artist. Returning to the main cabin I observed the great pompous Peek and his scrawny little daughters. Migraine was sitting at a table, sipping wine. He raised a hand at me. I pushed out on the deck toward the stern where I found Eckerd standing and Mlle Desclée crying. I jumped a high coil of rope to get to starboard, and there I had the fantastic drunken pleasure of hurling both canvas and cloth into the sea.

I never saw the portrait. It sailed across the breathless water and landed flat upon its back. The cloth rose a moment in the air and then it floated down, making a shadow that would take two weeks to go away. That is, I had made myself a public madman. The result of this insanity was that Migraine had unspoken permission to sit for his portrait with his door locked against me, and I could not bear the thought of them. I knew, with a madman's clarity, exactly what they did, and how they looked while doing it. And in the nights I must sleep amid the fug of the filthy day, oil, turpentine, their vile imaginary congress inside the pig's gut of my dreams.

II

The Piggotts' printers were very emotional supporters of the French Revolution and not even my tender father would shed a tear for Marie Antoinette or any of her ilk, but I was a child when first I heard of it, and so I secretly wept for all those children whose parents were made to bow before the blade. But Lord Migraine – I would have gladly shoved his pinhead through the window and let him see *the other side*, as the saying used to be.

He sat me in our cabin and coldly dictated to me as if I were a circus dog and he could utter whatever insults he wished to, and if it caused me pain as well, so much the better.

My Dear Little Mother, he said to me and I wrote it down. Dear Little Mother, my earlier letter was handed to a Calais-bound clipper. I imagine it must be in the dear rue Saint-Dominique by now, and I see it in your apartment, the Paris sunshine plumbing the honeyed grain of your bureau as you slit it open with that silver knife which Papa was given by the American who also brought the soda water. I have never forgotten that pink bottle we opened when we thought the world might be a happy place.

You will understand, dear Mother, that I was mad with grief when first I wrote and indeed, although I judge it best to be *of the party*, I still feel that half of my soul has been torn away. So must widows suffer, I imagine. The cruellest pain is not the thrust of grief but the moments of forgetfulness. A thousand times a day one thinks, Ah, I must tell Blacqueville, and then – in that instant – my friend dies once again. I will do my best to undertake the study which Father solicited on my behalf, and I trust I will not disgrace Blacqueville's memory in the eyes of those whose influence you used. It is no small thing to be granted exile without shame. No matter what reservations I may have about the character of the marquis de Tilbot and your power over him, you may be assured I will write a scrupulous report which will satisfy the new government as to my loyalty and diligence.

For the moment, he said (and I wrote) I have no penitentiaries or panopticons to interrogate and the object of my study is, of necessity, the creatures all around me, not prisoners in shackles but free Americans and I must confess, my little mother, that their country holds my interest for, although we may neither of us wish it so, the future of France will be found in their experiment and when the wave of democracy breaks over our heads, it will be best we know how to bend it to our ends rather than be broken by its weight.

My companions, he said, I wrote, are nothing if not charming but it is already clear that the Americans carry national pride altogether too far. I doubt whether it is possible to draw from them the least truth unfavourable to their country. Most of them boast about it without discernment and with an aggressiveness that is disagreeable to strangers and shows but little intelligence. In general it seems to me that they magnify objects in the way of people who are not accustomed to seeing great things. And these, you understand, are the travellers, the superior classes in this democracy. Reading that last sentence I see it is not quite true. There is an awful Jew with an actress I have heard he contracted through a misunderstanding and the pair of them are forever rehearsing upon the deck. Obviously this is a tragedy, for the Jew looks continually vengeful and the actress in a state of grief. There is also, outside the pale, my appalling English servant who has no redeeming feature except this calligraphy with which empty skill he manages to counterfeit both wit and learning. (You will not believe me when I say his nickname is Parrot.) This is his handiwork you have before your eyes. How strange to think that what lies behind this fine filigree is me, your blotted smudged Olivier whose natural hand belies his noble blood.

He said, I wrote – There are a great number of American girls aboard and if they represent their sisters at home I would say the country generally must lack in gaiety for they have, every one of them, a singular sort of caution that they express from their straight shoulders through their queerly rigid arms.

I thought, You little rabbit's arse.

He said, I wrote – They do not flirt and when they dance one feels the ghosts of puritans aboard, although I believe they are of the new sect of Unitarians and therefore very modern. There is one other young woman of interest, in no sense a candidate for matrimony dear Mother so please do not raise your lorgnette in that way. She is a Frenchwoman, a portrait painter.

A French woman, he said slowly, I wrote, who speaks in the rough and gravelly accents of Marseille. She comes aboard with her elderly pipe-smoking mother, a real old dame à la Victor Hugo with a woollen shawl and her chin always busy trying to reach her nose.

The most unexpected thing about her, Mother, he said, said he – Lord Pintle d'Pantedly, Lord Snobsduck – the most unexpected thing, I wrote, is that she has been in the drawing rooms of so many of our friends and I am sure that you have seen at least one of the portraits she has made. I mean the one of our neighbour, Catherine de Castille, I wrote, which the duc had hung in the foyer – am I right in remembering it this way? – so his new wife was the first person his first wife's old friends would see as they entered.

I know you always admired the portrait, Mother, although you thought it still unfinished.

I wrote, This same individual has painted two portraits of me now, the first being stolen by the English servant while in his cups.

I thought, I must not listen . I know the worst but cannot hear it.

In any case, he said, we were compelled to sit again. *Shit* again, I wrote.

He said, You know how tedious this is, Maman. I remember the stories you told of the boredom of your three sittings and how it might be relieved only by conversation. My little Marseillaise could not, of course, discuss the great matters of our religion, or pull apart the Jansenist tendencies of our beloved Bébé, but you will see how we made out just the same.

I wrote.

In my very ordinary cabin, a room so small, you would not give it to a servant, the most extraordinary events transpired and I will tell you of them.

I thought, You will tell her, little Pintle d'Pantedly. But I will tell her better. We will tell her together – Mother, I wrote, I know you share my revulsion for the philosopher's *Confessions*, and the last thing any of us wish to read is the general embarrassment of Jean-Jacques Rousseau's failures in the arms of Madame de Warens. My account – which I would never have made were you in the same room or house or even continent – has not the least element of failure about it.

I doubt I will ever send this to you, I wrote, for how can a son tell his dearest sweet most upright mother that he has, with no spoken invitation, removed the most intimate garments of a young woman who has run her sable brush across his very manhood and thus produced what the ancients, I believe, called 'pearls of joy'.

Dear Mamma, I wrote, I *rogered* her.

I looked up to find Lord Migraine staring at me. To hell with you, I thought. I laid her on the floor, I wrote, and when the gift was all unwrapped, found a willing partner, a Marseille animal, who refused to be contained by the narrow space between the bunks. What bruises she must have, Maman. She so struggled to take charge of all the business but I would not have it, and she was not sorry either and such was her pleasure and her proximity to the main cabin that she must take the damn cushion in her teeth. I swear she tore it, for there were soon feathers floating in the sunlight.

Lord Migraine cocked his head at me and waited for my pen to cease.

I wrote.

And all the while, my dear Maman, not two feet away, the puritans played whist. This is the servant writing to you, Comtesse, mother of Olivier. Your little Migraine is not whom you imagine, I wrote. He is vile. He has stolen my love. He has broken my heart. And I send you this news in that very same hand, that now and in the future, will declare myself your most affectionate son.

Adieu my dear mother. The wind is blowing from the west.

Later I placed blank pages in his envelope and ripped up my

madness and its carbon copy and gave them to the air but those words, cruel instruments made by none other than myself, continued to rub like sand against my heart.

III

You would say I was the perfect lover for a madwoman, and I confess to an attraction to that shadowed liveliness, those sudden passions, twisting stairs, violent updraughts that can break the wings of eagles in the tumult of a storm. That species never frightened me, although perhaps it should have. Did I drink too deeply from their pools of grief?

Mathilde and I first met when she was dispatched to tend to Monsieur's mural in the *petite maison*. It was grey and wet as Paris is in December. Here, clad in three pairs of heavy stockings, with a sheepskin rug forever slipping from her shoulders, she attempted to deal with the very poor foreshortening of Cupid's feet, an error not originally her own, although she owned it once she touched it with her brush.

Cupid, of course, was a central motif in many a man's *petite maison* and the Cupid in question was paying homage to Linnaeus and all the suggestive blossoms and insects the old man had classified and christened, in this case dragonflies, engorged, scandalously red, in a garden planted with a mixture of the fantastic and the exact.

Mathilde had not been pleased to be given this task. Firstly, the error was her master's. Secondly, her great talent was not with line but colour. Thirdly – although no one would ever guess this – she felt herself judged. By me! For my own part I assumed she looked down upon me as an oaf and ignoramus.

So she laboured – painfully embarrassed to be responsible for this deformed foot. All of womankind, she thought, would be held responsible for her failure to repair it. So she sat glowering at the wall, her cheeks an apple-russet red, her shapely upper lip marked with a faint charcoal smudge.

Monsieur was in Antwerp, playing the part of the most aristocratic bookseller ever born, and I had been left with the job of quieting his creditors, always an extremely complicated business and never, ever, something to be rushed at. The amounts were often in dispute and even his signature must not be taken lightly, so I was daily engaged in meetings with bankers and money changers, facilitating the transfer of specie and so on.

In short, I was not the footman Mathilde assumed I was. And how might I have possibly corrected this impression? *Please, Miss, come look at my engravings?*

As an artist I was certainly her inferior, but among the remaining items from the marquis de Tilbot's library was an etching after Mantegna's *Camera degli Sposi* which had served as my instructor in the ancient art of foreshortening. Thus I could witness her present struggles with an almost educated eye.

And of course, I found her very beautiful, and the colder she was toward me the more I wished to force her to see exactly who I was. And when she finally understood, why, then I would punish her for her impertinence.

When she arrived on her second day, she found the door unlocked. As she sat upon her chair she saw, as though pinned by Cupid's dart, a very nice pen rendition of the foot as it should be. There was no message and yet the meaning was quite clear. 'Here,' it said. 'Look.'

I affected to be very concerned with Monsieur's ledgers.

'Who did this?' she finally demanded.

'An artist I suppose.'

She cocked her head, seemed as if she might smile, crumpled my drawing, then placed it very neatly in the centre of my desk where, as her footsteps receded, it slowly opened like a flower.

Two hours later the mural was repaired. And then, of course, the point was no longer one of line or perspective but of the light and spirit that came from every corner of everything she ever touched. Even under the most sullen brown there burned a fire you would not tire of watching.

Mathilde brought to her canvases something that her master – who had signed the work himself – could never have approached. She would use a light body to underpin, perhaps a yellow white as a basis for a fiery red. Or she would lay a green-white beneath a cooler red and glaze it with a strong colour. These glazes were, where necessary, partly wiped off or blended with all sorts of colours in adjacent areas. Thus she created that suggestion of mystery which continually engages the eye anew and never tires it.

Two years later, when she painted Olivier de Garmont in our cabin aboard the *Havre*, what was most notable was not the rapidity of her attack – she had many patrons to collect before she landed – but that while working in great haste, she had produced a lustrous jewel. Lord Migraine's coat and embroidery, his very skin, even the pale blue silk draped behind him, held such luminous vitality that you would, if you were mad and jealous, think she loved her subject with all her heart.

When the work was done his lordship sat in the main cabin, affecting to read or – worse – to write, but it was very clear to me that he was squirming on the hook of his own desire while she, the demon, turned all her energy away from him. Thus the great French lover was cast into the dark. Then, in all her mad perversity, Mathilde selected Mr Eckerd for her attentions. It did not matter how the Americans were in love with her, and how they clamoured to be *done*, she would do no more than leave her book on the main table so anyone requiring a portrait could enter their address and she would call on them when she was in New York.

Whatever Migraine might have suffered was diminished by his ignorance. I, on the other hand, understood exactly what she thought about him, knew it with that deep intimacy of skin on skin. Mathilde was disgusted with herself. She burned with rage toward the aristocracy, and although it was her lot in life to flatter them, although her safety depended on it, it also made her ill. A portrait once completed she would, without fail, arrive home with an emaciated poet or a prostitute or a child she had found sleeping by the Seine. Maman would feed them, and she would paint them, dancers, odd pairs of women, men who slept in opium dens. In the world of these small canvases no one could be beautiful, and yet each was illuminated by that holy light glowing from beneath their injured skin.

Of course Eckerd said he could never pay her price and this was exactly what she wished. She stretched a tiny canvas and made his big nose bigger and emphasised the way it curved to almost touch his upper lip. She paid loving attention to his strange hair, the grey shadow across the top of his forehead where he had shaved his widow's peak and left a hairline black as boot polish. Yet to think of a hairline is to distort the picture for, by dint of comb and much pomade, Mr Eckerd made of his hair a kind of rug, terminating in a neat set of twisted tassels on his noble brow. So confident was he, so definite, that he made of his extraordinary appearance a wild and foreign kind of beauty which persuaded you there must exist a city where every man dressed himself in just this way. All the pride of this imaginary metropolis resided in the very direct and fearless eyes.

The sitter seemed not at all astonished to have himself portrayed in this way. Indeed, he sipped his absinthe and affected to show no interest in his audience. But the other passengers were titillated, and as the coastal blur of Connecticut became a grassy green, they made continual sallies off the deck to inspect *The Progress of the Jew*. At first they were amused, and then they were somehow not. Who can say why? By the time the *Havre* entered Long Island Sound, they had withdrawn their approval, not simply from the enterprise but from Mathilde herself. They revealed their hearts in their narrow

Yankee noses. At dinner on the last night I saw the pink and white Peek gaze upon Mathilde as if she were a cardsharp and he was regretting his generous bank draft which, as I knew, would be hidden in a most particular place beneath her skirts.

We entered New York by the back door next morning. Along the eastern shore I was presented with those very houses the Hero of the Vendée had offered to me, saying they cost no more than a cow. I may be mistaken, but there was one with ten windows which seemed to be the same dwelling Monsieur had pressed upon me. I could clearly see two children running across its lawns and I, with an awful guilty secret I will never tell you, felt a sharp pain stabbing like a skewer in my breast.

It was such pretty country – luscious bays cut into the slopes which were covered by lawns, a great variety of ornamental trees growing right down to the water, and so many large houses, which I would later hear called *cottages*. They looked like big boxes of chocolate, and from the windows the owners at their leisure could admire the brigs, gondolas, and boats of all sizes crossing in every direction.

I was, in the middle of all this beauty, so damnably lonely, and the sight of Mathilde and her mother broke my skewered heart. I stood on deck alone, my cold and lonely nipples scratching against the rough canvas of my shirt.

The *Havre* berthed at what was called the Cortlandt Street Wharf at the bottom of Manhattan Island, and I prepared to go ashore with nothing but a lifetime of bad judgement and my duffel bag. Edging forward, I kept a weather eye on Migraine and Peek who I did not doubt would do me ill. When the gangplank was lowered, I left Olivier de Garmont to discover the wonder of the financial instruments I had constructed for him like a clever box with hidden tendons, tricky mortises, and a secret lock you might take a week to find.

The American officials and police were lined up waiting in their shed. What they might want from me I could not say, but I had a very formal letter of safe conduct with so many seals you might think I robbed them from a prince. I showed these papers to a policeman.

'Bon Jour,' said he. He was as cockney as the Bow Bells.

'Hello,' said Parrot.

'So,' said the cockney American. 'You look like a very cheeky chappie.'

'That's me your worship.'

'And how did you come by a piece of paper like this?'

'My employer is a Frenchman. He's a lord.'

'Well is he now?' he said, and returned my documents.

'What now?' I asked. 'Aren't you going to write my name down?'

'Get out of here,' he said.

And that was that.

Outside, everything was confusion and bustle, hackney cabs and boardinghouse keepers, predators and prey, among them I saw Mathilde, Maman, Mr Eckerd and the actress, whose presence was being disputed by a porter whose way they blocked. Mathilde pushed her painting at Mr Eckerd. He wished to pay. She would not have it. He accepted finally, turning rapidly to hide emotion, while Mlle Desclée – clearly having no thought of how famous she would soon become – cast desolate eyes upon the hard stone blocks of Cortlandt Street.

OLIVIER

With whom else but Blacqueville might I have shared my amusement with America? Not the Americans who looked at me at every moment as if to ask, Are you not awestruck by the wonders you behold? Is this not a miracle? Do you not envy this, admire that? It was not until we approached the lower tip of Manhattan Island, when my friends found matters of their own to attend to, that I could no longer be distracted from the painful fact that my pockets contained no single gold coin, nothing but a verbose letter of credit composed in English by the hand of my enemy.

Mr Peek finally allowed himself to be drawn back into the deserted main cabin, where he sat himself in the captain's chair, donned his reading glasses, and peered down his thin nose at my *instrument*.

'Sit,' he said.

If there was a trace of middle-class self-importance in the performance, I was fully cognisant of the friendship that lay behind it. He turned the document so I might read as well as he, running his square-tipped finger beneath the salutation.

'The Bank of New York.' He smiled.

Nothing could be more convenient, he told me, for this was his bank, he was its president, and he had his offices a short stroll from the pier at Cortlandt Street.

'So,' I said. 'It is a simple matter.'

But he must read the whole document or he would read nothing, so he went very carefully from page to page – I believe there were five of them – and I waited, comforted by his scrupulousness, warmed by his aid and protection.

'Ah so,' said my friend, when he had reached the end and carefully pinned all five pages back together. 'What is the devil's name?'

'Who?'

'This servant we have to deal with?'

'They call him Parrot.'

'His legal name?'

'Perhaps Perroquet.'

'Larrit,' he said firmly. He removed his spectacles and rubbed his eyes. 'Who arranged this instrument?'

'My mother.'

'She must be a singular lady.'

I would not explain to an American what this noble lady had lost to the disgusting guillotine, nor would he learn that every night she lived the nightmare of her father's murder. She was singular indeed, but it was in no way amusing that she fought to save her son's life even when there was no threat to it. That was her scar. She gained it honourably.

'Did you ever trouble yourself to read what you were signing?'

'I am a lawyer, Mr Peek.'

An expression crossed Mr Peek's face, brief in its passage, like the shadow cast by a very small bird upon the waters of a pond. Was it impatience or something more insulting? 'Alas,' he said, 'there can be no prison cell for our Mr Larrit.'

'How so?'

'It is your mother's wish. She has made him what we would call a cosignatory with our bank.'

'My mother? No.'

'Your mother, yes.'

If he sought to unman me, he was a fool. 'Fortunately,' I said, 'you and I have met. What chance!'

'Indeed, it is most fortunate,' he said, but why was he so occupied in returning his spectacles to their patented case?

'Your bank will recognise me, of course.'

'Indeed, my dear fellow. I will take you personally. We can go together. You will travel in my carriage and I will introduce you to my manager.'

'This is such good fortune,' I said, 'for otherwise I would have been given not a penny.'

Peek then looked at me directly.

'Sir,' he said, with a formality that rather offended me. 'Sir, you have become my good friend on this voyage. It has been a great privilege to know you, and I trust we shall deepen our friendship further and that you will visit me and my family in our home. Certainly I will provide you with whatever further introductions you may require. As I said on other occasions, I am acquainted with the director of the House of Refuge, Mr Hart, and also Mr Godefroy, a governor of Wethersfield Penitentiary in Connecticut, and I will do everything in my power to help you carry out the task your government has commissioned.'

I thanked him.

'But dear Olivier,' he said, using my Christian name for the first time, laying his hand on my arm. 'Olivier, good friend, my bank simply cannot give you money with one signature. It is against the law.'

'Fortunately' – I smiled – 'I am a lawyer.'

'An American law, sir,' he said sternly, and I saw he would

no more query its justice than he would admit that the coast of Connecticut was the most shocking monument to avarice one could have ever witnessed, its ancient forests gone, smashed down and carted off for profit.

'We cannot arrest him,' said Mr Peek, as the *Havre* crashed into the dock and the Dutch captain ran past the porthole, pushing his way through the passengers, shouting in appalling French.

'*Easy as pie* was the term you used.'

'Indeed,' said Mr Peek. 'But now you need Mr Larrit to have his freedom. Without his signature, you cannot eat.'

Encountering the Protestant's alien eye, I thought, I have spent my entire life imagining prisons, pits, gallows, rats running across my fallen head. Why should I inspect one if I do not wish it. I will not leave the ship. I will go home immediately. Let them chop off my head if they like. At least I will be in France.

But Peek gave me his arm, and I, like a beast being led by a Judas goat, did as was customary.

'Come Olivier,' said the Staten Island farmer's burly son. 'We will find your man. We will make peace with him.'

I found the deck crowded with a musty malodorous humanity that had hitherto been kept below. Across their shoulders, behind their sad battered stacked portmanteaus, I made out New York – a great deal of bright-yellow sappy wood, a vast pile of bricks, a provincial town in the process of being built or broken. I put my goods into the care of a large black man. If he was a slave or a porter I did not know, only that he put my trunk upon his shoulder and tucked my valise under his arm and, with no regard for the delicacy of the first-class passengers, rammed his way down the gangplank, beckoning me to follow him. When I had, by necessity, mimicked the rude jostling of the nigger, I arrived in a limbo, not quite ashore nor quite on land, a long open-sided warehouse built atop a jetty. I looked for Peek. He was nowhere to be seen. Ahead of me I could see the servant's frightful hair, but by now the black giant had brought me to an official and delivered my baggage to his table.

Having opened each item to facilitate inspection, the porter demanded money.

I explained to him that I had only a letter of credit on the Bank of New York. Although it was clearly a ridiculous thing for me to do and I could imagine my mother rolling her eyes upward to see such behaviour from a Garmont, I showed the document to the damned porter whose huge black face contorted itself to the most frightening effect.

I asked the official to intercede, saying that if he would provide the porter's name, I would return tomorrow and give him the coin.

Anxious that my cosignatory was escaping me, I'm afraid that I rather thrust my letter at the official's face, thus causing unintended offence. He and the slave were then both joined in war against me and I was subjected to all the tyranny that a petty official can bring against his social better. As a consequence I was detained almost an hour while my possessions were carefully inspected, one by one. By the time the valise had been disembowelled and I had been interrogated about the exact nature of my nobility, how I stood in relation to the republic, and if I was for General Lafayette or against him – all of which I answered diplomatically, even though such questions had no more standing than a generally agreed desire that nobles were to be shown their place – I lost sight of both my ally and my servant.

When my ordeal was over I still had no *clinking stuff*. I was therefore compelled to carry my own luggage to the place where I saw Peek awaiting me. My progress was maliciously observed by the dull and hostile eyes of a dozen porters, not one of whom could be persuaded to rise from his haunches, not even by Peek himself who chastised the ruffians for their lack of hospitality to a friend of the revolution.

Mr Peek had sent his daughters and wife ahead, and when we two were aboard his coach he gave me a bulky envelope saying I could answer later the letter that was within. Understanding this 'letter' to be American banknotes, I judged this show of delicacy boded well for the manners of the young democracy.

We were finally compelled to share our ride with my trunk, the top of the coach being fully loaded with the Peek family's *souvenirs*. Did Marco Polo return with more? We lurched like a camel from the muddy apron out into the cobbled streets.

There is a street called Broadway where we found the Bank of New York which had much the same appearance as the Parthenon, a building where the elevation of the edifice serves only to remind you of its bourgeois intention. Here Peek effected my introduction to the manager who was every bit as servile as one might require. Promising I would come back with Mr Larrit, I returned to the coach in search of a suitable residence.

At first we passed only private houses but then came upon commodious shops of every description. I saw no museums or opera houses but was pleased to learn the different ways the Americans could spend their money on their Broadway, in jewellers, and silversmiths, coachmakers, coffeehouses and hotels.

Alas, my Mr Larrit was already established beneath the portico of Peek's preferred hotel. He did not notice us, so deep was he in conversation with the portraitist. We hesitated long enough to see the old lady step forward and administer a brisk and powerful slap to each of her daughter's cheeks.

The daughter looked one way up Broadway and then the other. After a moment all three of them turned and walked into the inn.

'Well,' said Peek, 'at least you know where your cosignatory lives.'

A little farther along Broadway he delivered me to a boarding-house run by an Irishwoman who was, nonetheless, thought to be a person of good character. Mr Peek said his wife and daughters had lived there for six months after their own house had been burned down. Here I was greeted very warmly by the lady and I confess I was not displeased to be under the roof of a fellow religionist. As she showed me to my quarters, she told me that the Catholics have a considerable establishment in New York. I asked her was it a religious country. She said the need for religion was felt more keenly here than anywhere else. Catholics and Protestants alike become fervent if they are not already. This I recorded in my journal, together with certain other observations about the nature of Americans.

That night I dined as the Americans dined, that is, I had a vast amount of ham. There was no wine at all and no one seemed to think there should be.

Next morning I was astounded to see women come to breakfast as if carefully dressed for the whole day. It was the same, my land-lady informed me, in all the private houses. One could, with great propriety, go to call on a lady at nine o'clock.

It was not yet eight o'clock when I stepped out to seek my servant. To a Parisian the aspect of Broadway was bizarre. One saw neither dome nor bell tower nor great edifice, with the result that one had the constant impression of being in a suburb. The city appeared to be made all of brick which gave it a most monotonous appearance.

I presented my card at Mr Larrit's inn and took a seat, a supplicant.

PARROT

Her cheek raised and branded with her mother's slap, Mathilde rushed into my arms, a steam engine, her tears as warm as tea. She was my thumbscrew and rack, I needed no reminding, but I was over four weeks bottled, stoppered, closed, and in our fifth-floor room, the industrious river in full view, the ships' rigging canvas slapping at their masts, I sued for peace.

The old maman affected not to notice our *negotiation* and was entering deep in argument with herself, placing one bag in one room and dragging it back again, wrestling with the rolled-up canvas, clanking and clattering with those beaten blackened pans she had carried like gold napoleons across the sea. With nod and nudge, she made it clear my only job was to hold her sobbing daughter, and my heart was brimming, one part rage, one cockalorum, all sloshing and gurgling and spurting through my chambers.

'I think I'll ask them where the market is,' she announced, the gorgeous old thing, bless her walnut face, her hammertoes. She closed the door behind her. She turned the key. Already her daughter's hands were dragging at my clothes and her upturned face was filled with cooey dove and tiger rage. Her mouth was washed with tears. I ate her, drank her, boiled her, stroked her till she was like a lovely flapping fish and her hair was drenched and our eyes held and our skins slid off each other and we smelled like farm animals, seaweed, the tanneries upriver.

She lay in my arms, exhausted, slippery, weeping with relief, and after what we had been through, what she had put herself through, it was *meet and right* that we should cry. We were washed up, our very innards showing like jellyfish upon the sand, and when – at long long last, at twilight – the beloved old lady returned from her exhausting travels in the English language, Mathilde announced she would remain in bed, her dark ringlets flat against her sweating brow.

Maman tipped me a wink. Thumbs-up. Well done. Did any mother ever care so for the welfare of her child?

Mathilde was still abed when we were visited by the landlady who announced we had a French gentleman most eager to meet with Mr Larrit. She had arrived all in a state about the importance of the visitor, her flinty Scots face quite plump with her excitement, until, that is, she spied my darling.

'What ails her then?'

'My wife is resting.'

'Your *wife*,' she said, 'has a fever.'

The landlady saw Maman smirk. At this she coloured brightly and closed the door, although this did not stop her returning later in the evening with a steaming bowl of chicken soup, on which occasion she boldly laid the back of her wrist against Mathilde's forehead.

Only when the door was locked against the possibility of more ministration did Mathilde rise. Then we sat at a little clubfooted table, and she and her mother passed severe judgement on the soup. My beloved's neck was red and blotchy, her forehead glistening very hot. At this point it will be clear to you that she was very sick, but

Mathilde was a container of many passions which raged through her veins and dreams like fire following the secret roots of trees, and it was not peculiar for her to be sickened by her passion, then rise next morning with her brow cool and her eyes clear. Even now she drank her soup with healthy appetite. She complained, again, about the grease. Everything seemed normal until she pushed her stool back and collapsed into my arms. I carried her to the bed.

And then, God help us, she was sick.

I smoothed her hair but she shrank back, reared, flailed. Her mother fetched water and a washer but this served like ginger on a racehorse's tail and the old lady could do nothing but withdraw and wait. So it was, less than an hour after we had so passionately declared our living love, that I sat on a bundle of Roman costumes, consumed with the fear that Mathilde was going to die.

And while I had, these thirty-seven days past, raged against her cold deceitful heart, now I could think only of our little nest in the faubourg Saint-Antoine and the happiness we had shared. I wished I had a God to speak to.

All that night we watched over her, all next day as well. I quickly learned to give thanks for whatever greasy soup or stew was delivered on a tray outside the door.

It was warm enough to leave our windows open, so we kept the air as fresh as might be possible in a seaport and it was only then, as wind off the river ripped through our small supply of candles and left us sitting in the moonless dark, that I heard the circumstances under which Mathilde had lost her father.

As a young man he had marched the road to Paris, full-lunged, moustached, howling the blood threats of the 'Marseillaise'. Throats he cut in plenty. He donated his right eye to the revolution and got nothing back except a dark and dreadful shell of bone. For *La Patrie* he had given enough.

Later, when Napoleon wanted him, he knew himself excused.

He was a veteran. He had a child. He would not go again. If anyone could make him go it was the gendarmerie, but by good chance these were men he had known since they had stolen eggs together, Jean-Marc and little Julian. He told them he would not go again and they dragged him from his screaming child, his boots making sparks along the cobbles in the middle of the night.

Within a year, he gave La Patrie the drink she craved, his hot garlic soup of blood which froze into the churned-up snow. He bequeathed his daughter a burning rage.

Soon the two women lost their home, first in Nîmes, then in Montpellier, then Arles, each situation worse than the one before. Finally they were slaves to an old woman in the village of Claret in Languedoc, dirt floors and walls three feet thick.

'Forgive her, sir,' her mother said to me. 'She cannot help it. Happiness is always taken from her. It is her curse.'

By the third day we could not hide the *symptômes*, even from ourselves, and we had a great fear of being evicted. That was the day Lord Migraine burst upon us, staring at Mathilde with such a sudden white expression that we clearly saw her disease.

'For God's sake,' he shouted at me, 'she must have a doctor.'

I thought, It is none of your damn business, but I was shamed. He now did what I should have, ran down the stairs three at a time. There was a great deal of shouting in bad English and worse French and then silence for a while. And within a very short time we were presented with Dr Halleck, a tall stringy fellow with buggy eyes and big ears and a great affection for his tailor. He arrived in the thrall of aristocracy. You could see it in the colour of his cheeks, his bright excited eyes, his open mouth as he looked around the room, its floor still littered with our battered goods.

'You are friends of the count?'

'*Oui, c'est exact,*' I said, as coldly as if it were the doctor who was enamoured of my wife.

'You are French,' he said.

'I am an Englishman,' I said, summoning up a set of vowels that would have graced a bishop's table.

Finally he turned his fastidious attention to my glazed and staring darling, leaning cautiously over her and doing everything he could but touch her with his hands. He lifted his bag onto the patient's bed and from its maw extracted a brown jar which he presented to me. 'It is a paste,' he said, patting at his grey hair, which rose like dandelion seed around his burned bald pate. 'You will use it to keep the air out of her sores.'

'She has no sores.'

But he was already closing his bag.

'What about your account?' I asked the question only to impress my general poshness.

'My compliments,' he answered, 'to your friend the count.'

'Well, what will I say is wrong with her?'

'Smallpox,' he said, and ran down the stairs as quickly as he could.

The doctor was an idiot. His advice was free but his paste was so cruel and irritating that we had to tie Mathilde's hands to the bed to keep her from scratching herself. When he returned the second day I was my true and natural self. That is, I advised him I would treat her better myself.

'I will have you thrown out of this house,' he said. 'Your wife has a contagious disease and is a risk to the public.'

I told him he could do that as soon as he pleased but he might begin by talking to the count. He went. I then departed by the servants' stairs, finding my way through the pig yard to Francis Bailey's Barclay Street drugstore, and there I asked the chemist for two bottles of olive oil. To hurry him along I said my wife had smallpox and I needed the oil quickly.

'Take it and go,' he said, handing it out and getting away from me. 'You need not wait to pay for it.'

Thus the maman and I bathed Mathilde's poor body until her calves were glowing and her sainted ribs were shining in the gloom. This done she slept, and stayed asleep for four long hours at the end of which time she woke and declared herself refreshed.

Mathilde remained ill for another week, but never again did she seem so close to death, and from time to time, usually around noon but sometimes in the evening, the French lover would come tapping on our door. I did not trust him for a moment, not even (particularly not) when I learned that it was he who carried our bundled linen downstairs where he forbade it to be touched until he had dropped it into the boiling copper and paddled it himself.

In any case Mathilde showed his lordship no encouragement at all. It was me, *Mon Perroquet*, she thanked for saving her and I held up her maman's little mirror so she could examine the recovery of her skin which would, in a very short time, show no more injury than a single small indentation in the splendid shadow of her nose.

You will say one cannot cure smallpox with olive oil.

In fact, one can. I did.

II

To the marquis de Tilbot,

Dear Monsieur, You always said I was ill-suited to my occupation and yet you understood my nature well enough, and with this knowledge strung me along from year to year, and I will not say I have not had an interesting life because of it.

To serve you, Monsieur, is one thing, but M. de Garmont knows not my history or abilities. He insults my honour. He entirely lacks your grace and spirit. He has threatened me, and made himself foolish in attempting to seduce my wife. For this last I would not be blamed for murdering him, so this letter is a less painful way, for himself, of sundering the connection.

I did not seek this new country you have exiled me to but, like Port Jackson many years ago, it does present me with a chance and this one I am too old to throw away.

That is to say, I must give my notice.

Yours faithfully,

J. Larrit Esq.

III

Determined to immediately free myself from Garmont, I was urgently in need of employment. I therefore visited printers on both Broadway and Chatham Street, but I had no etchings or letters of reference and the best offer I received was from Barnett Bros, who said they would inspect my work if I could provide a sample. I tried but did not please them. I then pretended I was also a compositor and was dismissed inside the hour without the thrashing that was offered in lieu of wages.

Finally I threw myself on the mercy of our hard-faced landlady who led me into a small dark parlour above whose mantel hung a likeness of a pair of pink-cheeked boys.

Here she seated her bony little self and studied Mathilde's *instruments* one by one. Finally, with her raw red hand, she pushed a single note across her desk to me. This instrument had been drawn by Mr Hill, the nail manufacturer, in payment for a portrait of his daughter.

'You must raise your wife up from her bed.'

'She needs her rest mum.'

'So she will need her room all paid for.'

'Yes, mum.'

'So,' she said, 'this bill is written on the Bank of Zion on Pearl Street. Take her there. Don't let her accept script. She must not take *any* notes issued by any bank at all.'

'No dollar bills?'

'When you have been in New York longer you will understand that there are many dollar bills that are worth no more than twenty cents. For now you must stick to gold and silver. Is her fever gone? Never mind. Say nothing about fever at the bank.'

'Mum's the word,' said I.

'That's the spirit, Mr Larrit, you'll be out of debt in no time.' And then, to my great surprise, she laid her fingers upon my cheek and I felt a little widow's hand, all filled with busy blood. 'Go,' she said. 'Before they close their doors.'

It was a dull grey Monday and the city was already counting its takings, whipping its horses, removing the jewellery from its cases. We set off for Pearl Street but managed to tour the perimeter of City Hall, arriving in Chatham Street where we had the surprise of seeing Mr Eckerd's *Tragedy of the Revolution* already advertised.

On board the ship there had been much talk about the healthy breezes on Manhattan. They must have meant the winds blowing from the arses of the New York pigs. Beekman Street stank like a shit heap, worse than the faubourg Saint-Antoine. We headed south, past Theater Alley, into a smudgy charcoal sort of maze in which the high-haunched New York pigs mingled with New York clerks, their collars all turned down and a great deal of vanity showing on their wispy chins. I mean the clerks. Mathilde was soon distressed and very hot, so then I carried her, and this attracted a group of white-eyed black children who guided us to Pearl and Wall and declared themselves insulted when I could not pay their bill.

The banking chamber of the Bank of Zion was supported by the most boastful columns, but if the name had made me think it would be the home of Jewish bankers I was a fool. On coming beneath its rotunda, we beheld a great symbol laid in mosaic on the floor, this being a triangle and a laurel and three stars which later proved to be the sign of American Protestants who believed their voyage had been more than equal to the Israelites'. Around this circle, like a great ice rink in its size and smoothness, were more columns, between which were placed some pale and ugly clerks, one of whom read Mathilde's *instrument*, once, then twice, then silently retreated from his pen without a beg-your-pardon.

We were left to wait five minutes and were finally interrogated by what the New Yorkers call a *baas*, a short man in a frockcoat and side whiskers who crossed the wide floor beneath the rotunda to ask whose *instrument* this was. There was then a lot of argy-bargy, a good quarter-hour of it.

'The gentleman wishes to load his trousers with a weight of silver?' etc., etc.

'The gentleman does.'

This baas then affected to laugh at our peasant ways, and I gave him the great smirking pleasure of observing how we divvied up our loot in three. It was clear it was past their closing time but only after we had shared our load did we permit ourselves to be escorted out. My pockets were so heavy I feared my trousers would fall down in front of him.

We strolled up Broadway and the evening sky was cobalt blue, the lamps yellow, the fires flickering red and orange in their *brasiers*. When I had lightened my load and tucked Mathilde into bed, I stepped out for a jiffy. I had no other plan than that I would quietly examine this place where the marquis de Tilbot had exiled us. Perhaps some oysters too. Why not?

I entered into the white-gas stream of Broadway, but could not see the silver North River and the dark East River flowing like mercury in the night, and how could I guess what was occurring, that very hour, in the unlit streets around the Bowery, where there was a murky smoking red-flecked flow of life – not ants but human beings, a living mass of men – roaring south toward me?

I later learned that the city fathers had locked about three hundred pigs inside the Canal Street pound. I had seen a notice in the street, but what were pigs to me? The city would no longer tolerate the swine whom their improvident owners let wander the streets where they relieved themselves in public and fornicated without shame.

The people's pigs had been stolen from them, and as a result there was extreme social agitation around the pound. All the angry owners of the pigs, some armed with hammers, others with crowbars, others with no more than a skinful of John Barleycorn, had been drawn like filings to a magnet, toward this enclosure.

So as I innocently wondered about the price of a dozen New York oysters, some hundred pigs were stampeding into genteel Hudson Square and a greater number of men were stumbling, falling, hollering. One wished only to retrieve his own pig and lead him home, another to steal a new pig, but most had no other ambition than to share the joy of the chase.

I heard them coming, I suppose, but I had lived so many years in Paris I thought the roar of voices to be nothing but a boxing match nearby.

On the corner of Broadway along Chambers Street, I saw a strange sight – a French noble whose cloak did not obscure the gold embroidery shining bright as Jesus in the gas. He carried a silver-capped stick in his inky right hand and an untidy pile of papers beneath his left arm.

I had forgotten that Lord Migraine was shortsighted, so when he did not see me I assumed he meant to cut me. Why not? It must be clear by now that I had no intention of being his second signatory. But then I saw he was not cutting me at all. He offered me his hand.

'Which way do you walk?' he asked.

As he was once again attempting English, I was slow to understand him.

'I trust Mrs Larrit is recovered.'

In the course of this very short conversation we had walked a block and so were on the corner of Murray Street when the swine and their fellows arrived on top of us. Murray was dark, but Broadway was lit from the Battery up to the Delphi Theater, so although I pulled him into a doorway, the bright light caught his fancy coat, and that was jewel enough to halt the whole stampede, or that part of it composed of a hulking Irishman and his Carib friend who immediately demanded that the aristocrat tell them who he was and where he came from.

'I am Mr Olivier de Garmont,' he said, in a haughty style not well matched to his situation. 'I am a friend of General Lafayette.'

To which the Carib wished to know how it was his head had not been taken off his shoulders many years before.

The little fellow stepped full into the light and, with that largeness of gesture that marks French theatrical speech, declared himself a student of democracy.

Alas, his listeners knew nothing of the French or the theatre. They were drunk and probably affronted that he did not have the grace to act afraid.

'Ye little curd o' moon spit,' cried the Irishman, and wrapped his arm around the slender neck and dragged him into Murray Street, wrenching him so violently that papers and stick went flying in the dark.

I searched for his stick and found it by its silver knob. By this time the two large men were sending him between them back and forth like a shuttlecock and singing in loud rousing voices:

Aux armes, citoyens!
Formez vos bataillons!
Marchons, marchons!
Qu'un sang impur
Abreuve nos sillons!

You have just read those words, written in a good hand. Migraine seemed not to understand the deadly intention of the song.

Silver knob or no, his lordship's stick was too light to be a useful weapon. Chance brought me a decent length of lumber, four inches by two inches, I would say. This *instrument* I brought down upon the Carib's arm.

Lord, what a crack.

Urgently the fellow held his limb against his chest, bestowing upon me, in complete silence, a look of inexorable outrage.

'Kindly bash the bugger, Jim,' said he, or words to that effect.

I was a fair height, and I was strong enough, but the Irishman was taller and heavier. I later read that he was a ferry driver famous for his foul mouth and violent possession of disputed wharfs. Soon he would be a millionaire. Now he was about to murder me.

The Irishman had raised his ringed fist.

'Lord Jesus,' interrupted the Carib, and sat down suddenly.

'*Allez!*' cried Lord Migraine. I did not have to turn my head to see the Frenchman's arm. It was extended parallel to the earth, and at one end there was a pistol with an eight-inch barrel.

'No,' I said, for I did not see how he had time to prime it.

'*Allez-vous-en,*' he said.

The Irishman began to laugh, and that was his miscalculation for it produced a flash of flame and he was violently pushed backward on his heels.

'You!' he said, clutching at himself. It was clear he had taken a ball in the shoulder.

'Now,' said my surprising ally to our two assailants. '*Maintenant rentrez chez vous.*'

It was clear I had much to learn about Olivier de Garmont.

OLIVIER

Despite the hostile nature of my financial instruments, I lived very well in my first fortnight in New York, firstly due to the allowance provided by Mr Peek, secondly by lunching at my boardinghouse, and thirdly by accepting the invitations to dinner that, as my banker friend had predicted, soon lay heavy on my tray.

There was a long treatise on American prisons I was duty-bound to write, and I certainly heard many original opinions during those nightly dinners whose guests had been clearly selected to provide me with every statistic I could ever wish to know. Being every day so occupied with notes, I had no time to consider a more flippant treatise: *On the Things Americans Put into Their Stomachs*. This *gastronomic* aspect of democracy has been quite overlooked in France, and I would propose to the young hack that he could do worse than devote a volume each to American breakfast, American dinner and American tea, also a heavy supplement on ham, for it is served in quantity at almost every meal. The publisher might profitably provide an addendum for supper, and also that afternoon feast of cakes and tea, the *goûter*. No doubt democracy will one day find its own Larousse and we will all be the better for it.

I called frequently on Master Larrit and was irritated to find him not at home to me. However, I was a French commissioner and therefore, without having done a thing to deserve it, I had American gentlemen making servants of themselves at every turn. If news of this did not reach Mr Parrot, then so be it. I had sent a doctor to his dying wife, but perhaps he had wished her dead and he was annoyed with me for interfering with his plans. He had frozen my assets and doubtless imagined me most upset, but by the second week I cared no more for him than in the general sense that I worked, as I was in conscience bound, to arrest the spread of his wife's disease.

A certain Mr Robert O'Hara had called on me the second Monday in New York. He clearly felt no obligation to provide any introduction other than last week's *Mercantile Advertiser* which he indicated I might be gratified to read.

I had so quickly adapted to the new state of *égalité* that I was far less disturbed than you might imagine. Indeed, the frank eccentricity of this introduction endeared me to the stranger who carried himself with an ease that I had not hitherto seen in even the wealthiest Americans. Ah, thought I, so this is it, a new world one can greet with pleasure.

The Man of the Future was of a middle age, tall, broad, bearded, with a great shock of dark hair which he brushed back off his high forehead in the 'romantic' style. He had rather to squeeze himself into his chair but once ensconced he made himself very comfortable indeed, crossing his considerable legs, sipping his tiny tea, all his features displaying his eager anticipation of my response.

We understand, I read, on the front page of the New York news-paper, *that the French magistrate M. Garmont has arrived on the ship* Havre, *sent here by order of the Minister for the Interior, to examine the various prisons in our country, and make a report on his return to France.*

To other countries, especially in Europe, a commission has also been sent, as the French government have it in contemplation to improve their penitentiary system and this means obtaining all proper information. In our country, we have no doubt that every facility will be extended to the gentleman who has arrived.

I smiled at my visitor, thinking, This article will make the banks obey me.

Mr O'Hara modestly inclined his head. He could not know I had no more interest in prisons than did my mother. As for the new government of France, the penal system of America was completely unimportant to them except in so much as the Minister for the Interior would insist that my report be both long and detailed. In this way I would be punished for taking up his valuable time.

Mr O'Hara waited calmly while I affected to reread the news-paper, privately wondering what I was supposed to do with him.

Then quite suddenly, as blunt as a gardener, he declared himself my servant.

What could I say? I did not know him. I immediately took refuge in excessive compliments, telling him that he spoke my language like a native, but his soft grey eyes acknowledged mine with such frankness that I immediately regretted my insincerity. His French had indeed been comical and disturbingly familiar. Yet it was surely a far more elevated form of speech than my English which had caused me endless difficulty since my arrival.

We then discussed the late season and the vivid leaves, and my visitor named for me the red maple, sugar maple, red oak, dogwood and sumac, whose colours are far more intense than those we are acquainted with in Europe. Seeming to continue on this subject, he produced a letter from a Mrs Dougdale. Between Mrs Dougdale's handwriting and my English, I understood only that O'Hara was, in some sense, an ambassador. I imagined she might be his mistress, but then he produced a gift from the writer of the letter, a severe black tract titled *Society for the Alleviation of the Miseries of the Public Prisons*.

So: she was not his mistress. My heart sank. The joyless Protestant appearance of the tract depressed me. The French commissioner, it seemed, was the object of Mrs Dougdale's veneration and respect. I was her champion. It was expected that I would be the French translator of the society's publication. I must devour whatever else was written on this upsetting subject.

I inquired where I might find a more suitable office than my boardinghouse.

O'Hara was my servant. He led me to the Athenaeum immediately. We strolled together down Broadway, which showed, to my eye, no sign of the two classes which we, in France, are so eager to keep apart. I would have questioned him but he was, quite unlike a Frenchman, without guile or secrets about himself. I was, I confess, disappointed to hear that he was disaffected with his democracy and had been brought low with *ennui*. He had recovered from this condition, he said, when the British burned down the capital in the summer of 1814, and he was then in such a rage that it was, for at least two years, quite invigorating. His ennui finally reasserting itself, he had sailed for Europe which he found advanced and backward both at once. He was, he said, more than happy to act as my interpreter, as it were, and I should know, he said, that all New York was drunk on the idea that a French nobleman was about to defer to their wisdom.

The Athenaeum reading room he treated as if it were his private business, and so it happened that, on the basis of no more than the write-up in the *Mercantile Advertiser* and Mr O'Hara's ill-informed excitement about my achievements, I was made a temporary member and – having received apologies that this could not be made permanent until tomorrow fortnight – I was given the freedom of the house.

How I missed my dear Blacqueville. In Versailles we had wrestled with our destinies, seeking to be great men when our very class was swept away. Misfortune and tragedy we knew already, but which one of us could have guessed it would come to this so quickly, one of us dead, the other kidnapped, transported to a society in the midst of such excitable self-invention that its best library had the heady quality of a drinking club.

I quickly occupied this democratic society at its highest levels, but how confusing this was, and the optimistic observer found himself one moment elevated and the next cast down in pure despair.

For instance:

No matter how strong their religious sentiments, or their passion about the reform of criminals, the Americans quickly revealed themselves to be obsessed with trade and money and beyond the walls of that particular cell they simply could not see anything that diminished their enthusiasm for self-congratulation. They had got their hands on a mighty continent from which the least of them could, by dint of some effort, extract unlimited wealth. There being so much to be extracted it scarcely mattered how or if they were governed, because there is no need to argue when there is plenty for all. The energy put into this quest for wealth left little room for anything one might think of as culture, and so marked was this lack that I would always, in speaking of the wealthier families, use the English term *middle class* and never *bourgeoisie*. There was, as they were continually pleased to tell me, no aristocracy required.

It is true that I judged harshly in my first few weeks, and yet my need was such that I would rather find their fabled city on the hill. Thus I persisted tirelessly, I will not bore the reader with a list of all the prisons I toured with the mayor and the rotund police commissioner, but let me name the Tombs, the House of Refuge for Delinquent Minors, Bloomingdale Hospital for the Insane, the Deaf and Dumb Asylum on Fifth Avenue, the Bellevue Almshouse and

Penitentiary, Blackwell's Island – all these visits normally accompanied by some twenty-five other gentlemen not one of whom spoke French. Delicacy prevents me from listing the dinners, the peculiar menus, the names of the ladies who lived only to marry and, when married, thought only of their husbands.

O'Hara, I thought, had *saved my bacon*. If there was to be a less than superficial understanding, I trusted it would come from him. I doubted another American could have understood why I was still unable to confront my English servant, lest the fellow imagine I had only paid for his woman's doctor to serve my own advantage. I would meet with Master Larrit, of course, but I was not yet prepared to so crudely place myself at his mercy.

There was – O'Hara said it – no need to sue for peace, but my Irish landlady had taken to placing my account underneath my door.

In my own country I would have been reluctant to accept O'Hara's money. I would have seen him as a rather shallow and perhaps raffish individual, but Peek had retreated to his farm, and without benefit of other advice, isolated by my language, depressed by my false situation, O'Hara appeared as a treasure beyond price.

He arrived at my rooms on the third Monday; that is, the evening of the day on which I had made my first real mark as French commissioner. I had that afternoon produced the first twenty pages of what would become known as *The Penitentiary System of the United States*, a volume whose famous first words – *Society, in our days, is in a state of disquiet, for which there are two causes* – presently lay on a severely Calvinist desk at the Athenaeum. I had begun that first sentence almost out of boredom but as I proceeded it seemed to me there really *were* two causes. And, dreary as they might be at table, the Americans were in a situation to do what the French had never done – experiment with their prisons and their prisoners. I had spent thirteen dinners and luncheons interrogating jailers and philanthropists. I had read Bentham and the duc de

La Rochefoucauld-Liancourt. Even so early, so asymmetrically, I was well equipped to consider the history of incarceration and its purposes. All of New York wished to tell me more.

O'Hara would guide me, I trusted him completely. Yet when the jovial Catholic pranced into my rooms that very evening, it was to announce that we would abandon our worthy dinner in the Bronx. He had taken care of this. Instead we were to go to?

'Is it Five Points?'

'Yes, but better than planned.'

He had originally proposed that we visit the iniquitous district in the company of a policeman but now he had a much better scheme which would leave us free to disport ourselves as we saw fit. That is, we would go armed. So saying, he flung back his blue-lined cloak to reveal a delicate rosewood box held in his hand.

He opened the lid sufficiently for me to see two handsome pistols nestled in the red velvet compartments of the chest.

'To show a rascal a pistol is so much nicer than going with policemen, cheaper too, and better company. Now Olivier, my dear, please pay attention, for what I have here is what the English call a *bloody wonder.*'

I have written publicly about the evils of the duel but when O'Hara set the casket before me, when he demonstrated the marvellous intricacy of its Yankee design, I was entranced. Here nestled two long-barrelled pistols and a variety of devices, including a dozen pink paper cylinders which were already packed with powder.

Each pistol bore an engraved shield bearing a coat of arms, a mullet encircled by a garter and surmounted by a ducal coronet, although O'Hara, seeing my attention on this point, misunderstood me so much as to insist that I understand the duke was by no means *légitime* and that I must not let that distract me from something of far greater import.

'You might not like our pompous speeches old chap,' said he, 'and we are in many respects a damned provincial lot, but you must admit this is a work of genius. This is an American patent.'

There was, in the case, a small compartment holding a treasure of small golden cones – *capsules fulminantes* as I understood the term. These small hats fitted onto a nipple mounted in the breech. This nipple contained a tiny channel which carried the flash to the cartridge. But that was not the end of the ingenuity of the Americans. Each of the pistols had two barrels, two locks, two triggers. When the two upper barrels had discharged, the four barrels were turned on a pivot thus aligning the loaded barrels with the locks.

'Well, it is not the equal of Voltaire,' I said, 'but it is a lovely thing.'

'I am not done, sir.'

He instructed me to close my eyes and I did as he requested, also holding my arms out ahead of me when he desired it. I felt the pressure of his hands as they brushed gently across my shoulders and lower back, and then, all at once, a curious sensation without an explanation, a firm saddler's embrace.

Next, a brandy-scented whisper, 'Open your eyes.'

On obeying I found myself encased in a leather harness into which O'Hara now fitted the patent pistol so it was held hard against my ribs.

'You look handsome,' he said.

He stood back to look at me, his leg cocked, his finger held to his lips.

'Very fine,' said he, and hurled his cloak from his broad shoulders to reveal an identical contraption. To this he now fitted the second pistol.

'Ten o'clock,' he said. 'My dear Olivier, I will collect you then.'

'All these charades and you abandon me,' I joked.

'I will never abandon you,' he said.

And I was suddenly very pleased, not only with his friendship but what it represented – the splendid American ingenuity which had, until this moment, been hidden by the rawness of colonial manners. This patent, this unheralded mechanism, was the precise equivalent of what Guizot hints we might discover in the social arrangements of the New World, something dazzling and generally much improved, a method of modern government like this luxurious pink cartridge in which all the explosive forces are kept safely contained, so ordered and original that one could place them next to an apple and simply admire how the colours played against the light.

'Ten o'clock,' he cried, taking my cheek between thumb and finger. 'Tonight will be your first night in America.' He meant, although he did not mention, Paradise Square, Black-and-Tan cabarets, Curlers Hook. 'The art of pleasure,' O'Hara cried, crushing me to his chest.

And then he was gone, leaving me with the reminders of tobacco and leather. Could it be in this giddy air that a civilisation might take its next substantial step?

I set out to remove what is, I now know, called a holster. What fastening mechanism there was I could not see, although I soon understood that it was high up in the middle of my back. Even with my shaving mirror I was unable to decipher its peculiar construction, and although I twisted, turned, lay upon my bed, and contorted myself like a corseted matron thrusting her backside in the air, although I made myself a vulgar sight, it was without reward.

I had no choice but remain captive for the next three hours.

I sat a short while in my armchair but was pinched and cut. I might have stood and studied had my books not been at the Athenaeum, and at length that was where I thought to go, to continue to ask how the American penitentiary system might have application in France.

On Broadway – my secret hidden by a cloak, grasped tightly all around – I appreciated the benefit of the corset for the female sex, for I do believe, on stepping out into the night, I was never so hopeful in all my life.

PARROT

I

I got copped on account of Lord Migraine's pistol shot, not by the police but by the *night watch* which is the local name for a pair of butchers in fancy dress. These clowns took possession of the weapon and announced they would put me in the Tombs, by which I understood a cemetery although it was soon revealed to be the type of 'advanced' American machine his lordship had been sent to study. It was a windowless sooty dungeon on Center Street. If there was no King of America, who would build so vile a thing?

When told that the prison got its morbid name from all the poor wretches who hanged themselves inside its walls, I wished never to go inside, but once I had endured the cold cobbles of Center Street, I was eager for a cell.

The night watch gathered like witches round a brazier and amused themselves by tossing me a fatty sausage from time to time. The smell of grilling meats was torture as they surely intended, but I was not a dog and would not act like one.

Somewhere before dawn an American juggernaut rolled into

the street and, as the nearside horse did its business at my feet, a small stooped man descended from the carriage. I had been expecting a magistrate, but his round-shouldered put-upon demeanour suggested a grocer's clerk crushed by the sentence of his dreary occupation.

The night watch became quiet but otherwise left the new man to his job which was to unlock a small right-hand door to the right side of the jail entrance. When he was gone inside, the night watch began to break their fire apart and one of them departed to the pump for water. Finally the fastenings of the Tombs jarred and rattled, and an awful door leered open on its hinges. From that dark portal came forth ten prisoners, a very sad and pretty girl among them, and they were led through the smaller door, presumably to stand before the man who had stepped down from the coach.

I expected I would then be included in their company, and I would then explain the simple fact that it was the French lord who had fired the gun and I was nothing but his servant.

Instead I was marched into the prison and left in charge of a warder, a tall well-made man with a handsome face, dead blue eyes, and a single frown mark, as black as charcoal, right above his nose.

Any gentleman with a good library, even Monsieur, would recognise immediately that I had been brought inside the dark brain of Piranesi who, being denied a career as an architect, used his burin to construct those satanic prisons which are known as *carceri*.

The warder informed me I had arrived too late for this morning's court sessions and I would do myself no favours by arguing the toss. He brought me deeper inside a high narrow machine. Piranesi's spiked wheels were nowhere to be seen, but who would need them when a prisoner's nostrils were tortured with the vile tarry smell I have since learned to call creosote but I knew pretty well as the smell of death and coffin wood. When I smell wild woodbine I'm once again six years old, standing in a field with my da. One whiff of creosote and I am in the New York Tombs and everything is suffocating hot because the contractor of firewood is a friend of someone who is a friend of someone who is no friend of the poor souls who suffer in this oven whose high glassed skylights are coated with dreary yellow tar.

From this dim dark distant place hung two wind sails, limp, useless. There were galleries of cells, one above the other, stairs at each end and in the middle, between the two sides of each gallery, were bridges, and on these bridges sat guards, variously dozing or reading or talking.

And at the very bottom of this space, directly in front of me as I entered, was the gibbet. If I had not been thoroughly frightened by then, I was now. Although every suicide inside the Tombs was politely hidden from the civilisation outside its walls, this gibbet was in sight of every cell. Outside on the street the citizens were innocent and kind, with the luxury of being distressed by copulating pigs. But here the chill of legal murder was in the air I breathed.

The warder was neither cruel nor lacking in civility. As he walked with me up the first flight of stairs I was put in mind of a Devon innkeeper taking a traveller to his rooms. He apologised for the condition a gentleman such as myself should find himself in. He listened sympathetically to my account of the shooting, had no doubt the pistol was not mine, and certainly credited my statement that it had been stolen by the night watch, not for evidence as they had told me but for profit. It was only when he understood that I had been robbed of my few silver dollars that his manner changed, although he gave me to understand that this change of mood was by no means irreversible, and I gave him the address of my boarding-house where I was sure Mathilde would do what the warder called 'the right thing'.

Finally he showed me to a small cell where the only source of light was a high embrasure. There was a simple table but no chair, and two beds one on top of the other. On the lower pallet sat a man, not tall or dangling in any way, indeed not like my father in the least, although it was my daddy of whom I was immediately reminded. And what an awful jolt it gave my heart. It was by no means the first time I should be set upon by that particular feeling – my father in some cruel incarceration.

The man looked up and gave an impatient shake of his head before returning to his book. When the door was loudly locked behind me I understood the prisoner's clothes were scattered about the floor of his cell, doubtless due to the absence of those hooks so popular with the suicides. It was dark as charcoal and the air was thick with the smell of coffin wood. There was no place for me to go but to the straw pallet of the upper bunk, and here I climbed and lay, as quiet and afraid as a forest animal that finds itself fallen into the innards of a dark machine, listening to the distant cries and upsets of souls as frightened and angry as itself. Inside the cell, silence lay like something lethal hidden in the hay. Against this threat I steeled myself until, after not so long a time, a feathery voice inquired diffidently as to the nature of my offence.

I looked down from my pallet, but there was not even a shadowed face to address myself to. I told my questioner pretty much what I had told the warder and to this he made no comment.

I thought it good manners to ask about his offence but he ignored the question and began to worry at the subject of his son, a boy of ten, who was being held in another cell on the tier above. As for himself he said he had no concern, for he would shortly be tried and thenceforth hanged on that device that had met me at the prison door.

'And what of your son?'

'Ah.' He sighed. 'If only something could be done about him. I would give anything.'

At this he stood, a big pale solitary fellow, with soft sloping shoulders and fair hair that was ruffled and thin and rather pecked at. I immediately thought the poor wretch a forger, for I could not imagine what else he might have done that his life would be taken from him.

'Has your boy no mother?'

He held out his big white hands in such a way that I thought of Dürer's engraving of Pontius Pilate. My thoughts flew toward the boy, and I imagined being in his position, frightened, alone, my daddy about to die.

'I will visit him,' I cried. 'I will not be held for long.'

This simple promise had a tremendous consequence. The prisoner's shoulders, so markedly stooped, were now drawn sharply back and he poked his head fiercely forward, his hope-filled eyes suddenly reflecting more light than you would think available in such a hole. A good man, I thought, would offer to adopt the lad. How vile of me to only visit.

'There would be profit in it,' he said. 'My word there would be.'

'No.'

'It is a great favour you offer, Mac.' My heart was wrung to see how he picked up his book – assuredly a bible – and carried it to that place where the light from the deep embrasure made a lopsided oblong on the floor. As he tilted the open pages I asked him what he read.

'The first and the best,' said he. His whole manner, as he hunched over his holy book, was of a poor pecked thing. Yet when I finally understood which part of Genesis he was taken with, I did not know what to do with the knowledge. For the place he went to for his comfort was violent and bloody – those alleged events I had once been forced to illustrate. It was the ghastly story of Abraham. 'Take your son,' he read from his bible, 'your only son – yes, Isaac, whom you love so much – and go into the land of Moriah. Sacrifice him there.' He grinned at me.

He closed his book and held it against his chest in some awful imitation of a priest.

'I will pay you plenty,' he said.

I thought Abraham a craven fool, his god a lord or worse.

The condemned man came close and he had a very nasty breath to him, an effluvium like sick, sour milk, the spirit of a dying child. From his moon-bright eyes I saw the truth – he wished a stranger to kill his son.

'Five hundred dollars,' said he.

I had no proper word of answer, just a black bag full of air.

'Five hundred, sir. Not paper. No Bank of Zion. There'll be no discount here.'

'He was a witness,' I cried. 'You devil.'

'I am a devil,' he said, 'and a rich devil too.'

I slapped at him, but he was swift as a frog.

'Oh, no need to rush,' he said, now crouched like a wrestler, hands on his wide knees. 'You've got a long night to think about it.' He dared to smile, flicked his tongue, and I pulled myself back into the dark, as far as I could with my white nubbly spine hard against the stones. I could feel the mad creature slithering around the cell below, hear his tiny voice reading his damned bible. I would not spend the night here. I would be murdered in my sleep.

I slipped down from the bunk, and he placed his bible on the table and stepped back toward the light to give me the clear benefit of his smile.

'You murdered his mother,' I said. 'And your little boy was the witness.'

He shook himself at me like a dog.

'That's why they'll hang you.'

He *purred*, but surely not. In any case, too strange.

'You think *I* will murder him for money?'

'Oh, I never said *murder*,' said the fellow, throwing up his big white washer-maid's hands. 'Good heavens. I never said that. You must only contrive to take the little chap away from here. He's a good-looking little fellow. You ask the warders. They never stop talking about him.'

He cocked his head and looked at me with one eye, as stupid as a leghorn hen. 'Oh, there is no need to murder him,' said he, 'just take him with you when you go.' He gave his pale feathered head a little shake.

I could not look at him. He tapped something metal against the bunk.

'I have the money, some of it. The rest I will have brought. They'll turn a blind eye so you can visit the lad – so to speak,' he said. 'Don't you think?' He insisted, but weakly, as if somehow waking and not knowing where he was.

God might have pitied him but he was vile and I wished to stop forever the bad milk smell of him, and I launched myself at him with my large strong hands around his neck, not guessing at his own strength until he near broke my wrists and got me in a hold around my chest and set to crush the life from me. No sound escaped me. My lungs were filled with dirty milk.

'Take him away from me,' he shouted as he killed me. 'Take the fool away.'

And then he dropped me on the floor and set at me with his fists and all the time he begged to be prevented from murdering me and he wept and struck me repeatedly around the head and neck.

I was unconscious when the warders came to drag me farther down into the darkness of the Piranesi pit.

II

They threw me in the 'crying room', so called because its door was bound with hay and hooper's steel, the lowest level of the Tombs, reserved for Negroes and that one small boy who had been a witness to his mother's death. I plucked and pulled at the hard-bound straw so it fell and floated, requiring only a flint to set the black and leaden air afire.

My beloved Mathilde was asleep in her bed, the sweet haze of moonlight on her hair. I had loved her and hated her and loved her once again, so now I wept for that boardinghouse on Broadway as if it were my childhood home. How many such homes had I invented – inns, church porches, printeries, crofters' cottages, stone beehives built by men in ancient time? I thought of the boy in his nearby cell, of Ganymede in the engraving after Rembrandt, the eagle's talons gripping the peeing baby's arms, and all below the terror of the eternal abyss and, in my mind, black-eyed Rembrandt with his eagle in the studio, dead of death and threaded through with cold cruel wire to make a living likeness, to bear false witness, to hold the dead wings high.

Such a child had I once been, a rabbit rug around my shoulders, tramping behind the Frenchman, down past Mist Tor, Over Tor, Sweet Tor, Yelverton where it began to rain, and all the low grey sky bled into the horizon and folded itself in the direction of my aching feet, me with my cloak, him with his one arm and his face scraped close so the bones of his cheeks shone through his living skin. In drear drizzle rabbit stink we arrived at Roborough Inn where my master spied a diligence waiting in the yard.

Monsieur walked into the yard and became a mute, rolling his eyes, poking in his mouth, raising his eyebrows at me.

'*Comprends-tu?*' he whispered. And thrust me stumbling forward.

I comprehended he dare not speak the language of our enemies, the French. And also that he wished the diligence to take us into Plymouth and so he steered me, claw on shoulder until he winkled out the coachman sitting in the stables puffing on his pipe.

The Frenchman stamped his feet to express frustration at his own dumb mouth.

To the driver I said, 'My da would like you to drive us down to Plymouth.'

'I've got *them*,' the driver said, meaning that he had a party come from Plymouth to lunch at the inn.

Monsieur produced a gold coin from his mouth and dried it on my shoulder. The coachman watched him, squinting all the while. He could not have understood the grunts and gestures, but he knew a sov when it was offered.

Very well, he could take us while the gentlemen had their lunch.

I had not known what war might mean until we got to Plymouth. Just past the Guild Hall in Wimple Street I heard the constant bugle calls and the tramp of soldiers, sailors shouting in the alleys of the Pool. Everybody looked as if they would kill everybody else. Poor tattered French prisoners of war shuffled beside our diligence, so close I could have stolen a hat if I had no heart. My giant companion boasted an idiot's smile which he used to persuade the driver to take us right into Sutton Pool, where the great battleships pushed their noses into the crowded centre of the town. The driver was then under the impression he had honoured his contract, but no, he must up to that eminence they call the *Hoe*. This Hoe was green and hard and naked of all trees and faced the open ocean from which blew a cold hard salty wind.

Very well, but fair is fair. The driver had an important member of the corporation abandoned in the inn, but Monsieur withheld his coin. Leaving the coachman to sulk, he strode to and fro on those windblown gravel paths atop the Hoe, and I was held hard beside him.

'What's he up to?' shouted the driver of the diligence. 'What's his game?'

Monsieur was surveying Plymouth, Devonport, Stonehouse, Stoke Temples, and those magnificent floating castles which had so recently set his fellow countrymen afire. If he was not a spy, he looked like one. I watched him wipe his watery eyes as he slowly took in the churches, towers, steeples, colonnades, porticoes, terraces, gardens, groves, orchards, meadows, and the green fields cut by estuaries. He fitted his claw around my neck. He shifted his attention to the gibbets on the lower path below the Hoe, on one of which there hung a man or what had been a man. I thought I could smell the gibbet but it was more likely the foul air blowing from the Hulks. I did not know these ships were prisons yet, but would see them later – floating hellholes draped with bedding, clothes, weed and rotting rigging – but this was the odour of the king's prisons. God save him. I will not.

Below the Hoe, leading down toward the ocean, there were a number of gravel paths, all crossing each other, and fitted with many flights of steps and crescent-shaped benches. Along the lower path came a platoon of soldiers and at the very front of the platoon eight more redcoats each one carrying an empty yellow coffin, and between the coffins and the soldiers walked four men in chains, and it suddenly struck me as I watched this horrible sight – that the man nearest to the sea and closest to the front was my own father, tall and gangling, dip-shouldered. I had not even the wit to raise my hand but as the party reached that point where they would forever disappear, he turned to look at me.

What the Frenchman understood I cannot say, but he scooped me up into the crook of his strong single arm and wedged my face into his hairy neck. He gave the driver his gold and grunted at him like an animal. Then he carried me, alone in my horror – more unbearable for being unclear – down a path until we were finally back among the armourers on the quay and thence to a second quay, where he lowered me to the flags and then onto a low wooden jetty, and there I found myself with a crowd of poor men and women all of whom were weeping pretty much as I was, and in their company I was persuaded into a longboat. I had no comfort from Monsieur's arm or the damp fustian of my fellow passengers who smelled like unhappy chickens after rain.

I had never been on a boat before. I had been no closer to the sea than a beach or two where my da and I had gone fossicking for useful storm wrack although we never found any more than a dented christening cup and oaken kindling sanded to velvet by the fury of the sea. We never bathed in the ocean, but rolled up our trousers and wondered at its treachery. One black afternoon at Falmouth, we had watched the lifeboat plough out into the storm and bring back the sodden wrung-out men who had once been sailors upon the *Dundee*.

We had seen sailors aplenty around the ports and had always been afraid of their air of hard hostility. They were missing eyes and fingers. They had killed other men, or so I thought. They were of the sea, and we were of the land, of hard tamped paths and the streams of Dartmoor with their *whisht*.

The ship's longboat pushed away from the jetty. Even now, my father was following his coffin or was dead from whatever vile thing they had done to him. The thought shackled my chest. Was he to be murdered for being an innocent accomplice to a forger? Was it even him? My young mind pushed against these gigantic thoughts as I left the land of England. There was no countenance divine. All the great ships in Plymouth Harbour were as tight together as creatures in a hive, all pulsing with the hum of war. We passed under the noses of the cannons, and the lapping sea was poison mercury beneath the grey sky, chicken guts and potato peels gathering around the towering hulls.

My sole protector was an enemy of England. He delivered me to the high black wall of the *Samarand*.

I wet myself halfway up the ladder. I was guided, piss-pant, limping, toward the fo'c's'le, past the cattle pens and boxes filled with chickens. Then the Frenchman gained access to the captain's cabin and was a mute no longer, speaking good French and bad English both. I was worried I would need to vomit and this was of more importance than Monsieur presenting the handsome captain with a palm full of Piggott's pound notes. Thus the currency trumped the navy, who would have gladly had the marquis de Tilbot, no matter what the complexion of his politics, hanging from a gibbet until his feet fell off his legs.

III

I was confined to a cabin not much better than a crying room, its entire length consumed by a bed as narrow as a plank. Beside this bunk there was a very squeezy space to stand and dress, and beyond this a dresser too shallow to accept the Frenchman's boots which must hang from a hook on the ceiling above his feet. It was inside this unhappy box young Parrot Larrit set to sea, suspended in a soupy atmosphere of socks and bacon. When the weather was rough my protector's boots kicked me in the face.

I had no notion of what and who awaited me.

First there was Dr Bingham, a frail and handsome fellow from Lincolnshire whose harelip was sometimes visible beneath his nest of pale moustache. By *sometimes* I mean the occasions he peered into my open mouth hunting for 'foul tongue'. The harelip is of no importance. I should not have even mentioned it.

Dr Bingham could not know the grief that wrung my heart. I wished to die but he administered an *emetic*, and after I had thrown up my guts – which he had warranted I would – he gave me a bright orange *purgative* which I tried to spit away.

He was a good man I'm sure, but by the time he had finished I was a hopeless shitting little animal and the captain had received the port admiral's order to leave the mooring. Through a grey curtain of nausea and stomach cramp, I lay in my hammock and heard the handsome Yorkshireman shouting that there was no damned wind and he did not see why he should abandon the harbour in favour of seasickness for all. He apologised for saying damned (so I knew there was a woman with us). I felt the keel scrape its way across the bar and, at the same time, dragging noise *above*.

I filled the chamber pot. I slept and woke with the bells of every watch. The *Samarand* lolloped with its sails flapping like washing on the line. I vomited and shat and wept. I did not have *sea legs* but had to reach the heads to empty my chamber pot. I woke at dawn to find myself attended by a stranger. She was short and plump and pretty and I was too gutted to be embarrassed when she wiped my bottom.

Mrs Bingham, the wife of Dr Bingham, spoke with the same soft Lincolnshire voice as her husband. I lay in my hammock. She lay on the bunk and stroked the inside of my wrist until I thought I would go mad. A day passed, and then a night.

I was woken by a cry of *Beds on deck* and the most horrid rattling dragging noises above my head. A man's voice cried, 'If I take the wings of the morning, and dwell in the uttermost parts of the sea.'

I slept. There was a mighty thwack of canvas and the whole ship groaned and screeched and then, at last, we were under way.

I curled up like a grub inside a leaf, not speaking, beset by waking dreams of my father and his yellow coffin.

A big bristly face inspected me: the Frenchman. His grey eyes reflected nothing but the little cabin and the bright speck of light which was the sea.

The winds soon grew fiercer and the seas larger, until the oily waves were like those I had once seen crashing in yellow foaming fury on the Devon coast. Except there was no coast, no *there*, no terminus, no restraint and the waters surged past us, over us, shaking not only our bones but the whole ship from stem to stern, sending great spurting plumes of spray across the decks, dropping a huge weight like earth above my coffined head. I had known loneliness before, and emptiness upon the moor, but I had never been a *noth-ing*, a nothing floating on a nothing, known by nothing, lonelier and colder than the space between the stars. It was more frightening than being dead.

I asked Monsieur, 'Where are we going?'

I could get no comfort from him, no purchase, so I slipped off him as from the hard black body of a seal and he played the mute even with our door shut fast.

How I yearned for some softness, even from the doctor's wife, but when she begged me to join the mess table I dared not accept for fear of what lethal secrets I might betray. When I finally did sit down to breakfast it was only because the ship pitched and threw me to the table from the heads.

'John,' cried Dr Bingham. 'Eat some porridge with us.'

'John,' said his little plump wife, and caught the Parrot by the hand and presented him to everybody excepting the first mate, who was otherwise engaged on deck, and Major Alexander, who had business with the prisoners. I did not know what prisoners. Below us, the seas surged across the pitching foredeck. Above, the sailors clung to the rigging like soft fruit in a storm.

Monsieur was eating an egg.

And there was the clergyman I had heard howling out the psalm. I had pictured a craggy grey-haired hermit, but he had pie-eater's jowls and the straight floppy dark hair of a boy. 'Your father has been worried for you, John,' said he.

My father.

The captain's flinty eyes were on us hard like a gamekeeper on a likely pair of poachers.

Monsieur towered silently over everyone at table, a frowning bull.

'Good morning, Da,' I said. I kissed him and felt the quiver of his foreign skin. He grasped my arm and I knew he never had a son to love in all his life. Who will care for me? I thought.

'This is a big adventure for a young lad,' said Reverend Potter.
Would *he* look after me?

'Your mother must miss you, John,' he asked.

'My mother is dead, sir.'

Monsieur's nose contracted so I knew I answered well.

'A new life,' said the doctor's wife, and patted my hand. Would
she look after me?

'An important job,' she said.

'Miss?'

'To be your father's voice. How very fine that is, John. What a
privilege it is for you.'

I doubt Monsieur understood a word. He bestowed on all a
ghastly smile.

The doctor flicked back his doggish hair as he examined me.
I smiled in the hope that he would like me for it.

The captain wiped his well-shaped mouth with his napkin and
leaned back in his chair. 'What will you be doing in Australia?' He
slid the sugar bowl toward my porridge and it did not rest until
brought up sharp against the table rim.

I thought, *He does not like me.*

'Dr Bingham,' he asked, not taking his eye off me for a second,
'what do you reckon of his nibs's colour?'

I turned to the doctor whose harelip showed like a sea anemone
in the morning light. I thought, Please do not send me to Australia.

'He is ill,' said the doctor.

'*Passez-moi le sucre,*' interrupted the clergyman.

'*Le sucre,*' I cried. Please do not send me to Australia. '*Passez-moi
le sucre.*'

The Frenchman squeezed my knee so hard it hurt, but he would
not look at me, only at the clergyman who did not have the sense
to be afraid.

'Ah-ha,' Potter cried. 'You speak French.'

'No sir.'

The Reverend Potter licked his plump lips so they glistened. 'I was admiring,' he continued, 'the way your father has his coat cut. I'm sure it is the latest thing.' He cast sideways glances at the captain, blinking at me like some silly lady's dog.

'I'm just a parrot, sir,' I cried, all cockney.

Potter bounced his bottom in his chair and the Frenchman, very slowly, as if to calm him, stretched his long single arm and laid it like a claw upon his shoulder.

'*Et quel est le but de votre voyage?*' the clergyman insisted, but he had not reached *voyage* before he yelped, and then I understood Monsieur, who was smiling in the most amiable way imaginable, had his hand like a gill hook in the chaplain's flesh.

Said Dr Bingham, 'You need fresh air, John.'

I escaped fresh air on that occasion, but the next morning I was escorted onto the poop deck by the doctor where I once more heard the cry of *Beds on deck*, and this time looked down to see the soldiers raise a great studded hatch on the deck and from this maw was produced, from the belly of the ship, a poor race of trolls and troglodytes who brought with them the most awful fetid smell. I watched in disgust and fascination as these creatures bundled their bedding up into the netting, and the boys – you never saw such boys, their eyes black as crab eyes, shrunken like black grapes unwanted by the world.

When they were all assembled, clanking in their chains, pressed tight onto the quarterdeck and surrounded by the soldiers with their guns and bayonets, the Reverend Potter performed the morning prayers, and this caused several of the men and women prisoners to kneel, thus making the most awful sound of chains rubbing on each other and falling hard onto the deck.

When we next came out for air I was afraid, not only of the sea but of that boiling black poisonous swarm, those *Australians*, in the nest beneath my feet. On that chill clear day they were kept below for their own safety, but I could hear the dreadful screams and shouts that went up every time the water came across the foredeck. I could not imagine who they were, except the awful creatures were in terror of being drowned.

Up on the deck, I wrapped my rabbit skin violently around me, fur in, crinkly side out. The seas rushed hugely by, sending fountains of spray to slap my face.

I held hard onto the lifeline and pressed against Monsieur.

Dr Bingham and the reverend were close beside us. The captain was seated on a large coil of rope, once more fiddling with his pipe.

There was a Mr Pillock, a new hand, at the wheel, and just at the moment when an unusually big wave overtook us, he allowed the vessel to broach to. In a moment the weight of all the sea, tons of it, fell upon me. It knocked the air out of me. I was drowned already, broken like a chicken wing, dragged and spun toward my death, and in the midst of that spinning sting I saw the reverend slide down the tilted deck beside me, and then Monsieur tackled the clergyman, and the coil of rope on which the captain had been sitting was washed overboard and snaked upon the sea.

I scrabbled at the deck. I saw the marquis de Tilbot swing his strong single arm around the reverend's neck. We slid down the deck together, toward the ocean. I saw the Frenchman give the clergyman a twist, a flick like a big fish might give with its tail. As I skidded down toward my death, I stuck my bony knees into the bulwarks. I was scraped from toe to knee. At that moment I thought the Reverend Potter was also still alive.

IV

The captain kneeled over the poor sodden body of the clergyman.

'Poor devil broke his neck.'

Monsieur held me. He poofed his lips at me. What did he mean? I was shivering, bleeding on his shirt. Was it because I said *sucre* he killed the chaplain? I felt the great hard sealy mass of him, his wet cold nose against my neck.

'*Mon petit,*' he whispered, in my secret English ear, in the lethal language, in the awful stinging sea.

By afternoon bright snakes of light were waving across the wardroom and my leg was bandaged and my chest was bare and I watched Mrs Bingham sew a mourning band onto my shirt.

At evening the chains scraped the deck like thunder and I watched the dreadful convicts marched seven times around the deck. A boy waved to me. I pretended not to see.

Next day, the day of poor Potter's burial, was the finest day we had since leaving Plymouth, a cloudless sky mirrored in the great ocean that lay beneath it like a sheet of glass. It was very cold. From the poop I saw some large fish alongside. The horror of that meal.

At the hour allotted for the ceremony, I returned to the poop deck with Mrs Bingham. Monsieur followed and stood behind. I could smell his sticky perfume as I waited for the convicts to be brought on deck. The Frenchman sighed. The hatchway was stoutly framed so the exposed woodwork was covered with broad-headed nails, so close together they made a sheet of steel and the structure was proof against being cut. Through this armoured throat the prisoners now came onto the deck, the men's heads blue and shaven, carrying with them that smell which Mrs Bingham said was their own fault as they would not holystone their decks as the doctor wished. They insisted on scrubbing them with seawater and as a result the whole of their deck had a sour stink like rags left in a bucket, sweat and pee and darkness.

They wore blue and white neckerchiefs, grey stockings barred with red stripes, and they were all in chains. Later most of the prisoners would have their shackles removed, but on the day of Mr Potter's burial the most fortunate were still chained on one side. I could taste the rust and steel of Australia inside my mouth.

At length the ship's bell began to toll in the solemn tones of a funeral knell, and the captain placed himself in the midst of all his captives. Twenty marines and their pricking bayonets made a wall around their backs.

Then two hard-faced bearded sailors emerged from a hatchway, followed by two more, with heads uncovered, bearing between them a long bumpy parcel tied up in a piece of sailcloth, with a great weight fastened to the feet.

Monsieur put his hand upon my shoulder, and I realised what the parcel was.

The bell tolled. The sailors marched in time, carrying the Reverend Potter round the ship till they came to the crowded quarterdeck, where a board was already laid to receive him.

Looking down on the captain's bared head I could see his naked scalp, fine hair lifting in the breeze.

'The Reverend Mr Potter had no family,' he began.

No sign of land, not even cloud to be mistaken for it.

'The Reverend Potter left a letter to a friend we know of only as Timothy. Let this be our lesson.'

There was a rattling of chains and a moan of misery which I took to be caused by their condition not the burial. I looked at Monsieur and was suddenly enraged to see his cheeks were wet with tears.

'He writes this to Timothy: You would have been much interested to see my schools in full working order.'

The smell was strong, even on the poop, a great stinking cloud of cheese.

'He writes,' the captain said, 'I appointed teachers from among the best educated prisoners, each one with his class ranged round him in the form of a semicircle, in each of which were some old and grey-headed men, striving earnestly to read and to write.'

The captain glared as if it was their fault he died.

'Did any of ye ever think he went back to his cabin and thought about your souls?'

He had a poor woman kneeling, crying. She was not young. It must have hurt to kneel.

'Listen,' he cried, his finger now running down the page, as if impatient with them all. 'Here,' he cried, 'here's this: Some of the convicts were reported to me as kneeling down to offer their private devotions before they retired to rest; and others used to assemble the young convicts to hear them say their prayers and the evening hymn.'

By now there was general weeping, and the chains would not be quiet.

'He is dead,' cried the captain. 'He is gone from us.'

The captain said, 'O death, where is thy sting? O grave, where is thy victory? With the full hope of a glorious resurrection, we commit this body to the deep.'

The two sailors raised one end of the board and the Reverend Potter shot down into the dark sea with a splash that struck my soul with horror. Then nothing was to be seen but a slight ripple on the face of the eternal waters.

I stood shivering while orders were given to the grey-striped prisoners. The boatswain piped for wind, which slowly arose, filling the sails, and the *Samarand* turned again toward Botany Bay.

Monsieur then took me into the ward and pointed down into the sea where there was a large dark fish clearly following behind. I held his neck and kissed his vile cheek. That's the Parrot for you. I wish he was another way.

V

I had slept on raw land, mud and gravel, suffered bruising hail, been frightened of ghosts and glow-worms, crawled in the musty tunnels to Mr Watkins' hole, but now, sitting at the captain's table after Mr Potter's murder, this was the worst.

There were waving weeds and rocks beneath us, fish with awful shapes and drooping noses, and the *Samarand* pushed through them, a creature bigger than a whale with weeping creatures in its belly. The seamen had whitewashed the smoky ceilings of the ward, and that dear homely smell carried the vividness of thatch and lumpy walls and stew given from the goodness of a stranger's heart. But that was all there was of comfort, and the salt air had turned from cold to warm in the passing of a life, an afternoon.

The Frenchman was sweaty and massive as a cattle thief, one of those hard wind-burned valley men who rule their herds with the power of life and death. Also at the table were the captain and the major and the quartermaster, all dressed for the service of the king, the palace, all the empire held in their golden buttons, lions and crowns.

Yet it was the harelipped doctor and his meek hen wife, the Binghams, who had suddenly taken possession of the table. Yesterday they had been two small bright-eyed birds, a plump smooth thrush, a long-necked egret, now death had nourished them. The loss of the reverend had diminished everyone, but the Binghams somehow shone. The young wife – luminous in the bleeding blackness of her mourning – now told the captain it was her Christian duty to be a schoolmistress in the dead man's place.

His cold and awful silence could not dull her small brown eyes one whit.

And it was the eyes that marked them both, the Binghams, their hidden wills, their completely unexpected certainty. Remember, I knew that doctor's eyes and never thought them threatening or strange. But now I witnessed how he riveted his attention onto the murderer. I thought, *He knows.*

And then I thought, *They all know.* The captain knows. The captain already knows he is a Frenchman. Does the purser know? The Major? I thought, They are playing with their stew, waiting for Rio de Janeiro, and then they will arrest him and put him in a ship in chains.

And who, I thought, will love me?

The doctor had strange long thin fingers and now he reached them out to touch Monsieur's sleeve. It was a peculiar action, inquiring, curious. Monsieur placed his spoon slowly on the table and gave full attention to the doctor's stare.

Bingham turned on me. 'Your father understands me perfectly. Is not that so?'

'I don't know, sir. I could not say.'

Your father now grinned at Dr Bingham, if that is what you call a naked baring of the teeth. He opened his mouth, he leaned across the table, he pointed inside, he made a moan, as if nakedly mocking his own impersonation of a mute, as if to say I could recite all Shakespeare to you but will not because you are a timid fool.

At the time I could not understand why he should take so ridiculous a risk, but when I was older I knew Marie-Jean de Villiers, *écuyer*, marquis de Tilbot, was one of those fighters who are never happy unless they are in some kind of hazard.

The captain had taken his bribe and kept his silence, but now sighed as if he was being pushed a pound too far. He toyed with his food, the poor grey beef clinging to its twig of bone.

'Come on, old fellow,' he said to Monsieur, 'give it straight. Now, are you ashore at Rio?'

Monsieur cocked his head at the captain, as if he were a clever dog, but if this was a joke, the captain would not share it. He turned to the major and the quartermaster and announced that he was not inclined to sail without a clergyman but that he doubted the streets of Rio would be packed with Anglicans. I saw he looked to Mrs Bingham as he spoke. But it was her husband he commanded. 'Doctor,' he said, pushing his chair back, 'a word on deck.'

I thought, He will arrest the Frenchman.

Monsieur clearly did not think so. He reached for the brandy bottle and filled his cup. It was I who witnessed the result of the captain's negotiation with Dr Bingham and knew that his wife had been granted her wish to be a schoolteacher. I saw Mrs Bingham marched through that dreadful hatch in the company of ten marines.

It was December. I should have been with my father roasting rabbit or perched up on the bar of some snug little house where I could draw an eagle for a penny. I retreated to the cabin and found the one-armed creature, battle-scarred, shirtless, wound tight as a post office clock. Finger to lips. Hands patting the air. I must shut the door. I must climb up on the bunk. Here, look, a length of timber he must have stolen. He jammed it under the handle of the door. So I was locked inside.

Then that awful smile, that missing tooth.

He reached his long arm to my hammock and dragged down my rabbit rug. From beneath the mattress he took a steel-shanked awl.

He planned to stab the doctor now, so I thought.

He whispered to me, 'Rio.'

So we would do a bunk. I let him know I understood. I had the stone in my pocket with his portrait on it. It was my only gift, my only wealth, my only thing to give. He took my rabbit-skin rug and held it this way and that, as if I were a bull to fight. Then he was a magician. He sat cross-legged at the head of his bunk, demonstrating how the awl could unstitch a doubled pelt inside which, snug as a wallet, was a sheaf of Piggott's five-pound notes.

'Pour moi,' he whispered, and slipped the money down inside

his pants. This trick he repeated three more times and when he was done, he took my hand and made me carefully feel the rug. Rabbit skins, as I am sure you know, are crinkly by nature, but now he led me to a place where the pelts were doubled and the crinkly feel must be accounted for by more than rough-cured skin.

'*Pour toi,*' he whispered in my ear. 'For you.'

He was holding my shoulders and looking at me very fond and I suddenly knew that he was about to run away and leave me.

In anguish, I produced my treasure and thrust it in his hand.

He accepted it with perfect understanding, so I thought. He held me up and looked at me as if I were a fish he had just caught.

'Very fine,' he said. He pursed his lips to make me quiet and then he brought my ear to his mouth. 'I come back, *comprenez*. I return.'

I looked into his pale spy's eyes, strangely moist and filled with all the light the porthole would allow.

Two days later I would stand at that same porthole and watch the bumboat as it set off for shore with Monsieur and Dr Bingham both aboard. They toiled toward Sugar Loaf then at a certain point, the sailors raised their oars, and the boat was swept back to the left and the marquis de Tilbot was gone.

'I come back. I promise.' But who could trust his tears?

OLIVIER

I

It was an autumn morning in New York when our peculiar little party gathered to one side of the entrance of the Tombs where – a low pawnshop being conveniently placed opposite the prison doors – the sun had been provided a pathway between the grim warehouses on the eastern side of Center Street. The pawnshop lay squat and mangy, barred iron teeth unchained and its boy or apprentice was stirring up a disgusting cloud of dust which drifted into the shadows before settling down again.

The leading actors of our company were Mr O'Hara (who had been my guide), the banker Mr Peek (my fellow passenger and friend), the servant's paramour, the paramour's maman, and of course that 25-year-old noble, previously of no reputation even in Versailles, who was now known to all New York as *The French Commissioner*. That is, myself, Olivier de Garmont.

In addition to those previously mentioned, our siege was abetted by a great number of top-hatted gentlemen – mayors, governors, commissioners whose names I have since forgotten. If you had been passing in your wagon or glancing out your counting-house window you might have reasonably assumed you had chanced upon *Old Europe Taught a Lesson by Young Democracy.*

The commissioner was always – whether on Center Street, in a Pearl Street oyster house or a horsedrawn omnibus – the honoured representative of his great nation. Of this he was continually aware and I can promise that he in no way – neither by his dress or manner nor his slightly narrowed eyes – revealed that he was freshly emerged from a night of horrors. For he – who had spent almost his entire life a student of his own noble Garmont courage, his Barfleur glory, having prepared himself to rebuff the citoyens from Paris – he, Olivier-Jean-Baptiste de Clarel de Garmont, with no other thought but that he, *The French Commissioner*, must not figure in a public scandal, had stood by while his own servant had been unjustly arrested.

So I confess. The awful Jean-Jacques Rousseau could not be more embarrassing. I, my father's son, had slunk away from the mob like a cat in a storm, my clothes torn, my papers scattered, skirting the brothels of Murray Street, past the College of Columbia, back around the block. All the way up Broadway, facing the fierce inquiry of the gaslights, I persisted with my justification – that it was for the glory of our nation that I ran away. I would have crawled into my bed like a weary innocent, had I not been confronted, on my return to the boardinghouse, by O'Hara.

I had kept him waiting half a bottle, far too long.

I was clearly in the wrong, but I did expect a cultivation, particularly from one who so despised his countrymen's lack of manners.

Once in my rooms, he listened to me very calmly as I explained that I had misplaced his pistol. He stroked his handsome beard and nodded, at first. But then he changed dramatically. One could blame the Madeira, possibly, or some hairline flaw in the marble of his character which, suffering new pressure from a new direction, split the whole asunder.

One moment he was nodding sagely. The next – good heavens – this huge fellow *hurled* his entire manly body on my sofa, falling like a cow dropped from a window. He yelped. His arm was broke. His tail was docked. He howled as if caught in a trap, and my neighbours were soon thumping on their floors and walls and ceilings. After two hours – the like of which I wish never to endure again – I had quieted him, and persuaded the timid night porter that he had the authority to give my friend a room and place it on my account.

Beholding O'Hara outside the Tombs next morning, with his moustache freshly waxed and his hair a glistening wave of fresh pomade, you would never, not for a second, guess what he had confessed to me. *That pistol had never been his to lend.* It had been *borrowed* from a certain Mr Astor on the understanding that he, O'Hara, would have it polished by a gunsmith he highly recommended. In other words, he was a scoundrel.

But there he was, basking in the sunshine on Center Street, as upright as a senator. The morning had begun very early and by this time, as he consulted his gold fob watch, Mr Astor's pistol was retrieved and was the source of no more public shame than a slight bulge disturbing his tightly tailored jacket. So O'Hara had been *made whole*, as the New York lawyers say, and he was engaging old Peek on that subject about which the people of Manhattan display more learning than any burghers of any other city on this earth, to wit, the price of property in Manhattan.

We were all waiting, of course, for the release of Monsieur Perroquet from imprisonment inside the Tombs. It was an event impossible to conceive in France, for I obtained this justice – and justice it was – with the distribution of dollars, not my own dollars either but those borrowed from Mr Peek who had personally arranged that the watchman – disrespectfully called a leather head on account of his helmet – be *tipped* and the two prison warders be *tipped* and certain other institutions be given a *gift*, and you would think this such a truly disgusting matter that it needs be transacted in the dead of night, but no. The beneficiaries had come straight from their homes or counting houses, the otherwise elegant Mr Peek carrying a small dot of egg yolk on his dimpled chin. Here they were, the Great and the Good of New York, intent on performing a charitable function.

The two Frenchwomen waited away from the swath of sunshine, nearest to the small door through which Mr Peek's emissary, a lawyer and comic novelist of some local renown, had disappeared. Although the females were occupied with nothing more than waiting they exhibited that strange intensity I had observed the night before when I had lifted my curtain to distract myself from O'Hara's snivelling. I looked down on great Broadway, as quiet and provincial as the rue d'Anjou, and found just two human forms, two women, one in grey, the other in blue, staring directly at my lighted window.

Downstairs the porter confessed he had already barred their way. *That sort*, he called them. I ordered the women admitted, and escorted to my rooms where the tough old creature whose cheeks were like a ruined apple fell upon me in oniony gratitude. The young beauty was more removed and steely in her manner. She would not weep or supplicate, and it was in that spirit she now stood before the jail in Center Street, where, as a bell was striking ten o'clock, the smaller prison door swung in, and from the shadow emerged the comic novelist and his big round balding head.

Bravo, etc.

A moment later M. Perroquet, slightly bowed, seemingly fuddled and confused by the complicated nature of his welcome, stepped into the light.

Then came a great wild female howl that stood my hair up and caught my breath. Mademoiselle charged, blue skirts flying,

with such *acceleration* she almost knocked her hero back inside the
prison walls. They stumbled, caught at each other. Reaching down
he held her waist, or worse. Reaching up, she grasped his head like
a pumpkin she might squash and drew him down to kiss him on
his prison mouth. Tsk or not tsk? I did not know what I thought.
I had not liked the fellow. I had been forced to wait like a courtier
to beg his signature, but then he came to fight by my side in honour
bound. Tsk or not tsk? He came toward us, his hand very frankly
around his woman's waist. He was tall and springy in his step. He
was older than he seemed. Both his left ear and his nose had been
remodelled somewhere along the way, in a war perhaps, or in a tavern brawl, and yet it gave the man a peculiar hawkish distinction.
He was a servant of the famous Monsieur with whom he shared
a certain hardness. He was wiry. His skin was much used, as if he
were a farmer or a botanist adventurer but there was a clear lucid
quality in his frank green eyes which showed a sharp intelligence.

'Thank you,' he said to me.

He bowed his head a little, with respect or irony I really could
not say. I noticed he was a great deal taller than I had imagined.

I shook his hand, surprised to discover I was so happy to see
him free.

'It is Mr Peek you should thank,' I said.

He looked to Peek, whom he knew by sight of course, having
travelled with him on the boat. He nodded, rather curtly I thought,
but then I noted that his cheek was bruised, so what gratitude did
he owe to anyone for his incarceration?

'I cannot leave by myself,' he said.

My English was not perfect. I thought, Naturally he wishes to
make love to her.

'Of course,' I cried. 'You have your freedom. It should never
have been taken from you.'

'Monsieur,' he said in that perfect aristocratic French he would mimic to disturb me, 'there is an innocent boy in great danger. He has done no wrong. He will be murdered if he is not released.'

But what could I do? I was not the *American* commissioner. I had already pushed diplomacy to its limits with my requests.

'No, monsieur,' I said, regretting my smile which must have made me look foolish and weak. 'I have not the power to empty prisons.'

'Then I return.'

Don't threaten me, I thought, but before anyone could hinder him, he had rushed back into prison and his woman was in a great flood of tears, accusing me of God knows what, her patois was beyond the pale.

Then *two* women at me. The language. All the pompous officials in great consternation. Two warders, big pale creatures, came out into the light, shrugging their meaty shoulders and holding their palms upward.

O'Hara consulted his watch again. I wondered if it was his property.

The novelist scurried back inside the door of the Tombs where he was intercepted it seemed, for his very comfortable backside remained on display to the crowd, as if he were a low comic in the rue du Temple. Peek took me firmly by the arm and moved me down the street, deeper into shadow.

From that distance I observed a general ruckus, the departure of certain governors, the arrival of some councillors, O'Hara's discussion with the paramour, O'Hara suffering a scratch from cheek to nose. I saw the distinguished councillors make their way through the traffic to stand in front of the pawnshop. Peek and I were now at the southern corner of the prison, where I assured him that the Government of France would not wish him to act in this case.

'My dear Jesus,' said he, a shocking expression from those lips.

The boy prisoner was brought out of the Tombs, although 'boy' does nothing to conjure the creature that we observed, a great hulking lad of fifteen with a long chin, a low forehead, and the most awful way of standing as if he were being beaten with a rod. He was a strong fellow, yet his shoulders were rounded, his hands brought so close together he might have been in chains. His eyes and mouth were queerly small, and he stared out at the passing scene as Mr Perroquet, placing his hand on the creature's shoulder, spoke urgently into his ear.

'This —' said Mr Peek but he was interrupted by a clerk of the court who explained to us that the boy's name was Joshua Boulton and he was required as a witness in a trial for murder. The court would be satisfied to give him to the surety of any of these gentlemen if they would feed him until the murderer was hanged.

While Mr Peek was silently considering this offer, M. Perroquet, his hair blazing in the sun, his hand still on the witness's shoulder, walked him to where the beauty stood. Those who heard them speak could not understand the language, but everyone saw that the woman gave the 'boy' some coins and put her lips to his cheek.

As the boy turned, I thought, He is being sent to make his plea. Then he seemed to imagine he had been ordered to talk to the gentlemen outside the pawnshop.

I called, 'No, come here.'

He started, stared in my direction, made a strange hop, and fled – the most ungainly rush, all crunched shoulders, pigeon toes, ducking, darting in front of a brewery dray, into an alley no wider than a knife. And he was gone, like a cockroach in the narrow dark.

In response to this, the fragrant Mademoiselle Mathilde Christian kissed me on the cheek. And Mr Peek proposed a *little ride*.

II

Even inside Peek's carriage, among the manly odours of leather and tobacco, the departed beauty remained in my mind's eye just as the light fragrance of her kiss stayed on my skin. Why this was so familiar, I did not know. Was it the drape of her light dress, with its very clear suggestion of the naked form? Or was it the sturdy well-formed calves, the little feet?

You see already where the 'memory' came from – Marianne, the wanton warrior of Delacroix, her pagan breasts bare to the sky, the musket and bayonet in her hand. I had seen her in that bloodthirsty painting at its *vernissage*. And the runaway devil with a pistol and those piles of broken bodies which made a mound, a plinth, a pulpit for the revolution.

As Peek's carriage macerated the fresh green grass which grew ever-hopeful between the cracks of cobbles, the banker placed his hand on my knee and declared himself well pleased that we had released my *cosignatory*. I was shocked he would think this entire performance had been undertaken for so base a purpose.

Certainly I could not say a word about Marianne. Nor was it proper for me to express my low opinion of a society in which money was all that might guarantee an innocent man justice.

This was not the better future I had sought with such faint heart. It was certainly not the system of American law as it had previously been laid out for me like precious silver at our municipal luncheons. Only the single egg spot on the banker's chin gave the clue that all was not as it should be at this interim.

My thoughts regarding Marianne, touching as they did both politics and philosophy, did not seem appropriate for the occasion. Yet I could not refrain from some observations on the subject of the runaway boy, for there was something vile about the creature's very form, as if his limbs, being bound from birth, had shaped him as criminal. One needed only to glimpse him lurch and slither into that narrow lightless lane to know he would return to the nest of contagion unreformed, and further spread the strain of criminality through the veins and arteries of his society.

Peek listened to this opinion politely, but when I had finished he patted my leg once more.

'Watch,' said he. 'He will end up president.'

In other circumstances I would have thought this insolent or mad. However, I beheld his high forehead, his noble nose, his strong chin, and recognised the proud man who told me he would not break the rules of his bank and that he held its laws above all those of common friendship. I had thought him the perfect specimen of Yankee puritan, and indeed I had recently discovered that he and his family were very strict about the Sabbath, and I had already seen him upset by a neighbour who had used a Sunday to split wood for his wife's oven.

'This boy was not a criminal,' he told me now. 'He was an innocent witness, and as such he was in great danger. It is better done like this.'

'He will end up president?'

'As Americans, we must allow the possibility. He may simply end up rich. My dear Olivier, this is not your ancient France. But if it were, that boy – if he showed similar initiative – might take possession of half the lands along the Loire. If he works hard. There are countless acres of America owned by no one, waiting to be taken. You want our American Avignon, it is empty. It is yours. I give it to you.'

I thought this childish and ignorant. I reminded him I had seen this boy. There had been not one fine thing about him, not even a cheap facsimile of nobility. While one might possibly take Peek and cast him in a play and have him, so long as he spoke only English, play the part of a comte, you could do no such thing with that lumpen child.

'That boy, Peek,' I said, properly eschewing the use of his Christian name, 'you cannot hold him up as the seed of a new nation. If he is your exemplar, the experiment is doomed.'

'Experiment,' he cried, laughing too violently for my taste. 'There is no experiment. We make this transformation every day. It is called *rags to riches*. Have you never heard of it? Why, I could put him in a house. I have a house for him. I could make that boy a loan. He could work and pay it back.'

'I do not believe you.'

'Well, don't frown so, my dear Olivier. If you do not like this boy, why not your valued servant or his buxom little wife?'

'I am not sure she is his wife.'

'So much the better,' he said, and I caught an odd excitement in those careful grey eyes. As so often, when we detect signs of base passions in those who we expect to be beyond the siren call, I was discomforted. 'There,' he said. 'I will put her in a house.'

I must have blushed, for he caught himself.

'Sir,' he said, 'you misunderstand me. Actuarially, she is superior. She is a better credit risk than her mate.'

I was becoming very weary of this national manner of joking, where the main point, by dint of boastfulness and exaggeration, was to make the visitor appear a fool. And all this in the service of some ignorant notion of American superiority.

'Why lend to either of them?'

'Did you not observe her on the ship?'

I thought, What did he see? What does he know? 'She was a dreadful flirt,' I said, 'as you must know yourself.'

'I thought her very able at her business.'

I suppose I made a face. Certainly I found the whole conversation so disagreeable that I expected he would understand and let it drop. But he was not French.

'Do you know how many women run boardinghouses in this city?' he persisted. 'Let me tell you: one hundred and fifty. I would lend to almost all of them. This girl. She painted you.'

Yes, I thought, and now I was embarrassed. In any case, she never finished anything one could put on the wall at rue Saint-Dominique.

'I know how much you paid her,' he insisted. 'I know how much the others paid. Now, do you know how many of her portraits one could commission in this city this afternoon?'

'If one were a fine painter, hundreds possibly.' I thought, Money, money, money.

'Did I not hear you declare yourself very happy with your likeness?'

Peek had been born on Staten Island but he was clearly of the Anglo-Saxon race, which, in these matters, likes nothing better than a pile of dead rabbits as the subject of their art. In any case, I could not discuss the art of painting with a farmer.

Peek was smiling amiably, and one could deny neither the deep power revealed by those grey eyes nor the amiability of his character and I reminded myself that he was indeed a rich man and a banker. Had I not seen his Doric columns?

We left the cobblestones. We journeyed through a dismal

streetscape of vacant lots and raw timber structures in such disarray that one could not tell if these were new houses being constructed or old ones pulled by dentists' pliers.

I had not known America would look like this. In my innocence I had hoped to find here a model for the future of France, or at least some sign as to how, if democracy was unstoppable, we might at least safeguard our future with certain principles or institutions.

Yet all I had learned was that when the mob was allowed to rule, a second mob sprang up beneath them, and the difference between the Americans and French is that the Americans do not need to steal from their fellows when they can roam the countryside in bands, cutting trees and taking wealth. Anyone can claim a site for his château whether he be a night-soil man or a portraitist.

'Look here,' Peek cried, and thumped his fist on the roof. His driver brought us to a halt in a forlorn place: the intersection of many tracks and roads, vacant lots, a blacksmith's forge, brambles, a stand of maples.

'See,' he cried. 'I could set her up there. She could have a studio.'

Mr Peek had seemed such a *straight stick*, but his stick now seemed to be like a dog's or duck's. In thinking this, of course, I was aware of what passions the woman had aroused in my own loins.

'Perhaps,' I said, 'it would be more sensible to lend it to her husband.'

'But you said he is not her husband. In any case, you might need to take that man away, no?' I refused to look at him. 'But she has a future here. I'll show you another spot,' he cried, banging on the roof until we left the desolate sight behind us.

I believe that was Union Place which later made Mr Ruggles such a grand man in New York.

As we rolled and bucked our way farther up the island, I was at once shocked and relieved to find evidence that the Protestant was not quite as severe as I had feared. I thought, He is going to put his Marianne in a *petite maison*. It was a joke on Delacroix at least.

'Mr Peek,' I said, 'my English is poor and sometimes I make a foreigner's mistake. I know you are a banker, monsieur. Am I right in thinking that you are suggesting you will loan money to my servant's mistress in order solely that she buy a house, and you do this – forgive me, I must be plain – with no ulterior motive?'

He looked at me and roared with laughter, slapping my knee again. I thought he laughed much too loud and slapped too hard. My knee was rather stung.

'You mean, sir, am I scoundrel or a fool? I am neither. Now look.' He drew a pencil from his pocket and thumped upon the ceiling, and when the coach had stilled he opened a notebook and began to write, speaking as he formed his letters.

'The business of land in Manhattan,' he said, 'is mathematical. I am a mathematical man. It is my hobby and my interest, and I do not mean arithmetic. Do you read Mr Newton's calculus, sir?'

'I know of it.'

'Well, first the A plus B. Arithmetic. Immigration to America increases thirty thousand persons annually. Seventy per cent of these immigrants come through New York.'

'I understand.'

'Then you understand too quickly. The workers stay close to jobs, the people with the money are moving out, here and here, farther from the city. Now can you read what I have written?'

It was as follows: $h(t) = Xit\beta$.

'The first equation,' he said, 'expresses the quantity of housing (in logs) as a linear function of the attributes X of housing unit i.'

Blah-blah, I thought. What this means I do not know except it has a nasty smell of freemasonry – the strange symbols, the mathematics, their use in the service of a prophecy.

'You could predict the price – Xit – of a Manhattan lot in any given year.'

A farmer spouting calculus. That is what it is like with Americans.

The moment you think you understand a man's character, then you are a foreign fool.

Ph(t) = −δt   βT = 0.

'It is Greek to me,' I joked.

'Ah but it *is* Greek,' he said, the autodidact.

'But no matter what the equation, it makes no sense to lend money to a debtor who will almost certainly default.'

'Ah,' said he, 'spoken like a banker. Spoken like my good friends who are busy lending money to each other, but your painter will pay me back for a year, for two years, for three years. I will do very well. The moment she defaults why it is back to Ph(t) = −δt   βT = 0. The land is worth a fortune. I have a house on Sixteenth Street and then I make money again.'

At which he thumped on the roof once more and we travelled for half a mile, after which he thumped again. We had arrived in a muddy track with a tall thin house beside it, all alone, with its arms and elbows pressed hard against its clapboard sides. From this structure a family was carrying tables and beds and mattresses and loading them on a cart, an operation that had clearly been in progress for some time. The harried man of the house kneeled to pick up a stone which he then hurled, his face contorted with a horrid rage, shattering the front window of the vacated cottage.

'Get your head down,' said Peek quietly.

I assumed myself a potential object of attack, but then I understood the banker wished to fetch the musket, which – together with an axe – was affixed to the carriage behind my head. In a moment he had set the charge and dropped the ball.

'Watch,' he whispered, and put his barrel out the window.

He fired.

I heard a whinny, a curse, and the cart took off down the road.

'Owning New York property,' said the banker, replacing the musket on its shelf, 'is a science.'

So I understood this house was his property and he had foreclosed.

Thus we descended to inspect the site and, while defending his right to resume his own property, I was shocked by Peek's animal spirits. Only then did I understand that his excitement was not caused by the eviction – which had, in any case, already taken place – but the plump pigeon he had shot from the carriage window. And even this I did not understand correctly, for the source of his most un-Protestant pleasure was that he had dropped the pigeon close by the horse and the horse had shied and bolted, thus removing his debtors from the site of their loan. And with this achievement he was as happy as a child. He held the pigeon high for me to see.

'Not bad,' cried he.

I thought, A little house for Marianne. It was a considerable idea that had escaped the attention of the revolution.

III

Several days thereafter I returned to my boardinghouse to find Master Perroquet waiting on the *stoop*. 'Sir,' said the former prisoner, rising slowly to his feet, 'I have decided to remain in your service until you are safely settled.'

'Indeed,' I said, thinking it impossible I had heard correctly.

'I have informed the marquis de Tilbot.'

It appeared that this strange hard creature was now dismissing me. 'That is damned civil of you,' I said.

The green eyes remained steady and unblinking, but could that subterranean expression be a smile?

'I thought so,' he said.

'Very well,' I said, thinking, I will not be dismissed by a servant, 'you must let me consider your offer.'

'While your lordship is considering,' he mimicked my way of speaking, 'perhaps he would enjoy signing some papers at the bank.'

'But I hesitate to intrude on your time,' I told the rogue, how I wished him still in jail. 'When might you be free?'

'Why,' cried he, all beaming good-nature, 'at once, immediately.'

What could I do but laugh? He laughed along with me, and perhaps his intention was benevolent for all I knew. It was still a mystery minutes later when the impossible villain and I were seated as equals at the Bank of New York. Here he produced a sheet of arithmetic which explained what he had earned by day and week, indicating Tilbot's customary tip. Was I being served or robbed, I did not know, or even care. I paid him. He signed. I drew an order for Mr Peek, to repay him all his loan. This too Parrot and Olivier signed together. Who could have imagined such an extraordinary world? I waited for him to declare that he had ordered some change in the financial instruments, but not a word, and how could I possibly ask him. I watched him saunter down Broadway intent on what further fraud I did not know, but I knew I would never see the crook again.

Yet the following day he was back at my stoop.

'You continue in my service yet?' I inquired not kindly.

Mr Peek, he announced, had invited me to visit him at Peek Farm for luncheon on the following day, a Saturday. 'When will we be starting, sir?' he asked.

We? I stared at his brand-new frockcoat and grey waistcoat. Then I saw the invitation contained the directive that I bring my servant and his wife. Peek would send a carriage for us all. My heart sank at the sheer awfulness of it – Olivier de Garmont delivering a woman like a common pimp. Quite clearly Peek had plans for her.

So I was completely prepared, on the morrow, to find the buxom Mistress Parrot aboard but I was not at all happy to learn that we must also be accompanied by her mother, who would chew raw garlic and parsley whilst giving her harsh commentary on the passing scene.

'*Broadway, puh!*' she cried, as we passed Canal Street. She declared it no better than a cart track in Aubagne.

I could hardly blame the Americans for the coarseness of a French peasant, and yet all this malodorous *égalité* depressed me awfully. She wished to converse with me, and I could not stop her. Could monsieur not see where a drunken coachman had argued the best way to get around a bog? Or cross that stream? And that disputed track – it set off as a detour, then wandered down the hill like a soldier who has lost his wits. He was drunk, monsieur, *sozzled*, there he is, off into the glen. Mathilde, *regardez* the wilderness, the *fol Américain* has built a house.

'Please, madame, I would prefer that you did not hit my knee.'

And then she was in a huff. It was too grotesque for words, and I certainly had no idea that this would be the most significant day of my life. It was October, and the trees were aflame with passion and all I could think was that the air was filled with moulds and fungi that would precipitate a *crise*.

It was not hot enough to make my nose bleed, but it was a very rough journey to Peek's farm, which was located at what may have become by now – if the New York Commissioners' Street Plan has any real authority – land bordered by East Forty-Eighth on the south and East Fifty-Sixth Street on the north. Emerging in bad temper from the wilderness, I found a silky driveway, a wooded ravine, a mature orchard, a clear narrow rocky stream running through native grasses. We rattled across a dam wall, came upon a rise from which we enjoyed the grand prospect across the East River to Blackwell's Island. Were my spirits lifted? Not at all. Along the shores of a little cove grew a number of pretty trees in low situations, quite green, very still, and through the leaves the white sand of a beach. I viewed them sourly. When, in a moment, I beheld the Peek mansion I was pleased only because its size reduced the old woman to stunned silence.

In the grand foyer I renewed my acquaintance with Mrs Peek and her stringy daughters.

'So,' said my creditor immediately, 'we must take the tour.'

This, it appears, is the American custom, to escort one's visitors from room to room like an auctioneer. Even the meanest object will have some story, and the grandest ones a price. I noted that the so-called library held no books, the furniture had been copied from engravings, and, of the six paintings in the thirty-four rooms, three of them had been painted aboard the *Havre*. And this was the home of one of New York's foremost citizens.

The arches into the dining room were trimmed with green and autumn leaves. Entering, one was immediately confronted by a great number of vases also dressed with autumn leaves. Everything, in short, was very gay.

The native flora was not, however, the room's chief decoration, for that was a friend of the two daughters, Miss Godefroy, a visitor from Connecticut who clearly carried in her veins the triumph of those Vikings who had raided the British Isles so many centuries before and whose miscegenation had produced such startling effects that three hundred years later they had been the subject of those mad maps of hair colour bequeathed to my mother by her brother Astolphe.

Seeing Miss Godefroy, my opinion of New York was changed immediately – that a creature like this one should walk the earth, straw-haired, blue-eyed, straight-backed, tall, strong, like a goddess but modest and gracious, perhaps even a little shy.

At the meal she was somehow placed between Mistress Perroquet and her mother while the Peek girls regaled me with what I do not know. I gave these two girls my full attention, noticing only that they both told me that Miss Godefroy was a daughter of Mr Philip Godefroy who sat on the board of the Wethersfield Prison. What could be more perfect?

There was food. We ate.

There was piano and flute. The Miss Peeks' voices had not improved since the *Havre*.

After dinner I strolled with the master in his grounds, admiring his pigs and discussing my forthcoming trips to Philadelphia and Albany, so the best part of the afternoon was gone before I found myself walking with Miss Godefroy. How this happened I have no idea. I was delighted, shocked that this impropriety should be so easily permitted, fearful my companion would notice how far we had strayed from the terrace where I noted Peek in deep conversation with Mistress Perroquet. I could not raise myself to protest.

Around us was the American autumn, in all its drunken wildness, like the colours of a savage or that impossible bird, the antipodean cassowary whose likeness Monsieur had sold to my mother while pretending it was a gift. Beyond the drive were carpets of green moss covered with red leaves. Miss Godefroy and I walked side by side, and now, so far from the house no soul could see us, she spoke to me quietly. In French.

Good Lord. What music, what an endearing way to speak. She was sorry she did not have her Molière so I could read it to her as it should be read, not in her poor colonial voice.

Was she flirting?

To ask the question is to not understand her.

She took each step as the first one of a dance. She kicked the red leaves and made them rise like birds. By the shoreline I saw Peek in close conversation with both Perroquets. What devilry he planned I could not say, nor could I hope to intercede. I had arrived, quite unexpectedly, in paradise.

Enclosed by a landscape that no painter could portray, before my eyes lay – or rather shone – magnificent New York. At every moment steamships passed.

America.

IV

There were now four letters to be written. The first, in every sense, must be to the extraordinary Miss Godefroy. I made several drafts, whittling it like a convict with a love token until all the tumult of my heart was hidden in its plain design. In fifty-seven English words I informed the angelic creature that I was planning, as soon as this week, to pay a visit to the prison at Wethersfield, Connecticut, and was hoping I might there have an opportunity to not only interview her father on the subject of the prison he commanded, but continue our conversation of Molière whose works I would carry with me in a fine edition.

Next, a short note to my secretary instructing him to transcribe this to a gilt paste card. To my relief he obeyed.

I then wrote to Miss Godefroy's father, introducing myself as the French commissioner and hoping I might interview him at his soonest convenience.

That done, I drafted a letter to the Quakers in Philadelphia who expected me on Crooked Billet Wharf this coming Friday. I cancelled them forthwith. It was to Mr Vaux I wrote asserting (not untruthfully) that I had heard so much in favour of the solitary system at their Eastern Prison, I thought it wiser that I first visit Wethersfield, Auburn and Sing Sing, whose different systems, all being of the whip side of the aisle, so to speak, would provide a firm basis of comparison with his Eastern Prison. I hoped this change of plan would not discommode him or Mrs Dougdale and the members of the *Society for the Alleviation of the Miseries of the Public Prisons*, but it would ensure I would finally come among them as a better educated man.

Only with Blacqueville might I have been concise: Dear Friend, I am in love.

My mother was not to be confided in, of course – she had never forgotten the case of the comte de Heudreville, who had returned to Paris with an American wife – and it made no difference that the poor creature was a Catholic or that her watercolours were of considerable delicacy. My mother's concern that I would *faire comme Heudreville* was so pronounced that seldom a letter passed between us where she did not inquire of the habits of American females. I was accustomed to replying in a manner that might seem, to those not privileged to know the comtesse de Garmont, unduly frank.

'Dear Maman,' I reassured her that Sunday night, 'I have been here in New York and am leading the most active agitated life it is possible to imagine. I am overwhelmed by courtesies, burdened by visits, etc., etc. If I can escape the pursuit of *my numerous friends*, I throw myself on my ideas, set myself problems to solve, and lay the foundations of a great work which ought someday to make my reputation.

'I take my place at table always served with meats more solid than well prepared, and around which are seated some very pretty persons, occasionally accompanied by some very ugly ones. You asked what is thought to be the great merit of women here. Well, Maman, it is this – to be very fresh complexioned. Beyond that they have very few – or rather they have none at all – of those exterior charms which contribute so powerfully to elegance of figure, and whose noble form so pleases the educated eye.

'I don't know why I speak of their physical qualities, for you did not precisely inquire after them, and they are above all remarkable for their moral virtues. In general they are of very severe principle and irreproachable conduct.

'Evenings I go out into society. I see several American families fairly often, particularly that of Mr Peek, our banker. He is the richest businessman in New York. I am received with infinite kindness in the Peek family. Mrs Peek is a charming woman, as attractive as can be and flirtatious as you earlier foresaw. But I do not know and shall never know if her coquetry goes further. I am to go in several days to visit the prison at Sing Sing, which is only a few miles from New York. From there I travel to Wethersfield, Connecticut, and its famous prison, attended as always by M. de Tilbot's man whose legible hand allows you to read this very letter.

'If I went into society with intentions of pleasure or seduction, I could regard as lost the time I pass here. But as my resolutions are entirely opposed to this result, I find only profit in it. In the first place I inevitably learn the English language, for although many women affect to speak French, there are at least twenty with whom I have to speak English.

'I expect to write at greater length when on my way to Mr Godefroy's prison at Wethersfield.'

Of this dissembling I was not at all ashamed. Was it not my mother who engineered my departure from my natural society, and now I was here, was I not still a man? I might be safe from the so-called July Revolution, but I was not safe from love.

I lay in bed, the cool linens against my heated flesh, in the most delicious frame of mind. When my countrymen imagined America, they thought of savages and bears and presidents who would not wear wigs. Who among them could have conjured Miss Godefroy in all her beauty of form and elegance of mind, her wit, her delicacy, her slender ankles amid those mad red leaves? Such were the unexpected turns of life, that I who had begun this journey in awful mourning, now lived again in the most delightful way.

I went to sleep very happy and in the morning, having been most surprisingly and properly waited on by Master Larrit, I directed that he copy the letters and have them dispatched by whatever was the fastest method. The good fellow undertook to spend his Sunday walking up to Peek's farm.

I tipped him generously. Shortly after, he was off inquiring about steamers to Sing Sing where Elam Lynds was – as I had heard a thousand times – using the labour of two hundred convicts to build their own prison. He would be the first step on my way to the Godefroys of Wethersfield.

By evening the servant had purchased our tickets at the slip, and had informed Mme Parrot that he would be away in pursuit of his duties. In all this he was exemplary, and there were no more signs of the rebellion I had glimpsed in his eyes aboard the *Havre*. He made inquiries about boardinghouses in Sing Sing and the climate in the mountains along the Hudson, ensured we were well provisioned, pasted labels on the trunks, and visited Schermerhorn Row so he would know exactly where we would board Mr Fulton's famous steamer. I did nothing more myself than attempt, unsuccessfully, three sketches of Miss Godefroy.

Then two things happened in quick succession. First I was visited by Mr Peek, who exhibited a coldness toward me that I found extremely odd.

Only when he produced my unopened letter to Miss Godefroy did I begin to understand.

'She has departed,' he said.

'So soon.'

'Exactly as expected,' he said severely.

I looked into his grey eyes and saw there a mighty stew and puzzle.

'She has returned to her own home,' he said. Then I understood. Peek was a father. He had sat me at lunch between his own two beauties. Had he imagined I would marry one of them? He was insulted on their behalf.

'Very well,' said I. 'Do you have another address where I might reach Mr Godefroy?'

'The prison,' he said.

I thought, You are an ill-mannered fool if you think you can stop me like this – and as for your dreadful daughters, are you a madman?

And yet I must soon begin the work of pacifying him, for he would be an inconvenient enemy.

None of this was pleasant, but then the morning post brought a most desperate letter from Mr Vaux in Philadelphia, in which he threw himself on my mercy, explaining that a meeting of fifty gentlemen had determined the course of my visit and it would be a distinct embarrassment to the cause of the penitentiary system in general and the Eastern Prison in particular if I was not at the Crooked Billet Wharf on the date I had promised.

So I must go to the damn Quakers. What agony to postpone the pleasure I knew was truly mine. For I had seen her soul, the excitement in her cheeks in which, illuminated by the glow of blood, were revealed the palest, finest, most exquisite markings – not freckles, not even of that genus.

In a great passion I wrote, it seemed, a hundred letters – to Mr Vaux, the Peek girls, Mr Peek, Mrs Peek, O'Hara, Mr Elam Lynds – but toward the object of my affections . . . I must be patient.

Very early on the following Thursday morning I was on the pier opposite Schermerhorn Row, where, with the low mist a perfect garment for my mood, Mr Parrot and I boarded the *Raritan* and set off in the opposite direction to the one my heart would have me go. That is, we churned our way to New Brunswick, then transferred to what had been advertised as a *stage wagon with good awning*, a disgusting contraption as it turned out. I was at Bordentown that evening, lovesick, sore and dirty, and the steamboat *Phoenix* was already at its wharf, tooting impatiently for us like a bull who wishes admittance to where he should not go. Finally, having spent ten dollars and twenty-six miserable hours, we arrived, soon after nine on a Friday morning at the Crooked Billet Wharf in Philadelphia.

V

As the *Phoenix* approached the dock I saw five severe gentlemen in those ridiculous clerical hats. Dear God, I thought, I hope they are not my *reception committee*. What dry and juiceless creatures, wrapped like ravens, furled like umbrellas in the low sad mist. Perhaps Miss Godefroy has a wharf at Wethersfield and it would appear the same – an identical honking of the geese, for instance, an awful mooing from the shore – but it would be *her* geese, *her* cattle, *her* home, *her* mist, each drop alive with its own aura. This awful hollow loneliness in my bones, this ache, would not be there.

To my mother's great distress I had become what is called a deist, but how I now longed for a Catholic household. It was not dogma I sought, but to breathe air of such subtle emanations that I might not even detect the true source of my own wellbeing. Now, I thought, I will be incarcerated in Philadelphia with Protestants who have built the kindest prison ever conceived, at a cost – I did not need Peek's equation for this – of two thousand dollars for every felon, at which price the state could equally afford to house them in a handsome riverside cottage with a dozen fat pigs and red leaves arranged in wreaths in vases every way you turn.

What use was this to France or me? I knew the answer but must still investigate, and after so short a time in the country I could accurately predict the room of documents, the pale grey ribbon, the bound reports that awaited me onshore, including but not limited to proclamations and *minutes* of those dreadful American *associations*. Was it O'Hara or was it Peek who claimed these free *associations* were the bones of their handsome democracy? Perhaps this is so in the giddy present, but let us wait to see them blossom as instruments of unrest and sedition. I will be gone by then, I thought.

And yet was not my hand playing with the letter to Miss Godefroy, a pristine article when it first left my boardinghouse, since spurned by Peek, defiled by his paternal hand, and now twisted and smudged by the ink-marked fingers of the lovelorn French commissioner? And what if my feelings were returned by Miss Godefroy? How catastrophic to be in love.

Master Parrot stood at my side at the rail. Was it solicitude he seemed to emanate? Had he seen me walk beside Miss Godefroy? Had he observed the colour in my cheeks? How diligently he had attended me on this turbulent journey, carried my trunk, secured my seat on the stage, belligerently pursued my comfort in the awful hotel.

The *Phoenix* met the Crooked Billet Wharf with a loud bang, and the Parrot's hand was on my shoulder. I thought, He knows I am in love.

On the wharf the members of the *Society for the Alleviation of the Miseries of the Public Prisons* awaited us – Mr Vaux, Mr Washington-Smith, Mr Devlin, Mr Weatherspoon, and another chap who I took to be their clerk, a deracinated Frenchman. I took particular note of this M. Duponceau, an old man of light frame, a little belly, a mane of grey hair, mouth ascetic but humorous, eyes clear and very lively. I thought, Did you fall in love, long ago, poor exiled creature?

Behold *the welcome of The French Commissioner to Philadelphia*. The Crooked Billet Inn stands behind us. A dog gazes at the sky. There is the usual confusion of meeting and greeting.

For me, there was only the question of how to introduce my travelling companion. 'This,' I said, 'is my *secrétaire*, Mr Larrit.' And found myself interrogated by that gentleman's frank green eyes. Damn the scoundrel, would he be amused by me? His face was marked with sun and wind and all manner of those rough irregularities that time puts on the bark of trees, but if he was forty or fifty I could not say. And of course it is inevitable among my class that time and time again we will conceive a generous affection for those who will later cut our throats.

In Philadelphia I learned that my boardinghouse had lost its roof the night before but that I should not be in the least concerned. The association's papers had all been saved, and there was now a new house set aside for my use. To this end we were to be conveyed by the queer old Frenchman, and later we would endure the amusements which are the lot of a French commissioner and would include, as time would show, a French play on Napoleon presented by an appalling troupe from New Orleans, a lecture at the historical society, a dinner at the home of Mr Vaux, and a musical soirée in the home of Mr Walsh.

We were dispatched by the Quakers with promises of a prompt reunion. Mr Duponceau then drove us in his own coach, so I was left to silently grapple with the problem of how to get my letter to Miss Godefroy. It was a very considerable concern that she had, at this instant, not the slightest hint of my warm feelings for her. Doubtless she had awaited a note and, receiving none, hardened her heart against me. How should I proceed? I had a thousand letters of introduction, but none to Godefroy *père*. The single person who might have performed this service – Peek – would not act against the *interests* of his daughters.

This problem whirled round and round as the wheels of Duponceau's coach brought us up in the direction of Chestnut Street where we would stay.

Philadelphia had been conceived in the style of an English rural town, one where houses and businesses would be spread far apart and surrounded by gardens and orchards. So thought Mr Penn – and Mr Penn alone. In the absence of others of a superior class to set the tone, the city's inhabitants, in pursuit of their own profit, crowded by the Delaware River and subdivided and resold their lots as many times as you can fold a piece of paper. Thus, while the grand centre of the town is often praised as the birthplace of American democracy, it is only at the waterfront that one views the consequences of majority rule.

It was a pretty cottage – the home of Mr Vaux's nephew, kindly vacated the previous day after the boardinghouse catastrophe – and so we three went to the parlour, as the main room of a middle-class house is called, while our trunks were stowed and Mr Duponceau – Frenchman that he was – produced a bottle of Burgundy which he indicated, this being a house of teetotallers, he would open and serve himself when the maid had left us.

Thus three unlikely characters were joined together, and I was pleased to interrogate our guide who was, he confessed, no part of the Quakers or their prisons but someone *trotted out*, as he picturesquely put it, to speak to those Frenchmen who happened to visit the birthplace of the nation.

We sat on chairs designed by a people who judged it a sin for a man to sit for long. I asked Duponceau where a Frenchman might buy a copy of Molière in his own language.

This produced such a sharp look that I suddenly feared him to be of that eccentric party of which my mother was a prominent representative – that is, those who still agree with the archbishop of Paris who, in 1667, forbade involvement with *Tartuffe* on pain of excommunication.

'Monsieur,' I said, 'if the name Molière offends you, I wish I never spoke it.'

'On the contrary,' he said, but his manner was not warm. 'It fills me with unlimited admiration. Generally,' he said, 'it is only Germans who defame the great writer. It was August Wilhelm von Schlegel who made a reputation by writing that Molière was a buffoon, that Racine likewise was of no account, that the French were the most prosaic people of the world, and that there was no poetry in France.'

His speaking voice was light and a little high, and together with his slight frame and lively eyes made one think of a schoolteacher, a priest, an antiquarian. He had that look you see in seminarians, that straight mouth, the bright grey combative eyes, fast as a twinkle, one of those clever little boys rescued from the farm or fishing boat.

'Wordsworth was as bad,' said the peculiar servant.

'Indeed,' said Duponceau.

A servant quoting literature, a Parrot, Perroquet. *A Parrot rather, for in my sence he talks by roat.*

'He went right off the French,' the so-called *secrétaire* explained to me.

'But how would you conceivably know this?' I asked.

'A light but cruel race, Coleridge called us,' interrupted M. Duponceau, and in so doing filled the servant's glass to spilling. There is nothing worse than those public fairs where one's tenants drink too heavily and forget, as the saying is, what side *their bread is buttered on.*

'Let me explain my reaction to your query,' said M. Duponceau, forcing his Burgundy through his teeth like a merchant and holding his glass – one of those American thimbles – up to the light as if to let his customers see the quality of the colour. My God, I thought, he is going to spit.

'It is very well known to those Quaker gentlemen that I have a library.' He swallowed. 'Beside my own linguistic interests – Chinese, particularly – I most highly value our great French writers. When I was a child in Saint-Martin-de-Ré it was the English language I loved, so the seminarians called me l'Anglais, but today nothing affords me more pleasure than to read Molière and, wherever possible, to dissuade my American friends from attempting any theatrical performance whatsoever.'

I thought, This is the man for me.

'For those not easily dissuaded, monsieur, I bring them to my table and read to them, aloud, in the only language in which it should be known. If I looked askance just now, it was because they once brought to my house a famous visitor, we need not say his name, of a family as noble as your own, sir,' and here he nodded his head and acknowledged that I understood exactly of whom he spoke. 'He was brought to me with an inquiry like your own. I lent this noble lord my copy of *The Misanthrope* and he, reading it while walking in the hills, fell asleep, was woken by a rainstorm, and fled.'

My God, I thought, this is wonderful. What is a little water damage in a case like this? I will get the copy from him. I will read for her.

'And it was destroyed,' he said.

Was this true?

Carefully I let him know I had been raised in a great library like his own. Of course this was gross flattery. His own library, by necessity, must be the collection of an exile, put together with great difficulty in thirty years or less. But I wished him to understand that the poorest item in his library would be safe with a Garmont.

When this got me nowhere I asked him to direct me to a bookseller where I might purchase a good copy of, perhaps, *Tartuffe*.

'Well,' said he, pursing his lips, 'that can be a subject for inquiry.'

So, I thought, he owns an edition of *Tartuffe*. He will trust me with it. He will. I will ensure it, and just as well, for I have no other scheme than to recite Molière upon the hills of Wethersfield.

VI

On the day following I was invited to a musical *soirée* at the home of Mr Walsh, a very distinguished Philadelphian. They sang well enough, which is to say that neither American men nor women figured in the concert, and all the entertainment was provided by an Italian and some Frenchwomen. The Americans, who are by nature as cold as ice, were throughout tempted to regard the Italian amateur as a lunatic, because he, while singing, gesticulated a great deal and assumed dramatic attitudes. The concert ended in some waltzes and quadrilles.

At its conclusion I was introduced to the redoubtable Mrs

Dougdale, who could not have been further from the emaciated figure I had imagined. She said she was perfectly convinced that the Negroes were of the same race as us, just as a black cow is of the same race as a white one. The Negro children show as much intelligence as the white ones, often they learn faster. I asked her if the blacks had citizens' rights. She answered, 'Yes, in this state, in law, but they cannot present themselves at the poll.'

'Why so?'

'They would be ill-treated.'

'And what happens to the rule of law in that case?'

'The law with us is nothing if it is not supported by public opinion.'

So, again – the majority.

There was not a drop of wine at the *soirée*, a lack I remarked on to my countryman as we walked through the streets of his occasionally handsome city. M. Duponceau said that the Quakers will touch nothing, but those of the other party are even worse, as they tipple, for the most part, on sweet Canary wine. Sometimes a port or Madeira is offered, although much of that is watered by the boatmen who see it as their right to sample the wares they transport. As there is some ancient enmity by the majority for the better classes, this 'tax' is accepted by those who must pay. Old Duponceau, speaking in an eccentric mixture of French and English, confessed himself the loneliest man in Philadelphia, for although he had a cellar of first-rate wines from Médoc, Graves and Bourgogne, none of his fellows would even *feign* to enjoy what he offered them.

I thought perhaps he had no palate, for what decent wine would survive the journey here? I asked what his guests refused.

'De Lafite.'

'Dear Duponceau.' I bowed to him. 'I would be honoured to be your friend.' At which the frockcoated Larrit seconded my vote – a sommelier, no doubt – and all three of us, quite suddenly, in spite of our very separate circumstance of wealth and education, were united by this fondness for *Patrie* and *Terroir* and fairly galloped along the streets of Philadelphia, a charming city, very favourable to those who have no carriage, since all the streets are bordered with wide sidewalks, and its sole defect is to be monotonous in its beauty.

All the edifices are neat, kept up with extreme care, and have all the freshness of new buildings, and M. Duponceau's house, when we reached it, presented its face to the street with a very Quakerish humility. The entire edifice was the work of saws and hammers.

There were two floors, no evidence of an attic, eight windows to face the unchristened street, and a door placed in the centre as if a child had drawn it there.

And so I entered, imagining I knew the character and standing of our host.

The hallway was as you would expect, not even a rug to hide its timbers. The walls were grey, the ceiling white, as in a nunnery. Only at its most distant extreme, almost beyond the penumbra of our host's lantern, was there a door to break the monotony of our passage. I followed him into a dark room redolent of some as yet unidentifiable luxury. Here I watched in blank astonishment as my exiled countryman, a little bent, moved from lamp to lamp and, with every lighted wick, revealed more and more of a library which, I now realised, occupied almost one half of the ground floor of this considerable house. Of its two longest walls only one was broken, and here by the single door through which we had entered. On these walls the source of the luxurious aroma was clearly visible – books, more books. At first I thought the smell buff-coloured, but it would not be that simple. And oh, the wonderful variety of those smells. Old copies redolent of the *ancien régime*, the glossier volumes of laboratories and gases, the American editions with floral perfumes, wig powder, candle wax, and all of them radiating glue and calf leather like tuberose on a summer's evening. I noticed a bright red cloth binding with the name of Diderot, but for the most part the spines were tan and beige and umber, each one holding the golden name of a philosopher or poet (and there was the great Lavoisier, beheaded in the revolution) familiar since my birth, and if the entire effect was contradicted by a ladder that had clearly begun its life in the unlettered company of a house painter, then could there be a better counterargument for a democracy where greed might tear the land apart but still the low could climb so high?

In the centre of the room, well curtained from the scrupulously moral street, was a green baize table and around it were placed, as if for the use of studious friends, four well-cushioned *chairs*. Our host pushed three of these into an untidy group, and here Larrit and I were instructed to sit and await the pleasures of Médoc. While Duponceau descended the stairs I imagined his cellar, like a deep reflection in a pond, a secret mirror of the library with dusty bottles in the place of fragrant books. Having learned that M. Duponceau had begun his life as a poor draper's son who had learned his English from the soldiers stationed in Saint-Martin-de-Ré, I was given one of those dazzling *visions* of America, sufficient to make one abandon one's necessary fears. I sat with my hands in my lap, contemplating the paint-splattered ladder with the kind of ardour more suited to a study of the lives of saints.

On the high baize table there were two books, positioned in such a way that I could easily read their spines, and it appeared to me that this placement was not accidental. These volumes, at about the level of my eye, had been provided like a book of poetry beside a visitor's bed. The first appeared to be one of those folio editions, so beloved by my mother, of antipodean botany, but it was the second I understood to have been chosen with my interests in mind: *Oeuvres de Molière avec des remarques grammaticales, des avertissements, et des observations sur chaque pièce, par M. Bret.* I took it to my lap. It had its own smells of goatskin and glue – one could imagine the artisans who made it, almost certainly in the service of a noble family – and it was very clear to me, leafing through the heavy paper, that they, who never read a book, had known themselves in the service of the eternal.

'Ah-hah!' our host cried from the door. He had two bottles in his left hand and a third in the right and with this latter treasure the dear bright-eyed madman pointed.

I thought, Do not shake the bottle, sir.

'There.' He pointed. 'There.' He shook. 'You have your *Tartuffe*, sir.'

Swiftly I returned M. Molière to his proper place while Duponceau, drawing corks, decanting, pouring with a splash that had the wine foaming like a bath – not elegant but doubtless efficient in achieving what he later called 'a damn good airing' – provided me an account of the volume's publication. I listened with some discomfort, thinking there are wine bores and book bores. I much preferred the former. As to the *Tartuffe*, what a great fool I would appear if I presented myself at Wethersfield with this monster edition in my pocket.

'So,' said Duponceau, who had finally come to the end of his educational address. 'So here is to the great Molière.'

'To Molière.' I drank.

'To Molière,' said Larrit, and, standing awkwardly, asked if he also might be permitted to examine the book. In speaking he assumed, in imitation of our host, a light and delicate if misshapen form of French, and I was given cause to wonder how the lines of *Tartuffe* might sound in the chamber of his parrot's mind. This was but a moment's speculation, and I was not sorry that a book would remove him from the conversation. Democracy brings with it tensions and anxieties I could never have predicted, so many of them, and more varieties than all the butterflies in the *Bottom Hundred*.

Duponceau and I chatted or chattered. I bemoaned the palates of the Philadelphians who had called his Médoc cold and sour. Miraculously, it was free of sediment, and rushed into my glass at that perfect stage of life. In a year it would be a dowager with a faded old corsage, but as it entered my mouth it was vigorous and manly, completely composed, its orchestra all present and correct. Oh, heavens, that such small things make a man so happy. I revealed to my host my plan to interview each of the forty-two prisoners in the Quaker prison. He told me it was well known that the cost of the famous outer wall was $200 000, a little under a third of the entire cost of the prison.

We finished a bottle and he decanted another.

'I have heard it asserted,' I said, holding high my glass, admiring its treasure – gorgeous garnet fading, toward the rim, to the colour of a brick. 'I have heard it asserted,' I said – although this was not true – 'that in general you have appointed incompetent people to run your undertakings.'

'*I* have appointed?'

'Have you not become an American?'

'Indeed, it appears so,' sighed M. Duponceau. 'And yes, what you have heard is commonly said. Seldom does the choice fall on an able man. All official positions are given for political reasons; the spirits of faction and intrigue grow here as they do under monarchies. Only the master is different.'

Throughout all this the peculiar Larrit said not a word. I thought, He is paid to spy on me. He is reporting to Monsieur, who is writing to my mother. Well, let him. He stood at table like an egret, his shoulders hunched, his wine untouched, leafing very slowly through the book. So strange was this behaviour, I did not know whether to keep my first opinion or to be upset by his ill manners.

'You are here to study the Americans,' Duponceau said, as he refreshed my glass. 'There are nice distinctions that may not yet be obvious to you, although this will be very clear in time, and here is one: our morality in France is shaped by each man's knowledge that he is shut in a certain sphere from which he does not hope to escape.'

I thought, He makes it sound like a prison.

'Here,' he said, 'the road to riches and fortune is open to every-body, no matter from where they start.'

I thought, Why must everyone tap my knee?

'So there is a restlessness of spirit and a greed for wealth which it would be hard for you to understand.'

I thought, *Miss Godefroy. Restlessness of spirit.*

'Yes, you must appreciate that everybody in America wants to grow rich and rise in the world, and there is no one who does not believe in his power to succeed. From that there springs a wearisome social activity, ever-changing intrigues, continual excitement, and an uncontrolled desire of each to outdo the others.'

'But in all this frenzy,' said I, 'what becomes of equality?'

'Equality exists only in the marketplace,' answered M. Duponceau.

'Good grief,' cried Larrit.

He was now kneeling on the floor, peering closely at the book.

Duponceau appeared distressed. I quickly changed the subject, asking where I might buy a pocket book or duodecimo of *Tartuffe*.

'I doubt they translate him,' said he, 'although they should, for there is a great deal in *Tartuffe* that you would recognise in Philadelphia.'

'I will read it in the language it was born in.'

'Then you must write to France.'

'I have no time.'

Duponceau cocked his head. I could not tell whether I had offended his notions of Art and Time or if he could somehow look into my soul and see Miss Godefroy.

'Very well,' he said at last. 'You must send your man to New York. You may be lucky.'

I thought, Good heavens, I cannot send him to New York. Who

could guess what Peek is up to with his painter wife? And yet look at him, I thought. He was *kneeling* on the floor. He was *sighing*, and *exclaiming*. Now he stood. With the rare volume in both hands, he turned toward us. I thought, His hair looks mad. I will send him to New York.

'I did this,' he cried.

He stood there: Brother Egret at the lectern, the book held wide in his big hands, his eyes alight, and on his face the most alarming smile.

'This work is mine.'

VII

It is a relatively easy matter to estimate a person's intelligence just by looking at him, or so I had thought until my interrogation of John Larrit in the library of M. Duponceau.

To see him there, his eyes bright as a boy's, the heavy folio edition held reverently in his weathered leathern hands, was to doubt one's own judgement.

'I did this,' he said.

Removing the folio promptly from his charge, I held it to the light. I had assumed he had spilled his wine but I found no colour on the paper except some tiny bits of shirts and petticoats which had survived the grinding of the pulp.

'Nonsense,' I said, irritated to have been unnecessarily alarmed.

He stared at me. 'It is not possible.'

Duponceau arrived to gaze, not at his own treasure, but at the servant. 'What is not possible?'

'These here are my engravings,' said the Parrot. 'Mine own.'

Gentle as a surgeon, M. Duponceau carried his book to his lectern. Here we could all three examine it, as the proud proprietor turned the pages. I read: *Sauvages des environs de la rivière Nepean. 1. Jedat; 2. Tara; 3. Nemare.*

'Where is the Nepean River?' I asked Larrit.

'In New South Wales,' he replied.

'So they are fancies, these faces?'

Outrage came storming to conquer his astonishment. 'They are drawn from life,' he said, and I saw M. Duponceau reach up, for he was a good head shorter, and place a hand between his shoulderblades.

Said he, 'What was your crime, poor fellow?'

Good Lord, I thought. I have shared a cabin with a convict.

Duponceau turned a page to reveal a page of botanical drawings very like the ones my mother so enjoyed.

'Then how did you reach Botany Bay, Mr Larrit?'

'By ship, of course.'

'How old?'

'I was a boy, sir.'

I could not believe I was party to such a conversation. I thought of the teeming criminal poor, millions of them, breeding in lanes, crowding in slums.

'You picked a pocket?' suggested our host, his voice marked by the greatest delicacy.

John Larrit shook his head and wiped his eye with the back of his wrist.

'Your father was transported?'

'Oh I wish he had been, sir. A certain gentleman transported me, so to speak. That's all.'

That's all? I thought. What vile business am I hearing?

'What was this gentleman's name?' I asked. I had never liked my mother's botanical drawings. Those strange seed pods with lips like women's parts.

'It would mean nothing to you, sir. You would not know him. He was a forger, sir. You would not know a forger.'

I thought, He never called me *sir* like this. I have become the *procureur-général* in this case, and he is guilty.

'A forger would be hanged.'

'He was never apprehended sir,' said the prisoner. 'I went on the ship an innocent boy, but I was found with forged notes.'

'In short, Mr Larrit, you are a convict.'

'No, sir.'

'You were transported to a penal colony. How old are you?'

'I don't know, sir.'

'Don't know?'

'I decided to forget. It would make me too angry to have lost so many years. I thought I will not count the days, and so I didn't.'

'Is that possible?'

'It was possible for me, sir. Off the boat they first put me to be servant for Major Grose who was temporarily in charge of the colony. Mrs Grose had wanted a maid, but there were no maids so she made me wear a dress.'

I thought, What story can this be?

'How long were you made to wear female attire?'

'More than a year, I think.'

'Was it one year or two? Surely you noticed the seasons.'

'It was cold and then it was hot. I suppose they might be seasons. But then they got a new forger sent to them. He was a Sussex man named Page. You mentioned hanging, sir, not on your life. They made him an architect, although that was never his trade. I was sent to work with him. We taught each other, so to speak.'

'And you don't know how old you were?'

'Perhaps I was thirteen.'

'An architect at thirteen.' I laughed. I thought it preposterous. 'And by fourteen you were an artist, capable of producing this?'

'Perhaps eighteen, sir. There were many journeys. We were sent to find a way through the Blue Mountains, and that was where those drawings are from.'

'You were an explorer too?'

'We failed at that, sir.'

'Eighteen?'

'Most likely. Perhaps twenty.'

'Perhaps twenty.'

I turned to the title page where I saw the authorship attributed to none other than the marquis de Tilbot, whom I had always known as the author of those very botanical engravings which had cast their gloomy shadow on my childhood.

'You, sir' – I now spoke to Larrit, and I was very angry – 'you, sir, are a scoundrel and a liar.'

'I am not,' he said, stepping back to lift his glass from the baize table and, standing with one insolent hand upon his hip, he drank it in a single gulp.

'You are a vassal to the marquis de Tilbot.'

'It would seem so, wouldn't it?'

'Then is he not the author of this work?'

'I believe the words are his, sir, but I could not say for sure. It is only the engravings I can speak for.'

'Then you speak falsely, for they are his.'

'A one-armed engraver?'

'Please be careful, Mr Larrit, lest you forget your perilous situation.'

'They are mine, sir. They were to be a gift to the Empress Josephine, or so I was told my him.'

'The marquis de Tilbot told you? Perhaps you shared a cell with him?'

'As I said, I was never imprisoned.'

'But you were confined in a penal colony.'

The rascal poured himself a spanking big glass of Château Lafite, and when he turned his eyes had changed, and they were narrow and nasty above his hatchet bones.

'Please listen to me, your lordship,' said he. 'If there is a scoundrel in this story it is that fellow named Monsieur, although in fact he saved my neck, and ruined my life, and rescued me again and I am, as a result of all these horrors which you could never understand, indebted to him. I had hoped to hide his name from you, but more shame to me, I failed. It was the marquis de Tilbot who passed forged money. It was he who abandoned me, abandoned me to a penal colony where I survived, sir, and saw human meat whipped off a living back. Do you know what the currency was in Australia?'

'The pound? The Spanish dollar?'

'Rum, sir. That was what it was. That was the place I was left in, and the place I tried to make myself an artist, and the place where the so-called marquis returned to find me when I was a man. Hello, said he. I don't know how he knew me. I promised I would fetch you, he said.

'Clearly this was a lie, except he recognised somehow the boy inside the man. I might not have known the old man neither, but for his awful arm and the fact he produced a keepsake I had given him, his likeness incised into a stone. This touched my heart in the most disquieting way, for I had given it to him for just this reason, that one day he would return and say, There you are.

'It was beyond the bounds of expectation that he would sail to Sydney to find me after all this time. But he was a spy, I must believe, and as a spy he had a dozen plans, not one of which was told to me. He and I had laboured through the bush like drunk schoolgirls collecting wildflowers, for he would take the seeds to Josephine at Malmaison, for what reason I cannot say. She was no empress by then. I don't know where the plates have ended up, although I know he sold the proofs without me ever benefiting. If this was to be a folio, he never told me, and if you saw me looking queer when I found the book, it was the shock of finding myself robbed. This book contains what I saw and tried to render. Perhaps he wrote the words. I doubt it. The only part he played was to instruct me on a way to draw a map of Australia. Here, sir. He can take credit for that, although, you see, it does not suit him to do so, for he has turned me into Captain Larrit.

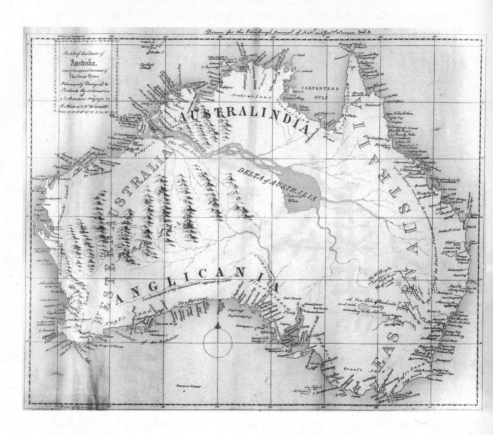

Carte de l'Australie entière, Capt. John Larrit, 1804

'I was not a captain, ever in my life, and I drew this fancy to his instructions. The *Delta of Australia* was his invention, I know because he changed the name so many times and caused me end-less trouble. If there is a sea where he says there is, no one has found it yet.'

'Why would he do such a thing?'

'Oh, sir, surely you know him.'

'Indeed I do, and have done all my life.'

'And what is his business do you think?'

'He is a noble gentleman.'

'He is a spy. But the map was not real spying. It was a counter-feit. It would please Napoleon, don't you think, to imagine all those fertile lands unoccupied? Why, we might have transported a million French felons to colonise the land.'

'Yet he rescued you, you said.'

'In his opinion.'

'And you left Botany Bay with him. Did he rescue you or not?'

'Like the Americans rescue their slaves from floods, so they will not run away. He bought me somehow. I was employed to record what took his fancy. We sailed to New Guinea and New Caledonia, and when the last ship came for us he said I could come home.'

'He rescued you.'

'He deceived me, as good as kidnapping. I had a wife by then, a house, a baby. In Botany Bay.'

'And where are they now?'

'How would I know?' he cried, his face now contorted, the tears flowing in great quantity. He retreated into the shadows and I stood with Duponceau, mortified on his account.

'How long ago was this, dear chap?' said Duponceau.

'He said I would remain a piss poor engraver if I stayed in Sydney. I was a guttersnipe. I had seen nothing of what could be done. He said I should take a year in Paris and I would see things that would make an artist of me.'

'And you went.'

'You know I did.'

'So you were made an artist.'

He laughed scornfully. I saw his hands hanging from his arms, alarming balls of fist. 'I was made useful,' he said, more quietly.

'What do you want now?' our host inquired.

I saw how my servant gazed at Duponceau while he considered the question, and you could imagine that all his life and travels were being weighed and evaluated and considered.

'To be still,' he said, and smiled.

Duponceau nodded, and ran his hand through his long unruly hair. 'Stasis,' said he.

John Larrit did not seem to understand the word. 'Not the road,' he said. 'Not the sea.' And I thought, He could be fifty, and I understood he told the truth and would have wept except I had no right.

PARROT

I was the one who should have been the French commissioner, I thought, following my duck-legged aristo through the wicket gate of the Eastern State Penitentiary, passing between clipped privet hedges into a central chamber from which seven long passages radiated like spokes on a Catherine wheel. On either side of every spoke was a long row of low cell doors.

Twice he touched me on the arm, as if in tenderness.

Everywhere about us was silence, although sometimes the thick walls gave a muffled clue to the living nightmares they contained, the distant *thuck* of a weaver's shuttle, the *ching* of a hammer striking steel. Behind every one of those numbered double doors – first oak, then steel – was a human soul, a mind in its bone cage, the centre of its solar system, burning with regret and rage, condemned to silent solitary labour, world without end.

This spoked device was a *machine of reform*, it had been explained to the commissioner in the lifeless garden. We were shown a black hood and invited to try it on. How bloody kind. This hood is the crown given to every prisoner at the wicket gate. He enters blind. He does not see the garden. He shuffles along the penitential corridor to his cell, alone, in terror, not knowing if his next step will be to a deadly fall, if he is alone on earth or surrounded by others in a castle ten miles long.

This Eastern Penitentiary is the work of the Quakers of Pennsylvania who would not tear a man apart or pour molten lead into his intestines as was done by the bastard kings of old. Instead, they work direct upon the *soul*.

I listened to Olivier de Garmont question the cost of construction. I was John Larrit, clown and *secrétaire* who had already lived too long, who carried paper and carbon paper.

The first poor devil we visited was seated at his loom and never ceased his endless *shuff* and *thump* the entire time he spoke. He offered a grimace and a shrug and reminded me of one I loved. He told us he had always liked to dance – a joke – he shuffled his feet before his loom. And as his lordship's servants must once have collected moths and butterflies, I collected this conversation for his important book to be titled *On the Penitentiary System in the United States and Its Application in France*.

Mesdames, messieurs, voilà. The very thing. *Les conversations pittoresques.*

'The prisoner had been there five years,' I wrote, 'and is to remain five more. He has been convicted as a receiver of stolen goods but, even after his long imprisonment, denies his guilt.'

'Add this,' his lordship demanded. 'Each cell is aired by a ventilator, and contains a *fosse d'aisance* whose construction makes it perfectly odourless. One must have seen all the cells of the Philadelphia prison, and have passed entire days in them, to form an exact idea of their cleanness and the purity of the air one breathes in them.' Oh, lucky man.

Of my own accord I wrote, 'He has a bible, a slate and a pencil.

His razor, plate, can and basin hang upon the wall. His bedstead turns up against the wall, which leaves more space for him to work in. He labours, sleeps and wakes, counts the seasons as they change, and grows old.'

We moved to the next cell, whose lonely inmate had smuggled in a cat or rabbit of which there was no sign except its dreadful smell.

The French commissioner's report was as follows: 'The inmate knows how to read and write, he was condemned for murder. He says that his health, without being bad, is poorer than it was outside the prison. He strongly denies having committed the crime which was the cause of his condemnation; otherwise he confesses readily that he was a drunkard, turbulent and irreligious. But today, he adds, his soul is changed; he finds a sort of pleasure in the solitude, and is tormented only by the desire to see his family again and give his children a moral and Christian education, something he had never considered.'

What pigwash, I thought, writing it down, correcting my employer's English. Democracies and monarchies, it does not matter – the world is filled with poor men tortured by the state. The rich make an endless supply of them, and when the Americans won their independence the king must find a new place to put his prisoners. So – Australia was invented by the British, that whole dry carcass, its withered dugs offered to our criminal lips. Now that, sir, is a place of penance.

In Philadelphia I wrote with my right hand but wandered in my mind, a mighty garden wild with weeds. I thought, Little Olivier is doubtless a clever man but has no idea what powers this sad bootmaker has locked within him. His lordship has, as they say, no fucking clue. In Sydney he would quickly become the proprietor of a stinking tannery. A drunkard, yes, who wasn't? Turbulent, yes. And irreligious, but a man with all life and hope ahead of him.

The previous night I had told tender Olivier about the flogging, but I said that only to ease the humiliation of my tears. It was a lie. I never saw a man flogged, thank Jesus, only a piece of human flesh glistening with black flies at the barracks gate.

I should never have left those shores, that's the truth.

I was tricked onto that ship. Worse, I *permitted* myself to be tricked because I understood myself to be a poor little boy, betrayed, abandoned, a victim of an awful fate. I always had it in my head that I must get home where I belonged.

I was a fool to cry at Duponceau's, but I was a much bigger fool to leave Port Jackson. I had a wife, a child, a home, but for all that I did not understand it was *my home*. She, my wife, would not call it home either. All around us everyone was the same – soldiers, convicts, even captains with their holds stock full of rum. *Home* did not mean *here*. That was *elsewhere*. When will we be in our real home at last? we asked each other. We manured the earth, she and I, and grew cabbage, and roasted tails of kangaroo, and held each other through the entire night, breathing that perfume that lies on the skin of young boys and girls. We swam at night, bare as God made us. We gathered oysters from the rocks and shucked their living juices down our cruel and eager throats. We laughed and farted. We had fevers and were well. We were at home, while waiting to go *home*, while missing *home*. We looked up at that cobalt sky, and out at the ultramarine seas, not seeing their beauty but only the cold empty distance between us and *home*. And so we made our lives, pining all the while.

In this way a self-pitying boy grew to be an artist, blessed to see what had not been seen in all of London. When I saw Duponceau's folio, I understood what treasure I had thrown away. I had been more talented, more decent. I had been a better man in New South Wales.

That was why I cried, but who knows why I cried? Her name was Aoibheann. I thought she was Eevan until we signed the papers. She was soft and Irish, fair-skinned, hair like my own, an angel with her swollen lips, her sturdy legs. It was really love and really marriage and even though the two of us built the house – she at one end of the saw as we cut the sandstone blocks – I did not consider it a real home, no matter the blisters on our hands.

The first day in the Eastern State Penitentiary I assisted the French commissioner interview four prisoners. I can think of no more disturbing labour – such a soup of gullibility and lies, horror and aristocratic imbecility. At day's end we were outside the crenellated walls and I inquired of my employer if he had some curiosity to taste the arrack, as this was the drink the prisoners had been destroyed by, every one.

'Indeed,' said he.

We turned into a low sort of inn, where we were given a flask of arrack and a water jug and two glasses.

Said he at last, 'I have a question.'

Said I, 'It is better we speak English here.'

'Would you undertake a journey for me? To New York.'

Habit made me hide my eagerness. 'As you wish,' I said.

'You don't mind then?' he said. I could not tell what changed his eyes, whether it was the awful stink of arrack or one of those peculiar niceties which seem to trouble the noble mind. 'I would have you find me a good edition of a French play. It seems you might know books.'

'Tell me what you want and how much you wish to spend.'

It was such a simple thing to say I could not understand why he was so long about it. On and on he went. 'You will see your wife?' he asked finally.

I thought, Frig me. What's this? 'With your permission.'

'She is a good woman?' he asked.

I thought, Why is he looking like that? His eyes down his long thin nose, those two red marks on each pale cheek. We finished our drinks and set off back to our lodgings. I thought, I will kill any man who hurts her name or body.

II

Arrack tastes like mothballs, castor oil, coffin wood, eats your throat and burns your brain, but – speaking of the Indian variety, delivered to Port Jackson on the *Amity* from Bombay – it has a more-ish quality that cannot be denied. Indeed, when Colonel Paterson allowed the captain of the *Amity* to sell his stuff, the entire colony became insane and I was hidden in the ceiling by his wife.

Of the American variety I have no right to talk – from what living plant or creature it has been fermented and distilled I do not know – but I will relate its effect on Lord *comte Nez Pointu*, who seemed sober as a Quaker when we returned to our lodgings from the pub.

After not too many minutes he was pacing back and forth above my head, and then he was up and down the stairs like old Mrs Hobbs attending to her dying master.

So – clippedy-cloppedy. Pillow held across the Parrot head.

Then it began to rain and I was imagining that bleak Crooked Billet dock in tomorrow morning's darkness, and the passengers on the *Phoenix* huddled like wet poultry beneath the awning. The rain lashed my bedroom windows, pebbles by the fistful, so it seemed. My bed had been made to fit a dwarf. Where was my beloved in the lonely foreign rain?

Comte Nez Pointu paced above my head. I could have killed the builder who had set the floor joists at four-foot centres. On the basis of no more than the creaks and groans I could have drawn you the whole, in plan and elevation, and was severely critical of all America for doing something I would never undertake in New South Wales.

The rain increased. I slept. I was woken as the front door slammed then blessed silence reigned.

I awoke to find a phantom with a lantern, dripping water on my face.

'Christ, what gives?'

He held up a new bottle of arrack, swinging it above me like a pendulum. This was an aspect of the noble Garmont I did not wish to see.

'What is the hour?'

'Not late,' he said, but was made a liar by the church bell. I dressed and joined him in the kitchen where every chair was a punishment, the bones of my arse already saying sorry to the oak.

'Now John,' says he.

John? I was never called John except by a magistrate.

He poured two spilling glasses, and drank without expression.

'I think John,' said he, 'you may understand the importance of your task tomorrow.' His cheeks and lips were cherry red in the charcoal of the night. 'You know who the book is for?'

For God's sake let me sleep.

I had seen the girl in public, drinking in every word he said. She was alive, alight, haughty to me but wet for him, one of those luminous *maidens* you see beyond the glass: bone china, do not touch. He did not need a book to court her. He could have thrown her on her back and done her in the rain.

I sipped in silence.

'How extremely interesting,' he said, 'to learn of your association with the marquis de Tilbot. I have known him all my life, but I have no idea either of his character or general occupation. Perhaps you will one day tell me what type of man he is?'

I thought, Be very bloody careful, my Parrot.

I allowed a little arrack to wet my lips. It was foul, a dirty brew, and the rain pelted at the window and I could hear a slow drip in the hall. The roof was leaking but it was not mine. My own property I lost on account of Monsieur. He said he would buy me another house. He said this first in 1814, then again in 1830. A house costs as much as a cow, he told me. And what of a wife and child? Could he replace these too?

I have dreamed of murdering him, driving a screwdriver through his eye. Carrying my own coffin, always, in the end.

'One last drink,' I said, and swallowed what remained. I stood.

'And you are content,' the comte Nez Pointu asked, 'in your life?'

His brown eyes caught the light of his lantern, his chin dimpled, his brow furrowed. Did he really imagine I would trust him with my heart?

'Good night, sir. Thank you for the drink.'

Five hours later I boarded the *Phoenix* in the dark. By then the wind had fallen and the dark houses along the Delaware were all crisp and straight and new against the fresh-washed sky. Who would guess their groans and cries?

The main deck of the *Phoenix* was today enclosed on all sides, stacked with casks and sacks like a Shanghai godown. I ascended to the hurricane deck. Up here you could see the engine churning, the connecting rod, caged in a strong and lofty frame, thrusting and turning like a bull. Here I came across two young fellows, no more than twenty, both dressed to the nines in waistcoats and tall top hats, busy with the task of strangling pigeons which they removed one by one from a wire cage before adding a new limp body to the pile between them on the deck. The other passengers being congregated below, the boys were undisturbed in their grim task.

I stood awhile and watched them and remembered the Jew aboard the *Havre*. I thought, I must get money.

The boys were busy but careful with their work, yet as their quick glances soon made clear, they wished to explain themselves. Clearly, I thought, they are on their way to market. They were both tall and lanky, fair-haired, red-cheeked, with low foreheads and high noses. In spite of which you might also call them handsome. They had been Dutch or German once, but now they were Americans.

'Off to Franklin Street?' I asked.

'Tell him,' said one.

'You tell him,' said the other.

They were on their way to the state of Georgia where they had bought two lots of land, which had recently been the territory of Creek Indians. Thanks to President Jackson these were now offered to settlers in a lottery. Or was it thanks to Jefferson the Creeks would leave the land? In any case – not being natives of Georgia they could not enter the lottery but they had got two lots from an agent, one of forty acres in Cass County which was said to be pretty rich in gold, and cost twenty dollars, and the other lot in Paulding County was two hundred acres, and they had a picture of a house they would build upon it and plenty of money to buy slaves and stock.

The taller one was named Dirk. He said he would have six children. He said there was no better place on earth than the *you-knighted states*, and he knew that because his ancestors had been poor men until now.

This did nothing to explain the pigeons, whose warm carcasses continued to pile up in the salty air, their poor black eyes containing no hope of the hereafter. I asked what they were up to with the birds.

Dirk said they had made a killing.

If he meant to make a joke, his face did not show it. He explained they had made *damn near one thousand dollars* and asked me to guess how they had done it.

I looked at their light bright eyes, their wet lower lips, their long raw hands, and could not imagine how, not for the life of me.

'You tell him,' said Dirk.

'Very well,' said the other, who turned out to be Peter and the son of Peter who had a dairy farm near the North River in New York until he sold it and now relaxed at a pub on the river at the place where the packet ships came in from England with news of the London Stock Exchange. It was their pa who saw that if they could get the London market prices from New York to Philadelphia faster than a horse, why, you could do very well indeed for what was in the London newspapers was, to all intents, the future, and if you knew the future you could be made a rich man with your winnings on the stock exchange. And to this end he had given his sons sufficient to rent fifty carrier pigeons from a gent residing in that city of Brotherly Love.

And that had been their business for three months, and they had made the thousand dollars they wished to have, and now they were off, but the gent who rented them the pigeons had refused to take them back on account of some clever cancellation clause (which was a great old birkin for no one wrote a thing). This bastard rentier was, at this moment, in his cabin, and they were eager to watch his face when he came to see their cancellation clause, now piling on the deck.

They said I should wait and see the show, but I did not have the taste for it. They had made me feel too old for pigeons or cotton or anything but being a servant to a waxwork effigy.

I reached the boardinghouse at dusk and found Mathilde and her mother gone.

OLIVIER

I

When dealing with servants, abandon all your normal nuance, irony, humour. Play no word games, nor make assumptions. Say exactly what service you require and then repeat it once and only once. In this way you will discover your servants are more intelligent than you supposed.

Whether he was aware of his habit or not, my father gave that advice, in pretty much those words, every quarter-day, and he continued to do so in his letters to me in America, an eccentricity perhaps, but no less valuable for that. Certainly I followed his precepts in dealing with my convict forger. In the case of his visit to New York, I specified the book I wished him to buy and the date of his return.

When he did not return on the Monday, his absence engendered considerable *weather* in my mind; first a fear that I had *propelled* him into a cruel domestic trauma; second a *rage* that he had not obeyed me. These two feelings may appear contradictory, but a hammer and a nail can make them all the one.

Beside all this, a circumstance had changed, which we will come to in just a moment. As a result, I had made arrangements to depart

Philadelphia on the Tuesday, travelling to New Haven aboard the *Zeus*, Captain Elihu Cammer. Until my fellow missed the *Phoenix* on the Monday this would have been easily done. The following morning, there were only two hours between the *daily* arrival of the *Phoenix* and the *weekly* departure of the *Zeus*, although with feuding owners, reckless races, and bursting boilers these timetables were at best approximate.

Still, I was a young man in love, impatient, sleepless. I could not pace in my house awaiting news. I would be down on the dock when the *Phoenix* was due to arrive. And if this meant I must pack my servant's trunk, then my father would never know I had kneeled before it. In any case, I had less curiosity about his possessions than the contents of a rat's nest. There was a great deal of strange paper which I had no time to read – maps, engravings of one sort or another. It was my own trunk that presented the greater upset. Who would have thought silk stockings were difficult to contain, a court jacket so resistant to lying flat. Naturally I made a hash of it, but I was now prepared for the dash to the New Haven steamboat, if Mr Parrot should present himself again.

Duponceau kindly arranged a Negro to transport my trunks and myself to the Crooked Billet Wharf with clear instruction he was not to leave my side. His name was 'James' which seemed immensely comic because he was black as coal, but it was clearly no joke to him and he looked me in the eye as if he were a senator.

'Yes, sir, Mr Duponceau,' said he. 'I will not leave the gentleman's side.'

This James was the proud owner of a coarse tweed suit, patched and darned about its knees and cuffs. He had very short trousers, two odd gloves, and a low-crowned broad-brimmed hat which he lifted at the slightest excuse. Once at the Crooked Billet, however, he clearly indicated that he would *not* unload as he had been ordered, but would instead remain on his box seat. He paused to lean forward and spit a bright yellow stream of tobacco, an action immediately mimicked by his horse's arse. He would safeguard my boxes, sir, as he had promised.

I had a mind to put him in his place but I heard a foghorn and understood the *Phoenix* might be early. Therefore, in company with a fishwife and a press of burghers, I strolled out on the jetty and peered into the mist and coal smoke which had democratically arranged its factions in stripes of brown and white, the whole illuminated most tremulously. From this spectral effluence appeared the *Phoenix*, looming high, klaxon loud. On the starboard side, as it drifted silently toward the dock, stood what might have been the emblem of America: frockcoated, very tall and straight, with a high stovepipe hat tilted back from his high forehead. I thought, This is the worst vision of democracy – illiterate, hard as wood, overdressed, uncultured – with that physiognomy I had earlier observed in the portrait of the awful Andrew Jackson – a face divided proudly in three equal parts: hairline to eyebrows, eyebrows to nose, lips to chin. In other words, the face of one who will never give any weight to the wisdom of his betters. To see the visage of their president is to understand that the farmer and the mechanic are the lords of the New World. Public opinion is their opinion; the public will is their will. This was on no account what I hoped to find.

The spectre raised a hand in salute and I realised it was my own servant. You can say this was due to myopia. I would say it was on account of fancy dress, the American habit of changing oneself from one thing to another which seems to be the national occupation, for they did not come all this way, as one of them said to me, 'to stay the way I were'. The air was perfumed by salt and industry. The rogue raised his other hand and in it I made out a thin oblong brown package which must certainly be *Tartuffe*. This was what I had waited for, what had kept me awake, and in a very few minutes he and I were side by side like partners, following behind James and his cart toward the Hitheren Wharf, where the *Zeus* was coaling.

When we were finally above the wharf I looked hard at John Larrit to see if he was damaged by his journey. Certainly his dress suggested he had become insolent, but seeing him at close quarters I relaxed sufficiently to wonder at the domestic situation he had found his wife in. I did not chastise him for his lateness.

'I have heard from Miss Godefroy's father,' I said to him, rather to my own surprise.

He smiled at me. 'Hey-ho,' said he.

'The letter came not two hours after you departed. Written on his own account without encouragement.'

'Everyone wants to meet the governor.'

'Commissioner,' I said. 'And you have the book?'

He patted the side pocket of his frockcoat. I could rehearse it on the voyage. I would know it word perfect before we were as far as Exeter.

'And all was well with your wife?'

'Of course,' he said, rather tersely.

We were by now descending a clay cutting to where the *Zeus* lay moored in a stench of mist and fish and coal.

The incorrigible James loaded our trunks together, side by side on his massive back. I thought, Should I tip him? Could he possibly be a slave?

'They did not have the *Cartouche*,' the Parrot said.

'They?'

'The bookstore had no *Cartouche*.'

'*Tartuffe*.' I smiled with difficulty, aware that he would sometimes, as the English say, *pull my leg*.

'It is no matter,' said he. 'Your lordship can relax.'

'*Tartuffe?*'

'He had a great stock in English translation, but I would not touch them.'

'Oh dear,' I said, staring at James, who awaited me, clearly in expectation of his reward.

'Your lordship need not worry,' John Larrit said, finally removing that dreadful hat. Said he, 'I found you a lovely edition of Molière.'

James held out his hand.

'*Bon voyage,*' said he.

Parrot looked at me tenderly as I shook the black man's dusty hand.

'You asked for *Cartouche?*' I demanded. 'Or *Tartuffe?*'

'*Tartuffe*, *Tartuffe*, of course *Tartuffe*. If the joke don't suit you, never mind. It is more a matter of what I have.'

He produced the parcel and it was coal-black James, still waiting, who produced a little penknife, cut the string and collected the paper.

Only then, as he shook the Parrot's hand, did I begin to realise what I was looking at.

'See,' said the member of the parrot family, 'it's a lovely edition.'

To all this James paid close attention as if to a game of shuttlecock.

'It is not *verse*,' I cried. 'Not verse.'

'It is Molière.' He shrugged, complacent, half educated in spite of how he mimicked me, not even clever enough to be afraid.

'It is not even a *play*. Did you not read it?'

'Your lordship, look at the pages,' he said. 'Please. It is a treasure.'

And then I saw, of course, he had bought me a pretty picture book. But how could I recite a picture book? It was no use to me at all. Every shopkeeper knows that *L'Impromptu de Versailles* is not even a proper play. The characters have no lines. They admit it themselves. They spend their time worrying that they have no performance for the king. It is all about how Molière will retaliate against his critics, but it ends with the king excusing them the command. There is no verse. There is no play. I knew my face was colouring. I was a beet.

'Dear sir,' said Mr Larrit, forger, thief, murderer, for all I knew. I reached for the whore's purse of a book, a flimflam filigree woven around the great name of Molière, and I thought of the Englishman's alleged pictures of savages and eucalypts. I wrenched the book free of him and made as if to cast it in the coal pit.

'It is a nonsense,' I cried, looking with dismay as the volume, against my wish, rose from my hand like a partridge frightened by beaters before dropping, stone dead, into the Delaware River.

My servant uttered a cry, raw and raucous as a gull. He cast his hat and coat aside and jumped. There was an awful splash. He disappeared.

I thought, Dear God, he's killed himself. I was the French commissioner. I could not be *tainted*.

But the colliers were clapping and the great hawking *bird* rose, spitting, snorting, coughing, holding the book on high, dripping wet, his eyes rimmed red as a kitten.

He would not look at me, not even when James and I pulled him up onto the dock. It was the Negro to whom he entrusted my Molière.

'Here,' said he. 'Protect it.'

And who was he to say protect it, but I gave James a silver dollar to retrieve my property, and thus we boarded the *Zeus*, a very silly pair indeed.

II

That Tuesday morning Captain Cammer's steamboat *Zeus*, carrying sufficient fuel to feed her boilers all the way to New Haven, departed the Crooked Billet Wharf. No matter its name, it proceeded out into the bay like a floating stack of firewood.

The picture was less dire below decks where I followed my servant's dripping path into a large public cabin with curtained windows in the style of a Broadway oyster house. Along the bulkheads on each side were banks of settees that would later be converted into berths. Aft of this cabin was the violent engine compartment, and aft of that two smaller cabins, one of which I engaged for my drowned Englishman who continued to hold his *L'Impromptu de Versailles* away from him (*like a pudding on a tray*, as the purser commented). For myself I took the deluxe cabin, not on account of its size, which was not so considerable, but for the big windows that stretched across the square transom stern.

Here, in this compartment perfectly constructed for the contemplation of the American sublime, was placed the inevitable machine, that awful monument to democratic restlessness – a rocking chair.

Oh Blacqueville, I wish you were here to see these Americans. They are the most turbulent, unpeaceful, least-contented people, far worse than Italians and Greeks. Clearly there is nothing less suited to meditation than democracy. You will never find, as in aristocracies, one class that sits back in its own comfort and another that will not stir itself because it despairs of ever improving its status. In America, everyone is in a state of agitation: some to attain power, others to grab wealth, and when they cannot move, they rock. They dig canals, they tear along the rivers in a rage of machinery, the engines pumping like sawyers in a pit, the shores denuded of their ancient trees. Napoleon restored the fortunes of France by plunder, and a similar economic principle is here being enacted, the mower splintering the scythe, the smokestack eating up the wind. And there will be acres more of it to pillage if Old Hickory has his way.

It is strange, in New York and Philadelphia, to see the feverish enthusiasm which accompanies Americans' pursuit of prosperity and the way they are ceaselessly tormented by the vague fear that they have failed to choose the shortest route to achieve it.

I have it from Duponceau that the restless Benjamin Franklin – who supposedly taught himself five languages, invented bifocal glasses and the lightning rod – is responsible for the awful rocking chair. I had that particular horror removed from the *deluxe* cabin and replaced with a comfortable wing-backed reading chair which would not rock no matter how heavily I sat in it. Having arranged all the papers on my bed, I spread my leather case upon my lap and there, setting all physical excitements aside, prepared to enjoy my memory of she toward whom the churning wheels propelled me.

I first took up the very gracious letter from Mr Godefroy. He wished, he said, to draw me to the other side of Sing Sing so I could witness the authentic Auburn style of penitentiary without the distraction of Mr Elam Lynds and his busy lash. This last comment I understood exactly. He was opposing the threatened cruelty of the Auburn system but was also against the Quakers. He hoped, I read – and this was perhaps the sixth time my eyes had crossed his sentence – that I would be a guest in his own home and make the acquaintance of *those members of my family as yet unknown to you.*

Dear heavens. Dear Miss Godefroy. She had spoken of me.

The door flung open, banging brass on brass. And there was Mr *Stasis* himself, his hair standing high, wearing a comical yellow nightshirt that did not protect one from his bony knees and big raw feet.

'I'm very sorry,' he declared.

Well, thought I, as I appraised the apparition, a kind of Holy Rooster.

'I am extremely sorry,' he said. 'I wished only to serve.'

Serve what? I thought. Dear Lord, look at him.

'I had no clue you wished Molière in bloody *verse*. You did not say so. Sir. You never did.'

'I said *Tartuffe*. Dear fellow.'

'And *Tartuffe* you would have had, but there was not a bloody crumb of him. The old Yankee said he had no call for *Tartuffe*. I did not believe him until he showed me he had almost nothing in the language. It was English floor to ceiling, books of the very worst kind. How to do this. How to do that. And bibles. And arguments about the soul. Shelves of them, and not a word you'd take some pleasure in.'

'You should dry your clothes.'

'I don't give a fart about my clothes. I care about your bloody book.'

'Mr Larrit, you will go away and be very quiet.'

'I am set to save your book,' he said, more quietly, searching in his pockets to no avail.

'If you must, please do it then.'

'Wait, sir. I will convince you yet.'

'Of what?'

'This *Impromptu* is your man.'

Did the idiot think I would take Miss Godefroy walking so I could act out for her a great man's failure?

'No, no, let it rest poor fellow.'

'Ah, but I have discovered sawdust,' he said, and was gone, leaving me with a mystery I had little inclination to investigate.

The book, being ancient and handsomely bound in calfskin, was clearly a fetish. He revered the *objet*, mistaking it for what it contained, an embarrassing misunderstanding such as the Negro James had suffered when he took that gentleman's black hat and placed it on his own grizzled head. Thinking himself elevated, he became comic. So it was with the agitated Mr Stasis and his *L'Impromptu de Versailles*.

At the same time I was touched by his remorse. It was the first sign he had ever given that he truly wished to serve me, and it suggested a happier prospect for the days and weeks when we would collate the pages of my interviews, transcribe them, and begin the first rough ordering of the French commissioner's report. I returned to my study of the character of Mr Lynds, who had placed a cut-throat razor in a murderer's hands and ordered the felon to shave him before the assembled prisoners.

'Sir.'

The Great Bird of the Antipodes had returned, dressed once more in a grey waistcoat although without his hat or shoes.

'There is no staining,' he announced.

'Staining?'

'Your pages will be saved. They are ready to be ironed.'

And off he went, barefooted, and I felt him running along the centreboard of the ship.

By the time he returned, the last of the sunset lay on the waters of Long Island Sound and I had lit my lantern and tried a taste of ginger wine. He stood at the cabin door, dressed in his frockcoat and wearing shoes. In his hand he held the edition I had been so very disappointed by.

'Sir?'

'Please enter.'

He stood before me, opening its pages one by one, and – had he been my butler and had the pages been, say, shirts – I would have been impressed with the rescue he had undertaken.

'You see sir,' said he. 'It is a beauty.'

'You are a clever fellow.'

He took my compliment solemnly. 'I know paper, sir,' he said, squatting down beside my chair. I had not the tiniest interest in that rare failure of Molière's, and yet I looked at what he showed me for as an *objet* one must admit it was a well-made one, the calf covers being gilt-tooled with a flower in each corner and a triple fillet.

'What chance to find this in America,' he said, peering as I expected at the engraving, a depiction of five actors on a stage.

'It is Holland paper,' I observed.

He smiled at me, so sweetly I hardly knew the man. 'Indeed,' said he. 'The engraver is Gravelot, but perhaps you also saw the crest.'

Americans were always drawing my attention to escutcheons. So I looked with condescension, I suppose, and was slow to understand that I was looking at the Bourbon coat of arms.

'You see sir.'

'I do,' I admitted, but hid my true astonishment, for this book was from the library of a Bourbon king.

'His Majesty liked it no better than you do,' he said, now having his turn to be amused by me.

'How much did I pay for this?'

'Two dollars, but it does not suit your purpose.'

'My purpose is my own private business.'

'You forget, sir, you told me your purpose. You wished to read the lines to Miss Godefroy.'

'I cannot read her lines from this, you puppy.'

'Of course you can.'

'Do not be impudent.'

'Of course, you know how to do your own business.'

'You think otherwise? Then show me how I would court her. What do you suggest?'

'Well, you tell the story.'

'The story of the play? It is nothing.'

'No, how you sent your stupid English servant to buy *Tartuffe*. He is an ignoramus.' He raised an eyebrow and waited.

'Go on.'

'The servant has no culture as you would expect. He returns with this ridiculous play. He has paid two dollars, more than it is worth. But then you discover it is from the library of your cousin the king.'

'Not my cousin.'

'Relation, no relation – it matters not a fig. You think, Has the rascal *stolen* it from the king? And do you know, my dear sweet American lady – you will whisper – Molière and his troupe in the play, the actors are characters, have been asked to perform for this very king. The one who rightly owns the book. Louis Quatorze.'

'Your French is awful.'

'In fact it is better than your own.'

'You will not tutoyer me! Tell me, clown, how can I recite this to Miss Godefroy?'

'You tell her how I performed it for you. You say, Miss Godefroy, dear,' and the rascal jumped three feet sideways. 'You see. This is how I do the different parts.'

'Now here is Mrs Molière.' He jumped a foot the other way. 'Where is everyone?' he cried.

'What?'

'I am playing all the parts,' he said, and jumped again. 'Molière is first onstage. He is calling for the actors – he shouts, Where is everyone?'

'Coming.' The Parrot jumped.

'Not here.' The Parrot jumped again.

'What's the matter with you?' He leaped back sideways and crashed against the cabin wall.

'You see,' he said, 'it is very athletic. You should do something that displays your calves.'

'This is not at all romantic,' I said. 'I am a French aristocrat. She does not want me to be a clown.'

'No, but it is funny, sir. You must admit that. You are smiling.'

'You want me to be a figure of fun.'

'She knows you are an aristocrat. What do you plan to do with her? She liked you. She will laugh. She will fall down laughing. Then you do the rest,' he said, drinking the dreadful ginger wine in a single gulp.

'It will take five hours to perform.'

'It is a short play.'

'Two hours.'

'Ah.' He raised a finger, and there was something very lively in those opaline eyes. 'Now your lordship is boasting.'

Just as I admitted that his company had become enjoyable, something clouded his expression.

'Is your wife well?' I asked.

'Fit as a scrub bull,' said he, a curious expression.

'The old lady?'

'Well also.'

'You were very comic, Mr Larrit. Where did you learn to read?'

'I learned from my father very young. He was a compositor.'

'I have it on good authority,' I remarked, 'that the compositor's genius is to recognise the letters without understanding a single word.'

'And who is your authority, my lord?'

'The comte d'Auvergne, I believe.'

'It is not true.'

He stood for a moment, looking out into the dark, and I realised I had spoiled what had been a very pleasant mood indeed.

'Perhaps you will settle in America,' I offered.

He held his hand close against the lantern to show me – what? That he had no wedding band? That his eyes were mirrors? That I should see some awful secret written on his leathern liver-spotted skin?

III

Clearly I did not lack curiosity about my fellow men, but my intuitions and sympathies were limited by the circumstances of my birth. A person like my servant was a foreign land, so although I might *very sincerely* wish to imagine him, how might I begin?

This question became more pressing when, after a dinner of fatty goose, Master Larrit carried a bottle of brandy to my room and made it clear that he and I should *shoot the breeze*.

'If only there were a chair for you.'

He shoved the papers to one side and sat himself on the edge of my bed. Then, holding up a forefinger in the manner of a low clown at a village fête, he produced a heavy tumbler from one pocket, holding it high between us while he poured a considerable amount. Continuing in the same broad style, he produced a second glass, and then generously rewarded himself with what was clearly cognac.

The first act done, he tossed the bottle on the bed.

We drank.

We smiled.

I thanked him.

But what next?

It was evident we must converse – he was set on it, he *demanded* it – but he clearly had no notion of how this game was played in society. So we were left toasting each other, with no commentary except that provided by the rude engine as it moaned and groaned and sent its endless *révolutions industrielles* to agitate our feet.

Still rather in the manner of an entertainer, he folded his ankle and rested it on his knee and one was left wondering what canary he would next produce.

'So,' he said at last, 'it is courting you go?'

As so often, I did not understand him immediately, but then I was all the more shocked by the personal nature of his inquiry. I had revealed far too much to him already, and thus I now rushed from his impertinent particular to the safety of the general. I asked him what his impressions were of American women.

He smiled and said he was a married man.

'They walk alone a good deal,' I encouraged.

'Oh yes,' he said, 'you will come upon them everywhere, or with their young fellows. Courting,' he said, grinning broadly so that I was almost certain he was imagining me with Miss Godefroy at Peek's farm.

'They enjoy a great deal of freedom,' I said. 'As married women they abandon it.'

'Ah, do they now?' said he. 'I would not know.'

'On the contrary,' I said. 'You are a married man, as you just observed. And you were married once before, you said. You had a child.' If this was cruel, it was no more than the cruelty of the bit we place in a stallion's mouth. It did its work.

'Aye,' he said, and rubbed at his turbulent hair.

In fact I did not wish to punish him but rather to ask, Who are you? With my own kind I would never have made so artless an entrée, but to him I said, 'There is a great deal to you, John Larrit.'

He considered me. 'It is a wonder how many lives a man can hold within his skin,' he said at last. 'I never expected to be quit of any of them. I never expected there would be a change, do you understand me? I have been a cork in the ocean, sir.' He smiled again, and I thought what a hell it must be to have no expectation of yourself, nothing but this endless, rootless freedom in which the bonds of family and responsibility could be so easily brushed aside.

'It was your father who was transported. The forger.'

'You do not listen,' he said fiercely. 'My father was a good man. He was funny and kind and *full of birds* as we used to say. He was my home. I thought the paths I walked with him would be my life. The birds and trees and weather of a particular place. I have never deliberately quit on anyone.'

'And where was that particular place?'

'In England.' He would reveal no more to me than that. 'I was transported by misadventure,' he said. 'You should understand. Your voyage to America was pretty much the same, I think. In my case they made a convict child of me, and I seemed doomed never to leave my exile. As it turned out, it would be in exile I would find my consolation.'

I assumed he meant his wife and child, but no.

'I could make art, you see. After a fashion.'

'You made illustrations,' I said, remembering the book in Duponceau's library. He looked at me sharply. 'I admit they were rough,' he said, at last. 'I was looked up to, but only for the lack of men who could do it any better. My master could not draw a chicken. My only decent teacher was a book of engravings owned by Mrs Paterson, but it was not fine. I could have done better. I knew I could do better.'

'Do you think there may be, in any case, a problem with art in a democracy?'

'Democracy? Jesus. Excuse me, sir. You cannot call a jail a democracy. It was a dictatorship, a cruel one too. They did not transport a man for showing at the Royal Academy.'

His glass was empty, but he filled mine first. The lantern had begun to sway.

'Very well,' I said, speaking as to an equal, 'but did you not observe the paintings on the walls of Philadelphia? They made me think that the taste for ideal beauty – and the pleasure of seeing it depicted – can never be as intense or widespread among a democratic as compared to an aristocratic people.'

'So you look at art, then?' he asked, and for a nasty moment I thought he was sneering at me. 'You own a canvas or two yourself, I suppose?'

'I was privileged to be born in a house of art.'

'Great painters, sir. Hanging everywhere you looked.'

'Indeed,' I said, and wondered if this weight of wealth and culture pained him.

'Turner's father was a barber,' he said suddenly. 'A plain old barber with a wart on his nose.'

'Turner?'

'An English painter.'

'Where did that thought come from?' I asked, amused by the wart as much as anything.

He tapped his forehead with his glass.

'You are correct, it is a privilege. I had a house in Woollahra,' he offered, rolling his tongue around the savage name. 'At night-time people came to be painted. As a result of Mrs Paterson's book I had too much attachment to chiaroscuro effects, but I was popular enough.'

I was embarrassed by the enormity of his misunderstanding. He stared at me, then drained the glass and held it beneath the swaying lantern studying a tear of alcohol as it rolled along below the rim.

'With brandy,' he said, 'there is always one last drop.'

Warily, I raised my glass.

'And you,' he said to me directly. 'Who are you?'

I thought, Here it is.

'You, sir, had one life, all of a piece, not a bobbing cork. Just the same, it aches in certain weathers, as if you were born with a shattered bone and had it healed.'

I did not know what he meant. I thought, How does he know this?

'Anyway,' he said, 'the damned marquis de Tilbot came to fetch me.'

'In Paris.'

'In Sydney. He had not seen me since I was a boy. That's right, a boy. He walks into the government architect's office and says, "Ah, there you are," as if he had seen me yesterday. "I promised I would return," said he, and I was pleased! Can you imagine. I was *pleased*. He was a big posh Frenchman with his sunburned skull now growing through his hair. He flattered my work. He needed me, he reckoned. I must come with him to botanise for the Empress Josephine – or she who had been empress. Can you imagine saying that to me? Just that word, sir. *Empress*.'

'What year was this then?'

'I was a fool. I thought I was being elevated. But I always believed I would return. I promised her.'

I would have cross-examined him, but he sighed and reached

across the bed where I had placed my papers. He then took up a single sheet which he laid on my tray and, taking a crayon, began to draw, frowning and showing his teeth. He occasionally wet his thumb in brandy and smudged at what he drew. He looked up, cocked a brow, returned to it. I wondered if I was being honoured with a portrait. I thought, He will not flatter me.

'Soon I will turn in,' I said.

He nodded.

'You understand,' he said, 'that she is what they call a genius.'

'She?' I laughed.

'She, Mathilde.' He looked up and held my eye again in that clear alarming way. 'The one who made your hanging johnny hard.'

I must never drink with him again, I thought. In the darkness I could hear the surf breaking on the American shore.

'A genius?'

'She paints only the light,' he said fiercely. 'There is nothing else for her.' He held up the sheet of paper. It was a woman's face, but not Mathilde at all.

'This is all I can do,' he said. 'I have no ability no matter how I work.'

I was, in spite of everything, impressed, not only with the portrait – a girl of twenty with a great deal of curling unkempt hair – but in the urgency and agony he brought to its execution. It was not art in the educated sense of the word, for it was really too disturbing – the whole, in its rush and incompleteness.

I thought, This represents the mother of his child. Her lip is swollen. She has been crying.

I understood that he was offering it to me, but as I reached to accept the gift, he snarled suddenly, showing the whole pink line of upper gum. His canines all exposed, he balled the portrait in his fist and threw it out into the night.

Later I heard him making an awful clatter in his cabin.

IV

When we finally crested the hill which had provided the last obstacle to my heart's desire, I understood, from the calm authority of the estate before me – its aesthetic balance, the good order of its fences, the clean white clusters of its barn and stables, its gardeners' cottages – and from the clearly expressed democratic idealism of the house, the nature of Miss Godefroy's inheritance.

My companion, until now rather sullen beneath his blanket, offered comment.

'My,' said he. 'You've fallen on your feet.'

Thus as always – just as one's sympathies were most engaged by him.

It was now November in Connecticut, and the savage splendour of the autumn had burned away. The soft maples were bare. Only a few apple trees held out green. An overcast sky gave a lovely grey flatness to a pond.

Approaching along the smooth pink road that swept so sweetly through the sward, it seemed I had finally stumbled on what New York and Philadelphia had refused to show, that secret centre of the new nation, that part that answered to its highest possibility. The Doric columns of the mansion seemed well earned for being so clearly thought, the statement of an aspiration, both noble and democratic. And I was not unamused, in the midst of this, to reflect that it had been a pretty ankle that had led me on, a generous bosom that brought me sweeping down this road, trotting toward the orchard, around the pond, to the long rolling sward across which a young woman ran and jumped, a fine athletic movement, as if it were not only the architecture but the body itself that spoke to the ancient Greek ideal. Her, in fact. Herself.

Old Farm, as it was modestly known, was such a delightful expression of America that I missed dear Blacqueville with whom

I might have dissected and reassembled its significance and who, even when lighthearted, would have had a great deal more to offer than English sarcasm.

Of the fellow I was about to meet I knew only what Duponceau had told me. Mr Philip Godefroy was of a southern family famously split among themselves on the subject of their own extraction, one party determined it was French, the opposition convinced they were Swedish Godfrids. Thus, they seemed to me, pretty representative of all Americans in that their connections with the past were of so little substance that they could be shaped and described almost any way they liked. Mrs Godefroy I understood to be an Englishwoman, perhaps of noble family. Duponceau had not been sure, but was certain that neither husband nor wife – both being busily involved in perfecting and improving what they saw around them – attached the least importance to crests or escutcheons. They were both restlessly opposed to slavery and in favour of universal suffrage. Mr Godefroy had attended Yale College and graduated a doctor but had never practised medicine having conceived a very definite theory about society and its relationship with nature, an idea made concrete by the *porch*, on which subject he would later occupy me in many hours of inquiry and conjecture. So although a porch might seem a small enough thing to you, in Godefroy's scheme it was at once a physical structure, a delineation of vast space and also a metaphor. The importance of the porch was such that not only the rich should have the luxury of enjoying nature but also the common man. In fact, he saw it as a kind of social engine, one which, when properly designed, would help a mechanic or farmer or labourer become more virtuous and educated.

It would be beneath a grander Grecian version of this humble appendage where I would meet my very erudite and handsome host and also feel my cheeks warmed by the presence of she who I affected to be unaware of.

She was taller than I had remembered, and although she had just returned from chasing with her dog and had a twig in her hair and a scratch on her cheek, she was far more pretty than I had dared remember.

Amelia – I do believe I never heard her Christian name mentioned by the Peeks – easily negotiated those social rapids created by Mr Larrit's ambivalent position – neither upstairs nor downstairs and sarcastic in between. She had a boy carry his duffel and billeted him in one of the bedrooms on the second floor, which, in the American fashion, were tucked in two low-ceilinged storeys behind the soaring reception rooms that distinguished the face of the house.

I did not thank her. I did not say a word to her. Instead, I furiously interrogated her father about the uses of the lash in Wethersfield. The dog licked my hand. I did not feel him. It required all my host's grace and humour to rescue me from myself, placing me in the care of his elderly manservant who, so Mrs Godefroy said fondly, laying her hand on the old man's shoulder, had begun heating water for my bath the moment he spied the dust of my coach 'back at Taylor's Flat'.

He had not been the only one working so assiduously for my arrival, for when I reached the room I found not only the steaming bath but also, on my bedside table, a copy of *Tartuffe*. I thought, She loves me. I kissed the pillow like a fool, inhaled the familial, familiar dust and wax. She will be mine, you are too far away to stop me.

V

Dear Little Mother, I hope by now you have all my letters from Philadelphia, and my account of the history of the servant you engaged for me. On this matter, I have a great deal to say, but as the days go by I become less certain of what that is, and as we have arrived at Wethersfield, Connecticut, I am hoping to have a vacation from his company.

We are at the house of Mr Philip Godefroy, a member of the Wethersfield Prison Board, which was the reason for my seeking him out, although this now seems to be the least of his accomplishments. He is the most naturally distinguished man I have met in America. He is well versed in all the political questions which interest his country and possesses the most precise understanding of the judiciary institutions of the United States.

I now spend all my time with him in conversations from which I have everything to gain. As soon as I am alone I write down what he has said. I have not yet met a single other person from whom I have drawn nearly so much. There are at his house three charming women, his wife and his daughters, Amelia and Catherine. Catherine is barely ten, but Amelia is closer to my own age and would give me terrible distractions if I had not, once and for all, made up my mind to have none. The two girls both have that white and rose complexion, occasionally to be found in Englishwomen but quite unknown in France. I have not yet seen in the United States such a velvet softness. It is impossible to describe. But why talk so long about her? Were I to continue you would think me in love, and the truth is I am not. In any case, I expect to be here another three or four days and by then I do not doubt she will have sung for me and, as on those other occasions, made my considerable willpower quite unnecessary.

I was, while in Philadelphia, entertained by a very wealthy and prominent family, all in such style you would never think yourself at the end of the earth. But the music. These people are, without contradiction, the most unhappily organised *in matters of harmony*. What the young ladies who regale me with this *musique miaulante* affect most are its difficult passages. You must think I speak of this subject with a sort of indignation, and that is so, but you must understand it is not simply the displeasure caused by detestable music but the feeling of moral violence to which one is subjected when forced to listen willy-nilly and to appear *pleased* as well.

So, my dear mother, you may rest assured that your Olivier has no plan to alarm you with an American wife. Ha. I know you never said so, but I know your heart, and I can tell it. Please be calm.

This evening or the next Mr Godefroy is to take me to the town of Wethersfield where I will attend a meeting of the citizens to elect their local officials. As this is in the State of Connecticut I do wonder if they will sing their state song, of which I now provide for you, dear comtesse, a small sample:

> *Yankee Doodle went to town,*
> *A-riding on a pony;*
> *He stuck a feather in his hat*
> *And called it macaroni.*

Olivier

PARROT

In the morning the mansion was colonised by children as numerous as rabbits, their boots slamming like horses' hooves along the
hallways. Everywhere I turned there was a Godefroy cousin or a
Godefroy neighbour, even some scholars from the local school where
the teacher had just broke her leg, they said, so her pupils had walked
six miles to Miss Godefroy to have their lessons. I would prefer to
be away from children, always. When, later, I chanced upon one
melancholy boy throwing stones against the outhouse, I felt a pain
like a corkscrew to my heart.

He has grown up without me.

Mine own.

Full well I know the anguish of the soul that knows not me.

II

Miss Godefroy poured tea for Olivier. She was like a willy-wagtail,
I thought, lifting up her feathers and singing, bless her. A bird in

the hand, bush too, her eyes alight, her laughter everywhere. *Come let us adore him*, Olivier de Garmont, the same cove who would die without his *Tartuffe*, who would destroy his *Impromptu*, who could not sleep for thinking of Miss Godefroy. Might not such a love-fuddled soul see a tiny chance to further things?

Well sir, no sir. I never saw a fellow go about his courting in such a wrongheaded way. He took one sip of milky tea, then marched off the porch in the company of the *father*.

'Well, Mr Larrit,' Miss Godefroy said to me, her pretty face revealing no particular sign of anything. 'I have work to do.' She also left the stage and soon I heard her fussing with the cook, ordering a donkey and cart be provided for the onion maidens, taking the abandoned children in control and setting them on their bottoms in the great reception room where she got them singing their times tables, all these things and more being done not all at once but over a period of time, at the end of which I heard a sad cello which I knew must be her own. I never listened to so heartrending a cry. Not even a Church of England organ could make you feel such misery.

I stepped off the porch and wandered round the back of the mansion where I smoked a pipe too bitter for much pleasure. I saw the splendid cattle. I noted the black alluvial soil which was devoted to the industry of onions. I beheld the so-called *onion maidens* labouring in Mr Godefroy's river flats. It was soon made clear to me that these were worldly women, very sure of their attractions. In any case, I was required in the library.

The two gentlemen were already awaiting me, facing each other from their leather club chairs. They gave no sign of hearing the plaintive cello.

Godefroy was as good-looking as an admiral. He had one of those voices you can hear across a running brook, but he had a nice set of wrinkles around his eyes and he looked straight at a man, this man, and shook his hand, not limply or (like poor Duponceau) too firmly. Was that his daughter fiddling her poor heart out?

'Here,' said he. 'Sit here.'

I had been provided a walnut table and straight-backed chair.

'I was in correspondence with Judge Welles,' my lovesick master began, and I set about my dreary dictation and wondered where exactly the cello was situated. I placed it in the open doorway between the hallway and the dining room.

'Ah, yes, Welles,' said Godefroy, frowning at the double doors. 'You will enjoy him.'

'Mr Welles has written that it is possible that a prison with five hundred inmates could make a profitable return to the state. This would be an attractive proposition to my government.'

The cello stopped. Then recommenced. There had been a creaking floorboard. From this and other evidence, I reckoned the musician had crept as close as the grandfather clock. It was a wild imagining: Miss Godefroy performing from outside the pale.

'We will look at the judge's arithmetic,' said her father. 'I do not recall a remarkable profit, but you must understand that at Wethersfield these things are looked at in relation to our onion crop.'

My master responded with an awful frown, all nose and brow, poor fellow.

'In Connecticut,' Mr Godefroy said, 'you will witness things you could not imagine in old Europe.'

Hear, hear, I thought. My master inclined his head, but when he looked up again he held me with his gaze and his cheeks were burning red.

Was it embarrassment drove Godefroy to snatch the onion from the windowsill? In any case, he was swift as a rat in the moonlight, opening his silver penknife, making two quick cuts, and removing from the onion's heart a good single slice, about a quarter-inch thick. This he held up between thumb and forefinger before the window.

'Is it not beautiful in the sunshine?'

How awful, cried the cello.

'Indeed,' said Olivier.

'You will think it a peculiar lens through which to view the world.'

'It is singular.'

'It is the robes of saints, do you see it? No? It is cool and watery-white edged with bishop's purple. And look, Mr Garmont, at that fiery nub of spring green at its centre.'

Mr Garmont stood, perhaps to be better convinced of its majesty.

'Now,' cried Godefroy, 'look further at the industry this humble fellow fathers.'

Outside the window I could see the onion maidens everywhere, their thighs and ankles, their straw bonnets bright against the dark black soil, the cello dark and urgent in its longing. Surely someone must say something.

Olivier squinted out the window, blind as a bat.

I cried loudly, 'Ah, your onion maidens.'

'A pretty sight, no?' inquired his host.

'Indeed,' said my employer, squinting more.

'I refer to the bonnets of course.' Godefroy laughed. 'And let me tell you about them. They came into existence because President Madison desired that we turn ourselves into a nation of manufacturers.'

The music stopped. There was a clatter with some bounce in it. I imagined a bow being thrown down the hallway. The host's story was then recited in a great sarcastic silence.

'This request,' said Mr Godefroy, 'was heard by a nineteen-year-old girl in Wethersfield. She looked at the spear grass which was growing around, free for her, requiring no capital. She harvested the grass. Then she boiled it, bleached it, moistened, fumigated and dried it to make it suitable for braiding. Then she made what are called Leghorn-style bonnets.'

'Might this be something that can be profitably undertaken by prisoners?'

'By prisoners? Oh no sir. What a waste. Her name is Sophia Cunningham and she is now a wealthy manufacturer. She has a patent for her invention. Can you imagine such a thing in France? She has changed her position in life entirely.'

At this point the cello resumed in dire complaint.

'Excuse me,' said Godefroy, returning to his feet. 'You shall see Wethersfield this evening.'

He left the room and as he did so the cello stopped. Olivier looked at me, his cheeks flushed, his neck red, and bestowed upon me – a wicked grin.

Godefroy returned and took his seat and I spent a long boring afternoon recording how the town meetings of Connecticut were conducted, on what their laws were based, how elections were held, to what degree the federal government affected their affairs, and how the *completely uneducated* majority in town meetings were stopped from tyrannising our host.

III

We had an early tea. Not a thing to drink but Adam's ale, which turned out to be water. Little Catherine asked the noble how did he like the French Revolution and his lordship told a story that made them all weep, Miss Amelia most of all. For God's sake, I thought, *attend* to her!

To me she said, 'It must be extraordinary to be his friend.'

After which she revealed that I, John Larrit, was expected to attend a town meeting with the Godefroys that evening. This was her father's wish for me. I thought, I want a drink. I thought, Who is he to give me orders? I was sour as a lemon tree when we came outside to find our carriages but then, in the twilight, I spied the courting count about to hop up into Mr Godefroy's slick two-seater. Enough, thought I, *go to her.* I knocked him so hard with my shoulder he nearly fell upon his arse.

He gathered himself and dusted down his bright blue frockcoat and patted at his ruff. I could have punched his pointy nose.

'Hello!' He cocked his head at me. 'What is it old chap?'

'Look to, mate, *look* to. You were stepping in the wrong carriage.' I meant he should sit in *her* carriage.

'You are an idiot,' said he.

I was a *what*? I pushed him in the chest. He staggered back two steps.

Godefroy descended from his gig and came toward me with his arm held out as if I were a horse in need of shooting. He got my collar and I shook him off, and all the time my eyes stayed on my so-called master.

All those weeping, prattling messages to New York and back. For Christ's sake, sir, get *in* the carriage. I was ready to give my notice.

'Now see here, Mr Larrit,' began Godefroy, and I thought I would knee his onions for him.

'No,' cried Olivier. 'He has had bad news.'

I thought, *Godefroy* has bad news? But then I understood it was me he was talking of. I thought, No, I bloody haven't.

'Is that not so?' he insisted, and held my eye.

I thought, Is he saying I am dismissed?

'That is true, John, is it not?'

'Yes sir, it is.'

Thus, my rage was explained and excused as simply as a case of measles, and everything continued as it had before. That is, Olivier de Garmont entered the racing coach of Mr Philip Godefroy, and I was put in with Miss Godefroy. What use was she to me? There were several snotty little scholars and her sister packed in as well, bringing with them a damp musty smell, a natural product of their occupation.

Miss Godefroy said, 'I am sorry about your news.'

'Thank you, Miss.'

'Is it terribly bad?'

'Yes, Miss.'

She sighed and sat with her hands clasped in her lap, and as the carriage set off I caught her perfume, very light, like an orange grove at evening, and there was no bad news but I set myself imagining that I must really have bad news and I thought only of Mathilde, and how I would die if I lost her. I was a fool to leave her side to serve the aristocracy. I read Tom Paine by candlelight, but for eighteen hours a day I was a vassal.

I would go home to Mathilde, I thought, as the carriage rocked me gently against Miss Godefroy and I could, through no fault of my own, feel the pressure of her upper leg or worse. I would turn in my notice. Olivier's courting was no concern of mine. When we arrived at the meeting hall I could have walked away into the night, but I followed them inside, still in the service of the Lord.

It had been my life's achievement to make myself into someone who could work no useful trade at all, to be secretary to a French noble, a messenger, not even a servant, not even a clerk, not anything you could describe, not an artist – although I might have been – a pimp for art perhaps.

These bilious thoughts bred amid the smell of leaf mould and autumn smoke. All around us lanterns bobbed, like a gathering of giant glow-worms emerging from the streets and flooding from the windows of the meeting hall, a church in fact, with its great white steeple shining in the night.

This was the kind of society the Dit'sum printers had envisaged, a kind of dream, and this was the country built on that dream, what Gunner and Weasel and Chooka and Chanker had discussed in the dusk at Piggott's printery. Yet we had never thought to see a church involved. Indeed, you could search all of England and never see the like. It was all wood: fine carpentry, and perfect mitre joints, and dowelling plugs instead of nails, and what was not painted pure white was plain waxed timber and the whole of its lower floors – for it had an upper – had its pews all divided up like a series of cages, each with a door. I was inclined to think of a chicken house, except it was not like this at all, and all the town – there must have been a thousand citizens – pushed in and sat in their places and there was a great certainty – a clarity, a plainness – which spoke well of them in spite of the religious aspect.

There was no stained glass, just clear panes, as if you might be expected to look out and witness the saints kneeling on the lawn beside the baker or the library.

There was no pew named Parrot. I abandoned Miss Godefroy to her friends, aunts and children on her lap. They asked me to be with them but I was better by myself. I had grown up hard and solitary beneath the stars, that was our conceit, mine and my da's, that we were not people who hid the wonder of the universe with ceilings, like a cloth across a cage.

At this moment I witnessed the arrival of Olivier de Garmont in the church. He was not higher than Godefroy's shoulder but he seemed to give off a certain light. Doubtless the blue jacket surrounded by so much black and grey. His bright white ruff, but something else, a glowing skin, an elegance of manner – *aristocratic! call it that!* – he bowed and moved as if he were a visitation, a most glorious apparition, being taken in, moved from one hand to the next, to the centre of their hive, and I was jealous of them, their bonneted wives, their church, I hated it.

And thus I sat, the sole occupant of the pew, and listened as their selectmen reported to them, and as they all – and it did seem like all – had something to say about the collection of a tax, or the new assessment for the school, and the question of those who must make their payment in kind. I never heard such boring tripe in all my life.

It was moved that the ground be broken in spring.

It was moved that the tax be raised in advance.

It was moved that the government road should stop at the township border.

Every time I thought it was the end, there was more, and the people of Wethersfield were never in a rush so even when the old boy stood up to explain how the town could patent the onion, and even when they explained to him the onion was the work of God and therefore not included in the patents, and even when he explained that these onions had their distinctive nature on account of his father and uncle who had 'bred them up like lambs', no one moved to throttle him.

As was common, my seat had been made by someone who disapproved of sitting and by the time Godefroy stood and introduced the French commissioner, there was no feeling in my bum.

But Olivier, Lord Migraine. He was aglow, his cheeks red, wreathed in smiles. He wiped the corner of his eye. He declared, good grief, he had come home. It was the greatest evening of his life. And when he left they made a space and he came down toward me in all his glory like a bride.

OLIVIER

By the time of our arrival in Connecticut, the once detestable Parrot could have no other name than Friend. He was certainly imperfect, as friends must always be, often very irritating, but he had aligned himself against the mob, suffered both jail and Philadelphia, ministered to my pain, and made me laugh. When, on the carriage-way of Old Farm, he pushed me violently, in full view of our hosts, I knew myself the object of a strange and savage love.

My noble blood urged me tell him, *All is well dear old fellow, I have caught her eye, she has brushed my hand,* and yet every single action I performed was calculated to hide from him the truth.

He was my most unusual friend, but he had first been the marquis's man, and he could not possibly have occupied this post so long without honestly delivering what was asked of him. As was clear on the first night I saw him in Versailles, he was a specialised creation. Under the marquis's influence he had become convict, maid, architect, cartographer and botanist, although never anything but what the marquis wanted. He may have been an ultra-royalist spy. He had been Monsieur's clerk and *secrétaire*. He had, this very year in Paris, packed his trunk with carbon paper, and who knows what other *matériel de l'espionnage*. He had been dispatched to America to protect me, yes, but also the Garmont name, a task that involved, more than anything, alerting my mother to affairs of the heart.

As I hope I have made clear, my mother was a religious woman, an ultra-royalist and an aristocrat, but in certain matters she could be as shockingly direct as a peasant. She would never ask her servant, Is Olivier enjoying himself, but rather *Is she a Protestant?* and *Ont-ils baisé?*

In my letters I could make the most exquisite American woman appear repulsive to her eyes, but I could not expect M. Perroquet to dissemble on my behalf.

I had already been careless and indiscreet, but until we arrived at the top of the hill and looked down across Old Farm, and I beheld the great acres and gentle hills spread before us, and the arm and elbow of the Connecticut River embracing the onion fields, the deep alluvial soil, the fat red Friesians at pasture, only then – well before the town meeting – did I realise how seriously my courtship might be taken. This was not Versailles. It was not a question of crossing the boulevard de la Reine in search of *les plaisirs anglais*.

Thus I had entered Old Farm with that prickling feeling in my neck, such a *frisson* as when walking tipsy along the high walls of the Seine at night. When I heard the cello I knew I could easily fall and break my neck.

In brushing this young woman's hot hand I was flirting with something that was unimaginable, and if I had fallen in love with America generally, then I was both engaged and disturbed by the daring and beauty of Amelia Godefroy. I found myself almost numb with desire and terror. At any serious level, such a liaison would be unthinkable, but there was no other level from which to choose.

To arrange to meet and talk together in private would, in France, have been a matter of some complication, but America was not France. In the United States, Protestant doctrines combined with a very free constitution and a very democratic social state; in no other country was a girl left so soon or so entirely to look after herself. There were no chaperones to deceive. There was no great difficulty in arranging to walk with Amelia Godefroy. I did not misunderstand this walk at all, for in truth I had gone on certain other walks and had observed that the American girl never completely ceases to be in control of herself. She enjoys all the permitted pleasures without losing her head to any of them. And her reason does not loosen the reins even though she often seems to hold them loosely.

In short, I had no one to deceive but my own servant who would still be sleeping at the hour appointed.

The morning was cool, and the ghostly cattle walked in a blanket of mist which lay across Amelia Godefroy's own small herb garden and wrapped itself around her pastel cloak. Her raw woollen bonnet revealed a perfect oval face with very definite brows. Her nose, she might forgive me saying, was somewhat pink, but that was as befitted the climate, and it was a very nicely shaped nose sitting attentively above a perfectly swollen upper lip. She had been cutting thyme as I approached, but now she set her basket on the stile.

For a moment neither of us said anything, and in that extraordinarily familiar silence, a dove cooed. She laughed frankly, then was embarrassed and drew on her gloves.

'Perhaps I can show you my father's landscaping. It is best I call it that, or else you might not notice that anything had been done. My father,' she said, not caring to hide the mischief in her eyes, 'wishes to prove that man can be civilised without geometry. He has a thesis' – how I *adored* that lip – 'but it is much more pleasant to walk through the landscape than listen to its explanation.'

Soon the pair of us were plunging into the Godefroys' neglected grasses which were, in all their autumnal collapse, an extraordinary contrast to his barbered trees. These last he had gathered in two elegant platoons of perhaps twenty each, standing at attention in a field of late mown grass. The design allowed low-lying reddish shrubs to exist in a territory between the wild and the cultivated, and these were arranged with borders which sometimes pushed their way like a coastline into the lawn and at other times into wild grass. In this same mood the master had embraced the natural forests, added water features, paths, and carriage roads, all in a way that would blend in with the natural beauty. Even the gardeners' cottages seemed to grow out of the natural surroundings. In my mind I saw my mother's eyes, as they might, in appalled triumphant secret, seek mine across a dinner table.

Miss Godefroy had led me to the tamped yellow path along the river. 'Tell me where you live,' she asked. The path was so narrow we must be careful not to bump each other and we were as careful and careless as you might expect. 'I have never been to France. I cannot imagine what it must be like.'

'We live very much in the past, I fear.' I spoke not *quite* sincerely, for I affected to mock my country, a bad habit for a French commissioner, but one learned on the job. And yet I spoke truly for we French had not yet cleared a way forward from the past. We were stuck in the slough between what had been and what might be possible, and whatever avenue we sought was mired with mud and blood and the horrors of misrule. We fiddled here. We fiddled there. And all the while the great lava flow of democracy came inexorably toward us.

'I was thinking last night of your fields,' she said softly, 'and how they have surely been farmed for centuries, so there must be – am I right? – a certain softness to the contours, even the hedges and ditches.'

When last night had she thought this? Lying in her bed? My ditches.

We pushed on along the river, heedless of where we might arrive. Yes, I thought, she imagines our fields very well. 'Your town meeting rather shook me to my bones,' I said. 'I am still reverberating.'

I thought, I should not have said reverberating. I might as well say I dreamed about her all night long.

I felt myself blushing, which of course only made it worse. 'What exactly are we discussing, Miss Godefroy?'

'Democracy in America,' she said. 'You were interrogating me.'

'Very well.' I smiled. 'Does the government never subdue your town? Do they not think this association dangerous?'

'There is always danger everywhere.' She smiled.

I said, 'But your town meeting is an old practice? You have never clashed with the central government?'

'Our fathers founded the town before the state. There were Wethersfield town meetings before there was a United States.'

'Then I have a question. It may be impertinent.'

'Oh please *do* be impertinent.' She laid a hand again upon my arm. 'No one is ever impertinent in Wethersfield.'

'Was it a town meeting that tried and convicted your witches?' This was what Blacqueville would have called a *blurter*. I said it only because it had been much on my mind. 'I am sorry. I have been ill-mannered.'

'On the contrary,' she said kindly. 'I have been too light and frivolous. Those women were murdered by a theocracy. There was no democracy involved. It was a terror, but not an American terror.'

If she had been briefly cool, then she was cool no longer. Her eyes were bright and liquid. I thought, Good heavens, here she is.

She said, 'Who could not be moved by the fate of your dear grandfather?'

Not for the first time was I taken aback by the lucky boldness with which these American girls could steer their thoughts through the reefs of lively conversation.

'Of course,' she said, 'we are not grand or cultivated. We must seem very provincial to you.'

I thought, What does she feel?

'A little provincialism is very much to be desired,' I said, then saw her blush. 'In France,' I insisted, 'we have suffered from centralism: the revolution, Bonaparte, you see.'

'You will have what you desire,' she said, and abruptly turned. Good God, what did she mean? I watched her slender back as she led me along the river. Beside us a cormorant, blue sky mirrored in its glistening back. Here: a fir tree. She ducked low, and I followed into a dark and spiky little wood, my heart racing very hard. We emerged in a considerable field, its extent being some thirty acres, curtained by forest, no human being in sight. I held out my hand to her and she took it quite definitely and together we walked toward the centre of the field. I was on the other side of the earth, invisible to that fierce eye.

I thought, Might I live here? In this town?

'But what of envy?' I asked her. 'If the majority is to rule, what of its desire to level?'

She listened, but only to that part of a conversation that cannot be detected by the ear, and she heard me very well indeed and when I opened my arms she came slowly to me, her chin lifted, her eyes narrowed. Her lip.

Who would not envy me? I thought. Dear Lord, I thought, as I breathed the mad warm air directly from her nose.

PARROT

I

The dark horse was lurking on the stairs. Good Jesus, did servant ever suffer such surprise? I pretended not to see him but I don't know why I bothered. He had no shame.

'*Bonjour,*' called he as he retired.

Bon-bloody-*jour* indeed. It was not long past dawn and his stockings were wet up to the knees.

'*Bonjour,*' said I and returned to my plain white room and sat upon the bed.

He with his dachshund eyes, I thought. A stallion after all.

I would have happily waited for his orders and it was only the fear of missing breakfast that drew me eventually down the stairs, and then – in the library – blow me down if it was not the sneaky French commissioner, and sitting *in my place* was the lovely Miss Godefroy, her white muslin alive with sun, ready with her quill to take dictation or, should I say, my job.

I laughed. I smiled, but I knew not what I thought: You dog, for one part. But also: She should be careful with that ink.

I asked my employer would he be needing me this morning.

'No,' he said.

'What shall I do?'

He raised his brows in such a way as to make Miss Godefroy laugh. Why would I let myself be offended? It was a lovely day and the pale blue sky was feathery and pretty as a mother's china. My time was all my own so I set off for Wethersfield, but I had not walked two miles when my other master – that is, my stomach – issued loud orders to return.

At the midday meal I once more inquired would his lordship be needing me. He answered no.

In the afternoon I observed him return to the library in the company of Miss Godefroy. This time her father sat attendance. Had negotiations begun already? Who can imagine what was said?

At the evening meal, I asked would sir need me on the morrow.

But tomorrow was the Sabbath. Christ, it turned out to be an awful thing. The lady of the house had been, until this morning, distinguished by her relentless busyness, but now all that was extinguished and when she sat at table I had a chance to see her, in the flesh, as the saying is. Even in the unforgiving light which streamed through the eastern windows, it was clear that Mrs Godefroy had once been a raving beauty. But something had frightened or disappointed her, or perhaps the rigours of being a God-botherer had turned her bottom into stone.

His lordship, on the other hand, was very perky and I observed how adoringly Miss Godefroy looked at him. She had snagged an aristocrat, and she was pleased about it. He was talking on and on, as always, leaning forward, cocking his head, mispronouncing every English word he knew. Miss Godefroy thought him perfect. Did the Indians have a religion, he wished to know, or was it what they would call a cult?

The mother then replied. 'I am afraid the French commissioner will find us heavy and stupid.'

'On the contrary madame.' He smiled, showing off his noble manners.

'This is our day of rest,' said Mrs Godefroy bluntly. 'A very different day, I am certain, from what you have in your own country.'

She meant he was a Mick and she would burn him if she could.

'I shall do very well, madame,' my master answered, smiling at each and every one of us in turn. 'I like work better than Sunday amusements.'

At this I found it necessary to kick his shin.

'Just so,' said he, understanding me perfectly, biting his lip in the most thoughtful manner. 'Everybody to church.'

'Some go to church, but most to chapel. I am not quite sure Wethersfield has anything in the French style,' said Mrs Godefroy.

Miss Godefroy was blushing, furious, staring at her plate.

'I am a Christian.' His lordship smiled, applying a Catholic amount of butter to his Protestant bread. 'I can join all Christians, no matter of what denomination, as brethren in their devotions.'

'Indeed,' said Mrs Godefroy. 'Then I would say your doctrine is rather broad.'

The family, quite clearly, had scuffled at these crossroads more than once before and now Miss Godefroy, very bright of face, addressed her mother. 'Of course you will worship at Mr Farrar's?'

'And you will come with us?' the mother asked.

I understood nothing except there were preachers named Poole and Farrar and they were on opposing teams.

'I will go to hear Mr Poole,' the daughter said. 'And if the gentleman,' she added, with a slight bow across the table to Olivier de Garmont who sat showing his clean teeth to one and all, 'will keep me company, I shall be most happy to show him the way.'

'Mr Poole is a worthy divine. I have said so before.'

'Oh dear,' said Mr Godefroy, looking from wife to daughter as a mood descended on him like a Dartmoor mist.

'Yes dear Mr Godefroy,' said his wife. 'Mr Poole is a grander man in the pulpit than Mr Farrar. But alas he is almost Unitarian.'

'That is, a reasoning being,' said Mr Godefroy, smiling.

I did not get the joke, but I was chuckling sociably when Mrs Godefroy swooped on me. 'And you, Mr Larrit, where to?'

'With my apologies,' said I. 'An atheist.'

The French commissioner frowned at me. Miss Godefroy bowed her head but I could see the edge of her bright eyes as they looked up from under her brow. Perhaps she was amused but her mother seemed likely to never look my way again. I was upset to have been rude to the lady of the house, although she could not damage me as severely as my employer who would not tell me what my future held.

After breakfast I stood alone on the great porch and observed streams of worshippers move across the landscape to their different destinations like ants before a deluge. Two hours later I saw them all return. Then it was the dinner hour. Then afternoon service. Then teatime. Then evening service. Then supper. Then Mr Godefroy read a bible chapter, Lord knows which one.

So what was my future?

Not a word.

That night was cold and the blanket thin. When it was finally Monday I went eagerly to my desk, only to find it already occupied by Miss Godefroy.

'Good morning, Mr Larrit,' cried she.

'Am I required?' I asked my employer.

'No,' said he.

I inquired was there anything else he wished to tell me. He said that there was not. God damn them. I needed paid employment.

I returned to my room, reflecting on the general thoughtlessness of aristocrats. They never imagine a man has a life of his own. When they are done with him, then it is over, and when they want him, then he must come back again. So it had been with the marquis de Tilbot who had walked into the architect's office like he had been away twelve minutes not as many years. 'Come up-country,' he said. 'You are a clever chap, it will make your name.'

Well, who does not want to have a name? 'But I have a family,' I said.

'And you will return to them with money in your pocket, royal ribbons on your coat.'

And what did I know of him that would make me trust his word? Nothing. He could eat a trout alive. He was a spy. For a frightened boy to believe him was one thing, but what about a man?

Eight months later, having suffered dysentery, tropical ulcers, and a continual anxiety about my wife and child, having bashed my way through the worst of Queensland and New Guinea, I arrived in what was then Porte de Bergamote where I fully trusted I would get a berth on a Sydney clipper, but there had never been a ship for Sydney in Porte de Bergamote, not then or ever, and Monsieur was loudly astonished I would imagine there ever could be at a time of war.

But *voilà*! We could both get a berth to Marseille.

'As you know,' he said, 'your engravings were commissioned by the Empress Josephine, and she insists you call on her at home.'

As a result of this and other lies, I began to have foolish ideas about what would happen to me in France. I wrote to my dear wife. I have no copy of my letter but fear it was filled with too much empress and insufficient heart. In any case this stupid act had her take the boy to Melbourne with that famous liar, Ted Spence.

The composition of that two-page letter was the most stupid thing I ever did, and all my life, as now at Wethersfield, this memory made me grimace and cry out.

I went downstairs again and demanded, 'Are you dismissing me?'

He was in the library reciting opinions, his head back, his eyes half closed.

'No, no,' Miss Godefroy said. I did not think this was her business. She was not married to him yet.

'I have an important job for you,' said his lordship, still reclining.

'What is it?'

'I will tell you later,' said he, and I thought, He has no more clue than a blind pig. He will send me *up-country* perhaps, and what of my own life, and my own happiness?

I walked into Wethersfield that afternoon wishing only to get the burn of arrack in my throat. The town was dry, I was told three times, and just as I was getting in a mighty rage about Jesus Christ and all his ministers, I entered a likely doorway and found a landlord mixing sherry cobblers. Blow the man down.

After I had tried a cobbler, he made me what they call a *cocktail* after which my natural temper came hurtling back. The landlord then begged I try his *pick-me-up*. Having obliged him, I was ready to ask him the role of religion in a town where they burned people who did not know their catechism.

To this he responded with a doleful kind of hymn, sung in a deep bass voice – *Damnation! Oh, damnation* – and this provoked a croaking laugh from an individual who now began drowsily rocking herself in a dark corner.

'Not salvation,' said she who may have been his wife. 'Damnation, damnation,' and off they set, the pair of them like Christmas carollers.

I finished my pick-me-up and thanked the pair of them for improving my idea of Connecticut. Then I set off to discover the whereabouts of Old Farm. I was most fortunate there was a moon to light my way home, or perhaps it might have been better if I lost my way, for on ascending the stairs I went into my master's room and shook him violently awake.

II

I opened my eyes the following morning and beheld Olivier de Garmont – his silk gown, his surprisingly athletic legs – standing at my bedroom door. The light was bright as all the Christian faiths and his nightgown was like a dirty rag.

'How do you feel, Master Larrit?'

'I am ill.'

'I would expect you are.'

'What have I done?' Oh dear God, I think I tried to murder him. Why then would he smile? His phiz looks like he has been dining in a coal scuttle.

'I said, Mr Parrot, that you must take a vacation, and for some reason that made you very angry. You had a cocktail, so you said.'

I had not known what a vacation was, but I recalled my boiling rage at him, and what sort of poor character he thought I had. 'You offered me money.'

'Of course. You were demanding money.'

'I must be employed, sir. I wish to work.'

'I said I would not dismiss you but you must go away and I will pay you.'

'That's it!'

'You recall what next you did?'

'You accused me of blackmailing you.'

'No, I said I would pay you even while you travelled to New York. It is a vacation. Vacation is an old English word, I do believe.'

'You thought I was a spy. You wanted me to go where I could not witness your hanky-panky. You thought I wanted money.'

'You did want money. Do you remember what you did?'

Following his eyes, I surveyed my room. 'You have been at my trunk.'

'No, sir, *you* have been at your trunk.'

The lid was open. There was a mess of paper, all my papers, and black flakes everywhere, like Dit'sum on that awful day, the sky full of nightjars and alive with burning currency. Here around the bright white Christian room were my carbon papers, all destroyed. What nightmare had I woken into?

'Please sir, what have I done?'

My master came and sat upon my bed and peered down his thin straight nose at me. It was not hard to imagine him in a court of law. 'It turned out you had not been writing to my mother. Nor sending her my copies.'

'I can't do everything.'

'Indeed. Thank heavens.'

'I need my job.'

'And you have your job, John Larrit. Now perhaps you should fetch some soap and water and we will discuss your *vacation*. It is a word you deserve to know.'

He touched my head. I wish he hadn't. He departed and left me to confront the disarray. I had done battle with the Devil and his dark and glistening scales lay all around. It is possible that I had tried to stuff an aristocrat with carbon paper but I never dared to ask.

III

That week the captain of the *Zeus* blew up his boiler and burned his first-class passengers and killed a horse innocently engaged in towing a barge along the western bank. It was therefore announced I would leave for my *vacation* by stagecoach. I was honoured to be invited by Mr Godefroy to be his guest aboard his one-horse chaise.

'*Trot up!*' cried Godefroy.

And we were bloody off, racing for the crest of the ridge. What a view: the waving noble and his adopted Godefroys, all those black loamy acres of *Old Farm*, soft drizzle showing on the feathered mountains, sixteen shades of grey and pale, while below, from north to south, the rain marked the surface of the stream like shoals of whitebait rising in a boil.

I did not doubt we would see an *orangerie* down there before too long.

We sped down onto the flats, through Dartmoor drizzle to mist to stinging rain. I was dressed as I wished Mathilde to see me – in my waistcoat and top hat and spivvy grey frockcoat – although, studying the driver's wardrobe, I discovered I was underdressed.

Godefroy was fifty-five years old and a saint of his church but he was also what they call a *hotspur*, pushing his horse through the needling water with his teeth gleaming and his eyes bright, wrapped up like a coachman proper with that snug and cosy perfume of the oilskin all around him.

Having been abandoned at the inn, I was turning in damp resignation in the direction of my own pneumonia when I heard a *thwack* and felt a *thwap* across my head and shoulders. It was his oilskin coat.

'Bon voyage!' he cried, and I could not even thank him for the gift, for he was already up the road, standing in his shirtsleeves, *giddyup*. If he would do this for an atheist, I reckoned he could manage a Catholic for a son.

I therefore set out with my spirits high, enjoying the blissful prospect of my forthcoming *conjugation* and the subtle pleasures of the scene. It took a little while for me to understand that, though I might be dry from throat to ankle, I would be very cold. For hours interminable, for days finally, I sat atop a heavy coach, always rocking on its leather thoroughbraces, swaying around the curves, lurching over the hills, passing with perilous tilt the heavy, slow-moving, canvas-covered freight wagons, never arriving before sunset at our inn, and then cold to the marrow of my bones.

The inns were flea-bitten, the beds were hard, and the owners of the stagecoach service, like the landlords, were set to avoid all unnecessary costs. As we approached each tollgate the driver blasted his cornet trumpet. This was a signal to another coach, owned by the same company waiting on the other side of the barrier. It was also a sign to us passengers that we must soon get our bags down, and sometimes there was a wheelbarrow to assist us but mostly there was not, and then we must carry our belongings through the toll, paying our three cents, and board a new carriage on the other side. I thought fondly of the *Zeus*.

On a Sunday evening I arrived at Manhattanville and discovered the coach would go no farther till the morrow. To hell with it. I purchased a fat lamp from a tinker and set off on foot. God knows what sort of muck was in my lantern, it gave off the powerful stink of tannery or what are called the noxious trades and I suppose I was drenched in it by the time I arrived at the place where last I saw Mathilde.

On being sent to New York from Philadelphia, not so long ago, I had found her absconded from the boardinghouse and I was caused considerable distress until I located her, and then I felt far worse. God save me. She had gone and bought a *house*, feme sole status or some such nonsense, which meant she was not married and could do what she pleased, including contracting to buy a *dwelling house* in the jungle – they called it Sixteenth Street although it was nothing but a rutted track. The house was timber, what they call clapboard. It shook at every step, and that was bad, but this was worse – she had no money except what she had made hawking portraits on the boat.

In spite of this Mr Peek had sold her a house, and if you don't believe it, then I did not either, but we must. For Peek had played Shylock with her, himself lending her the capital and loading her to breaking point with every type of extra fee, compulsory insurance, brokerage, advance payments on taxes I am still sure that he invented. This was why I could not lose my job – my wages stood between her and debtor's prison, not to say foreclosure. And through all this time, of course, I loved her, and yearned for her, and my bad-smelling lamp gave off just sufficient light to guide my way toward her bed. Sometime after the bells rang ten, I forded the muddy little stream and stood where my beloved had bought her house.

Sir, it was not there. It had been. Now it was not. Except one crooked chimney stack. And a heap of half-burned wood. I waved my lantern like a fool and found a corner of scorched silk I thought I recognised, a cooking pot the old lady had transported. The night air smelled of wet ash and my noxious lamp. I found a wooden cross stuck in the earth, just two feet tall, most likely a cat or dog but awful just the same.

I was gutted as any trout, grey liver lying in the ash.

And there I stood, a stinking grieving factory illuminated – chiaroscuro – when I saw another lamp in whose penumbra I could make out two pairs of unlaced boots. It was a very young couple, almost children.

'Where is she?' I demanded.

The girl took the lantern from the boy and held it up to me. 'Where is who?' she demanded.

'The Frenchwoman.'

'Are you Mr OK?'

'Perroquet?'

'Mr OK?'

'Yes.'

'She said not to tell it to no one else.'

'Good,' I said. She was alive. 'Very good.'

'How do we know it's you?'

'I will speak to you in French.' I was mad and desperate. I knew this made no sense. I thought I would have to give them money. But they retreated to parley and when they returned the girl said, 'Go on.'

'Ne me faites pas perdre mon temps,' I said.

They gave me the address of the Broadway boardinghouse but by the time I got there the landlady had sold to someone else. The night man was new and did not like my smell and if I had not woken the maid I might have suffered more losses than a man can bear.

So, God knows what hour, but off into the night once more. My lantern ran dry and I abandoned it downwind from the Collect. From there I was at the mercy of the clouds and finally, by misadventure, fell into what I later learned was Bestevaar Kill or Manetta Water, and I cursed and lurched along its bank nearly to the North River where, by sheer chance, the stream ran along the side of the house to which I had been directed. Dear Jesus thank you whoever you are – a small dairy farm with its name carved in the gate.

Fearing I would be savaged by the dogs I could hear flinging themselves against their chains, I followed a moon-pale driveway with high grass in its middle until, having barked my shins and poked my eye, I got myself up to the porch.

'Mathilde?'

'Who is it?' It was a man.

'John Larrit.'

'What do you want?' Yes, I thought, here I am again, in the middle of the night, and who will love me now?

'Mathilde.'

When the door began to open I already hated who was on the other side of it. I kicked it but it was held hard by its chain.

'Eckerd?'

'No one of that name.'

In the lantern light I saw the Jew from the *Havre*, his wild and foreign beauty, the smell of his pomade, the grey shadow across the top of his forehead.

He saw me, of course he did. He rolled up his lip beneath his nose, as if my smell had caused offence.

'I am here to see my wife.'

He opened reluctantly, as if he did not remember me. But there, on the stair behind him, holding a candle and wrapping herself in her blue shawl, stood the woman I had come to see.

'Oh my dear, Parrot,' she cried, and ran to me, kissing all of my face and eyebrows and complaining about my smell while in danger of sucking my very eyes inside her mouth. My soul, oh how I had missed her, and her combustibles, her turpentine and linseed oil, and all the time I could feel this queer soft tapping on my shoulderblade, not her.

'Dear Monsieur Perroquet,' said Mr Eckerd. 'Most welcome to our house.'

IV

Tildy smelled of sleep. What was happening in this house I did not know, but I took good note of the Jew's very fancy gown, a silk peacock embroidered in gold from neck to hem and the whole less well secured than I would have liked. We passed down a wide central corridor, decorated like a post office, by which I mean, busy with packages and portmanteaus and all the signs of recent arrival or imminent departure. Nothing was secured or settled except – where you would expect a hatstand – there was a large fresh-smelling portrait of Eckerd in this very gown. He was posed seated in a cane chair, legs apart, leaning back. She had put him next to a sloping attic window stolen from our home in the faubourg Saint-Antoine, but out the window was another country, a broken wilderness, fallen trunks, splintered yellow roots, a part of a man's leg. No one would buy a work like this. It was foolishness extreme to do such charitable labour when you have lost your house to fire.

'What happened to your canvases?' I asked.

She referred to Eckerd.

'Burned,' he said.

I looked to the Jew and he caught my eye and held it very hard.

Said he, 'Not a single specimen survived.'

Tildy broke my stare and drew me into the kitchen, a big old room with a brick farm floor. While Eckerd watched us from the doorway, she held my hand against her mouth. Mr Eckerd fetched me an arrack in a deep-blue glass which I would have rejected had I sufficient character, but my entire body was frozen and exhausted and I took three of them in a row, waiting while he filled the thimble to the full.

Mathilde set to heat water for a bath. I observed Eckerd and how he stood, his feet astride, arms across his wide and wire-wool chest. I wondered did he plan to watch me at my toilet. When Tildy moved to take down the tub from its hook he rushed to help her.

I asked her where her mother was.

She smiled at me and melted my heart and held her hand to her ear and thus drew my attention to the old familiar breath.

'What caused the fire?' I asked, but that most reasonable question came out sounding false or coded. I could not be myself.

Again she looked to Eckerd.

'Tell him,' said he.

She told me her mother had been frying fish and spilled a pot of burning fat. It was lucky she was not burned to death.

I wished with all my heart to hold her and love her but why did she need his permission to tell me everything? When the bath was ready Eckerd retired to his bedroom – I noted where it was, on the ground floor, at the back. But even when the pair of us were alone together I was very distant with her and insisted I wash myself while she sat on a chair and looked at me. We were silent, irritable and sad.

I found dry clothes in my duffel and we went up the stairs, conscious of every brush and accidental bump, questions, accusations, one step at a time. At the top of the landing there was a door, a light shining underneath.

'No,' she cried, as I reached for the handle.

Naturally I entered.

In the corner, sitting cross-legged before a canvas, I beheld a creature more awful than any of the twisted hacked-up beggars who haunt the Église Saint-Sulpice. His forehead was high, his skull hairless, and all his face was scarred and tattooed in such a way I thought the burning fat must have spilled all over him. However, this creature was not newly made, but ancient, and his pale blue eyes peered out from his own tattered skin as if they were prisoners inside the trunk of a blackened antipodean paperbark. I stared at him and the dead bird he was painting – gold and black, as big as a blackbird, its beak partly open, its legs and claws tied tight around a rack, and the whole of the poor thing threaded through with an armature of wire.

He held his brush in the air, clearly waiting to be left in peace.

Matilda drew me back across the corridor and there I found a pallet on the floor and all her pretty quilts and shawls which had wrapped and tangled us so many nights. I did not yet set down my duffel.

'Let me show you,' she said.

Along one wall there was a ladder such as they use in apple orchards, by which I mean you would need to recruit Tom Thumb himself to walk the upper rungs. This implement Mathilde now used to poke at the ceiling, thereby lifting a trapdoor and shoving the pointy end of the ladder up into the attic dark. Ascending until the rung could not accommodate a single foot, she reached inside and brought down a canvas about three foot by three foot, in other words a tight fit even on the diagonal.

'I'll take it.'

But she kept it hidden from me until, now on the floor, she flipped it around. Dear Jesus what was this?

Why Mathilde, I thought, you have made a portrait as charming as burned milk – the monstrous little man with his pale eyes peering from the devastation of a war. His face dire black and delicious pink, a horror, a bad dream. He had a bird upon his rack, but not the one I had seen. Along its base was carefully inscribed, like holy writ in Greek: $h(t) = Xit\beta$.

The creature's eye was bright, those long blue feathers shone like silk, the man's skin was made from paint, thick, stirred, brown, red, a mix of raw and cooked.

'Dear Jesus.'

Even I could see the genius of this horror. No one would buy this, ever. She dared me to say it. I would not. I praised her, in a secret fury at her selfish artist's will, but I praised truly, although it would remain in some secret hole a century and thence it would be taken out and burned.

'*Cher Perroquet, tu m'aimes toujours?*' She held my eyes, her face wreathed in that familiar grin, and she was as a Venus and a gargoyle all at once, the Devil dancing on a wire between two steeples over fire. When she was like this she was a goddess, bare-breasted, bright-eyed, drunk on liquors a mortal should not touch. How could I resist her?

And so I placed my duffel down, and we loved each other once again, and made an awful scatter of the quilts, and lay in each other's arms and talked, and only then did she reveal to me the financial balance of the fire. Mr Peek, in his frenzy to take every penny from her, had forced her to buy insurance from his own company, not only for the house but for all her paintings which he, having paid top dollar for his own, now made her value highly.

And then there really was a fire, and the insurer, as usual, had no wish to pay. So he came to her boardinghouse and accused her of burning it herself. That day Eckerd engaged for her a brainy Jewish lawyer, and in the end Peek (or the Hand in Hand Insurance Company) paid up. At the same time he was happy to inform her that neither he nor anyone else would insure her ever again.

But this was of no concern to her, she told her Parrot, laying her head upon his chest and tickling his nose with her fragrant hair. I should ask her why.

'Why, my beloved?'

Because she had sold that block of land, the same one I had stumbled around with my lantern, to Mr Ruggles. I should ask her who was he.

'And who is Mr Ruggles?'

A rich man who added it to his parcel of land north of Union Place, and she was very well provided for by the fire. It had worked out perfectly. So now they had bought this farm, which was very cheap because of the gruesome murder done here.

'And who is *they?*'

'In partnership,' she said.

'With who?'

'Well it must be Mr Eckerd, of course,' said she. 'I cannot insure in my name.'

'Do you have this in writing?'

'But have I not been clever? Can't you see? You thought I was a fool, but I am not. It is an agreement with Eckerd, my darling,' she said. 'I trust him.'

'And who is this Apollo?' I said, nodding to the portrait on the floor.

'He is a partner also.'

'And how do you know him?'

'He is a good friend of Mr Eckerd.'

She was ridiculous. Impossible. Desirable. My body was aching and exhausted, but I could not sleep, not even when she did. I snuffed the candle and lay in the dark, aware of the sweet musty odour of her body, the thin yellow knife of light beneath the door. I closed my eyes. I saw the carriage lurch. I was haunted by my jealousy, my doubt. I saw the endless yellow roads, and a vision of the burned man, labouring at his exquisite bird. He was so grotesque, and yet so troublingly familiar, the way he sat, his tortured forehead unnaturally high, his back straight, his legs folded. Like a bad tooth I could not keep my tongue from, in the end I knew I must address it properly. Carefully I separated myself from Tildy's white, rose-tipped breast. I slipped from the bed and drew a quilt around myself.

When I opened his door the second time he looked approximately as he had the first, except I understood him as Mathilde's portrait taught me to, the pale, pale eyes, their queer determination, the flicker around the melting mouth that might have been a smile or sneer.

'What's your name?' I asked.

'Who wants to know?' he said, and I heard the burr of Devon in the vowels.

'Mr Watkins,' said I, 'I am the boy.'

V

Watkins held me away from him, clamping my forearms, and all his melted features shivered like an oyster or a quaking bog or tarry bed. Who would have expected his feelings to be quite so strong?

'Marie,' he called, in such a tone as if to say *Quick, bring the net*. 'Marie, raise yourself.'

I expected Marie would be a child, but she was a slender old woman and her fine bones and clear kind brown eyes were lively in the dancing light.

'Marie, it is the boy.'

The stranger in the doorway smiled at me so brightly, so familiarly, she might have been my long-lost aunt. Carefully she set down her candle on a chair which, like every other object in that smoky unsettled room, had only recently arrived in a rush from someplace else and had no useful connection with its fellows. Quiet as a cat, in grey woollen socks, she moved to hold my hand and I was embarrassed to feel her private skin against my own.

'So there,' said she, and gave me a little shake. 'I don't know why you look so shocked. He was always going to do it. Nothing would have stopped him.'

Then she stood beside Watkins with her long plain hand hung across his shoulder, more like a girl, I thought, and there was such sweet affection between them, I knew she must be his wife, and yet the Watkins I had known was a bachelor and who would marry him *after* he had been so cruelly burned?

'He has spoken of you often,' she said, kneeling to place a lump of coal into a brazier whose crooked tin chimney teetered upward and out through the open window. Her English was not English to the ear, and I was reminded of the speech of Walloon printers whose trade had taken them across one too many borders in the dead of night.

'But of course,' she said. 'It was a surprise to me, to hear an ink-stained little boy should carry such a gift.'

'And that you have taken a French wife,' she added.

I thought, What gift?

The burned artist shook his frightful head. 'Very nice,' said he. 'Could not be happier.'

'We have talked about you so often,' the woman said. 'The little printer's devil running through the woods. We prayed for you.'

I thought it queer that Watkins was religious, but a man who walks through fire is entitled to believe in fairies should he please.

'They were shooting at him,' he said, as if I had not been there.

'You were like a rabbit,' she told me.

'He was like a rabbit.'

They were very moved, each reaching out a hand to me, while I, in confusion and embarrassment, shyly made myself available.

'I do not remember you,' I admitted to the woman finally. 'Forgive me.'

'You knew me in a different way,' she said and I wondered could she possibly be the girl at the *Swan* who I had delivered the dockets to, but there had not been sufficient years for that girl to have become so old. I had been in Dittisham in 1793. Thirty-seven years had passed since Piggott's printery had killed my father.

'I was Mrs Piggott,' she declared.

Good Jesus, I thought. Strike me dead, I never saw a soul *less* like the awful Mrs Piggott, the tightest, smallest, driest, least affectionate creature ever born.

'No,' I said.

'You must let me know my own name,' said she, and from Watkins' shaking mouth I understood this was most definitely Mrs Piggott. Yet was not Mrs Piggott *old* so many years before? How could she be transformed into this supple lady with shapely white feet, teal silk gown, and a complexion which could carry that single highlight, the kiss and blessing of Vermeer?

She had been just a girl, she soon told me, when they took her husband off for hanging. She had thought her life was ended then.

I had harboured hatred for her all my life, she and her awful husband. I felt it must show in my eyes, so I turned toward the burned man's canvas which was as crisp as he was churned and charred, and which displayed, to the most elevated degree, the achievement of that ambition he had confessed to me so long ago. I will produce a book, he had told me, containing all the birds in the world. Or did he say America?

And there it stood, a miracle, like the Baby Jesus in the manger – one bird, one painting, one jewel in the pigsty of a house with fluff and dust and rat-shit pellets in the corners.

'It is beyond anything I ever saw,' I said.

Watkins began immediately to push the praise away and, instead, gave full and passionate credit to America. He and Marie had arrived impoverished, in such a damaged state, knowing no one of any influence, but what was bestowed upon them were twenty thousand unnamed birds. These came, like the land itself, with the opportunity to profit from them, not handsomely perhaps, and it sometimes made Marie sad to see his artworks so dispersed, and not always to those who might appreciate them.

'Look at us,' he said.

'Look at *him*,' she said. 'God bless America for that.'

Everything I knew, everything I thought I knew, was now called into question. Had she been his lover all the time? Did she crawl along that passage late at night? For if Mrs Piggott had snaked through the intestines of that house, who else had crawled and slithered, and if she had been a lover with a hot sluicing heart and soft hungry lips, what else of my history had happened in the dark?

'But you,' he said, 'who got away unscathed. What are you doing? What have you done?'

There were no more seats available than an upturned bucket and the chair, so we stood near the brazier, and the former Mrs Piggott attended to it carefully, arranging the coals like flowers in a vase, eking out the fire as poor people do, but when I saw their eager heated faces, like Rembrandt's shepherds, I understood they had, with years of continual conversation, gloried and elevated the little Parrot to something that Parrot would never be: that is, an artist.

'Enough,' I said, and truly the pain was awful.

'You are too modest.'

'I am a servant! Nothing more.'

'Aye,' said Watkins. 'Art is a hard master.'

'Stop!' I cried. 'Did you not once tell me I was not an engraver's bootlace?'

But nothing could shake him. 'Well, think how big your head would be by now.'

'It is clear,' the woman said. 'You have grown up very nicely.'

'Madam, I am forty-nine years old! Yes sir, no sir, two bags full. A servant.'

'The curse of great facility in a child,' said Mr Watkins, 'is that it easily produces laziness. I was the same. Thank Petey, I was taken down a peg or two.'

His face moved like a shaking sort of bog and I guess he was laughing, but for myself I could have ripped my face right off my living bones. What torture to hear that a life had been available to me that I had not been man enough to live.

Again I sought refuge in his canvas – the blue-winged bird, the white-ringed eye, the beak, the crunching locust. I felt bilious, and very very sad, to have arrived in this great new country with my heart and my pockets and my life so very empty.

'In any case,' I said, 'we can discuss my work another time for it is late. Fate has given us the opportunity to spend many hours together.'

And so, without even having the politeness to ask them how their unlikely marriage had come to pass, I bade them goodnight and slipped into bed beside Mathilde whose throaty contented murmur should have reminded me of all the sweet and sweaty comforts of our convivial conjugal life, but now, on my back, straight as a plank, staring into the inky ambiguous air above my head, I was cut and twisted by a considerable sadness in whose particular rubbed and layered charcoal I recognised the dye of jealousy. All around me in that cold and empty house art was being made such as had not been made before. These artists showed themselves each day more remarkable than the day before while I, who had apparently been granted talents in plenty, had wasted and abused my gifts.

How can you love a woman and be jealous of her? By this

light my admiration of Mathilde took on another hue, and I lay awake listening to the condemned cattle become restive with the dawn.

I had thought myself a young man until then.

VI

What pleasures I had expected of my *grandes vacances* must stay as private as Long Island oysters in their blue and ashy shells, but finally the morning came when I woke to find myself alone in heaven and Mathilde departed to her linseed shore – some five feet from my hand. There she once more scraped and rubbed and pounded at two yellow faces glowing from a muddy ground.

I nuzzled her neck, inhaled her sleep and tobacco smoke. She murmured in her throat and kissed my lips and eyelids, and I soon understood I was put out to pasture *on a promise*, as they say, from a genius of the female sex.

Down in the brick-floored kitchen my lovely screw-spined mother-out-law gave me her garlic welcome – a tin cup for my tea and a slathering of white lard and salt on a heel of black crust bread. As for conversation, Maman was occupied arguing with her Pennsylvania stove, riddling and raddling and poking and punishing it, until – seeing me about to take my breakfast out on the front porch – she sternly ordered I must never show my face out there as this access was reserved only for the clever Jew.

She spoke to me like that? Well, bless her muddled head. I was a fool to be offended, and I was much too exercised by the gentleman who had his portrait painted with his legs apart. I carried my tea and the huge burthen of my pride and jealousy up the cold and dusty stairs. Mathilde made it clear she would permit just one final kiss, well never mind, ma'am, that will be enough for now.

She wished to know why I did not visit my old mate Watkins.

Damn this, I thought. I came down all the way from Wethersfield, and now I am sent out to the back paddock for the day.

Across the hallway the second great genius of our age donated me a bright blue eye from his crusted mussel shell of face. He asked me how I liked his heron wing and was it not about the best heron wing that man had ever made? The back of his hand was like those knurled Australian banksia seeds, scorched lips and scumble, but he had maintained the maiden treasure of his palm and fingers, petals the colour of white English rose. He held them up to me, an awful sort of vanity, I thought, a badge. Such arrogance in the midst of such misfortune. The very same man who had told me I was not worth a bootlace.

I asked him was there any wood to chop.

He did not suggest that was beneath me. He said his wife was eager to natter with me about 'old times'. Dear Jesus, what a thing to call those nightmares. I found her on the back veranda. She who I had always thought of as *old Mrs Piggott* had turned out strangely glossy, slender and collected in her form. With bright birdie eyes she greeted me, looking up from her fresh-killed herons. She sat on a three-legged stool, behind a narrow bench, and arranged the deceased, smoothing out their cooling bones.

She looked up at me in the way of a woman interrupted darning socks, pausing as she threaded fine wires through dead flesh. It was sunny in the yard but all her labour was conducted on the chilly damp back veranda, on whose greasy black floors the previous inhabitants appeared to have butchered many beasts. A line of rusty meat hooks were suspended above her head. Like beads, I thought. RIP. In memoriam.

Perhaps, at that moment, when I was back among my own kind, amid the blood and tallow of New York, young Olivier was standing on Godefroy's uplifting porch. I drank cold tea and made a cigarette and watched Mrs Piggott play with dead things. I leaned against the veranda post. I wondered how my thin-nosed Olivier was doing with his beautiful American.

Mrs Piggott bent and twisted the wires to raise the birds' inquiring heads toward me, as if to say wotcha, chap.

She asked me did I wish to have a free ticket to Mr Eckerd's theatre. It was a roaring show about the French Revolution. As if encouraging me to leave, she nodded at the dappled muddy path which led from the veranda beneath the sumac, thrust through the tangled rosehips and beside the maple.

I asked her would she mind doing me a favour.

She said she was happy to oblige.

I asked her would she tell me about my father. It was surprisingly hard to say those words.

She laid a small soft bird upon her aproned lap. She was silent a moment while she measured wire from beak to tail.

'As long as you live,' she said, and one bright eye held me like a pin. 'As long as you live, so does he.'

She clipped the wire, and I had no idea what was being said between us. I was a grown man but frightened as a child to imagine what those blue doll's eyes had seen.

I said, 'What brought you here?' In other words, please tell me anything but what I asked.

She pushed her wire in up the birdie's bottom and, by dint of pinching and massage, managed to bring it out the beak and thus she was able to twist its head to look at me.

'What brought me here?' She laid the dead creature beside her clogs and set to measuring and clipping wires. 'Your father was a fine brave man,' she said. 'While you live, he lives,' she repeated.

Everything in me wished to know in which way I was like him, but I lacked the spine. She had seen him die, I knew it, but I did not want to live the horror of that day, the soldiers marching with their cheery yellow coffins while Monsieur tossed his sovereign with his single hand.

'Afterward,' she said, and I knew she meant *after I saw your pater murdered*, 'afterward I had nowhere else to go but the place I did not wish to see again. Do you know,' she said, 'I was never Mrs Piggott in any sense at all.'

I did not ask her how that was and never would. I looked at her, with her wire and birds and clogs, and I breathed the fall air and river wrack and lard, and I had no wish to descend into the maze of this peculiar foreign life. You can go mad that way, imagining the lives of others, all crowded in like a universe of stars all murmuring and crying with their dreadful want. 'I returned to the printery,' she said. 'There was nothing but smoke and ruins and banns nailed on the trees announcing the punishment by hanging for a counterfeit. I made a gruel of flour and water and crawled down the fallen stair, and got in underneath like a cat set to die beneath a house.'

She was a young woman who had witnessed awful things. The best and worst she found beneath the ground floor of her former life – the burned man who would be her soul mate, as she liked to say, the luvvy she would sit beside the livelong day, grinding him his colours, frying his whitebait crisp and toasty as he liked. She found him there beneath the earth line, broken like burned roast pork, whimpering and shaking, his hair become part of his skin like you see the grass in crusts of farmer's cheese or stoneware jugs.

She saved him, or they saved each other, with a bath of the tung oil old Piggott had laid in for his floors, although it beggars belief how she moved the man without killing him and how he went about the business of eating and making waste inside this oily womb. The tung turned his open wounds a horrid colour. Sometimes it appeared that she was poisoning him, and then she would order him out of it, and then she feared he was dying anyway and so he must get back, and if I had a generous heart I would relate their struggles as winter came – frost and snow, starvation, fever – list every one of their ruses, their will to live in a sea of counterfeit and war and suspicion, but my lesser pain must blot them out.

Down the end of Perry Street, within earshot of the slapping riggings, pigeons cooing, the perpetual upset of cattle brought for sale, sat a small aproned woman with a pair of handy pliers. In 1793 she had recovered her best purse and scorched it in a bucket and in this had placed the most serviceably burned counterfeits, and thence she took herself to a Catholic priest, and the priest himself took her to the Bank of England and insisted they replace her 'widow's mite' as he was pleased to call these thirty pounds.

There was much more than thirty pounds available, but it was her understanding that they might be hanged at any time and she was very cautious, only using this ruse one final time. Then she got her seeping stinking luvvy in sailor's clothes and thus, assisted by the revulsion and pity of all who saw him, got him on board a ship to America. He had no dowry but his burin and those bright blue wilful eyes.

She was very frightened of America, of the Comanche and Cherokees who cut the private parts of men and took white women as their wives, she told me, but Mr Watkins was frightened of nothing. How will we eat? she asked him. He said nothing better could have happened to them because America had more birds than all the world had ever seen before and he would engrave every one and print the plates and bind a book which would go to every rich man in the world.

What do you know of rich men? she had asked him.

He knew nothing, of course, he was a Devon boy. He told her there was not a rich man presently snoring over his Madeira who would not want folios of pretty birds to show his friends. He said there was not a jumped-up Bradford millowner who would not wish this book, three inches thick, gilt-tooled, morocco-bound.

And who was Mrs Piggott that she would believe him, the silk-worm, burned, crusty? You would not even know him human but for his weeping skin. Later she saw an engraving of a poison fish, disguised as a stone. She wondered what she recognised, and it was him, her luvvy.

He was carried in a litter by sailors – 'There you are mate,' the litter bearers called – each one thinking this was himself burned by oil at sea. Thus he was nursed like a precious creature all the way to New York. With his livid secret hand he drew their likenesses. He told them he was the author of *The Illustrated Compendium of Birds*.

'And what of the great book?' I asked.

'It would never have been possible in England,' she said.

VII

Sooner or later, one day or the next, the muddy path from Mrs Piggott's birds led me to that ill-loved stream and finally persuaded me through a stand of bright red sumac and brought me sidling sideways, not quite honest-looking, up onto the King Street footbridge.

And here I commenced my *grandes vacances* or *tour*.

First I circled around to Greenwich Street where I could inspect the front door of the house. With GEO WILLS BLACKSMITH behind my back, and the late-afternoon sun lighting up the east side of Greenwich Street, and the masts of the great ships filling the sky above the west-side rooftops, their rigging in constant bickering argument with the wind, I addressed the front door, pretty much, I suppose, like a bull standing at the gate that separates him from his herd. If this sounds comic let me say that the farmhouse was as funny as a murder site or butchery, and it had been both. Even the broad spreading beech tree, which might be a thing of beauty in Wethersfield, had been gnawed by frightened cattle. The front door was secured with a padlock and chain threaded through a rough wide hole. For all that brutal practicality, some unknown punter once had hopes for this house – around the door were set expensive glass panels, composed of amber leadlight about two inches square. The transom contained a stained-glass peacock.

As I assessed my new bolt-hole, the winter sun slipped round the upstairs corner of the inn behind my back. The peacock was thus suddenly, violently, ignited – Dear Sweet Jesus Come Again in Glory, or words to that effect. I retired to the Bull Inn in a frame of mind where I could have found a fight with almost anybody. I sat myself on the window bench where, before the first glass of rum, I witnessed the clever Jew emerge, crowned by the peacock, framed in golden lead-light splendour, his strange hair gleaming, his eyes cut against the light. I raised my glass. He did not notice me. He stooped to lock his chain, wiped his hands with his kerchief, and walked into Greenwich Street, a man of rank and purpose. How different was my own situation.

All my life I had moved forward. No matter what misfortune I had faced, I always knew how to continue, and even when I lost my da, I had confidence I could negotiate the day, the tide, the force of the wind or river, to end up somewhere, carry my burden to the next place, wear a dress if need be, but always be a man, be in the flow of life, hurrying toward a destination, the evening rise of rainbow trout, a home, a wife, a child, a meal, sweet sleep, breathing the air of a lover's neck, and always with the strong certainty that I was Parrot and, being so, was a proud distinctive chap.

I had still thought myself so blessed when the sun rose that morning. Had I not breathed that Frenchwoman's skin, the linseed oil, the turpentine? I was happy when I rose to stand naked to observe her rubbing and scrubbing at her portrait. I did not think myself useless. That is, I woke as Parrot, he who is loved to death, is agin the government, a Jacobin, a socialist, a man of the future, a traveller on the tides of history, subject to the laws of Newton but not to those of kings, a subject, yes, but always in proud and personal rebellion. Such was my distinctive character that lords and counts referred to me by name. The Empress Josephine was almost of my circle. I was true to myself. I was *not no one*, if you please.

But when I sat in the Bull Inn on Greenwich Street and saw Eckerd lock his door, I suddenly *comprehended* that the entire house was occupied by people who had occupations suited for the present age. They lived in the New World, and what an awful shock it was to finally understand. I was abandoned to this New World, but I was a habitual servant to a dying breed. I might be on my *grandes vacances*, but I was of no damn use. I had no art, no trade. I had travelled all my life to arrive here, but here was an abyss. I was beached on the corner of King and Greenwich, a creature with no purpose in the world.

I had three rums, awful stuff, stinking of raisins and sweet as baby's sick. I paid. I left. I walked quickly to escape the Hudson's unrelenting wind, and soon enough I was on Broadway and all was business – barrow boys, bankers, whores in a hurry with something on their mind. This was not Paris where you might drift uselessly from place to place, affecting to carry your wit and learning in a conch shell up your bottom. There were no *flâneurs* on Broadway. They were a hundred per cent business and they banged against one another like marbles in a lottery barrel.

I tried a burlesque and imagined myself a man of leisure, but everyone in the street was working at a plan, and I would not be a market for their enterprise. I rushed downtown and called in on the old boardinghouse, inquiring for mail. No one knew me. I headed across Park Row and there, by mistake, found myself confronted with the bloody banners of Eckerd's play. Of course I turned away.

The oyster bars were open before noon and I ate a good two dozen, observing how they shrank from my lemon juice, curdling in horror from their fate. I chewed them without any pleasure, while my own grey matter shrank back from the awful fact that I had no purpose on the earth unless it be to embrace a pretty woman, to raise her off the mattress with my arms beneath her spine and cause her an hour of pleasure before she set to paint again.

I headed out along Downing Street, treading carefully amid the shit on the broken banks of the Manetta Water, and by the time I was in the stand of red sumac by the back gate of Mathilde's house I was admitting to myself that I missed the company of Olivier de Garmont. I never thought I would think such a thing in all my life. When I came into the kitchen I discovered that the old lady had produced a mighty stew. The rich vinous fumes made my stomach growl as always, but I was not as always, no longer the Parrot who had left that morning. I was some poor wretch who has lost his station, returning home with a misery he cannot share.

VIII

Mathilde had an eye, and you could normally rely on her to notice the light in *my eye*, or where I looked as I chewed my food or changed my mind. But she was living deep inside her tar-pit paintings and arrived at table with that wild and startled look you see in artists when surfacing at dusk. She wore tall fuzzy socks up to her sweet round knees. She had not brushed her tangled hair. The skin around that eye was bluish, taut, her pupils very large.

I knew she had not washed her hands for she was still wearing fingerless gloves – the kind market women wear to count the change – chrome yellow and ultramarine marked her nails and nose. She smiled at me, showing me her rosy gums, the tiny imperfect incisor with the pointy end.

I smiled but at the same time I was thinking, She only dares do these things because someone else is paying for her. I meant those frightening canvases which no one could expect to praise except a lover, or some genius from another star. To paint like this was to shove an unacceptable fact beneath my nose.

Soon I discovered her removing her paintings from their hiding place. I inquired if she had a buyer.

'I am making money,' she said. 'Don't you worry, monsieur.'

'Monsieur?'

'Monsieur my darling.'

I touched her little woolly hand and felt her icy fingertips.

'How are you making money?' I asked.

'Come to the theatre on Friday night,' said she, 'and I will tell you then.'

By theatre, of course, she meant the business set up by the Jew, and I felt so sad I could have cried.

'You'll come? You promise?'

'I promise,' I said. Then I thought a rum and milk might improve my horrible mood, so it was out the back gate, through the rusty sumacs, up onto the bridge, and into the Bull Inn where I was confronted with about fifty roaring men – merchants from the Tontine, clerks, loungers, racetrack touts, reporters – all squeezed in and shouting and writing in their notebooks or on butcher's paper, pressed against the next chap's back.

To the publican, I said, 'So what is this?'

Said he, 'It is the packet *Waterloo* released by customs.' And he nodded beyond the crowd where the smoke-yellowed windows had been thrown open to reveal the busy wharf, the windy river.

'But what are these men doing?'

'What are they doing?' He was a big cheeky red-haired Irishman with hard-used cheeks. 'They are getting the news from England. That chap there is from the *New York Sentinel*.' He listed the names of all the newspapers, and as he spoke I spotted the tall stringy fair-haired lad I had last seen strangling pigeons. He was not seated but had one knee rested on a chair and a little stub of pencil between two big fingers. At a certain moment he looked up from his labours and caught my eye and gave me an indication that he would be with me in a tick.

The blood-cheeked Irishman was very happy to keep me tippled while I waited. I asked him could he get me paper and pencil which he very cheerfully provided, and for a while I occupied myself making a picture of the scene.

I wish I could tell you all my old skills returned or, better, that new ones had developed in the years I slept, but of course that is not true. I had made nothing useful of my life.

Soon enough the pigeon boy returned, depositing himself heavily, laying his inky hands flat on the table.

'Hello friend,' said he.

For that, I purchased him a sour mash whiskey.

Then we sat turned sideways, his back to Greenwich Street, his pale scuffed yellow boot resting along his bench. Generally, the shine had gone off him – that is, he had swapped his grey suit and waistcoat for denim and coarse wool, and there was a much harder set to his mouth and a glint to his eye which made his high nose flinty and warlike, although I was sure he never meant to convey that particular expression.

'Back in the pigeon business?' I inquired, for I had not forgotten how he got his stock prices from the English newspapers and flew them up to Philadelphia.

'I'll be quitting soon enough,' said he.

I was about to inquire as to his brother but changed my mind. 'Then back to Georgia,' I suggested.

'Ah, you remember.'

'Cass County and Paulding County,' I said.

'That's all sold,' he said.

'Good price, I hope?'

'No one ever paid more than I did,' he said. And then he told me how he and his brother Dirk had travelled to Georgia as they had intended, taking up the lot in Paulding County which was very pretty in its situation – black fertile land, a little swampy, but excellent for cotton (as was the opinion of other holders moved there recently from Louisiana). Among their neighbours, the family of O'Grady had been very hostile at the get-go but when the men had all wrestled they became friendly and the O'Gradys were soon ready to teach the business of cotton as they understood it.

They had settled only two weeks when, without having had the time to sin against another human, they and the O'Grady wives and children were set upon by savages, and although they were well fortified in the O'Grady household, with logs driven five feet down into the earth, and although Dirk shot more than five Creeks and Peter himself a certain three, they were finally overwhelmed and men and women were slaughtered and children had their brains bashed out. Dirk had been pinned to the ground with a spear but instead of murdering him directly the savages cut the soles off his feet, and the last time his brother saw him he was running tied behind an Indian horse and screaming Lord-give-me-mercy.

'Dear heavens,' I said, wondering how Peter had been saved but never asking.

'I will see them all in hell,' said he. I supposed his brother must be dead.

'So you are back in the pigeon business.'

He looked at me directly, and I wondered if his eyes were bulging more than a month before. He was mad or sad or frightened, which I could not tell.

'I was ignorant,' he said. 'Now I have been studying up on the savages. I wish I had known this before, but they are not all the same.'

'There are different tribes I've heard.'

'Quite so.' He nodded his head. 'The government of Texas will give you what they call a parcel, about one hundred thousand acres, so they say. One hundred thousand acres and no trouble.'

'That seems an awful lot.'

'It's a different country,' he explained. 'There are tribes there who are peaceable. Not all, but some. The agent says this is much easier doing than the Creeks.'

'I have heard there are some very wild tribes in the Texian country,' I said.

'Yes,' said he. 'I'm not a fool.'

And he then pushed at me a piece of folded paper on which he had made three columns: FRIENDLY, HOSTILE, HARMLESS.

I was an Englishman, the servant of a Frenchman. I knew nothing of these matters but there are very few men who are harmless when asked to give away their ancient lands.

I asked him would he not rather have a good business in New York.

'No,' he said, 'for I hate pigeons more than you could ever know.'

'Not pigeons.'

'Well I don't know what else there is available,' he said. 'I do pretty good out of pigeons, but it is no work for a man.'

'Oh you could do a lot better than pigeons,' I said, not really having an idea but thinking, Parrot, you are in America, you too must do something with your life.

'What?' said Peter, suddenly alert and holding my eye very hard.

'Oh, I couldn't say.'

'You have a plan,' he cried. 'I see it.'

'Not really.'

'You have a plan. It's clear.'

He now began to pay attention to my awful drawing.

'You cannot keep it from me,' he cried grabbing so violently it tore in two. 'Why, it is terrible,' he said, and returned a half of it as if in confirmation.

He was not incorrect, but I had drunk four glasses of rum and curdled milk, and my life, generally speaking, seemed to stand on very shaky ground and I would not have trusted his opinion of a dollar bill.

'You tore my drawing,' I said.

He tried to laugh.

'You mutt,' I said, and thereupon I leaned across the table, and with a style more powerful than graceful, I brought my fist to the attention of that wet and baleful organism on the right side of his beak.

OLIVIER

To form words with my own hand is to reveal myself to the world as a disgusting kind of cripple who must, in dragging his limb across the paper, arouse both pity and disgust. It must always be a shock to receive a letter from Olivier de Garmont, a young noble whose hand might be reasonably expected to be blessed with elegance and beauty as a right of birth. Imagine the recipient as he innocently slits an envelope and is made privy to the esteemed noble in a state of calligraphic dishabille.

Amelia Godefroy's hand, in contrast, was a very fine and graceful instrument, and I had imagined she would replace Mr Parrot as my *secrétaire*, and then all three of us would be most content. Indeed, when her father whipped his buggy up the hill, when the servant cried out a great halloo as if he were at hunt, no one was happier than Amelia. She showed it too.

For the next two days we worked very peacefully together, occupying the library with all the calm content of a married couple. I laid out, in French, what I understood of the American

justice system and thought myself blessed to have my misunderstandings corrected before they were committed to the page.

She was a very cultured young woman, but being American she
was also very practical and no one should have been astonished that
a portion of the administration of the farm already resided in her
hands. That she might not, at the same time as possessing all her
graces and virtues, be familiar with the arts of letters or diplomacy,
can hardly be thought surprising in the circumstances, and yet it
took me a day or so to understand that she, in all her very sweet
Christian enthusiasm, had seriously underestimated the amount of
labour required as *secrétaire*. I rather think she had seen the service
as similar to that she might render an elderly aunt who – her once
blue eyes now clouded, her knuckles knotted and woody – wished
to write to her sister about last Sunday's sermon, a good deed I had
been moved to see her perform.

But I was ridiculously happy to give dictation, to show off the
workings of my mind, and, like a bowerbird building a mound to
entice his mate, to construct, as only a Frenchman really can, the
most lovely artful sentences, rippling threads of argument that
dazzle even while they lock themselves in place. This sounds a
mite grandiose or mad, but did I not hear her sigh? I certainly saw
her bosom rise when the subject was no other than the degree to
which the towns of America protected themselves from central
interference.

She permitted me to dictate the case of Missouri, where the
citoyens elected a goat to the senate, so little did they respect the
role of government. This they sent to Washington where Andrew
Jackson had it served for dinner. Later I understood this was not
true. I deleted the paragraph but one cannot remove the memory of
my wicked pleasure, to display myself and see the quiver of response.

I was the peacock of Wethersfield and very pleased to be far
from France.

As the days wore on, and as my beloved moved from the break-fast room to the library with less alacrity, and as I understood the occupation was duller than she had anticipated, I saw it would be necessary to fetch my servant back from Babylon. To this end I dispatched one letter and then others, all addressed to him c/o the New York Post Office where he had promised to inquire each day.

I then tactfully professed a weariness with that which I now referred to as the *opus horribilis* and in so doing gained a great reward on earth – the opportunity to explore Wethersfield, although this turned out to be more concerned with mechanical matters than I might have expected.

Our first call was a visit to the new corn-husking machinery Mr Godefroy had purchased just the year before. We stood in drizzling rain, watching the monster fed, and there was no shortage of neigh-bours and workers to explain, again and again, the wonders of the mechanism. The sole voice of dissent, and the most complicated and eloquent one, was Amelia Godefroy, who provided a perfect example of that poignancy, that surprising melancholy, that unex-pected nostalgia to which Americans are so vulnerable. Their past is so brief and yet they are conscious of an ideal world, a perfect nature disappearing before their eyes, sentiments one would more reasonably expect in an aristocratic rather than a democratic society.

So, Miss Godefroy, on the subject of the corn shucker, her arms folded inside her oilskin coat, the rain running down her lovely cheeks: 'Before this excellent invention which my dear papa is so excited by, the corn was hauled in good weather to the barn, and then in wintertime the young people went from farm to farm in the evenings making a party out of the husking. The person who husked a red ear earned the right to kiss his or her sweetheart. This was a way of making work pleasant. It has been replaced by what you see before you now – this solitary worker husking corn in a cold December field.'

The red ear. How could I not love her?

I now formally released her from the chore of her dictation and, as is obvious from this appalling page, took on the task myself, trusting that the Parrot would eventually rewrite it, but then why am I now writing it in German?

When Amelia asked why I was using this ugly language and not my own exquisite French, I immediately asked her did she read German? As I had intuited, she did not. I said it was an occasional exercise for me to write in German, to keep myself fluent, but really what I needed to discuss was this business of Amelia and what to do about her, for she is a completely delightful, alarmingly different woman, as unlike a Frenchwoman as it might be possible to imagine while at the same time every bit the equal in her wit and beauty, and I do know why I am writing in German, of course I do.

Amelia is not only wealthy, she is a hundred times more splendid and desirable than any other woman I have ever met.

What has been occupying my mind is the subject of marriage. I had thought I could avoid it, even while I flirted with it, but now it appears more certain and more serious, I find myself in the position of the coy bride. Let me explain in confidence: *laß mich erklären im Vertrauen*.

As a result of her father's reformist enthusiasm for the porch he had caused to be built some five cottages, positioning each one where the aspect was thought to be particularly *improving*. And there the little houses waited, above the lake, gazing down upon the wonders of the river – whose secret ripples and hidden shoals were instructive as metaphors within the glory of the Protestant God – waiting to reform the characters of those who never seemed to come.

Perhaps Godefroy had imagined well-behaved prisoners ending their term at Wethersfield, and perhaps there would have been, had he not suffered conservative enemies on the prison board. In any case, these romantic cabins were all empty and it was Amelia's great pleasure to escort me into them, one by one, and do a turn of the rather cobwebby room while pretending we had just arrived to be reformed.

I had imagined I would be able to write what followed but even in this German language, even with no other reader but myself, I am too shy. I cannot, even inside this seashell, confess what urges she wished us to be reformed of.

PARROT

Peter von Gunsteren lent me his handkerchief to stanch the blood of combat. Two rums later he was confessing he had a girl whom he was required to marry in Philadelphia, and it would be a favour to him if I would deal with the New York end of the business which involved not much more than sitting in a tavern all day long. The only strict requirement was that I should never be late for the English papers.

I told him I would think about it and stepped out into the hustle of Greenwich Street, enjoying that bracing, head-clearing feeling that only a fight can properly give you.

Having nothing much to do except make a third inquiry about my mail at the post office, I wandered, using my freedom to consider who I was and how I might be better. I headed along King Street, away from the waterfront where it was very cold and beastly, and the poor Irish girls, clad only in silk and gooseflesh, had their complexions turned the colour of a plover's egg. Soon I was down on Chambers Street, with the wind hard against my back and pushing me toward the post office. Here, under the rotunda, my sparring partner waited on me, a long-armed beetle-browed clerk dressed for his chilblained life behind his counter. He wore three woolly jumpers, and mittens like my own Mathilde.

'Nothing for Larrit,' said he at once.

This was all as previously, and I don't know why this occasion would be any different, except I suddenly had a vision of his lordship's handwriting. Lord God, what a frightful sight it was!

So I returned to Mr Woolly Jumper and asked him was there a letter for a man named Carrit.

'You always ask for Larrit,' said he.

'Now I'm asking Carrit.'

With great reluctance he returned to those pigeonholes to which he had affixed so many labels and handwritten instructions that he had made of his simple job a puzzle no one else on earth would ever solve. He came back empty-handed.

'Then Jarrit,' I inquired. 'Or Garrit.'

He stared over my shoulder so indignantly you might imagine he saw a phantom queue behind me.

'Garrit is it now? With a G?'

'Try that first.'

Soon I heard him give a sort of bark. Then he threw a number of envelopes across the countertop.

'Smudged,' said he, as if I did it.

'And blotted,' said I.

'They arrive like this,' he said.

'I do not doubt it.'

And for a moment the pair of us were joined by our severe judgement of the calligraphy. Our alliance was brief, for he would not permit me to read them at the counter, or in the cosy little corner where the ladies got their mail, so it was out in windy old Chambers Street that I learned my services were urgently required back in Wethersfield. My first response was to feel an immense relief. Far removed from conjugal relations, I would be spared this awful unmanned feeling that comes from having no useful purpose on the earth. This was not a long-lasting satisfaction. Indeed, by the time I had got myself to the wine merchants on Pearl Street (where I went to order the Montrachet he wished me to shake up on the coach), I saw my trip to Wethersfield as no more serious a solution than a job in a pigeon loft.

The pigeons might occupy my days I supposed. I might save enough money to have a shop. But how would Parrot end his days behind the counter of a shop?

I squatted on a stoop on Broadway reading old Garmont's awful smudgy scrawl, not without affection, for he, in being so distant from my prickly presence, seemed to have forgotten exactly who I was. Thus he not only gave me the expected orders regarding wine and banking but confessed his personal feelings toward both his hosts and their nation. He loved beyond reason. Of course he judged them very fiercely for the blot of slavery on their luminous constitution, but how fine it was, he wrote in the very next sentence, what enormous pleasure there was in walking down a good paved street in Massachusetts knowing no one was planning to chop off his head.

This he spoiled by adding: *I don't know, dear fellow, if you can imagine it.*

Well that is a question I will answer for him before this account is over. But on that day, I walked the cold street imagining only myself, thinking of pigeons and making money, wondering what it would be to spend my life writing stock-market prices on paper and banding them around the legs of birds. When hats were blown past me I did not chase them. I pushed into the face of the wind and, with my ears freezing and my forehead numb – for I had no hat of my own – I arrived back by the river with its lumbering carts and horse shit and poor cold girls and sailors drunk before lunch and at the Bull Inn I asked permission of the Irishman to inspect Peter's pigeon loft.

Having seen us fight, the landlord knew us to be friends and indicated the window from which I could reach the ladder to the loft.

Squatting in this disturbed air, with the wings hitting the back of my head and my nose pinched up against what the New Yorkers call a shitstorm – an accurate description – I recalled Dirk and his brother wringing necks as if they had no souls. I had been brought up with a better idea of myself than this.

I washed my hands and face in the Hudson River and then I set off once again on one of those walks where the greatest part of your aim is to convince strangers – touts, thieves, barrow men – that you are a busy chap on an errand of great importance. Thus I was a fraud and the only true thing I knew was that I would not return to a house where I had no pride or purpose. By evening time, my very shins exhausted by the day, I came back down Chambers Street and then down Broadway, turned into Park Row, and found myself confronting what I secretly had known I must – a great banner on which was painted in heroic style, Marianne and the charging bourgeoisie. Dark had fallen now and the banner was illuminated by violent roaring faggots arranged along the top of the high steps. In this light was revealed the work of some ash-faced bible-basher who had painted across Marianne's naked bosom in a style so artless as to be an assault on anyone who has ever touched a breast or brush:

THE DRAMA OF
THE REVOLUTION IN FRANCE
AND
ITS CHILDREN IN AMERICA

There I was hailed by the impresario. He stood above me and below his sign, his scimitar lips casting a frightening shadow on his features until the moment of a smile revealed a more perfect sweetness than one could hope to find in a mother's kiss. His moustache was waxed. His glistening rug of hair shone in the yellow flares.

Eckerd was a salesman. He was an American. He came down the steps like a dancer, prancing a little sideways to fit his shoes to the narrow tread.

'So there he is at last,' said he, 'the father of the play, the midwife too,' he said. 'You were there that awful day. Only you know,' he said, 'in all the world, what we have done. I am so pleased. No one knows but you. Please come. There are special seats and, afterward, all sorts of surprises. This play,' he said, examining me closely with his gleaming foreign eye, 'will change your life.'

OLIVIER

Larrit, I hardly know how to address you from this distance. Indeed, having just begun my chapter *HOW DEMOCRACY AFFECTS RELATIONS BETWEEN MASTER AND SERVANT*, the matter is of some concern. I do wish you will soon return to attend to its legible transcription, and then you will find yourself more in agreement with me than with anyone else in Wethersfield.

I cannot think what has become of you and confess I wake several times each night, alarmed by the powers I have entrusted to you, not least your stewardship of my New York bank. Perhaps it will amuse you – although I hope not – to see your master dangling on this particular hook. And yet there is no other person I should trust more than yourself, and no matter what early difficulties we knew, I have never been unmindful of the long and faithful service you gave M. de Tilbot. Surely you would expect that I know a great deal about your service to him in the years after his properties were forfeited. I have been many times reminded of the scrupulous and honour-able way you attended to the breaking up of his father's folios, and with what discretion and commercial judgement. That a noble lord should be reduced to surviving as a bookseller was too much for him to bear, and you, I know, undertook this liquidation on his behalf and left the most particular accounting of the transactions. This the marquis de Tilbot was keen to impress on me when he offered your services. Do not think I accepted his gift ignorantly or lightly.

Perhaps you have not felt your value is apparent to me. Believe me, you have proved yourself to me time and time again, not only when you stood by my side against the mob but even when I least appreciated it. Your purchase of the *Versailles Impromptu* was one such incident and I have successfully copied your comic enactment, together with a string of commentary which pretty much follows the path that you indicated.

All this makes your failure to return a source of concern, for trusting your integrity, being needful of your assistance, I hardly know what to think except that harm has come to you. Are you ill?

I have completed these chapters in readiness for your return:

* *INFLUENCE OF DEMOCRACY ON WAGES*
* *HOW THE GIRL CAN BE SEEN BENEATH THE FEATURES OF THE WIFE*
* *EDUCATION OF GIRLS IN THE UNITED STATES*
* *HOW THE EQUALITY OF SOCIAL CONDITIONS HELPS TO MAINTAIN GOOD MORALS IN AMERICA*
* *SOME REFLECTIONS ON AMERICAN MANNERS*

Thus some thirty pages are already here. For the present they lie atop the tall black spines of Mr Godefroy's *Virgil*, and I am reminded by the flickering of the fire – the same warm light that brushes Miss Godefroy's cheeks as she turns the page of her novel – of the fire's double nature.

Monsieur, I wish to say to you that you have been, and I hope will continue to be, of immense service, and as the long days progress and I labour on this book, I feel we are both, you and I, partners in a matter that represents your own cause as well.

I will write for you, whenever you ask for it, the most useful letter imaginable, one that would have the presidents of America wish to have you as their trusted confidant and friend, and once your service to me is at an end – well, I wonder if this is what you will require. Consider this, as you chart your course, for I doubt there is a better letter for you than the one I plan to write.

Dear Larrit, I have been travelling out from Wethersfield on more than one occasion, having traversed the most primitive wilds, with no sign of any human soul. Last week I came upon one of those poor settler's cabins where one's first thought is to pity them the plainness of their existence, the lack of cultured society, or any of the comforts that even the peasants of Orne might take for granted. But here, as one such fellow pointed out to me, it is the opposite of France where land is beyond price. Here land is taken freely, and it is only the labour of the family that is bought dearly, but what one finally comes to understand is that one is talking to the lord of the manor, and if one's eyes can see the dense wild forest as his domain, one sees oneself much as I might see myself at the château de Barfleur. This, monsieur, may be a life you would consider, and if that were so I would assist you in every way. The cost to you would be somewhere in the region of forty chapters of transcription.

It was in the midst of this profound solitude, some miles beyond this settler's cabin, that I thought of the July Revolution. I cannot say with what violence the memories of the twenty-ninth of that month took possession of my spirit. The cries and smoke of combat, the sound of cannon, the rolling of musketry, the still more terrible tolling of the tocsin – the entire day with its enflamed atmosphere seemed suddenly to rise out of the past and place itself as a living tableau before me. There was a sudden illumination. When, raising my head, I glanced around, the apparition had already disappeared. But never had the silence of the forest seemed colder, its shades more deep, or its solitude so complete.

As you and I walk these American streets it is perhaps best you are aware of the present state of Europe which my father writes 'seems to be that of a volcano ready to explode'. Coincidentally the administration of justice in France is moving to curtail my eighteen-month leave of absence, and here I sit before the fire at Old Farm, the fire crackling merrily and Miss Godefroy, as I write, laying down her novel on her lap and smiling at me and at her mother, who has revealed herself to be not so bad a soul, glancing from one to the other of us before returning to her crochet hook with something close to contentment. I do not suggest paradise – she and Amelia have, this very night at dinner, suffered a loud and distressing disagreement on whether Christmas was a pagan feast or no. This I am sure is a question of little interest to a declared atheist, except that the Godefroy family has ordered me to issue an invitation to you and your family to visit at that time of year.

My immediate thought was that this was one of those American misunderstandings. For would you not agree with me that in aristocracies masters and servants share no natural similarities and although wealth, education, opinions and rights keep them a great distance apart on the scale of human beings, the passing of time winds up nevertheless tying them closely together, so much so that they would both agree they should not share table at Christmas though they know each other better than any other pair at that table. Long-shared memories keep them together and, despite their differences, they have grown alike.

Here in Wethersfield, where I am as unexpectedly content as I have ever been, we would find our ideas questioned at every moment. They believe that aristocrats will mingle with the common mass, while I despair of seeing the end of that noble class. My dear Miss

Godefroy believes that the European will one day mingle with the Negro. To me this is a wishful delusion and nothing one observes can possibly support it.

For all that, will you, dear sir, be so kind as to attend Old Farm at Christmas? It will require no second reading to understand your services are required by the master of us both, I mean the book.

Also, if you please, two cases of that Montrachet and whatever gold coin you think safe to travel with.

Olivier de Garmont

PARROT

When Eckerd said his play would change my life, I expected he would somehow shatter it. Still, I followed him.

It is said in Paris that Americans do not like the theatre, that they go to church instead and never drink. The truth was found on Chatham Row where, inside Eckerd's Elysium, I found a theatre like a wedding cake and the gods more Greek than Christian. That is, as Eckerd led me to my seat, a lady's stocking floated down, as gentle as the seed of a dandelion. I mean, the audience was *mixed*, and had bought their tickets for different reasons, some as simple as thumping their boots and singing '*Yankee Doodle*' whenever they got bored. There was a gross of bankers and their families but also a good sprinkling of those wispy-bearded New York clerks and their girls and mechanics and British sailors ashore and a party of blonde Germans staring at the curtain so they would avoid whatever wickedness was being presently enacted above their heads.

The Elysium was red velvet like a knocking shop, a kind of maze through which the great Eckerd guided me, touching my elbow like a tiller on a shallow run. He was so circumspect, so delicate. From his fingers I felt a dreadful sort of pity, as if I must be kindly killed.

'Sir,' said he, 'your good bride.'

I was a stupid man. I felt an awful dread. I clambered over merchants' knees and stood on their wives' squeezed-up little toes – poor peas in pods too small for them. Mathilde took my arm. She was warm against my side, her soft breast against my arm.

I thought, Clearly it is Eckerd who is coughing up the money. I said, 'Young Olivier has been writing to me.'

She plucked a pigeon feather from the shoulder of my coat and examined it closely. Did she see I was a pigeon not a cheeky parrot, a lackey who carries messages bound to his scabby skinny legs?

Mathilde asked me did my master wish me to go back to Wethersfield.

I said, 'Where is the money coming from?'

But the curtain rose, and she was saved.

The backdrop showed an idiot's idea of France from a bad engraving. Never mind, it did not matter. Mlle Desclée was beautiful, unrecognisable beneath her powdered wig. Her English was a treasure, an entire language learned in something like eight weeks. She was an aristocrat from somewhere on the Mississippi, or so I guess, for she sounded like the captain of the *Zeus*, who was Natchez born and bred.

The play yawned ahead, eternity.

Mlle Desclée's lover was a bourgeois revolutionary. If he was a historic figure who can say. He was a London actor with the hair of Danton but he was lightly built so I wondered was he Robespierre but he did not have that fellow's priestly turn. In any case, it was clear that the playwright, taking the example of Shakespeare, did not care to be constrained too much by history.

Mlle Desclée had a fine and noble house painted twenty feet

tall. This I examined closely. In certain aspects I thought it the Empress Josephine's Malmaison, even to the gum trees out the back.

There was a scene with a great herd of actors all calling for Mlle Desclée to be guillotined. The audience were surprisingly upset. This would have puzzled my father's friends but it was the human factor I was later told.

Mlle Desclée sang. It suited her.

The lover sang. It did not suit him half so well.

But all in all, Eckerd knew his Americans, and he delivered his hero and heroine in front of a backdrop which faithfully represented the city of New York. Here both hero and heroine declared the revolution won.

I thought it awful. But the audience *went wild*, as Peter von Gunsteren would say, throwing fruit and nuts.

I rose. A firm white hand was laid upon my knee. I thought, She loves me. Then I understood I was being instructed to stay seated for reasons stated thus: CODA: THE FREE BIRDS OF AMERICA.

Darkness fell. There was a flute, I think. A figure materialised, so slowly it seemed like one of those pictures that appears behind the eyelids when they close. It was the actor who had played the part of lover. The lights dimmed and brightened, and there stood, in the same bright green garments as the lover, our very own poor twisted charcoal Watkins, like a tree blossoming after fire.

'Good God,' I cried. 'What's this?'

It was our sensitive friend exhibited in his monstrosity. He stood alone, uncomforted, a paintbrush in his hand. Some lout laughed, and then the audience took refuge in a certain hush of horror.

But he was not Tiny Ted the midget or the lady with three legs. He was Algernon Watkins, an artist of the first degree, and as the idiot audience shouted its amazement or upset, I bawled out my rage against it all.

He was a great artist, not a clown.

Mathilde whispered that Watkins represented the troubles of the revolution and the promise of America. If so, it was in no way clear. Watkins sold his engravings in the foyer. I thought, He is not a circus dog.

The commerce was very brisk and occupied the best part of half an hour. Afterward, we were led up beyond the balconies, past the ropes and pulleys where we were escorted into the small apartment Eckerd had built beneath the roof.

I will come to this apartment presently. It was a minor miracle, and was later famous in a murder and divorce. But at the time I set upon the owner angrily, for I had seen Watkins sell an engraving for fifty cents. The unlikely connoisseur was a gentleman with grey striped pants and long frockcoat. He folded the precious print in four and slipped it inside his shirt.

'It was unbearable,' I said to Eckerd.

'I am not an artist,' he said, and I refrained from saying that was evident in every aspect of the play. It was grotesque to attach poor Watkins like a tail.

'I am not an artist, but I look after my friends,' he said.

So he had not given a damn for his play. I suppose I had known that when I saw him make it up. He had chopped and sawed and nailed it, like a man making a tannery on a riverbank, adding Watkins to the script as if he were an outhouse or a shed.

Eckerd questioned me until he understood exactly what my objection was. He was very civil. He poured me a glass of bright red sparkling wine.

'So,' said he, placing the glass in my hand. 'You disapprove of what I do. But what would *you* do for Mr Watkins? Or for your wife?'

Of course I had no answer.

He smiled, raising his glass. 'The stage is clear for you. Please go ahead.'

When I turned my attention to Mrs Watkins, I understood she had been shaking her head at me these last minutes past. I looked to Watkins and saw his furrowed features twisted on themselves, the pink scar showing his upset. It was Mathilde who came to my rescue, who took my hand, who owned me with a kiss upon my rough-shaven cheek.

'What a shame it is,' said she, 'that you must go away.'

Let me explain more carefully where it was we were.

II

Being inside Eckerd's secret apartment was like being inside a whisky barrel, or beneath the ceiling of a barrel-vaulted church, or taking shelter under a tight-clad boat turned upside down against the storm, a kind of ark.

It was very high, above all the scenery and ropes and pulleys, and very dry, just beneath the roof.

The ark had room for just one animal, a cat. It was what they call the Egyptian breed, grey in colour with very cool blue eyes. Max, his name was, more like a monkey than a cat, with a comic monkey turn that had him leaping from a cupboard and landing on his master's head. This was a good joke when it was not your head being landed on, but I was soon extremely put out by his manners in respect of chamber pots or lack thereof.

There was no facility for washing, cooking, or other personal matters, and although the whole was draped and hung with rugs and fabrics such as an artist might use to create a scene, and although there was also a long low settee where you might pay a poor girl to be an odalisque, there were also a number of straw pallets arranged on the floor, and these suggested a church at a time of war or flooding. On one of these Mrs Watkins now sat, a blanket wrapped around her lap, making a cushion for her husband's tortured head. I quickly sensed that my six companions were parties to a plan from which I had been excluded.

At first I was relieved, but then I was very bloody irritated to understand they had been selling art when they might have benefited from my experience in the world. They did not know a bloody thing – not even Mathilde – about the services I had performed for the marquis de Tilbot. Can you imagine them selling Watkins' birds for fifty cents?

When I saw that oaf tuck the engraving into his woolly underpants . . .

In any case: a room like a boat. Straw mattresses. Rugs. Odalisques and so on. Then – all along the gentle golden walls, stacked in some cases, pinned in others – a great number of works of art, including those paintings Mathilde had removed from the Greenwich Street farmhouse, from under my nose, from above my arse. Now here they were, with Watkins' engravings to keep them company. Also to be noted very bloody *bene* was the Egyptian cat who sprayed first one canvas and then another while no one bothered to tell him to mind his manners. I was exceedingly annoyed to see artists party to this pissing.

I bathed my tongue in sparkling wine until my organs cooled. Most politely and carefully I asked my Good Companions – Did they think it spoke well for their character that they were prepared to sell Watkins' engravings for fifty cents?

Eckerd would not take the bait.

Nor could I argue with Mathilde.

So I turned to Mrs Watkins who was busy stroking the short soft hair on her husband's head.

I asked her what that engraving had cost her, the one they sold for half a dollar.

'Me? Dearie me, not a penny.'

'But was it not a warbler?'

'Yes it was, dearie.'

'Then did you not invest a great deal of courage on the banks of the Missouri River?' I knew of what I spoke, for her doting husband had lectured me at length. I knew the cost of that engraving – the horrid ulcer that still grew down to her living bone.

Mathilde said they all valued art. They thought of nothing else.

'Then why,' I asked, 'does Watkins have his plates here to be corroded by the cat?'

If a sigh is a reply, he answered me.

On a low bench in a corner by the door there were more plates, higgledy-piggledy, not even protected by a sheet of paper. I took the uppermost one which happened to portray, by chance, a spoonbill parrot.

'Return that, sir.'

'Why? Do you not know me?'

'Return it.'

'Please,' said Mathilde, 'my dear Parrot. Please do not be thin-skinned.'

She tried to take the plate. I would not permit it.

Watkins raised his head and screeched as I carefully wrapped his copperplate.

Mathilde shook her head.

Eckerd asked me what it was that I intended.

I said he must accept that the theatre is each night washed into the sea, it sinks, it drowns, so even the great Burbage is forgotten. But we can pull down an entire country and chop up the king's heart and fry it with the kidneys, and still the paintings will survive.

Watkins said I should read the parable of the talents.

I said he could wipe his bottom with his bible.

A great number of words followed and it was only when we quietened down that I understood my friends were – on the basis of some secret understanding – to sleep the night on these pallets on the floor. What could I do but lie down also with the copperplate safe beneath my head? And there we all stayed, grubs in blankets, not knowing what we would become. In the night a huge wind blew through the theatre below us. I heard it moan, and something crashed. Then it was inside the walls. Then Mathilde came onto my mattress and clamped herself around me like a padlock. I held her and felt her breath beneath my chin.

III

No chamber pots that I could find, although I had been up and searching often in the night. I was ready to use the wine bottle when I heard a tread upon the stairs.

Thank the suffering Jesus, I thought. Someone was fiddling with a chain. Stuff me with little green apples. There was Eckerd – I had thought him sleeping behind my back but now he was in front of me. Someone had been stuffing carbon paper down his mouth.

'It is done,' he said.

'Give me the damn pot.'

'What pot?'

'I am about to burst.'

'In the drawer,' he said, and I saw smuts of carbon on his glittering gold coat. He had no explanation, only newspapers beneath his arm.

'Show me the drawer,' I cried in the midst of a general resurrection of the bodies on the floor. 'Give me the pot.'

This was delivered from behind my back, a tin bucket in the hand of Mrs Watkins. It seems the custom was to step out on the landing, but as no one instructed me I did my business as modestly as the circumstances permitted.

When I had time to pay attention to the others I found them in deep contemplation of the *New York Sentinel*. Naturally I assumed it was a write-up of the play. This misunderstanding was strengthened by Watkins' agitation which suggested that his engravings had a bad reception. Eckerd and Mlle Desclée looked rosy in comparison. They perched on the settee and Mathilde leaned over them, frowning as she always did when called to interpret long stretches of the English language. Meanwhile Maman looked from face to face to read what effect the news was having.

FIRE AT MURDER HOUSE

It was Rapid and Caused Consternation for a Time
Property of Mr. Eckerd
Much Loss Averted

The house at 565 Greenwich Street which was made notorious in living memory by the hideous Muldoon murders was last night burnt to the ground in a conflagration so fierce it was, for a time, expected to destroy an inn on the other side of Greenwich Street, which is, at this point, some 25 feet wide. The Bull Inn, a great favorite with captains of the London packets, was saved thanks to the enthusiasm of its patrons. The timber yard of Mr. Fachetti lost its fence, and a small quantity of cedar was consumed.

The owner of 565 Greenwich Street, returning home from Eckerd's Elysium, of which he is the well-known public promoter, soon became a highly visible and valiant member of the bucket brigade and showed himself, in his desperate efforts to protect his property, quite careless of the gold tuxedo which many of us have seen beneath the footlights.

The cause of Mr. Eckerd's clear distress was, it was soon

known, not only the loss of his recently acquired dwelling but a collection of letters from many European artists and musicians. Also missing was a historic tiara, once the property of his grandmother. Neighbors joined Mr. Eckerd in sifting through the hot ashes, where, not without numerous burns, some of which were judged severe, a certain quantity of melted gold was recovered. Although this metal will, of course, bring a not insubstantial price as specie, its value is expected to be only a fraction of the melted treasure.

Mr. Eckerd appeared too distressed to discuss this loss, but Mr. Peek of Turtle Bay, a director of the Hand in Hand Insurance, confirmed the tiara was insured by his company. He would not disclose the value of the lost item but did disclose to the *Sentinel* that Mr. Eckerd had recently, at his own insistence, placed many other pieces of jewelry in the vault of the Bank of New York.

'This might have been so much worse,' Mr. Peek said. Mr. Eckerd was a very fine example to the public, he added, for he had recognized that insurance of property, while wise, could never return a beloved object. At a time when the building was still smoldering, it was still hoped that the tiara's five diamonds would be recovered and that these, together with the price of the recovered gold, would go some small way to covering the loss.

———————————

The story continued, but by now my companions had lost patience and, having been somehow launched into a fantastic frame of mind, set about pouring whiskey and making toasts in such a raucous style it would be easy to imagine oneself aboard a pirate ship.

To Mathilde I said the following: 'But this is the same Peek who said he would not insure you.'

'That's him,' said she who sometimes called herself my wife. 'And he did not insure me either.' She laughed again, and her old mother poured herself a dram and lifted it high and Mr Watkins, who seemed to have been mostly afraid that someone would be burned, took his whiskey in a teacup.

'You have burned down your house,' I said to her.

She replied by flinging her arms around me and setting her whiskey lips upon my own. 'Not mine, my Parrot.'

'Was there a tiara?' I asked Eckerd.

His answer was to reach into his cloak and produce some melted gold, but he could not stop smirking at his cleverness.

'And this is what you had to keep secret from me?' I said to them. 'I suppose you have paste jewellery in the bank? There was never a valuable tiara. You melted some gold. You burned down the house. You are scoundrels, all of you.'

'We are *artists*,' said Mathilde. 'We have a right to live.'

You have no idea how beautiful she was and how her eyes glowed, but I did not like her at this moment, and this was not exactly a moral point. I understood her to be saying she and Watkins were artists and I was not. This might be true, but it stabbed me in the heart.

Watkins avoided my eye.

Eckerd, however, did not wish to flee my gaze. He floated in it, basking.

'And when Peek sees you two together? Your game will be up.'

'He never has,' said Eckerd. 'He never will.'

Of course this was why Eckerd used the front door while the rest of us used the back. I had been tricked, insulted, weighed beside them and found lacking.

'So then, this is Art.'

'Art in America,' said Mathilde.

'Well damn you all,' I cried, and the old maman sat down as if pushed.

'No one here knows quality,' said Watkins. 'No one will pay us what we're worth.'

'Would you rather have the lords and nobles back? What is democracy for? Not so we can rob each other. Or cheat.' I said *cheat* and felt the teeth in it, the cleat, the cut, the eat. I thought, My lover cheated me, my wife. 'You are no better than Lord Pintle d'Pantedly. He thinks the common man is stupid. He thinks there can be no art in a democracy.'

But Mathilde would not be doused by me. She flung her arm around the room. 'This is art,' she cried. 'We made this.'

'But your argument is just the same as Garmont's. He says you cannot make art, he is wrong. You say no one can recognise art, and you are also wrong.'

We snarled at each other like a pair of dogs.

What were the roots of my rage, I hardly knew. I had failed to use my own talents as my companions had. They thought they were my betters and I feared they might be right. They were arrogant. They were wrong. They thought that they alone could *see*. They had promoted themselves to be aristocrats of the senses. In this role they felt entitled to steal whatever gold they wished from public coffers.

'Fifty cents,' I cried, and picked up the printing plate that I had kept safe throughout the night. 'Here's two dollars.' I threw the coins onto the mattress, where Mrs Watkins snaffled them. No one moved toward me.

I further wrapped the printing plate, two more sheets for good measure, tied it up with string, and dropped it in my duffel bag which Mathilde, to her credit, had moved out of the house before she burned it down.

Next I kicked off the top of the wicker basket in which Mathilde kept her supplies. She had never seen me act like this before. I threw out the jars I found inside, and then removed that little sack of wax-paper twists which she, being always careful with her money, wrapped around her leftover paints. These I took possession of, and a brush or two as well.

'I was not born to be a thief,' I said to her, 'and neither were you. If you burn down another house I will come back here and burn down your bloody theatre.' I repeated this in French and Mlle Desclée began to cry.

Good, I thought, let them bawl.

I lifted my duffel to my shoulder.

Mathilde cried, 'Don't!' but failed to specify. She had an awful fear of the police, so perhaps that was it, but when I left the theatre I had no more dealings with authority than to make one last visit to the post office before I left New York.

No sooner had I appeared beneath his grand rotunda than my old friend with the wool jumpers hailed me.

'Ha,' said he, and was soon referring to the labels on his holes, and then held out a long thin article, not exactly an envelope but a letter folded and contained the way the nobles do in France.

It was addressed in a hand I recognised. If Monsieur was writing letters I feared the guillotines were being taken down and scrubbed and oiled.

Lettre de la comtesse de Garmont
à l'attention du domestique de l'honorable
Olivier-Jean-Baptiste de Garmont, actuellement à New York

'*Du domestique*,' said my woolly friend, without much care to the niceties of language. 'I have been thinking this must be you.'

'It is, mate. Yes.'

He leaned so close to me I could smell his onion sandwich.

'It is in French,' I said.

'All of it?' As if he had not already steamed it open.

'It is.'

'You won't be reading that too quickly,' he said, 'Why don't you take it over there where the ladies get their mail? There's no one to complain of you this early.'

M. Perroquet,

            I write to you at the behest of the comtesse de Garmont, who, being prey to all the natural feelings of her sex and having in addition become advised, whether directly or indirectly I do not know, that her beloved son is set on making a marriage in no way advantageous to that noble and ancient house, begs you to use whatever tools you have in your possession to have her son returned to her.

Being acquainted with that gentleman's strong character from birth, and expecting that he will not confess his American attachment, I have no doubt he has placed himself in a situation where the good counsel of his peers can never reach him. Thus she who gave him his life now invests her hopes in you, fully understanding that his salvation should probably be undertaken in the same forceful manner whereby he was put aboard the *Havre*.

However, as he is presently, she understands, many miles from a port, and being himself most clearly in that unbalanced state of mind he may call 'in love', she has asked you to communicate to him that his tutor and old friend the abbé de La Londe is presently dying. She hopes this will shock him out of his bewitchment. In the moment of greatest shock she would have you encourage him to take a coach to whatever port is nearest in order that he should speed to the old man's side. Yet I am conscience-bound to tell you that the abbé passed away last week.

Perroquet, what you are to do with this request is for you alone to decide. I would not encourage you to any criminal acts which, being undertaken on American soil, might be far more dangerous than any of my actions at Le Havre.

If you do receive this letter you might let me know c/o the one in Brussels where I may spend the winter. I have a copy of the Baillard which makes me very happy. The morocco is not of the quality of the treasured item we let go, but the prints are exceptionally fine, there being a greater density in the blacks as a reward for patience.

Tilbot

OLIVIER

I

It was a considerable surprise, in the middle of a gloomy afternoon, at a time when I was nodding before the fire, to see Mr Larrit looming, not as I sentimentally remembered him but as he really was: weathered cheeks, coarse hair, frank eyes, and that careless habit he had of leaving a few long hairs unshaved around his Adam's apple. He had not brought the Montrachet and, like a servant in an American inn, made no apology except to assure me it would be here by and by.

When he had settled his 'things' (in truth no more than the usual bumpy duffel bag), he returned to the library and, without taking the trouble to close the door, announced he had a proposition to put to me.

Of course servants do not, in the normal order of things, put propositions to their masters, and yet it was not his use of this word that alarmed me, but the very clear direct expression in his eyes. To put it coarsely, he looked like he had something 'on me'.

'A penny for your thoughts, John Larrit.'

For answer he patted my arm.

Perhaps this behaviour had been encouraged by my friendly letters, or was simply the unfortunate consequence of his spending time among Americans. In any case, I answered coldly. 'You may put to me your proposition.'

He said he understood I required a great deal of labour from his hand and he would honestly perform it, writing for as many hours a day as I could reasonably expect.

Reasonably? I thought. *Un moment*, dear Blacqueville.

'No, no,' said he, although I had not spoken. No, he promised to rise early and labour late, but he would require a horse and three hours of every afternoon to be given to his own endeavours.

I asked him what endeavours and he answered that his proposition was to leave the house when the family sat down to lunch and return in time for supper. I thought, Would not even an American democrat be offended by this presumption? He said he would rise at four each morning and, being absent for the hours he had decided, work until nine at night. He invited me to do the arithmetic although there was no need for he had already done the calculation. It was a bargain for me.

'Indeed,' I said.

He could not have been deaf to my tone, but he stared at me directly and I thought, He has something 'on me' certainly.

I had confessed everything. If he had forgotten what I told him in my madness on the steamer, I had reminded him in writing. Of course the scoundrel imagines he can stare at me like that and then demand to be provided with a horse for some endeavour he will not name.

'Wait,' he cried, seeing the expression on my face. 'This is all to your advantage.' He then explained that the horse would allow him to spend more of his time labouring in the library and a great deal less along the road to Wethersfield.

His time? This was a very modern concept he had learned. I was far too angry to ask him what business he might have in Wethersfield. I said I would talk to Mr Godefroy about the horse.

But he had already spoken to *Miss* Godefroy and she, without consulting his master as she might have, had been very happy to oblige him. In a democracy, it seemed, one could not go against a servant's will.

Thereafter John Larrit performed his duties as he had invented them for himself.

Sometime later, a week or so perhaps, it was reported that Mr Godefroy's black mare had been seen in the shed adjoining Mrs Dover's boardinghouse, and so poor Godefroy had a very urgent need to establish that the horse was not there on account of any business of his own, nor was he in unseemly congress with Mrs Dover whose reputation, it was widely agreed, was not beyond reproach. Godefroy was very cool with me when giving me this news and I was very sorry to be the cause of upset for the man with whom I wished, one day, to form a close association. He left it to me to reprimand my servant, who naturally swore that he had no relationship with Mrs Dover except to rent the shed from her and he undertook to ensure that the shed door was always closed in future.

My good Amelia chanced upon this conversation which another of her sex might have thought judicious to leave alone, but as in other controversial matters, such as Christmas and her opinion of the educational qualifications of President Jackson, she surprised me. Taking up her usual chair by the library fireplace, she reached for her English novel and rested it upon her knee as if it were a bible upon which she would make John Larrit swear.

'How was your time in Wethersfield?' she asked my man.

'Very good thanks Miss.'

'I suppose it was on a private matter that you ventured forth?'

'Yes Miss.'

'But you looked after our Molly.'

'Next time I will have a feed bag for her.'

'She has a stable, I heard.'

'A shed. I rented it, Miss.'

'Did you meet the landlady at all?'

'A moment.'

'They say she is handsome.'

'Yes, very.'

'It would not be the first time she gave a stranger shelter.'

'Will that be all sir?' he asked me, colouring.

'Yes,' I said. 'Please leave us.'

When he had gone Amelia said, 'He looks at you in such a cheeky way, don't you think? What have you just given him permission for?'

I said I had given no permission, and if anyone had been permissive it was she who gave him the horse.

She put aside her book and stood as if to leave. 'My father thinks Larrit has smuggled his wife to Wethersfield.'

And then, the minx, she kissed me, and held my hands, high, so they would almost touch her breasts.

Said she, 'It must be very nice to have a wife,' referring frankly to those pleasures which she had hitherto invited but denied.

'Indeed,' I said, for what else could I say? She had such a bright engaged intelligence, and such beauty, that one would think her, in France, to be an aristocrat, a woman like Mme de Staël, although not burdened with her flirtatious reputation. Here in Wethersfield, she could also be seen carrying feed for her chickens, not playing the farm girl but running a considerable business of her own. She would not marry a man who did not love her and a man who loved her could only make that clear by his proposal. There was no question in my mind that I must, sooner rather than later, overcome my sense of duty to my mother. I must eliminate all those ancient lines that led me to this point, sever that root to the Clarels and Barfleurs, everything by which I secured my place on earth, my hope for glory. And yet of course my past in France was not secure at all, nor could my future be when, even now, my own kind was once again regarded an enemy of the state. If this mortal danger was a privilege of rank, why should I not cast it from me?

Was not the American democracy preferable? Was not the French turmoil the result only of its inevitable path toward democracy, a treacherous confluence where the river of nobility met the ocean of equality? Was it not better to inhabit the future than the past? And if the future appeared half made and raw, was it not also peacefully free of politics and parties? In America there was nothing like our schisms, our ancient blood-drenched hatreds. I could discover no discord here more serious than the manufacturing states bickering with the agrarian about a tariff.

Life in rural Wethersfield was never without amusement. For instance, I soon discovered why the horse was kept in Miss Dover's shed. Larrit had become engaged in a business with the printer Mr Cloverdale who housed his presses in the lane behind the widow. Soon it was clear to everyone that Mr Godefroy had no relationship with Mrs Dover. But then the entire village was alarmed to learn that my servant was demanding Cloverdale order in paper of an unheard of and expensive kind. No one had seen this paper, let alone felt its weight, but its price so offended something in Cloverdale's Protestant soul that he must take his anxieties to a town meeting (of which it was judged better that I be left in ignorance). Here at the meeting house there appeared many citizens who apparently feared a counterfeit was to be committed, a type of fraud such as had become common recently.

No one came to me as they should have. As a result my servant was called before the village in the middle of the afternoon. There he was asked what he wished this expensive paper for.

He laughed at them outright, asking them what did they imagine he would do.

They did not like to say.

Thus, in the same church in which I had been so moved by the marvels of democracy, the servant publicly quizzed the printer who was soon revealed to be not very much of a printer at all, and the town was shocked to hear the questions he could not answer, and alarmed to learn these failures would have disqualified him from his trade in London or even Hartford. As for the expensive paper, the servant had already fetched it himself from Boston and used it before the printer's very nose.

He who is sometimes called the Parrot then left the meeting and returned with a coloured etching of a bird he was not prepared to name, allowing only that it had been seen in the lands of Texas, and although it was commonly agreed to be very like a spoonbill parrot, its colourings were another matter, being carmine at its head and sulphur blue at its tail, and as luminous as a phoenix or some beauty in a myth. The exhibition of this etching in the meeting produced a silence of such length and intensity that even the most prayerful would swear it had been never equalled in the long religious past. I am sorry to have missed it, this proof that God had blessed America with such a wonder. The bird itself must have seemed a miracle, a breathless holy sight, and it is for this reason, perhaps, that Wethersfield soon found itself without a printer and there was no newspaper until after Independence Day.

At this period I was engaged in writing the difficult chapters about the American judicial system, no simple matter for a French lawyer. I was daily perturbed by my servant whom I found continually staring at me, as if there were something he could tell me if he wished, but need not if he did not wish. Many is the time I found him with his lips already parted, before he seemed to change his mind.

This came to a head on an afternoon turned suddenly dark with a snowstorm, and the rest of the family out of doors dealing with this unexpected circumstance.

I looked up from my chores and found again that clear direct stare.

'Yes, sir,' said I, and laid my notes down. I thought, I will give the chap his notice. I am sick of him.

'Sir,' said he, and rose.

I thought, Good grief, the impudence.

'What is it that you wish to say? You may say it. Be done with it and go.'

He hesitated.

'Continue.'

'The abbé has passed away.'

I slapped the rascal's face for such a filthy lie.

II

In aristocratic nations, it is not unusual to find, in the service of the great lords, servants of noble and energetic character who do not feel the status they suffer, who obey their master's will with no fear of arousing his anger.

In these circumstances it would be unthinkable for the one to strike the other.

In a democracy, however, both parties know that the servant may at any moment *become* the master and that he has the ambition to do so; the servant is, therefore, in both parties' understandings, no different from the master. But even this unstable promise of equality will not serve as an excuse for striking Larrit as I did.

Indeed, one does not require the intelligence of Machiavelli to recognise it as unwise to invite combat with an Englishman of his type, orphaned, abandoned, therefore forced to inhabit close quarters with the most depraved type of creature, a servant through necessity although having the misfortune to imagine himself called to higher things, who must become, inevitably, a resentful character whose body, in the singular case of the man before me, will carry the clear marks not only of the wind and sun but the bar-room brawl and perhaps – unseen – the lash. Even his distinctive nose, quite handsome in its way, may not have been the one his parents gave him. In short, John Larrit was the sort of narrow-eyed and haughty character on whose account one might wisely cross the road.

I had seen his eyes blaze, most memorably aboard the *Havre* where I twice had reason to fear he would kill me in my bunk, but now I observed – after a first highlight of anger – not hostility or belligerence but an awful sort of hurt. Silently, stolidly, he considered me, and I could actually *see* him thinking, of what, I could not say, but the thoughts themselves were as unarguable as clouds crossing a pale green sky, drifting, changing form, blocking out the sun from time to time. Before this uncanny spectacle I stood, a master, yes, but also a child, waiting to be taught the consequence of my savagery.

'You loved him then,' he said at last.

'Who told you this?'

'You, sir. You could not have made your point more forcefully.'

So, he shamed me. I apologised to him from my heart.

'Well, sir,' said he, 'a man must do something when his father dies. If he does not, he will feel the pain forever.'

'He was not my father.'

'But there is no doubt he was worthy of the blow.'

I thought, What is this to him? Was it a trick of light that his eyes appeared so moist? 'Who gave you this bad news?' I demanded.

'It comes from France' – and he gave full pause before admitting that which I might not have known myself – 'from your mother.'

My mother, I thought. My mother. My mother who loved me so intensely, who could never hold me very long but could never let me go, my mother whom I pinched because I could not share her with the world.

I said, 'Does it not seem strange that my *mother* should confide this awful news to you? Has she ever *noticed* you? Why would she not tell me?'

'In any case, her request was of a slightly different nature.'

'How different? What exactly do you mean?'

But he was like a horse, shaking his head at the approach of the bridle. 'To reveal that is to break a bond.'

'But you and I – do we not have a bond?'

He touched his reddened cheek, waiting a discreet moment before glancing at his fingertips. 'Call a spade a spade,' he said. 'She wants you home.'

'And I should sail to France to stand by a grave? It makes no sense. My mother would never give this news as an enticement to return. If my old confessor was dying, that would be something else, but I would not cross the world to lay my hand against a stone.'

'There you are then. That's it.'

'What? You mean he is yet alive?'

'Your parent might have preferred I suggested that.'

'Damn these riddles!' I cried, but he had his sense of honour and it made him stand excessive straight. 'Do you intend now to raise my confessor from the earth?'

'On my honour, he has passed away.'

I thought, God save me from the scrupulousness of servants. She wants me home, of course. I thought, She would say anything that served her ends. She has heard I have been sporting. But how could she have heard?

'Were you sent along to spy on me?' I demanded.

His eyes hardened.

'Not you? Then who has been reporting to her?'

This question would never be answered satisfactorily, although for several years I suspected Mr Peek whose daughters I had unintentionally insulted. He had been recently in France and having, as he was pleased to tell me, 'gotten myself about', may have been the source. But this really made no sense, for my mother would never have received an American of his type. Most likely, I had betrayed myself with my dissembling letters. My mother knew my heart was easily touched. She knew me judgemental but also passionate, my senses readily excited. If I had only had the wit to *admire* an American woman or two, if I had admitted a single intellect, a melodious voice or two, she may not have so clearly understood the love that I was hiding. As the Parrot coarsely observed when describing her intuition, 'Your mother sniffed the fillies in the air.'

In any case, the comtesse de Garmont had somehow perceived her son's matrimonial intentions. As a result the game had reached a dangerous stage and I was delivered, quite unprepared, to that place above the cataract where life-and-death decisions must be made. There might still be time to catch a branch, but did I wish it?

Finding myself suffering considerable emotions I turned to stack the fire which had, as always at Old Farm, been neglected by the servants. The great logs being almost exhausted and the kindling in poor supply, I had excuse to make a considerable task of it but finally I must reveal my own eyes to my servant. He had folded his hands in front of his apron and I observed the crescents of red and yellow paint beneath his fingernails. Being irritated by these marks of absence, I set to get him back on track, to now take the dictation he had so much avoided.

'Now?' he inquired.

'Now,' I ordered.

But even as I spoke, my mind was in another place. This tactic of the comtesse had forced me to confront myself. I loved Amelia Godefroy with all my heart. I would die rather than be parted from her – but she would be destroyed by noble France. I had been, so many evenings, drunk on the possibility of America, but was I in love with America or Amelia? In this – dear wild wonderful girl – she did not help me. For while I might wax rhapsodic about the simple direct democracy of a town meeting, it was Amelia who took furious issue with President Jackson and his treatment of the Indians. It was she who, affecting not to disturb my concentration, slipped papers beneath my library door. Had I answered these written pleas I would have had my nation prevent Jackson's scheme to have all previous treaties with the Indians denied. I would also have departed for South Carolina that very morning. There I would learn what it was to spend all one's life, from first breath to last, in chains.

Was this what I wished to marry?

How could you not love the woman who wrote these lines? But if I married her, I would join the Union in every sense. Then would not Jackson's crimes be mine as well?

In my own conversations with my beloved, all was turbulence, one moment tender kisses and the next the president was a tyrant and the next he was a brave and honest man who would remove the people's gold from the First United States Bank where it was being used to oppose the people's will.

My heart and mind were in turmoil, yet I could not cease my labour. I ignored the bell to lunch and my *secrétaire*, although clearly agitated, did not demand his afternoon in Wethersfield. It was suppertime, and both our stomachs in chorus, when I bade him set the quill aside.

He begged permission to light a pipe – a new habit – and when he had his long legs backed hard against the fire, he announced that he must now travel to New York and could not be sure of his return.

I could not lose him now.

The job of work I had begun in America had its roots in the flinty soil of penal servitude. Had that not been my public intention, to come to Wethersfield to study the administration of the prison? But once here the prison seemed a minor task and what was growing in Connecticut was a second undertaking, and no matter what its author's lacks, his foreign ignorances, his inevitable confusions, I had reason to believe my study of America would stand for many years to come. It would act as map and compass to my countrymen as they negotiated the violent onset of democracy. What business was more important than this? Not Mr Parrot's, certainly.

As to the engraving he showed me, I never saw so gaudy a thing and I was reminded of the painting of Thomas Cole – a tedious man – whose autumn landscape had already brought an alarming garishness to Mr Godefroy's foyer. The colours of the American autumn are, in all their splendour, the most magical thing you ever saw, but they are of a very raw and independent nature, wild beasts in their way, creatures who will not permit themselves to be made tame in art. Indoors they are rude and gaudy – one wishes they had left their accordion and muddy boots outside – and that was the vulgar nature of this singular engraving that poor John Larrit, who had already suffered very much in his long life, now staked all his store on. It was nothing much more than a circus bird but he stood before me full of hope, like a boy in a fairy story, off to make his fortune in the world.

I had grown very fond of him and was exceedingly sad to witness his conceit.

III

'You have lost your wife,' Amelia said, flicking snow into my face. 'It is weeks ago he left and you have been in mourning ever since.'

'He is my servant, not my wife,' I said, although of course I understood the joke. Also it was very true – he had ended up a very useful chap.

'Only a servant?' she said. 'Then that's easily fixed. We'll get a new one.'

She stooped to pick a small grey rock from the white crisp blanket at our feet.

'Your lordship's rock,' said she, smiling to reveal that charming slender shadow between her two top teeth. Why was this apparent defect so entrancing?

'Shall I warm it for you, sir?' she asked, and proceeded to blow on the rock and hold it under her arm and I thought that tiny gap was really the master stroke in all her face, although how this absence could create such a sense of character, of liveliness, of blessed mischief was beyond my understanding. She was a Rembrandt not a Hals.

We had come to the long ridge of Gibson's Hill, named for a settler of living memory, and all of Old Farm was spread before me like a gift I might unwrap if so I chose, the snow-dusted onion fields, the cow pastures and woods, the idealistic cabins with their porches and, beyond these steep white roofs, the crooked elbow of the Connecticut River beside which I had wandered in ignorance and love, not daring hope this day be granted me.

My darling was clad in sturdy tall boots and a long native bear-skin coat, but on her head she wore the bright red bonnet she had adopted when the locals were still hunting deer. This framed a face that, in all its Greek perfection, recalled the Hygeia which stood on my father's desk, its secret life hidden behind her pale pink mouth which, applied with winter oil against the cold, glistened like those lips which made Elisabeth Vigée-Lebrun such a favourite with Marie Antoinette.

'He has gone on to other things,' she said. 'You should be happy.'

How could one not be content with this extraordinary beauty, this grand sweep of life and all the centuries that might be lived within the landscape now considered?

'Your Larrit,' she said. 'He will make a fortune, you will see.'

'If I am sad it is not because I have lost a servant.'

'Dear Olly,' she said. 'Don't be ashamed to miss him. I have observed the pair of you together. It is really rather sweet. You are a very noble noble, dear.'

My beloved annoyed me, I admit it. Yet so it is between couples of the deepest and most enduring affections.

'He is my servant,' I said. 'The person I grieve for is my confessor.'

Then, all at once, the rock was a rock, and all frivolity was cast off in the snow, and she had taken hold of both my hands and was insisting I acknowledge the grief I had hidden from her all that time.

Why I should keep this secret from she who would console me, I cannot exactly know, except I had spent the weeks in a state of chronic loneliness that was oftentimes unbearable. When I smelled the sweet Virginia tobacco on Mr Godefroy's coat, I was reminded not of American things, not of the nullifiers of South Carolina and the sin of slavery, but of Bébé whose bristly cheek had so often brushed against mine, a caress made more intense by its almost painful roughness on my pale child's skin. How the strong must love the weak, I thought, that he cared for me like a squawking sparrow in a nest. He ran that I must learn to follow, swam that I might not drown.

He was gone, his body in the soil of France, leaving the world entire a foreign place.

Side by side we tramped the ten miles to Wethersfield, and thence another three miles to see a small red schoolhouse where my beloved sometimes came to teach the farmers' children. Amelia had been, from our first encounter, a believer in the principle of education in democracy. On this point we argued freely, with curiosity and humour, but I could never see, and would never see, not if I lived to be one hundred, what use she found in the English novels she made these rural children read. For what can a society learn from Jane Austen except that it is a very nice thing to become married? To my shame, I kept this opinion to myself, but always with the intention that we would discuss the matter properly when we were nicely settled with each other.

The road from the school led up a considerable hill where a great amount of snow had accumulated, calf-high in places. I was more than a little excited by her splendid strength, her pink cheeks, her shining smile, the dear comic faces she made when the snow, on occasion, fell inside her boots.

There was a place below the crest where the downhill coaches pulled politely aside so as not to spoil the momentum of the uphill traffic labouring the last quarter-mile to the crest. On a shelf of dark rock we caught our breath and contemplated that plain white sheet on which a glorious history might be writ, perhaps by those very two who stood there now, young, childless, their futures still unimagined.

She said, 'It is not good for you, to be cooped up in this way.'

'Oh, I am happy enough.'

'You are very sad, my dearest, as you just confessed.'

'That will pass,' I said, wondering if that miracle might not have been achieved already.

'You have no one of your own kind to talk to.'

'I have you.'

In response she surprised me, as she had done on other occasions, briefly – mischievously – brushing, as if by accident, that item of anatomy which proved me not her kind. And having done that, the imp set off walking up the hill. I followed her in some confusion, knowing that I must amend my chapter on the manners of Americans.

'You are a devil,' I said, kissing her.

'I might become an angel, in God's eyes.'

And thus continued our conversation on the subject of matrimony. It was always present, and never quite declared. Yet when she said *angel* I pictured, as she intended, Amelia Godefroy dressed in white before an altar. Thus our language was functional enough.

Hand in hand, we walked downhill, with the smoke of Old Farm rising from behind a stand of poplar. We spoke not of devils or angels but about Bébé and my peculiar childhood and she persuaded me to once again describe for her the Seine, the orchard, the *Bottom Hundred*, my mother's house in the rue Saint-Dominique.

In attempting to conjure all this I was constantly aware of the weakness of my powers of observation, and yet I caused her to see *something*, see it vividly, and I was moved and comforted by her excitement.

She said, 'One day I will walk through the *Bottom Hundred* with you.'

'It is a world away.'

'Then we will travel worlds away together,' she said. 'And I will spend years and years seeing everything you have seen, with your eyes, my eyes too. I will walk across the Pont Neuf, sit at a café in the rue du Temple, hear your mother tell me how you were when you were a child. I cannot imagine how it will be, but very old and very cultured.'

'Oh my darling, you would not wish that.'

'But I would. Why should we not live in France?'

Here, at this moment when I might have been most considerably alarmed, I was overjoyed. My heart beat fast. I embraced her, held her slender graceful form inside the furry feathers of her coat, pressed myself shamelessly against her. 'Do you propose to me, my wench?'

'A hundred times already,' she said, and inside the cave of her mouth it was very warm and soft.

'But I am the one who must propose to you. Or is that one more custom you Americans have abandoned?'

'It is a fine custom,' she said, and what a smile, what a mixture of delicacy and mischief, some hint of Caravaggio in her Bacchus cheeks.

'But should I not ask your father?'

'Indeed,' she said. 'But you must ask my permission to ask his.'

And so it was agreed, and all my grief smothered by this, this joy that she and I could think of nothing better than to walk in the woods by the Seine and together we would botanise and I would show her all the algae, lichens, fungi, mosses and ferns Bébé had had me classify, not because they were most beautiful or rare but because Linnaeus's plant taxonomy was based solely on the number and arrangement of the reproductive organs.

The dear tender priest chose for my attention those parts of God's creation with no obvious sex organs, the class Cryptogamia, the only 'plants', as I was to learn years later, 'with a hidden marriage'. It was not any sense of propriety that kept me from relating this to Amelia, but rather the fast rush of our conversation, for now a certain door had been opened between us, and she confessed that she nightly dreamed of France, of its soft green grasses, the gentle landscape made by centuries of cultivation.

'In my sleep everyone is speaking French,' she said.

It was then, before we reached the long curving drive into Old Farm, that I imagined my mother as she heard my beloved's way of speaking. I saw the glitter in her eye, the slight lift of her upper lip. As we opened the wide gate to the property, I pinched my mother's arm and watched her outraged eyes.

IV

Early on the following morning, complaining that his office fireplace was choking him, Mr Godefroy brought his trays and folders into the library.

Godefroy was a big man and of athletic frame, and although you would never think him anything less than cultured, there was a comic aspect to his occupation of a desk – his big legs squashed in underneath that walnut octagon. Physically, he was better suited to leading his men in raising a barn or pulling down a bull.

Among the chores pressing him that day I can recall a letter to his friend Biddle at the First Bank of the United States, new proofs of a treatise on workers' housing, the latest shot in a sometimes contentious exchange with the manufacturer of the corn shucker, and the response he must make to a commissioner's inquiry into the justice of various punishments meted out at Wethersfield Prison. This last item appeared in no way ominous, and in truth I paid it very little attention. I was hard at work on the bigger subject of America, and if my present chapter owed something to my host, it was not something I had discussed with him.

'Among the small number of men who are engaged in literary works in the United States, the majority are English, if not in origin then in style. Thus they transplant into the democracy ideas and literary uses which are current in the aristocratic nation they take as their model.' I was, even as I wrote, aware of the scratching of his quill as he endeavoured to persuade the manufacturer, by dint of both argument and illustration, of the change he wished made.

In other words, there was a great deal going on in that charming room with its merry fireplace and the deep-silled windows with their views of the late February snow, but not so much that I could not sense him gazing at me constantly. I was, without this help, acutely aware that I would soon have to speak to him.

He had shown, during every moment of my visit, the most agreeable and cultivated manner, but I never forgot that he was a passionate Republican who could never have imagined this French noble might become his son.

'Do you have a French expression for cabin fever?' he inquired at last.

I could, of course, supply several, not only in French but in German too.

'We should take a trip,' said he. 'We should get away.'

I wished to go nowhere, to do nothing but finish my chapter and see my beloved. I was, at that moment, in the best place on earth. 'Indeed,' I said. 'We must.'

'Six more weeks and there will be dogwood blooming in Atlanta,' he said. 'We might be there to greet it. You will find a different America down there, I promise you.' He had by then turned and was standing over me, smiling down. For a dreadful moment I thought he intended to read my manuscript. I sprinkled a cloud of sawdust on the pages.

'That sounds an excellent idea,' I said.

'Well, frankly, I am pleased to hear it,' he said, 'for you cannot stay in Wethersfield and know what is happening on the Mississippi or understand the passions in South Carolina where, at this very moment, there are otherwise intelligent men gone mad and marching in the streets, declaring they will fight to separate from the Union.'

At that moment my dear beautiful beloved entered.

'What say you to this?' he asked her, holding out a drawing but I observed his eyes joining her to me, and saw her warm smile in return.

Blood rushed to my cheeks.

My darling made some comment about the corn shucker I did not exactly understand but which clearly concerned the utility of her father's emendation. Watching this picture, the seated father with the high forehead, the eyes turned up toward the thoughtful girl, her handsome features softly illuminated by the field of snow, I thought of her meeting with my mother. It should have frightened me, but it amused me to imagine Amelia Godefroy politely passing the cogwheel of a corn shucker to the comtesse de Garmont.

Amelia crossed the rug and stood beside my desk, resting her hand upon my shoulder.

'So what do you say?' she asked.

'Say?' I asked, alarmed that there would now be some frank

conversation performed in some violently efficient American way. I was not ready, not at all.

'To my father's invitation.'

She looked deep into my eyes and I saw what she had done. She was conspiring to send me away with her father, to keep us locked together in a carriage until the matter of our marriage was raised and settled once and for all. Of course there would be democratic opposition to my nobility, but how could Amelia's loving determination not excite my pulse and predict the strength of our union?

Nor was I unaware of the enormous benefit this travel would have for my greater work which, no matter how much I wished to stay here at Wethersfield, could not possibly be completed without venturing into the nether regions of America.

These travels of mine are, by this time, generally well known, being a considerable part of *Morals and Manners in Democracies*. This present narration, therefore, will not repeat my existing accounts of the explosion aboard the *Comet* behind the barrier islands, our meetings with the *Creeks* in Georgia, or the astonishing discovery of President Andrew Jackson sitting quite alone in his rather plain salon.

As for Mr Godefroy's great appetites for life, they have no place in either book, although it is a caution to any foreigner taking the pulse of this nation, that I would never have guessed at the depth of his character if I had known him only in the Protestant propriety of Wethersfield.

Once we were in the free and open air of New York State, he whom I hoped to be my father bloomed spectacularly and did not once cease to astonish me all the way to Virginia, where it proved necessary for him to fight a duel in which he behaved with extraordinary courage and dignity. When his poor henpecked opponent, having missed his shot, awaited his death, Godefroy fired into the air.

Whether that individual's honour could be said to have been

restored, I would judge quite unlikely, but what is certain is that the book I laboured on so long would never have been written without Philip Godefroy. And if I must here record lighter, more personal matters, let it be said that Godefroy was on good terms with those on all sides of the great questions. We dined with Mr Biddle of the First Bank of the United States before calling on Andrew Jackson who was set on destroying all the bankers' power. We enjoyed the hospitality of Mr Calhoun and the great good humour of the diminutive Van Buren.

Through all this very long and sometimes arduous journey, during which we were often delayed by the most appalling roads and had not much better fortune when we took to sea and river, I wrote constantly to Amelia and she to me. These letters, being both passionate and intelligent, made me all the more certain of the correctness of our course.

V

We were in South Carolina by the time *the subject* could be approached but even then there were impediments which I would ask you, like Godefroy and myself, to tolerate a while longer.

I forget the name of our hotel except it was considered the best place in Charleston. Godefroy had written to secure our lodging while we were still in Georgia.

What he wrote I do not know, but clearly an impression had been made, for although we arrived late at night we were greeted with much bowing and scraping and a boy was sent to the chef with an order to keep the fires alive. The landlord then held us under close engagement – I presumed to cover any likely delay in the kitchen – so by the time we were seated at table we knew he had purchased the cellar of the late Thomas Jefferson and had himself driven all the way to Monticello to collect his loot, sleeping beneath his carriage on return as he feared he would be robbed of his treasure by bandits or oenophiles or worse.

Who knows how much he paid for his fifty cases? More, certainly, than he could afford, for we had been but a moment in the dining room – a place of extraordinary pretension – when he was looming over us ready to discuss his *carte de vin*. He was a confusing man to consider, a meaty military-looking fellow with the manner of a bully but at the same time unctuous, a character echoed in the decoration of the dining room, a high-ceilinged hall with a gallery from which were hung the flags of all the nations. Against this manly bluster were opposed a great number of floral displays too strongly perfumed for their situation.

He presented us each with his wine list explaining, ha-ha, that it would have been a deal longer if my countryman Lafayette had not had such pleasure from it. I thought him tedious.

Godefroy raised an apologetic eyebrow as the man happily recounted how the late president had died impoverished, and he had managed to get a great bargain from the estate.

'The prices, monsieur,' the landlord said to me, 'will gratify you, I am sure.'

Grave-robbing to one side, the list saddened me, for it was not what you would expect in the cellar of a head of state. There was a Bergasse, a wine mixed together in some cellar in Marseille which was labelled claret in the English manner, also some Blanquette de Limoux, a great deal of Minervois and Languedoc. Only a Beaune Grèves Vigne de l'Enfant Jésus seemed to rise above the ordinary.

Godefroy declared I must choose, but I declined, saying I was a stranger in his land.

'You are practically family,' he said, with what degree of calculation I do not know. I fancy we both blushed.

I judged the moment had arrived.

'Monsieur le commissaire, permets-moi de me présenter.' This, at that

very instant, came from our neighbour who was dining by himself.

I thought, Who dares to speak to me in this familiar tone?

I regarded the milky well-fed form and prissy little beard which I was told belonged to the French consul to Louisiana. If he was a diplomat he was also a boor for he had discovered my business when there was no decent way he could have done so. He ignored the most important man in my life and tutoyered me, inquiring of my family, my friends and relatives when he could not possibly be of our circle. In return, I paid him some empty compliment about the city of New Orleans, and returned my full attention to he who I intended to make my father-in-law.

'Excuse me gentlemen.'

Godefroy ignored him and filled my glass. I drank too quickly. Godefroy poured again.

'Monsieur le commissaire,' our neighbour insisted, 'do you wish to have an idea of the public administration of New Orleans?' Only then did I understand that he too had been drinking Jefferson's cellar and was already well invested in a Barsac. He was, as the English say, *two sheets to the wind.*

'Examine the streets of New Orleans, monsieur – what holes, what lack of order and alignment. Yet ask me, what is its revenue?' His eyes were awash with some strange emotion, as if daring me to snub him.

'What is its revenue?' said Godefroy pleasantly.

'The revenue, sir, is one million dollars. But into what hands it passes, God only knows.'

There was a Negro servant standing close by, his tall slender back reflected in the mirror with the flowers. Who knows what goes on in a Negro's head?

'Read the names of those who compose boards and councils of Louisiana – obscure people, lawyers of the third order, village intriguers.'

I looked to the citizen of Wethersfield and saw his colour rising.

'It is the lower classes,' said the ridiculous consul, 'who have the majority in the electoral colleges. They choose from their own kind. They eliminate one position to ruin a man and create another to give a living to a friend.'

At this Godefroy rose from his seat. 'To democracy,' he said firmly, and raised his glass.

The consul rose unsteadily and brushed some substance from his waistcoat. 'Democracy.' He raised his glass, but we neither of us saw him drink.

Godefroy remained standing, glowering down at the consul.

'I apologise,' the consul said at last, but a Frenchman would have been insulted by the tone. 'My opinion is obviously mistaken.'

'Indeed sir,' said Godefroy gravely. 'Indeed it is.'

Now the consul raised his Barsac, leaving a sweet viscous shine about his plump red lips. 'There is one merit of the American system that one must not deny,' he said.

'One?' asked Godefroy who had remained standing.

The consul did not know enough, I thought, to be afraid. He plunged on.

'Without force as it is without skill.'

'It?'

'*Le système démocratique, naturellement*. It is as without plans as it is without energy, as incapable of harm as it is incapable of good. It is powerless and passive. It lets society *marcher tout seul* without trying to direct it. Well, in the present state of affairs, it is perfect, no? In order to prosper? America does not need either leadership or deep-laid plans or great efforts, but liberty and still more liberty. The reason for this is that no one yet has any interest in abusing liberty. But wait, monsieur. It may take a century but *le fou viendra*.'

Did Godefroy understand the final insult, the prediction that a lunatic will come to rule America? God save us, it was clear. 'To liberty!' roared my friend, beckoning the hovering landlord while glaring at the sweating consul.

I ordered the Grèves Vigne de l'Enfant Jésus, wondering if the cork would be pulled before the duel.

'Je te présente mes excuses, Monsieur le commissaire.'

We ignored the consul and there was a very tense period when he remained beside us, swaying slightly. Our restraint was finally rewarded by a loud theatrical sigh and the sight, reflected in some dozen gold-framed mirrors, of his most unsteady departure from the room.

United as we were by outrage, neither of us said a word until the Beaune was poured. It might be expected that the first mouthful would make me yearn for France and all its refinements, and yet, was I not already intoxicated by Jefferson's Bergasse?

When, in excitement and affection, we had toasted each other one more time, I remarked to Godefroy that there had been periods in France when one would never dare make such a speech for fear of imprisonment or even death, and that in all the wretched consul's ignorance and sarcasm he made the strongest argument for democracy I had ever heard.

'To liberty,' I cried. 'To America. To beauty. To the future.'

I was drunk, of course, but I spoke *in veritas*. How moved I was to see my sentiments so welcomed. Amelia's father leaned across the table – a large table, but he was a large man – and took my hand and locked it fast.

'At the end of the day,' he said, 'you either love a man or you do not.'

Not knowing what to say, I attempted to raise my glass, but he did not wish to be interrupted.

'When you talk of America like that, can I take it that you would reside here?'

'Who would wish to live in the past?' I answered.

'Am I correct in assuming it is in Wethersfield that you would dwell?'

My heart was beating very hard. I was perhaps too much aware of the Negro waiter at my side.

I replied to Godefroy that I wished to live very close to him and his family.

He said, 'But I am assuming you will one day marry.'

'Exactly,' I cried.

He smiled. I thought, I have done it now, but had not allowed for his being American. One must speak directly. 'Sir, may I ask for your daughter's hand in marriage?'

He raised his glass, his eyes glistening. 'You cannot imagine,' said he, 'how happy I am. I will tell you the truth, dear Olivier, I thought you planned to take her away from us and I really thought that I would die.'

Somewhere about this point the consommé was inserted into the scene.

'No,' I said, 'she is a flower of America. I don't believe France would bring her happiness.'

'It is you who will bring her happiness,' he said. 'Is it not the strangest thing, that my daughter would become a French aristocrat?'

If the consul to Louisiana had been present he would, doubtless, have taken issue with this particular point, but the honourable gentleman was snoring in the parlour beneath the stairs.

'I could never have imagined,' Godefroy continued, his voice thick with feeling, 'that after all the long sad journeys of my family, it would end up thus.' And he then related to me the most extraordinary story – his father had been a bootmaker and his wife's family been driven from her home in Scotland.

He held my hand and would not release me.

VI

My darling –

The night before last I was so happy as to dream of you, embracing you with such intense and rapturous affection that I awoke. Now in a waking state of equal happiness I am rushing toward you with open arms. We sleep but little, and our bones are very sore, but apart from your dear father's insistence that we travel the extra distance to Albany, where he feels the July Fourth parade will make a real American of me, there is no delay, and we expect to come careening down into Old Farm on July eighth at the very latest.

Your father informs me that the meaning of Amelia is *industrious* which I do not doubt is true but I have a second name with which to christen you and I will say it in your ear when once again I hold you in my arms.

Your husband in his dreams,
Olivier

PARROT

Dear Sir,

      I did the service you requested. I can now report that his lordship is aware that the abbé de La Londe has died and that his mother wishes him to return to France. However, he continues in his present situation where he is satisfied with the library and its window, which contains almost eight hundred acres with onions and dairy and a pretty part of the Connecticut River.

      On parting we wished each other well, as the saying is.

      You made no inquiry of my health but let me tell you just the same. I am well. Having departed Wethersfield, yours truly is now engaged in labour quite different from that which you intended me to perform and for that reason I am sending to M. Olivier de Garmont all the financial instruments you entrusted me with. The accounts are complete and all in order, although the bank should be communicated with in terms of the signatories. You are perhaps aware that his lordship has abandoned lawyering and has convinced himself he is a famous author. There are those at Wethersfield capable of rendering all secretarial services. Of other services it is not my place to comment.

Sir, you said it was for me to decide what I would tell his lordship and now I would like to allow myself the same privilege in respect of your good self. Sir, there is no use for me in service in New York. It is not that the Americans do not have servants but I would imagine there are very few masters with your elevated requirements. So here – you know me pretty well – I have a business proposition. *Do not burn this.* What follows will both amuse and benefit you. If I know you at all – and who could anticipate you better? – you have opened the accompanying tin box and discovered there engravings of a quality to astonish you. You nod your noble head. You agree I do not exaggerate.

Sir, when I reflect how many miles I travelled on your behalf and how often my job was to deliver some priceless item from your late father's library and to receive for it a few sous, a pittance, all because history had left you with ashes for inheritance, there may be some pleasure to be obtained in the thought that you might profit handsomely from the sale of these beautiful coloured etchings by a Mr Algernon Watkins. These are the equal of any ancient book you ever mourned.

As I write to you, my business partners and I have, as yet, only five of the engravings for *The Birds of America*. What you hold now are the pulls but still you may judge the quality. We have priced them here at two dollars for each print and ten dollars for each number, a complete volume of one hundred prints is subscribed in New York at the following prices:

LOOSE PRINTS $189

HALF BOUND $225

FULL BOUND $234

These prices are all established by me with my knowledge of the European trade and your needs concerning it. I am told the

British sovereign is five dollars but of the currencies of Europe I may be not so well informed.

Mr Watkins and his associate Mr Eckerd have both aided me in writing up a prospectus for the work which, as you will have already seen, is printed on Whatman Turkey. *Nota bene*: The watermark of each sheet contains the date. Mr Eckerd, who is known until now in the business of jewellery and theatrical production, has found it 'not challenging' to obtain orders in New York, Boston and Philadelphia, and that in a space of time extremely brief. I offer you some names which may mean nothing to you but accept my guarantee that these are *big cheeses*: American Philosophical Society, Massachusetts Historical Society, Yale College, etc.

What do you say? The price is so friendly that you could add a twenty per cent icing for your efforts. You know the likely buyers better than anyone on earth, and I refer not only to France but all of Britain, from Westminster as far as His Grace the Duke of Buccleuch of Dalkeith House, who I recall cheated us awfully over that folio of Dürer which I delivered for you one pleasant sunny day.

Sir, birds such as these have not been seen in Europe on air or paper. The value of novelty will be clearer to you than to myself, although I will never forget tramping the viper-infested jungles of Queensland in search of exotic flora to draw for the amusement of the Empress Josephine, as she had once been.

After so many years your servant, to write like this! Sir, the world is topsy-turvy, I do admit. Do not take it as an issue of presumption of equality but rather understand that we, each of us, have an appreciation of the engraver's art, and the pair of us, in our different stations, knows what it is to be far from home without shelter or sustenance. In these circumstances we have aided each other on more than one occasion. Sir, I have secured a house which is, by the bye, the mirror image of the establishment you once told me I could buy for the price of a cow. I will not haggle with you about

the Herefords but am very pleased we have room for Watkins, our
engraver, and his French wife. We employ three American colourists
who are sometimes assisted by my wife (who mostly continues, at
my insistence, to be engaged in her own distinctive canvases, which
you shall see when the market for the engravings is established). We
look out on the river as you promised me, but I am sure you never
dreamed we would create for you such opportunities, first for the
greatest aesthetic pleasure, second to satisfy that enlightened
passion for the engraver's art, third that you, in your old age, will
have the means to keep table fitting to your station.

What do you say?

Let me quote from our prospectus: 'To those of you who have
not seen any portion of the author's collection of original drawings it may be proper to state, that their superiority consists in the
accuracy as to proportion and outline, and the variety and truth of
the attitudes and positions of the figures, resulting from the peculiar
means discovered and employed by the author, and his attentive
examination of the objects portrayed.'

Sir, you know every educated man in Europe will want these.

But let me put it to you man-to-man so you will see. I had no
sooner secured this grand house at Pleasant Creek when Mr and Mrs
Watkins arrived from Manhattan where they had just that day taken
delivery of a Golden Eagle, which had been caught in a spring trap
set for foxes in the wild mountains of New Hampshire. It was late
in the day and I understood that the artist and his wife had eaten
little, but Watkins could think of nothing more than entering the
studio my wife and I had prepared for him. There, with no other
light but candles left by the previous inhabitants, he set to work
and continued all night, firstly outlining and then working fiercely
with his pencils. We all thought him sleeping, but when I had my
morning grub I went to look at the eagle and found our valued
artist seized by a spasmodic affliction, and even after we fetched

the doctor the sickness laid the poor cove low for several days. The artist surviving, he continued. Fourteen days, sir, in a frenzy such as I warrant you never saw outside a circus. Had you been with me you would have cried. Monsieur, *that* is an artist, and how I wish he is the one I had set before those Australian flowers and niggers.

His lordship Garmont was always of the very loud and firm opinion that nothing of worth could be made in this new country, and I hope I never disgraced myself by arguing against him. But you are in Paris, sir, looking at our engravings, and if there were a Charles X still on the throne, I know you would be straight out to chat to M. Pétain at the Royal Château of Saint-Cloud.

Sir there is wampum to be made, and plenty of it, for which we can all thank the bounty of nature, but there is a greater richness still and that is the hours you will spend – for I do know you sir – in silent perusal in your library. There is an added advantage to the purchase of this work, and that is, should there be a spill or other misadventure with the Chambertin, the artist vouches himself ready to supply a new engraving, to you if no one else, at no charge at all.

I expect the mails are slow to reach you and it may be, when your eyes finally fall upon my words, that many months have passed since I wrote them. Therefore could I ask you, sir, if you agree with my assessment of the commercial aspects of this publication, that you communicate at your earliest convenience. I have persuaded my partners to invest a great deal of their *very hard won* capital in this scheme and there is hardly a day goes by when one of them does not, on the advice of some idiot dealer or collector of stuffed butterflies, come to believe that my plan cannot work as I have promised. The Americans have all manner of opinions as to what the French will buy, one fool swearing that it is impossible to sell a print of any bird in Paris and that ants and caterpillars are all the go. From London they have more information, but no better in quality, and so you can imagine what great utility there would be in a letter of encouragement from your noble name. It seems to me, looking at the quality of Watkins' work, not at all mad to fancy that our mothers – yours and mine, high and base – gave birth so that at this point in the history of the universe a great work of art should be placed in the grand institutions of France and America and Britain, and in many other places besides – I know you have noble connections in Austria, for instance.

I do remember, as a child aboard the *Samarand*, being very frightened that I would be abandoned by yourself – I gave you your portrait on a stone which you were nice enough to make a keepsake – and today I can admit to feeling something of the same, and although I am not fearful as a child and the item I place in your hand is worth the attention of a king, we must each recognise the need for our continued profitable relationship.

Perroquet

OLIVIER

I

How would one expect the victors to celebrate the anniversary of the Glorious Fourth, that impossible date when the tides of history surged and, having finally receded, revealed crowns and broken sceptres amid the flotsam on the flat sand. Here the new words, until now unimagined (*I am the future and shall serve thee*) shining in the wet dawn light.

After that tumult, that burst sac, that spilled blood, with that price paid and the impossible attained, would you not, on the yearly feast, assemble your brave soldiers and their sons and would not each wife and mother, with golden threads and scissors, bind those epaulettes and braid, not to the torn and bloodied remnants of battle but to cloth entirely new, the honourable costume of a great nation?

The Glorious Fourth.

What banners.

Behind the banners we will expect the new philosophers, the new statesmen, the composers of genius who may have been blinded in combat or even deafened by cannon roar but who can still, in the ceaseless ringing silence of peace, compose the triumphal and the pastoral and thus make hymns for the shining malodorous people who now march from awful serfdom to the light of day.

'It will make you American,' Godefroy said.

What peace was I offered in those words. And I refer not only to dear Amelia, her hair the colour of spun gold, but also the silver cornfields of Connecticut.

Independence Day would be my baptism, and my marriage would somehow be my christening, but it was hard to conceive the Glorious Fourth on the inglorious third, which we spent on a long slow mucky ride to Albany, mud to the axles and bullocks commandeered from an old Dutchman who did not mind renting us his oxen because ploughing, he said, was useless in the mud, and he would rather rescue us than destroy his fields. He said – nay, everybody said – it was most unusual weather for July but having travelled a good deal by now and having suffered a typhoon and hail the size of eggs, I would say that all American weather is unusual.

We arrived in Albany in filthy darkness, nothing to eat but eggs and the inevitable toast. Attempting to complete my diary before bed, I managed to spill my ink across the carpet. Doubtless this damaged item will be valued at one thousand dollars by the morning.

At daybreak I was awakened by artillery explosion, a horrid sound for a Frenchman of my age. Forgetting my accident the night before I left dark blue footprints from my bed to the window where I understood Independence Day had now commenced. I flung aside the lace curtains and found the day was glorious indeed, the sun bright, the sky blue. Those wedding-cake buildings had been washed clean and the small square outside the boardinghouse was a brilliant shining green. Every house, every window, was decorated with the stars and stripes.

Huzzah! I cried, wishing my new wife were at my side.

The conversations about the ink were astonishingly civil. No one would accept a sou. Then my future father waited for me at the table with the bright eyes of an uncle, one of those imaginary chaps who arrives with splendid surprises on your birthday.

'Eat, eat,' he cried.

It was a short while after dawn but there was already a crowd trampling the grass on the square, eager, I thought, to find a good position for the parade. I was slow in understanding that this *was* the parade and these were the dignitaries. And what were they doing, do you imagine? Why, they were deciding who had precedence in the parade.

How extraordinary, I thought. 'Is not your precedence set?'

'It will be soon,' said Godefroy.

'But this is not the first Independence Day.'

'Oh, no,' said he, 'but the precedence is different every year.'

If I had been myself I would have laughed, but I was the guest of a great nation. I ordered a chop as was suggested, but had little time to eat it as Godefroy's friends Mr Azariah Flagg and the lieutenant governor arrived and I was required to join them as a dignitary in the procession.

'But I am a foreigner,' I said. 'I have no right to march with the citizens.'

'You are one with us,' they cried.

I was most excited, I confessed, and what a very peculiar and blessed feeling it was to stand safely inside the revolution, so to speak, to be on the unquestioned side of good.

The great day was in no way what I had anticipated as we toiled here through the mud. The gold thread was nowhere in evidence. There was nothing grander than a small militia escort, that is, quite rightly, the national guard of a country in which the military spirit is absolutely unknown.

And yet I did not laugh at this lack of martial splendour, and not merely from good manners, or my own private commitment to

America, but because there was such a spirit of gravitas and I was very moved to see the plain uncultured people in their pride – the deputations of all the trades and associations of the city, triumphantly turned out, bearing aloft the emblems of their professions.

Good Lord, I thought, my mother would die. But in this world my mother did not live.

It was completely original, without precedent. First came the fire department, all nine companies of men. At the front were twelve of the straightest and strongest. They carried on their shoulders, like pallbearers and just as solemnly, a miniature fire engine which was at once the most magnificent toy and also the Virgin Mary being carried through a village on Assumption Day.

Next came the association of printers carrying a carmine silk banner with letters in gold font worthy of a prophecy.

Next was the Albany Typographical Society which boasted a float as big as an opera stage and on it a printing press and a bust of Franklin, whom I mentioned in connection with his rocking chair.

Dear Blacqueville, you were a dreadful giggler. How comic, you would have thought, to see this solemn participation of the industries and trades. There was no king or parliament, no nobles of the sword or robe, instead an Association of Butchers and an Association of Apprentices, and you must allow that these emblems are very natural to a people who owe their prosperity to commerce and industry.

Mechanics Benefit Society. Carpenters Architectural and Benevolent Association. Some fifty societies with their various badges, banners and implements of art.

'How splendid!' I declared, ashamed of my own insincerity, poleaxed, in spite of my wiser self, by the absence of splendour, imperium, *gloire*. Where one might naturally expect imperial guards there were red-faced Carmelites, about fifty, in snow-white frocks tied at the neck and wrist with green ribbon.

The foreign visitor was looking for the past and there it was, before my very nose – Godefroy and the comptroller, their eyes shining as they saluted an old American flag, bullet-torn, a brave survivor of the War of Independence. It flew from a wagon occupied by four ancient soldiers who fought with Washington. I am told they are honoured and preserved like holy relics, so why does no one think to darn their trousers? Such was the confusion of my response to Independence Day, my feelings flying back and forth like blackbirds trapped inside a church. Here the dust and dirt, here the gold. There the beggars, here the lords, here the merchants giving change. Who are you, Olivier de Garmont, to drive them from the temple?

Oh for a bicycle of gold to race you up and down the streets, for in my privileged position, much of the parade was hidden from my view. So let me escort you on foot to a Methodist church which had the appearance of a drill hall in a Catholic country. Here a magistrate, who in America performs functions analogous to the *procureur du Roi*, read the Declaration of Independence.

Here then. A truly fine spectacle. A profound silence reigned. Thus the magistrate's voice became the voice of the Congress as it reviewed the injustices and the tyranny of England with great warmth and dignity. You could hear and *feel* the murmur of indignation and anger circulate about the auditorium. When the magistrate proclaimed the justice of the cause and expressed the founders' resolution to either succumb or free America, it seemed that an electric current made all our hearts vibrate.

Here one could feel, to one's very bones, the return of an entire people to the moment of their birth. In this union of the present generation with that which is no longer, and sharing for the moment all its generous passion, there was something deeply felt and truly great.

Oh that it had stopped there.

Alas, a lawyer next stepped up to deliver a harangue, and thus the great day turned to farce as *The Great Bore of Albany* was obliged to mention every single country in the history of the world. Thus he evoked everything boastful, uncertain, uncultured and boorish that might mark the ascent of the majority. If he had an idea – and I suppose we must admit he did – it was that all countries are coming back or will return to liberty. How could I not compare this fool with the great Guizot. How might I not, against my own emotional resistance, recall the wit and learning of Paris, and when the speaker – in order to impress the crowd with the greatness of America – referred to me, the French commissioner, as some sort of proof of his nation's prestige, I was as ashamed of myself as I was revolted by his presumption.

I had come to Albany as a convert to an altar of liberty, yearning for my perfect union with its great historic soul. I had believed it might be possible to live my life completely careless of how democracy might harm me. I aspired to become one of the rivulets – nay, streams – that makes the river of the people roar, to lend my gifts and privileges to the highest idea of civilisation the world had ever seen. When I had stood at Godefroy's side and heard the Declaration read, my heart had raced, hair raised on my neck.

But then the *awful* lawyer. I had entered the church a convert. I emerged as the son of the comtesse de Garmont.

It is not always wise to tell the truth, but now I will tell it – I was not at all moved to see the float with national banners of France, Belgium, Poland and Columbia. I did not like the silly platform with its working press and a boy in leather apron handing out the Declaration of Independence.

It is a painful thing to think that which you do not wish to think. Thus: a float with a Clymer printing press over which soared an eagle and in its beak a scroll, with the motto *vérité sans peur* – truth without fear.

What pride they showed, those members of the New York

Association of Morning and Evening Journals. And what made those men so righteous? Why, it must be all the coarse insults, the small vilifications, the impudent calumnies which fill their papers every day.

On the right was the Goddess of Liberty, supporting the American flag, on the left a full-sized figure of a slave, bound in chains, who having burst the shackles from one arm was reaching toward the printing press for emancipation.

But only reach! For how many years?

I had become a corrupted actor, a kind of cad. I placed my hand at Godefroy's back and shouted that the scene was charming. My breath was very difficult. Amelia awaited me. These people, I reminded myself, are the heroes of the world. They have not yet finished what they will achieve. And I am with them, of their number, aroused to feel their shoulders touch my own. What makes a democracy bearable? I asked myself, wondering if I had sufficient ink left in my bottle for my evening's work.

II

Being too impatient to wait for the maid and very eager to abandon Albany, I bathed in cold water and was refreshed. Alas, it was some hours before Godefroy emerged and I saw he was in no hurry to reach Wethersfield. On the contrary, he had already planned a diversion that would take us to a waterfall.

It was only then I finally grasped what the attentive reader will have understood already – that this elder of the puritan community did not like to be at home. He would prefer to spend his days sharing wine or ale with councillors and aldermen in as many towns as there were along the Hudson, all down the Mississippi to the sea. Why, even here in Albany, it seemed there was much that could occupy us for the remainder of the week. The governor's room, the golden corridor, the senate staircase, the senate chamber, the assembly chamber, the court of appeals room, the new state library with 150000 volumes and the Clinton papers – Clinton papers, sir! He had already arranged for me to handle a sword once belonging to General Washington!

In explaining why I must rush to Wethersfield, I painted myself, not incorrectly, as the lovesick fool. This flattered his paternal vanity to such an extent that he must hide his pleasure behind his table napkin.

'You would depart without inspecting the Museum of Military Records and Relics?'

'Alas.'

'Sir, it contains eight hundred battle flags of state regiments, with several ensigns captured from the enemy.'

'Sir, there is no battle flag can compete with your daughter's charms.'

'You will not be kept from her too long,' he said, 'for we can take the steamer down to the town of Hudson. Tomorrow we will see one of the great wonders of the world, then home. We will have some bad roads, but nothing worse than you have had en route.'

'We can take the steamer?'

'Indeed,' he cried.

'Might we not have saved ourselves a lot of mud to come here in that way?'

'If we had wished. Of course.'

'Then, pray, why not?'

'Because,' replied Philip Godefroy, 'you are an American now, and you must take the rough with the smooth.'

I did an excellent job of disguising my feelings. Sometimes I think it is the sole talent of the aristocracy.

Much later I came to understand that we had travelled by land so that my future father-in-law could avoid passing Sing Sing prison.

The steamer to Albany would have berthed there, and the French commissioner would have been compelled to make an inspection of that fabled place of incarceration. As to why Philip Godefroy wished to prevent this meeting, it is now well known that the governor of Sing Sing sat on the commission to investigate Wethersfield Prison, and that the results of this investigation were the cause of Mr Godefroy's fall from grace.

The steamer was raucous, filled with mechanics and other celebrants of the national day, all in their cups by noon. I recorded the scenery – the pleasant residences and villas on the riverbank, the early signs of unregulated greed and devastation. This was to be my new country, and I observed it was profitable all the way to Hudson.

Once landed, I took to my bed, pleading a stomach ailment, although the disturbed organ was in fact the heart. All night I dreamed I was still on the steamer, pressed in by mechanics and their wives who were roasting a cow on the deck. I got in a great rage with them for this stupidity, swinging an oar about my head and striking them so hard they flew into the river, which they possessed like a great mass of poisoned fish floating on their backs.

In the morning we went by coach to Kaaterskill Falls, a journey which gave Godefroy a new excuse to praise Thomas Cole, the same one who had bored me at the Godefroy table and whose *Autumn on the Hudson* contaminated the natural simplicity of the Godefroy home.

On the subject of the falls, I am told Mr Cole has written volumes. I have only a steep climb, a scramble, the wild prospect of dense dark laurel pines slashed by brilliant birch and, through this screen, the stream – olive-green water, soft as velvet. There was a hawk or eagle circling at one stage. The sky was blue, the rising breeze crisp for the time of year. We crossed a small wooden bridge on which was nailed a rusty kind of money box in which Godefroy deposited some coins. In a moment I saw four wild streams descend from a glistening shelf.

With what power and weight they leaped into the abyss. I heard Godefroy shout, saw his eyes wide with pleasure and astonishment.

Both Godefroy and the trail insisted that I continue, across a landscape of flat rocks, blueberry bushes, and dwarfish pitch pine.

And there were the Kaaterskill Falls: a great sheet, plunging to the depths, immediately provoking thoughts of suicide. My host would not dream of stopping. What choice did I have? I would not be a coward before this man. My chest was tight. My throat closed. Great Phobos, my blood spills across your altar stone.

Kaaterskill is from the Dutch word *kaater*, which means *lynx*. The first pitch is two hundred feet. Then the creature gathers itself for a new leap: its living blood surges across fifty flat feet, plummets for another hundred, jumps about from shelf to shelf. God save me, why had I come here? Godefroy and I lay side by side.

'What fun,' he cried.

It was fun enough for anybody, but then the father of my bride insisted we should get ourselves *behind* the falls, all the while crying to me that in summer it was usually 'not like this', when of course it was exactly *like this*, or worse than *like this*, for now the wind rose so violently it almost blew me to my death. We crept out across a bridge of rock and then, already soaking wet and shivering, stood in a place unimaginable in waking life, behind the falls, our faces assaulted by a choking spray.

'Now you are American,' he cried into my ear.

There was no air in America, only this great suffocating mass which would wash me clear away. I pressed my mouth against the rock behind me, and so could almost breathe. But still there reigned, in this dark heart, a terrifying and foreign obscurity. I cannot describe the awfulness of the murk or the horror of the sharp steely ray of light that then appeared, giving no comfort but rather an idea of the vast chaos which surrounded me.

So great a fear. No explanation. This terror accompanied me

beyond the darkness of the falls. Godefroy escorted me safely across the little bridge, but even then, inhabiting an ink-black cloud of melancholy, I could not speak. So it would continue all through dinner and all that night when I was tangled in my bedclothes with the Albany parade. The mass of America would suffocate me.

Then again: my poor Bébé was dead.

Then again: I was certain a civil war was about to start in France, bringing with it many perils for the very ones who were dearest to me. Was it their deaths I suffered beneath the falls of Kaaterskill?

And at the same time, through all this horror, I loved Amelia, and in the inky night, like one cast out and damned, I sought her generous breast while her white gown wrapped itself around my neck.

III

Unless we had planned to fish for trout in every stream from Kaaterskill to Wethersfield, I doubt we could have devised a less sensible way to get back home. There were hills so steep we had to walk behind one another, narrow roads where two coaches could not pass, pinches so tight it might take an hour's manoeuvring to get the muddy carriage around a corner.

I had not been well since the awful parade. Since my public crisis under Kaaterskill Falls I had become much worse. I wished I could sleep but as I could not talk and sleep then sleep was not permitted. I did what I could to hide the full horror from the father of my future bride. We agreed that I had suffered a 'strange fit' at Kaaterskill, although it was not really strange to me. The rising of the temperature of my thin-walled vessels, the pressure in my heart, the great giddy circular confusions, the rasping of the bronchi – these were my old companions.

The roads were filled with choking dust. The carriage was hot and airless. But still I must not fail the test for son-in-law.

Vigorously I admired the rivers, the mountains, the new pastures of Great Barrington, the civility of the inn at New Marlborough, each of which I tried to love.

Perhaps it would have been enough to love Amelia, and then her father, and then the land itself, and so on. Yet I felt myself honour-bound to take all this wilderness and ignorance into my heart and embrace it, trusting that it would show, in time, not the coarseness and vulgarity of the Glorious Fourth but something new and fine and worthy of the Declaration. For had not these same woods given birth to the intense spirituality of the puritans and was that not, already, more noble than the *enrichissez-vous* of the July Monarchy?

But how many parades could I truly bear to witness without being sick?

And how could I live without my France?

How would I learn to breathe in this awful heat?

I had inherited those wandering choirs of blood which rose singing from my neck and cheeks, congregations of heat that I had seen destroy my mother's cream and silk complexion and send the servants clattering up and down the stairs.

I wondered out loud whether I might not be in need of bleeding.

And this is the thing with Americans, for it was no sooner said than Godefroy had his stockings and his shoes off, the coach was stopped, and he was wading into the bulrushes beside a pond. There he stood, laughing, his splendid white scarf trailing in the water, pointing out a viper fleeing, as if from Good itself.

Then he was returning to the coach with some six leeches latched onto his sturdy calves and these, with great skill – for he had studied the science of medicine at Yale – he removed without tearing his flesh, and – with the leeches still alive and happy – placed two on each side of my nose, and the last two on my forehead.

Thus the dear, dear fellow brought me peace, and as we travelled the last half-day to Wethersfield I dreamily recalled Odile with that curious scoop she had made to catch the leeches. How she had loved to cast the engorged creatures into the fire. 'Go, demons. Burn in hell!'

As we came out of Wethersfield, along the long river road by Old Farm, Godefroy gently removed the *vieilles amies* and threw them out into the summer air, and I felt myself safe, in loving company, quite equal to the challenges ahead.

The coach made its final climb to Chapel Hill where we found the great gift of America lay spread before us. We paused while Godefroy climbed out the window and stood on the box beside the coachman where he took the reins himself and cried a great halloo, and then we descended, galloping at a fearful pace. I did not attempt to convince myself that I loved that tree, that gate, that arm of river. I no longer placed these new affections on the scales, comparing them to those I might once have felt in approaching the château de Barfleur.

The hydraulics of my system had been adjusted. I could now believe that my affection for this place would not lead to the dismantlement of the château de Barfleur as the marquis de Tilbot had lost his family seat which vanished from the earth like a carcass set upon by ants.

We raced toward the Godefroy home and left behind us a great orange plume of dust like a feather in the cap of a chevalier. In the summer dusk I spied a figure in a long white dress walking through the fields from the direction of the river.

'Amelia,' I cried.

The coach halted. My future father was already there to help me down. He steadied me, a hand on each shoulder.

'Hold on,' he demanded. Then, wetting his kerchief like a nurse, he removed some flecks of blood the leeches had left upon my cheeks.

'Go to, sir!' he cried. And I could not keep from laughing as I set off through the garden, into the orchard, beside the onion maidens who laid down their hoes. The wide grass meadow was like a racetrack and I sprinted toward my beloved, who, without abandoning her flowers, and while holding her skirts from the unclean pasture, called my name. How sweet it sounded in her voice, her lovely lilting American intonation.

And thus we met – in the middle of a great arena – with the onion maidens all applauding and laughing and my family of Godefroys hooraying from beside the carriage.

And here she was, her hand in mine, this astonishing bright-eyed Viking beauty with her arms filled with those snowy-white hydrangeas which grew wild beside the river.

Her eyes filled with love for me, her mouth was ready to receive my kisses – and then I saw her expression change completely.

I thought, God, she has seen the confusion of my treacherous French heart.

'Olivier,' she cried, and her mouth was red with blood.

I was Olivier-Jean-Baptiste de Clarel de Garmont, and my nose was bleeding, my heart was burst, a great red stain of crisis presented itself, as public as my shirt.

IV

There was something awful about the blood which had soaked my linen shirt, spread across the flowers, smeared my beloved's mouth. There was no way to make light of it or do anything other than endure the profound embarrassment throughout the Godefroys' wineless evening meal.

Of the matter of the betrothal, not a word was said and I did not judge their reticence improper. Instead I observed how the very definite passions of Amelia's family were diverted, transmuted into a great blooming excitement about matters completely unrelated. The topic was not material. It might have been corn huskers or grasshoppers, but what was closest at hand, what was forever churning over in every room in all the land, was President Jackson's threat to remove the government's deposits from the First Bank of the United States and distribute them among a number of smaller banks. He wanted to do this, he claimed, because the money was the people's and the First Bank of the United States used its wealth to act against the people's government.

On this issue a very angry Mrs Godefroy and her daughter opposed each other with a violence I had not previously witnessed at their table. Godefroy attempted to tell his stories of the road, but the women's dispute was so intense that all he could do was cut the boiled beef very fine and chew it slowly.

When this field of battle – that is, the very pure and proper table, eight feet by four – had been cleared and scrubbed by the two sisters, my beloved and I were permitted to retire, first to the porch and then along the gravel paths that began as a formal grid at the poplars before twisting themselves among the strangely artless topiary and thence stretching into the wilderness and along the Connecticut River which held its dark and bleeding shadows to itself.

My arm lay across her light and level shoulder. My ribs knew the aching softness of her breast. There was nothing except our feet upon the path to break the warm and luscious quiet.

'How exactly have I offended your mother?'

'Well of course you know.'

'My nose.'

'Your lips, you silly.'

We could now hear the distinct sound of a smaller rill or stream entering the large. 'Then here, I repeat my crime.'

'No, my sweetest, this is private. It was the public aspect that was criminal.'

'I will be her son-in-law. She knows that. She had your father's letter?'

I turned her chin to me and this time it was she who kissed me, her mouth so soft and labial, so engulfing.

She smiled and laid her nose against my own. 'Perhaps your kiss was too Catholic for her taste.'

'Catholic?'

'She is in a fret I will become a Catholic. For her it is much worse than turning French.'

'But a Catholic is a Christian,' I argued, more than a little dis-ingenuously. 'Can that be so terrible to her?'

'Nay sir, worse. Besides, she knows only the Irish who are beyond salvation.'

'No, really. Tell me. It was the nose.'

'I don't suppose it helped your case, poor nose.'

Here, just at the river's bend, there was an oak log which Godefroy had ordered adzed to make a self-improving bench. We sat.

'In Catholic countries,' I said, 'we are far more proper than Mrs Godefroy knows. My own mother would look at the habits of American women and find them scandalous. This walking out, for instance.'

'Oh' – she sighed – 'we are so provincial. I wish it were not so.'

'I wish it only as it is.'

There followed a long and private moment, very lovely, only interrupted by the antic stuff of nature, a leaping fish or diving bird, either one would sound the same to me.

'In truth, I would prefer to be Catholic,' she said.

She said this so lightly, I could not help but snort, an ugly noise I now suppose.

'Why do you laugh?' Her generous smile did not disguise the hurt and I rushed like a fireman to undo the damage, explaining that it was always shocking for a Frenchman to see Americans treat the questions of doctrine, which we in Europe had disputed so bloodily, as so light a matter. I proclaimed myself no longer a Catholic, although I carried with me, like old moss, Catholic tastes, sensibilities, and certain of our ancient prejudices.

'But it will be essential, will it not?' she asked. 'If we are to marry I must become a Catholic.'

This was a matter I would rather not discuss on the banks of the Connecticut River, and instead I persuaded my beloved onto the fresh scythed grass where I spread out her hair and kissed her clear blue Viking eyes.

Said she, 'I cannot wait to see your home.'

I covered her eyes and felt the lashes tremble like moth's wings.

'We could not stroll like this in French society,' I said.

'But we will be a married pair. You forget the difference.'

'Yes,' I said, and laid my hand against *that place*. She brought her own warm hand to rest upon mine awhile until, languidly, she lifted it to meet her lips.

'In that little chapel,' she said, nuzzling what Blacqueville always called *la snuff box*, that small well between the thumb and fore-finger. Naturally I was slow to understand she meant we would be married at the château de Barfleur.

'Which chapel?'

'Where your poor Bébé prayed,' she said, and ran her lips along my thumb.

I did not answer. There was nothing I could say.

'You are thinking about Bébé?'

I was thinking like a lawyer with an argument to win. 'But should an American marry in France?'

She looked at me sharply, drawing her hands to hold her arms. 'Why should I not? I will be a Catholic.'

'No darling, I mean myself. I will be American. I pledge myself to you entire.'

She laughed. 'Dear Olivier, what did my daddy do to you? Did he bathe you in the waters of Natchez?'

'He compelled me to drink the awful wine of Thomas Jefferson.'

'No, my sweet dear beautiful man. Look at your lovely nose and those perfect lips. Look at your eyes. I can see the moon in them.'

'I am not a woman. You must not admire me like one.'

'No, you are a de Garmont.'

I did not correct her or admit, even to myself, the jarring note. She should not, of course, have used the *de*.

'You are a noble count, my darling, and you are a huge curiosity to all the onion maidens, who are astonished you do not have two heads and beat your servants.'

'There are no nobles in America.' I said this meaning: I shall be one no longer; it is impossible.

Clearly she was not attending to the argument. 'Yes,' she said, 'I cannot wait to see my mother's face when she thinks it through.'

'What *through* my pet?'

'That I will be a Frenchwoman. What will she do when this dawns upon her?'

'You will be a Frenchwoman because you are my wife, as I will be an American because I am your husband. When your mother sees me by your side in Wethersfield she will not think you French.'

'But we will not be married in Wethersfield.'

'Why on earth not?'

'Because we are to be married in France.'

'No.'

'You said so.'

'I swear not.'

'My darling, do you not think I love you with all my soul? How could I demand you marry in Wethersfield? I would not cut you off from all you are. You are a de Garmont. Would I be the knife that severed the cord to the mother of your life?'

'You do not say the *de*.'

'Dear, do I embarrass you?'

'Don't be silly.'

'Yes, I embarrass you.'

'No.'

'That is why you will not take me home to France.'

Of course the first part was not true, but alas the second was. I could die of love inside her sweet white arms, but I could not present her at the rue Saint-Dominique. We would be made more miserable than poor Heudreville who drowned himself like a peasant in his well.

'We will be Americans together.'

'Please do not say that, Olivier. You are not American. As for me, I am a creature just being formed. I am not anything except provincial.'

'Why does anyone think this a bad thing?'

'So you agree! I am provincial.'

'Better a life among provincials than to be victims to the centralists. My darling, do not pout. This will be the great civilisation of the world. France will never do what America has already done.'

'You do not believe that.'

'Believe? I insist.'

'You insist I am a provincial and you will not take me to France.'

'Yes,' I said, exasperated.

'Then goodnight, sir,' she cried, and ran off into the dark.

V

Why is it that a strong and happy man can be so easily laid so low that he cannot find escape even in the pages of a beloved book, where instead of the expected comfort he feels only the cruelty of the guillotine, the demonic pounding of the printing press?

I loved her so.

I did not love her country. It excited and repulsed me, but I would live there. I would die there. I would see only what was good. I would *do* good. I would make my name in America. I would make myself *into* America. I would write the first great book describing the great experiment.

Except I could not. Because she would not have me.

Downstairs I came upon her father wandering about the house with his lighted candle and his great hairy thighs showing beneath his foolish shirt.

'Do you have a brandy?' I asked him.

'For God's sake, man. You must stop this. For my sake, please.'

Had we been companions travelling, I should have insisted on the drink. Instead, I obeyed like a child and thrashed like a beached shark on the littoral of sleep, and when at last the moon lifted the tides, I drifted out and then was washed back to discover a human body lying all along mine own. My head was lifted as an invalid is given soup. And then what strength boiled in my blood. For I was fed, not by the huge cold silver of an heirloom spoon but by my fiancée's living lips, which now sought to suck, bite, rip, devour me like a *pain saucisson* and just as I rose to embrace my wild good fortune, she slipped away. The door closed shut.

You might think me happy.

VI

Sometime later I heard footsteps downstairs. I thought, *Amelia*. Without aid of a candle, with no guide other than a banister, I made my way. Doubtless my legs were as ridiculous as Godefroy's. I did not care. I discovered the light of a candle visible beneath the library door.

Here I found, not Amelia, but her father, seated at the chess table with a whiskey bottle and a single glass.

'You look absurd,' he said. 'Sit down immediately.'

I understood my tent peg was showing and I obeyed without protest. He fetched a second glass and filled it.

'I will not make her miserable.' He stared balefully, his eyes wet and swollen, his grey hair standing at peculiar angles. 'I am her father,' he said. 'I will not.'

The whiskey was coarse but I took comfort from the burn.

'I apologise,' I said. 'I mean nothing but the best for her.'

He filled my glass another inch. 'I made you promise not to take her away from me. You are a good man, Garmont. How I admired you for that sacrifice.'

So he saw I had my good points. He was not against me.

'You know I love your daughter.'

'That I do.'

'I am prepared to give up my past for her, my country, everything.'

'You are an extraordinary man. I will be proud to call you my son.'

'Then sir, it is as I said to you in Charleston. It is not my noble character that makes me say this, but it is nonetheless a fact: we cannot be married in France.'

'You do not understand. I have withdrawn my objection. She shall marry where she pleases.'

'Mr Godefroy. It will not work.'

'No, no, she will turn Catholic. Her mother must get used to it. There, that's it. It is done.'

'It is not a question of religion sir.'

'Then what is it a question of?' he cried. 'Not me, certainly. There is no impediment. I will sail to France tomorrow if she so directs it.'

'French society has none of your vigour, your love of innovation. It is looking backward while it marches to its doom.'

'What are you saying?'

'I have no intention of being insolent.'

'Slap my face, man. I do not care. I have been wrong.'

'They will not be able to grasp Amelia's originality.'

'Amelia, original?'

'My mother, my father, the family. Their lives are circumscribed.'

'Circumscribed?' he asked, looking at me directly across his glass and then placing it, extremely carefully, on the table.

'Should I be more blunt?'

'You mean they are snobs?'

'They have a way of living.'

'Snobs.'

'You may think them so.'

'Well, to hell with them sir. Did they never meet Ben Franklin, sir?'

'Indeed. But we must marry here, in Wethersfield.'

'And to my daughter you will say, You are not good enough for France. What of Lafayette? He never said we were not good enough for him. He was a noble, sir, in case you forget.'

'And I would say you are twice as good as all of them.'

To a stranger this conversation might be thought to be proceeding badly, but I had reason to hope for a favourable result, for Godefroy, no matter what his passion, was a man who liked an argument, and if he sometimes began in confusion he would finally fit the whole together.

However, it was at this point, when the pieces lay in confusion between us, that Amelia entered the room, not in her gown but fully dressed, with her hair drawn up and held in combs in a way that emphasised the handsome severity of her jaw.

'I heard you.'

I thought, She looks rather like her mother.

'Amelia,' her father said, half standing. His tone was suddenly quite mild. 'You promised not to do this. How long have you been listening?'

'Long enough to break my heart.'

Then Godefroy was fully on his feet and following his daughter from the room. I heard them on the stairs, his bare feet, her leather soles. A door slammed. Then began the striding to and fro above my head.

I drank my whiskey and poured another. I was still in the chair when the sun's first rays struck Old Farm, so harsh that I turned my back on the spectacle, arranging my chair to more directly face the bourbon.

It was around this time that Godefroy returned.

'I am so sorry, old chap,' he said. He was dressed to do business for the day and I understood my situation from this as much as anything he said.

'I will pack my things immediately,' I offered.

'There is a good inn at New Britain,' he said. 'I will take you there.'

Dear God, the Americans are brutal. I was dispatched like a wounded doe, killed with a fast hard cracking of the neck.

PARROT

The marquis de Tilbot was turned into a pedlar, and it suited him to be the representative of Watkins' birds, perhaps not quite as much as spying, but it fitted his character far more comfortably than cadging invitations to the châteaux of his old friends. As to whether he understood the artistic worth of what he was selling, I was never exactly sure for it is very hard to resist the notion that a man who praises you has a good brain connected to his eye.

My dear M. Perroquet, he wrote to me, this is all fine work, indeed the best I ever saw, and the Devil take the Duke of York for saying otherwise. If John Larrit & Co. can continue this excellent production, your name will go farther than we might have ever thought. My father would wake from the dead to think of our association, but this is a mighty enterprise and I have managed, on the strength of my widely trusted opinion and the evidence supplied by the recent birds of Delaware, to procure forty-three new subscriptions, a number I am still astonished to see before me on the page.

Hereafter, I think, you could increase the price as much as twenty per cent and if you agree to this I will increase my percentage also but by a smaller amount, perhaps seven. Be assured this shall result in no diminution of appetite among the future subscribers. Should such a thing occur, which it will not, then I would take it upon myself to make up your loss. You know my word.

I am still in Bruges and have taken an additional five subscriptions for the *second* volume, being completely successful in every approach except for a certain banker I am sure you must remember as his wife had a high opinion of you in the past. I am positive you cannot have written to her, so I am puzzled as to what has caused this female to so turn against our enterprise. She now wishes her husband's subscription cancelled. She told me that what folios she has received are so very bad she could not think of providing them *houseroom*. I took this news as if wounded, but later enjoyed a glass of genever and allowed myself the luxury of imagining what past devilry of your own had caused this.

Herr de Kok, burgher of Bruges, was shown up to my apartments but half an hour ago, so for a short while my quill has been dry. With all the peculiar character of his nation he set very directly to business: that is, *he subscribed*. So please, M. Perroquet, please find him a handsome clean copy, well coloured – twenty numbers with the sheet of title, page of contents and subscribers' names – in a good portfolio with silver paper for the whole. Pack it as you did the recent shipment. It is well worth the extra expense.

I thank you, by the bye, for the portrait of your house on the handsome river. It was much admired by the comtesse de Angerbaud de Texerau who, in unison with her daughters, deemed it *of the period*, whatever that might mean. I took great pleasure in asking them if they remembered you, my servant.

What, the awful one? they shrieked.

In America, I said, this is his house.

What fun! They were quite beside themselves with the most

exhilarating mixture of wonder and outrage, and the younger daughter would not be quiet about the perfection of the bridge across the stream and demanded to know who was your architect.

All three of them were very taken with Mr Watkins' 'White-headed Eagle with Eggs', which I unpacked in their presence and I do believe we may have three subscriptions here although the business will not be pleasant as the comtesse cannot buy a ticket to the Comédie-Française without haggling like a peasant. I thought it best to withhold from view that work which is to me most fascinating. You know what I mean – that small hand-coloured engraving of your exceptionally handsome wife who, as much by her pose – the hand resting, just so, upon her stomach – as by certain subtle changes in her figure, gives every indication that you are to be, at your considerable age, a father. I have understood this engraving, I hope correctly, as a personal memento, a gift in celebration of our unusual friendship. Tell me I am correct? I am completely confident of this assumption, for who would buy a portrait of a woman enceinte I do not know.

It is my hope that you are able to quietly accept this unfortunate development, but perhaps in America, as you earlier reported, everyone will live forever, so if you should consider to remain there you will see your child from womb to altar. The eyes of the children of old fathers have a sad grey quality which I have observed on more than one continent. Perhaps it is not that they inherit an old man's wisdom, but that they are born knowing they must soon say farewell to him who gave them life. I have no children of my own and have not regretted it a single day. In any case there would be nothing to pass on to them except this awful title which has caused me no end of trouble all my life.

You, M. Perroquet, now appear to be in a markedly different situation. I will not insult you by suggesting you will be rich, but I advise you to emulate the wasp as you plan for this child – is it not true that wasps paralyse a spider or other insect for the young to feed on? Then, although the parent has long gone, the child of the wasp grows up in plenty. If I am wrong then never mind. It is a good principle anyway. Watkins must surely know.

In any case, your wife is extraordinarily handsome and there is a way she stands, with her shoulders back, the wind lightly lifting her hair, that encourages me to think she will bring forth your American children in the best possible humour, with strength and vigour. I am thinking of Watkins' notes to his engraving of that nesting eagle.

The attachment of the parents to the young is very great, when the latter are yet of a small size ... But as the young advance, and, after being able to take wing and provide for themselves, are not disposed to fly off, the old birds turn them out, and beat them away from them.

Here, some advice from an old man, or older – for I am almost eighty years of age and have lived hand-to-mouth for sixty of them. Have no more children.

But you are a devil, far too subtle and secret for one of your position, and I expect you will go on living as you wish or as chance will wish for you.

Taking into account your note of the present unreliability of the American currency, I am shipping the specie, insuring it as you have required.

Monsieur

II

We bought our farm out along the Bloomingdale Road, although when I say *farm* I do not mean anything like Hoagland's but rather a collection of gorges and wooded hills on the banks of the Hudson River some three miles south of Harlem Heights. In addition to the ancient wonder of the Hudson we had one very serviceable stream which we were told was called Ratskill but which we renamed Pleasant Creek, which indeed it was.

It was here, in the haze of a summer afternoon, where the eye found itself sunk into humid jungly greens, that Mathilde was once more endeavouring to prepare a canvas from whose heart would glow the light that was everywhere around us. She was in the upstairs studio with a velvet curtain hung to keep dust away from the colourists – three girls who were busy with their birds in the same long room. The correct preparation of a canvas was a continual bane to my extraordinary darling, and I had lived with her through the days of chalk, half chalk, oil, even graphite. This was sometimes an agony to us both, although I was generally, as they say of husbands, *good*.

On this particular day she was at it with a pumice stone, abrading a surface she had earlier sized with glove paring. After this there would be more lead white, then the never-ending pumice, and who knew if this would ever hold the light of this Indian summer afternoon? The light of this country was its greatest joy and burden.

Looking up from her furious attack on the glove parings, she spied a man proceeding toward Harlem along the dusty road. Immediately she stamped her foot three times on the floor, for she, who had once acted so rashly, was now in constant anxiety lest she be paid a little visit by insurance agents and their spies.

I came out my front door like the lord of the manor, which I was, even if our grand estate was all ravines and jungle, yellow clay, not a beast upon the place except a cart horse by the name of Biff. What came toward us was no insurance agent. Indeed, the creature was proceeding more in the manner of a beetle with a ball of dung, although this latter item turned out to be a very large trunk such as gentlemen are used to taking on their voyages.

I was very slow to understand the traveller was my Lord Migraine, his red face covered by clay dust, attempting to convey a burden which had already long defeated him. He shifted it from his left shoulder to his right, onto his back, now placed it down and rolled it with his hands, picked it up again and rested it on the rail of our little bridge.

I ran out to help him like the greatest lackey ever born, but when I arrived in front of him I was too embarrassed to say a word. I got his trunk onto my back, and without a single word of greeting, or any inquiry as to how he had got himself into such a state, I lead him to our house.

I did not need to be an Oxford don to see his marriage prospects had gone up in flames, and of course my heart went out to the poor coot. Yet that common bodily organ is as complicated as a spinning jenny, and when he appeared before me in this way, with all his braid torn, and his bare skin showing through his hose, there was, God forgive me, a certain sinful joy in it. Of course I am not a heartless bastard. I was not gratified to glimpse his pain, but I suppose I was as full of myself as the next fellow, and I was just a little pleased that the posh shine had been knocked off him. In that moment, in the middle of a steamy afternoon, it seemed as if he had come to be with us, to be *like* us, to share our fortune. That made me happy. I should be thoroughly ashamed.

I seated him on our one good chair at table and Mathilde gave him tea and bread and butter and he ate three slices which was all we had. Maman already had a drum of water boiling (so she could scald and pluck an unlucky Canadian goose, shot while flying miles up in the sky), and this I commandeered and carried down beside the house and filled our tub and then brought it to a nice temperature with a little bit of Hudson. To this pretty spot I did then escort the poor human and he still uttered no sound other than a small cry as the water touched his feet, which had broken blisters as rough and raw as orange peels.

There was a great pleasure in caring for him, and I was not alone in feeling it. Mrs Watkins took the wagonette up to Harlem, to the inn, hoping to find good wine for her countryman, and Mathilde was already in his trunk, searching for clean items to replace those he had arrived in.

'He has no servant,' she later whispered, so I knew what a mess his trunk must be and that he had been sent away from Wethersfield with no assistance in his packing.

I washed his hair and found it filled with grit and gravel and twigs, and so dirty it took three goes to have a lather rising, but when it was done I towelled his brainy noggin and his hair rose light and curly as an angel in a church.

'I thank you, Master Larrit,' he said.

'You are welcome,' I replied, although I did think a *Mister* would have gone down better on this particular occasion. I had a great and childish passion to tell him, I will look after you, to say, This is my own house, this is my own dear wife, this is my successful enterprise. Here you can stay safely and write whatever book you like.

He said, 'I would be obliged if you could find a bed for me.'

Mathilde's maman had heated her black iron and pressed him a shirt and there were now cleanish stockings and trousers available and so when he was decent I escorted him inside and up my stairs. You see, I thought, I have so many rooms. He must be gobsmacked.

'Just wait one moment,' I said, and I left him standing in the upstairs hall while I asked two of the pretty little colourists if they would mind to share a bed that night, and of course they were happy to give up their mattress to a French noble. I came out and found the hallway empty. Then I heard his shoes fall and understood he had lain down in our room.

A moment later my former master was sound asleep. By the time I had brought Mathilde to see the sight, he was gently snoring. We stood together, she and I, my arm around her shoulder, the pair of us smiling like fools, as if he were our child. My dear father and his friends would have risen from their graves if they could have known, but Mathilde and I were proud and happy for him to rest awhile in such a large and handsome room – big windows open to the breezes from the Hudson and the walls holding aspects of the river, oil studies all of them, my darling's continual grappling with the fleeting colours of dawn and sunset, the clear clear light of noon, and the warm whiskey haze of this very afternoon.

Mathilde and I had shared many mattresses but this was our first bed, purchased from a family travelling north upon the road. Who had slept in it I was careful not to ask, but it was a bargain and very beautiful – ornate cast iron with a brass sun at its head and four moons, one at every post.

And here he now lay, our friend, our guest, Olivier-Jean-Baptiste de Clarel de Garmont, in our care and under our protection.

Mathilde's work in M. Proudhon's studio had left her with no single reason to be sentimental about the aristocracy of France, but when I saw her eyes I knew she was moved by this most impossible of friendships, perhaps the only example of its type the world had ever seen.

III

Apart from Watkins, who had been out of temper since the punter in Bruges refused to give his folio houseroom, we were very satisfied to hear his lordship snore, and we thereafter ate our shad soup very quietly and, like a household of aunts who have nursed a beloved nephew through a fever, tiptoed up and down the stairs in a state of general happiness. And of course it was Mathilde and I who shared a pallet on the floor.

In the night I threw a quilt across our visitor.

At dawn he was still sleeping, so soundly in fact that I suddenly feared I might be unable to evict him. On this subject I must say a word or two because – sir, madam – I treasured that bed and the room it occupied. There was not a morning when Parrot Larrit did not wake and see the river from those two big windows and understand what a miracle his life had been. There was my beloved wife, her stomach blooming, her lovely little nose above the sheet like some very pretty and *exquis* animal safe in her burrow, knowing there was not a soul on earth would harm her. And here were her small canvases arranged on the right-hand wall like a hand of patience. So although I was honour-bound to offer every care and comfort to young Migraine, I had no plans that he would lie in my bed a second night.

Thus it was, very early, at an hour when I would normally have enjoyed a cup of tea and watched the cormorants glide like deadly fish beneath the surface of the Hudson, I set out to make a bed. Even as I laid out the planks of yellow pine on top of the trestles, I was well aware that I had promised this same timber to Watkins for his shelves.

I had only just measured off the bearers, had not even lifted up a saw, when Watkins appeared beside me in his flannel gown, his bare toes curling upward, his bright blue eyes ignited by the heat of my offence.

He was a great artist, as he knew himself, far greater than Cole or even Church. He was formally superior to all of them. He had a better sense of rhythm. His placement was so keen, his studies so fastidious. I have known him to require Mrs Watkins to shoot sixty-four of one species to get the perfect specimen.

Yet he could forget, as he forgot now, that there were others in the world, and having wrestled all of fate and circumstance to reach his new position, he would not stand aside for anyone, although there were many he would be well advised to consider, not least Cloverdale, his engraver, who had produced fifty-five of our first sixty plates, and also the colourists and artists, let me list them now before they disappear into the endless night: Bessie Coady painted flowers, foliage, and insects for thirty-five of the prints; 'Pretty'

Cudlipp coloured more than fifty; Mathilde at least forty. I myself coloured prints beyond number, not counting all those tiny gifts I made him so carelessly, like #150, the Red-eyed Vireo to which I added an extra twig and spider webbing.

All of this Watkins was pleased to forget, and he would never, not even at the height of his fame, thank a soul except himself. Sometimes this led him to actions both puzzling and amusing. For instance, he had carefully arranged three fire-insurance plaques along his studio wall. I suppose he saw them as some strange proof of ownership. Certainly he refused to see that they incriminated him, as either an arsonist or a coward, depending on your point of view. These mementos should have been chopped up for kindling, but when Mr Eckerd, who owned forty-two per cent of our corporation, was appointed to make this request on our behalf, Watkins flew into a rage and would not speak to him.

I did not require this genius to tell me that yellow pine was a poor material to make a bed. He did so just the same, hopping from one foot to the other, thus appearing like one of his own creations, the poor sad wisps of hair like grass in a rocky place, the colours of skin so thick, embossed in raging scarlet and vermilion. I was reminded of the backsides of monkeys in a state of passion.

Poor Watkins' abnormalities had been branded on him by Lord Devon's fire, but he had always, I believe, been marked for this greatness. When I first saw him, inside his lethal priest's hole, I thought of him as a silkworm. But now I would say he was more like a spider and it would not matter how many times you tore his paper or stole his pencil, he would find new paper, charcoal, watercolour, pastel, chalk, eggwhite, clay. He would start off again. It was his nature.

I often thought, *I pity you*, but although his appearance invited our compassion he lived far beyond its reach. He was a genius and a tyrant and would thank no one. He would work slowly when there was a rush and be a storm of activity when there was no reason. He was cosseted, like a robin's egg in cotton wool. Thank God he had a wife who loved him, who protected him from the world – and us from him.

At length he went away to find his porridge and I was thereafter lost inside my labours for an hour or so, and I was finishing my second mortise when I heard my bedroom window slam shut above my head.

Oh dearie me, I must have woke our guest.

I went to discover his lordship standing at his washstand writing in his book. I had expected, on account of the window, to find him out of temper, but all I saw was the deep, deep injury about his eyes. Perhaps it was simply shame, but it was a look I had never seen in him before.

He told me he had slept well.

I told him I was constructing a new bed and would have it for him by that night.

'Oh,' said he, 'I am quite happy here.'

Well, do me sideways, of course he was! I considered him standing in the middle of my lovely room, the northern wall holding the river light in canvas squares, not finished works but lively studies, the point of each being to see what the ground beneath the paint would do. There were far too many to describe, but here is one – the light of evening like a sheet of copper. Lying beneath, submerged like a bed of luminous sand, is a magic ground, the engine of the light. Just as I looked out the window at the dawn light on the Hudson I could gaze on the works of my beloved and know her sweet ambition was to imitate the colour of the very air.

This was *my* place, *my* palace, not his.

Je suis tout à fait heureux ici, merci,' he said to me. Mathilde would later make a joke of it and say to me, when she refused to share her wine, 'No thank you, I am perfectly happy as I am.'

I returned to my yellow pine, and I was now just as annoyed as

Watkins was, to find myself forced to use the oak – which had been saved to make new runners for our press – for the legs. I was a fool, I thought. I was a lackey, I knew, and yet none of us could doubt the poor fellow's human injury, and we ministered to him as well as we could. Maman darned his torn stockings and laundered his linen. Mrs Watkins, who was nervous of the wild coaches in the city, took the wagonette to Pearl Street to see if she could unearth better wine than Harlem offered. Then, in the afternoon, she offered to take him to a spot where he could shoot some game and I saw them go off together, the noble very jaunty in his walk, carrying Mrs Watkins' precious weapon as if it were his right, surely not understanding she was the shootist our entire enterprise depended on.

Later in the afternoon when it was very hot and I was admitting to myself I had turned our pine shelves into an ugly misshapen thing, Mathilde interrupted me. About the bed she passed no comment, saying only that our two hunters had come upon a group of deer, and his lordship, somehow imagining he would be arrested as a poacher, would not raise the gun.

Then had the plucky Mrs Watkins snatched the weapon from him and shot the creature through the heart. For having thus secured our dinner, she was berated, in her first language which sounded to her much crueller than her second – she heard that she was a foolish woman and would face the magistrate for her crime, and on and on.

Abandoning my sorry carpentry, I caught the poor sore horse and put him back into the wagonette and then Mrs Watkins and I set off together to secure our game. I cut off two legs and we took the remainder to the inn at Harlem Heights where the landlord, a Dutchman nicknamed Pegs, pretended he did not want it. In the end I settled for a bottle of brandy, for I had no time for butchering today.

Our house was not normally a place of high emotion, and the day had been exhausting, and yet the smell of roasting venison seemed to improve all of us, not least Watkins who, sitting on one of our two chairs, was very busy with the nose bag, as they used to say at home.

As for himself, he clearly took notice of the variety of boxes and crates we assembled at our table, but when he was invited to take a chair he did not protest.

Apart from that, he was gracious in every way. He took possession of his captain's chair and engaged with every one of us, not least the printer and the colourist who boarded with us. They, for their part, were charmed by him, his interest and knowledge of their country often surpassing their own. My own response was perhaps more complicated for I heard the same tone he had used in Philadelphia to ask a prisoner, 'Do you think the yard annexed to your cell is necessary for your health?'

Indeed, you will read a very different account of the dinner in his own book, for in the so-called appendix there are five pages titled 'An Account of Settlers at Harlem'. (I have taken care not to repeat any of those very original observations, they are his alone and shall not be poached by me.)

When he had finished eating, he rose and proposed a toast to all of us, in both French and English, very charmingly using words like *stonkered* which produced much merriment. He spoke beautifully, with a grace as distinctive as the minuet. Standing in his carefully darned stockings he specifically noted the quality of cooking which was superior to anything he had tasted in any home for the previous year, although in fact the meal was very simple, there being, besides the venison, a salad of wild greens and last year's potatoes. He spoke most enthusiastically about the construction of the house and its picturesque position, and if he could not bring himself to praise the wine, he made the effort to tell us how it reminded him of a journey to the Loire and the most delightful little village which must be no more than a mile from the place where the grapes were grown.

I did not mind that he admired the grain of our table but not the table itself. He was a noble, after all. Also, this was a man whose entire soul had been pulled out of him as if it were a long thin gut of shrimp. A fellow must admire both his courage and his grace.

Finally, however, I understood that he intended to say nothing about the most remarkable aspect of our situation – that the ruined Watkins and his wife had produced art which his lordship knew – because I told him so – was being sold in Paris at prices one could hardly credit. He also knew that my wife was now painting whatever she pleased, not to flatter the vanity of clients who would not know a painting from a potato but in order to plumb the luminous mystery of New York light. As he remained silent on these two foundations of my life, I became annoyed.

IV

Between the house and the Hudson there lay buried a long shelf of what is known to ignorant labourers as Manhattan shitz, a diamond-hard grey rock which thrust itself forward from the topsoil and thus, with walls of earth bound hard with roots, left clear a most perfect place which had been named, not by deliberation but by common usage, Picnic Rock.

It was here M. de Garmont and I retired after our meal of venison, each carrying our brandy in the only vessels available, two sturdy teacups such as you find in the town cafés.

It was at that hour, when the last skerrick of colour had left the water and it lay below us lapping in its secret life, while above us the night sky which, in fact or in imagination, showed the deepest darkest stain of blue. I could just trace the outline of the farther shore which I knew to be the Palisades, those cliffs which in the morning, in the eastern sun, would glow a luminous gold. So here we sat, in paradise I thought, with our backs against the grassy bank, our legs stretched out, savouring our brandy and the aroma of fresh-cut lemon which – Mathilde thought this a wild extravagance – my companion used to keep away mosquitoes.

He sipped his brandy a second time and said it was made pleasingly *rounded* by the thickness of the vessel which he was far too polite to call a cup. He understood, he said, for the first time, that certain brandies must have been taken, from the earliest years, in vessels of this thickness, which served to counterfeit viscosity and were therefore, as it were, part of the taste.

In short, the drink was rough enough to blind a sailor.

The bats, swooping low, added their black wings to the uncertain patchwork of the other blacks. The screech owl began, as usual, and I was somehow pleased my companion did not ask its name for he would have *disagreed* with it. I had already transcribed his essay on the problem of naming plants and birds in new countries and how screech owl and prickly bush, for instance, sounded like the language of children.

The brandy was not half bad if you would be patient with it.

'So,' said he. 'I have arrived here at an important moment in your life.'

'You have.'

'A fork in the road, I think it is called.'

'It is.'

'You have a business.'

'Yes,' I said, thinking, He is finally going to acknowledge what is going on here before his very nose where he finds us, like the first people on earth, recording the nature of our inheritance.

'The business of art,' he insisted.

'It is a business of the highest sort.'

He was quiet.

'Do you not agree?' I asked him, for I was truly impatient with his politeness and evasion and if he talked about the art as he had talked about the brandy I would break his neck.

Finally, he said, 'Dear chap, no one else will tell you, so forgive me. The paintings are awful.'

I laughed.

'You are in love. The paintings are awful. I lie in bed in that bare room and there is nowhere else for my eyes to go. I have studied them for hours.'

'They are not exactly paintings.'

'I agree,' he said.

'She is experimenting with the New York light.'

'The same sun shines on everything. It is the same light here as in France. It would be ridiculous to believe any different.'

He appeared to be looking at the sky. At first I was furious and then I thought, He is shortsighted. He cannot even see the stars, poor devil.

'When you love a woman you impute to her the virtues you desire.'

I thought again, Poor devil. He loved Miss Godefroy to distraction. He loved all the damned Godefroys. He would sit at table looking from one tight face to the next, smiling with his happiness.

'Come to Paris,' he said suddenly.

I had heard him very well, but I answered the way fools do, 'What?'

'I will pay for you.'

'And leave this?'

'You are a remarkable man,' he said at last. 'You have discovered your own genius. When you leave America you will still be a remarkable man. You have a house here. Well, I will set you up in one at home.'

You might think I was outraged, but I am worse than that, for I was flattered, although of this my tone gave not a clue.

'What, a hermit's cottage, that sort of thing? Like Rousseau? I believe he was always put up by nobles.'

'Exactly.'

'They say he gave away his children to the orphanage.'

'Fortunately you have no children.'

'But I do.'

'No!' he exclaimed as if it were of death I spoke.

'Oh yes, and a wife, and her mother as well.'

'So,' he said, then paused. 'Ah.' He sighed. 'A business.'

What complication of emotions crossed his face I will never know, but he, urgently, unexpectedly, clamped his arm around my shoulder and pulled me roughly to him. The lemon smell was very strong.

'Well,' he said as he finally released me, 'there is no place for me.'

We sat in silence. I did not know what to think or say.

'It will not ripen well.'

'Sir, she is my wife.'

'I do not mean your handsome wife. I mean this, democracy. It is a truly lovely flower, a tiny tender fruit, but it will not ripen well. You will see.'

Poor devil, I thought. Is it not obvious to him that the people are making their own future very well? What of our little factory? What was that? And had he not been on the brink of living here himself?

'I tried to love it,' he said. 'I could not.'

'What did you see upon your bedroom wall?' I asked, a stupid question but I was embarrassed by his pain and wished to cheer him.

'I saw the awful tyranny of the majority,' he said.

You bloody sprat, I thought. I said, 'Does your lordship wish me to write this down?'

'Sarcasm does not become you, John Larrit. Listen to me well. In a democracy there is not that class with the leisure to acquire discernment and taste in all the arts. Without that class, art is produced to suit the tastes of the market, which is filled with its own doubt and self-importance and ignorance, its own ability to be tricked and titillated by every bauble. If you are to make a business from catering to these people, the whole of your life will be spent in corrupting whatever public taste might struggle toward the light, tarnishing the virtues and confusing the manners of your country. Dear John Larrit, this is harsh and beastly. I mean nothing but kindness. Bring yourself away.'

'America is new.'

'Indeed,' he said, and I frankly loathed the certainty of his judgement. He might go away and write a book about this, but what could he know from so short a visit? The time it would take to make this nation would be put in centuries and it did not do to come prancing around in your embroidered vests and buckled shoes and even if the *New York Sentinel* reported what you said, it did not mean you knew.

'These people are not the same as the people you distrust in France. They will be educated.'

'Oh dear,' he said, and held his head in his hands and I could not tell if this was because he thought it a very bad idea or if he considered education impossible and expected our people would all grow up ignorant and their children after them.

'From what will they get their culture?' he cried, 'the newspapers? God help you all.'

You think I will say I punched him in the nose, but I knew his heart was broken. I pitied him his nightmares. How dreadful it must be, to spend your days in terror of the common people, expecting them to tear out your entrails and burn them before your eyes.

Of course he apologised, but even when he apologised he went on to treble the offence. It was his opinion that the common American people preferred their leaders to be as undereducated as they were themselves.

'Ah, but they elect great men.'

'Have you met Andrew Jackson? I have. He is a woodsman, an orphan. Mercy on you all.'

'Then he is a miracle, and there will be more of him.'

'Yes,' he cried, and he had changed now, for there was none of the early condescension. He was no longer reclining but sitting, and his voice had risen. 'Yes, and you will follow fur traders and woodsmen as your presidents, and they will be as barbarians at the head of armies, ignorant of geography and science, the leaders of a mob daily educated by a perfidious press which will make them so confident and ignorant that the only books on their shelves will be instruction manuals, the only theatre gaudy spectacles, the paintings made to please that vulgar class of bankers, men of no moral character, half-bourgeois and half-criminal, who will affect the tastes of an aristocracy but will compete with each like wrestlers at a fair, wishing only to pay the highest price for the most fashionable artist. Do not laugh, sir. Listen. I have travelled widely. I have seen this country in its infancy. I tell you what it will become. The public squares will be occupied by an uneducated class who will not be able to quote a line of Shakespeare.'

Miss Amelia Godefroy would not love him as he wished, he was flayed alive, and in his pain he revealed only his pessimism concerning the possibilities of life. I was hurt, of course, but a man could not be angry with a child of the awful guillotine.

'I'm very sorry,' he said. 'I have behaved disgracefully.'

He stood. We embraced. He gave me the cup, the brandy pretty much untouched. A screech owl cried, despairing, hauntingly lovely. He sighed and walked up to the house alone, poor sausage.

DEDICATION

I have observed in the libraries and binderies of Paris that a book for gentlemen should carry its dedication at the start. Here, straight off, the author thanks some noble lord or lady without whom, etc., etc., but as I, Parrot, am now the citizen of a democracy and have not lived in his lordship's hermitage, I will place my dedication here, in a very kindly spirit. Indeed, I would offer it as solace for my tortured patron, for patron he was, even if he did not know it at the time.

I dedicate this account of our lives and travels to Olivier-Jean-Baptiste de Clarel de Garmont in pretty much the same spirit that his mother, or more likely the abbé de La Londe, offered him comfort during the fearful nights of his childhood. To him I say, in the fullness of my heart, Sir, your fears are phantoms.

Look, it is daylight. There are no sansculottes, nor will there ever be again. There is no tyranny in America, nor ever could be. Your horrid visions concerning fur traders are groundless. The great ignoramus will not be elected. The illiterate will never rule. Your bleak certainty that there can be no art in a democracy is unsupported by the truth.

You are wrong, dear sir, and the proof that you are wrong is here, in my jumbled life, for I was your servant and became your friend. I was your employee and am now truly your progenitor, by which I mean that you were honestly MADE IN NEW YORK by a footman and a rogue. I mean that all these words, these blemishes and tears, this darkness, this unreliable history – although written pretty much as well as could be done in London – was cobbled together by me, jumped-up John Larrit, at Harlem Heights, and given to our compositor on May 10, 1837.

Acknowledgements

This novel began when I read Alexis de Tocqueville's prescient *Democracy in America*. In the following three years I was nourished by a hundred other works, most notably Pierson's *Tocqueville in America*, Jardin's *Tocqueville*, and Hugh Brogan's delightful *Alexis de Tocqueville* which was published just in the nick of time. The author's debt to Tocqueville himself will be obvious to scholars who will detect, squirrelled away amongst the thatch of sentences, distinctive threads, necklaces of words which were clearly made by the great man himself. The very fanciful use I have made of these artifacts may not suit everyone, but as the world of Tocqueville seems to be filled with dissenting voices, it may not be inappropriate for a novelist to assume a minor place in the back row of that full-throated choir.

Naturally I read a great deal other than Tocqueville, and there are some who have recommended that I provide a bibliography, an instrument that seems as useful to the reader of a novel as a hammer is to a dolphin. Nonetheless I have posted a list of those books I remember reading while I worked. This is on my website at petercareybooks.com.

Finally, it is a pleasure to thank Frances Coady, Sonny Mehta, Ben Ball, Angus Cargill, Diana Coglianese, Meredith Rose, Lydia Buechler, Jean Marc Devocelle, Gabriel Packard, Vanessa Manko, Francoise Mouly, Ivan and Claude Nabokov, Lucy Neave, Ruth Scurr, Paul Kane, Patrick McGrath and Maria Aiken, Stewart Waltzer, Mike Wallace, David Rankin, Grant Hamston at The State Library of Victoria, and David Smith at The New York Public Library.